MANSION
BEACH

ALSO BY MEG MITCHELL MOORE

Summer Stage

Vacationland

Two Truths and a Lie

The Islanders

The Captain's Daughter

The Admissions

So Far Away

The Arrivals

MANSION
BEACH

A Novel

MEG MITCHELL MOORE

WM

WILLIAM MORROW
An Imprint of HarperCollins*Publishers*

HarperCollins books may be purchased for educational, business, or sales promotional use. For information, please email the Special Markets Department at SPsales@harpercollins.com.

FIRST EDITION

Library of Congress Cataloging-in-Publication Data

Names: Moore, Meg Mitchell, author.
Title: Mansion beach: a novel / Meg Mitchell Moore.
Description: First edition. | New York, NY: William Morrow, 2025.
Identifiers: LCCN 2024025106 | ISBN 9780063336964 (hardcover) | ISBN 9780063336988 (ebook)
Subjects: LCGFT: Novels.
Classification: LCC PS3613.O5653 M36 2025 | DDC 813/.6—dc23/eng/20240624
LC record available at https://lccn.loc.gov/2024025106

ISBN 978-0-06-333696-4

25 26 27 28 29 LBC 7 6 5 4 3

To my family and the people of Block Island

MANSION

BEACH

Host: Welcome to *Life and Death on an Island*, produced by All Ears Media. I'm your host, Milton Anderson, and on this podcast we're taking a deep dive, so to speak, into life on a small island whose population increases nearly twentyfold from winter to summer. Last week you heard from several restaurant owners about the challenges they face hiring and housing their workers, many of whom come to the island on J-1 visas. Next week, law enforcement discusses how the increasing number of underage drinkers is threatening island summers. Today we're talking to four members of the Block Island Town Council. Some of these members believe a mysterious death last summer was related to issues of overdevelopment, landownership, and excessive life-styles on the island.

If you could each begin by stating your name, your age, your profession, and what, if any, your relationship was to the deceased.

Betsy: I'll start. I'm Betsy Meyers. I'm sixty-four years old. I've taught English at the high school for thirty years. I'm one year away from retirement. My grandson, Henry, was the general con-tractor for the four houses Buchanan built last summer off Beacon Hill Road. Never met the deceased personally, not one-on-one to have a conversation with. But I saw her. We all did. She was quite memorable, with the hair and all. And I sure heard a lot about her.

Evan: Evan Miller, thirty-five. I own a store in town. The Hangry Angler? We sell fishing gear, and we have a sandwich shop in the back. I might be biased but it's the best meatball sub on the island. No relationship to the deceased, except observational.

Kelsey: Kelsey Amaral, twenty-seven. Nurse at the medical center here on the island and also at South County Hospital. The meatball subs at the Angler are *fire*, by the way. I grew up on the island, left, swore I'd never come back, and here I am. I went to one of those big parties last summer. It was insane. When I was a teenager, a party was a six-pack of beer and a bonfire on the beach. We'd barely even heard of hard seltzer. I leave, I go to college, I get a nursing degree, and suddenly people are having like raw bars and champagne at their parties?

(Pause.)

The deceased? I didn't see her. But, yeah, looking back. She must have been there. Right? She must have been.

Lou: Lou Carpenter, seventy-one. I run a fishing charter out of Old Harbor Charter Dock. Right near where the ferries come in. Every year I say it's my last year. My daughter's telling me to retire. And every year, there I am, same as always. I love the water. Did I know the deceased? I didn't. But if you ask me, it should be prerequisite to coming to an island that you know how to swim.

Evan: Like, a swimming test at the ferry dock? Uh, I don't think we can do that. We can barely get a noise ordinance passed.

Lou: Why not? The city of Venice started charging an entry fee. I don't know why we can't institute a swimming test.

Kelsey: Lots of people who know how to swim drown. I was on duty when they brought her in. The body had been in the water for hours before it was found by that dog walker.

Betsy: It's always a dog walker. I watch a lot of true crime, and let me tell you. It's *always* a dog walker that finds the body.

The previous summer . . .

JUNE

NICOLA

For the first three nights in her rental cottage, Nicola tries to ignore the sounds of the parties that reach her from the grand house next door. The thump of music, the highs and lows of traveling laughter, the general rumble that signifies a crowd.

Rental isn't accurate. She isn't paying a penny. *Borrowing* is the word that fits. The cottage belongs to the father of her cousin's wife—her cousin's in-laws, the Buchanans, are the Boston Buchanans. If you move in certain circles you will have heard of them. Buchanan Enterprises is the biggest property development firm in Boston.

Nicola doesn't move in these circles, but she now occasionally lingers on the outside of them. It was a Very Big Deal when her cousin David married into Taylor's family. A boy from Minnesota, a prankster, an extrovert, the son of a discount furniture shop co-owner (Nicola's dad being the other owner), who sometimes got into trouble but who also got into Yale. Taylor and David met during freshman year, and except for a brief hiatus in their early twenties, they've been together ever since. They are the kind of couple whose perfection people are constantly remarking on: Taylor so blond and porcelain-skinned, David tall with a Kennedyesque head of dark hair. In fact, more than once the similarities between Taylor/David and Carolyn/JFK Jr. have come up.

A little over two years ago Brice Buchanan, Taylor's father, happened to visit Block Island from a friend's yacht that docked at New Harbor for the night. And what did he see but a small, relatively unspoiled place—New England's best-kept secret, some called it—crying out for development. Brice Buchanan, is, according to some, 80 percent to blame for what the island's old-timers, its year-round residents, and its longtime summer renters and owners see as a burgeoning recklessness.

Residents have lots to think about, on an island like this: coastal resiliency, shoreline erosion, rising sea levels. Moped rules. But those things are not top of mind for Brice Buchanan.

Buchanan bought David and Taylor's house as well as the cottage Nicola is currently living in with plans to tear down and rebuild the latter; in the meantime, David pulled a string or bent an ear or called in a favor, and so here she is. The cottage has basic furnishings—these too will go when the cottage does—and a simple set of kitchenware, all of which suits Nicola perfectly, because aside from the patio furniture and a bed, what more does she need?

Happenstance, a breakup, and a dramatic career change have brought Nicola to this place. She recently started a job as an intern for the Block Island Maritime Institute, making her, she's pretty sure, at twenty-nine, the Oldest Intern in the History of the World. She tries not to think about this most days; some days, she can think of nothing else. She also tries not to think about the law degree she's no longer using, the live-in boyfriend with whom she's no longer living, and the school loan payments she's no longer making, except for the very barest minimum to keep her out of default.

She tries not to think about the day she told Zachary she was moving out.

She tries to think instead about how close she is living to the ocean, and how, if she plays her cards right, she'll never have to put on business clothes ever again. She thinks about the seals that gather at the north end of the island, and she thinks about how, if you really look at them, they seem to be looking back at you, as if they're about to ask a philosophical question, or relate to you the secret of the universe. As if they can see into the very center of your soul.

Nicola comes from a loud, boisterous family in Minnesota, where she never got to visit the ocean or watch seals. She grew up with three older sisters, the four of them born over a span of six years. They were the kind who barged in on each other in the bathroom without compunction and shared jeans and nail polish and gossip. They fought and made up on a daily—sometimes hourly—basis. When Nicola's family and David's family combined, as they did every holiday, most weekends, and summers at the family cottage on Pokegama Lake, the kids numbered seven. Which means Nicola has been very good at sleeping through distractions, until now.

To combat the noise from next door she tries every trick in the book: AirPods, a noise machine, a fan, an app that plays soothing ocean sounds designed to put one to sleep. (Ironic, this last one, because if only she turned off these electronics she might, in fact, hear the actual ocean.) But all to no avail. Not even a speck of avail.

After the first party, she's irritable. After the second, she's bleary throughout her workday. During the third party, just after midnight, the last straw bends, then breaks the back of the proverbial camel.

"That's it," she mutters to nobody. She switches on the bedside lamp, rises from her bed, removes her statement T-shirt (a polar bear sweating on a tiny iceberg with the words NOT COOL above), dons a bra, and then puts the polar bear shirt back on. She turns on the light on her phone to guide her across the grass—already dew-kissed— and to the house next door.

As it turns out, she doesn't need the phone. Holy hell, the lights from the house are more than plenty. The house is lit up like a— well, like a house where every single light is on. There are people everywhere, just everywhere: spilling from the open back door to the slice of lawn between the house and Great Salt Pond, moving in and out of the shadows in the side yard, and even crowded on the dock that points like a finger out to the pond.

"What the major hell," she grumbles. She knows she sounds like an old crank, but some people have to work in the morning. Two shadowy figures move past her, both laughing, and she says, "Hey!" and then says it again until one of the figures turns toward her and says, "Yeah?" in a voice more curious than challenging.

"What's going on?"

"Party," said one of the figures, male. A vape pen moves in and out of his mouth; the smell of weed is prevalent.

"Well, yeah. I figured that much out. What I mean is, what's the occasion?"

"No occasion," explains the companion, female. "There are parties here all the time."

"All the time?" Nicola is perturbed . . . and maybe a little envious. "Who knows enough people to have a party all the time? On a small island?"

"Oh, you don't have to know her to come to the parties," says the girl, and the male confirms this, saying, "Half the time you don't even see her."

"Half the time you don't even see who?" Nicola's astonishment and perturbation begin to hew more closely to frustration. She feels like these two are talking in riddles she's too tired to solve.

"Juliana. Juliana George?"

"Should I know who that is?"

"She's like totally famous," says the girl.

"As what?"

"As what, again?" The girl turns uncertainly toward Vape Man.

"Tech stuff," says Vape Man, with great (possibly unwarranted) confidence and authority. "I think? She started that company . . ." His voice trails off.

"Right," says the girl. "I can't remember the name of it. But it's really good for our platforms, being here." As she says that she lifts her phone at a very specific angle, and she and her companion press their heads together and look up. The flash goes off.

"Well, what's the company do?"

"Not sure," says the girl vaguely. "But she made gazillions. She invented something?"

"Or discovered something," offers the companion.

"Right. Or both? Or maybe it was an app—"

Nicola scans the scene. There's no hope, she can see now, of asking the party host—Juliana George, whose name, she thinks, might ring a bell; she pictures a magazine cover, a sharp suit and bright lipstick—to be a bit quieter.

"I've never seen her," says the male. "And this is my third party in ten days. Hey, is that a polar bear?"

Nicola glances down at her shirt and says, "Yeah."

He nods and says, "Nice."

The shirt had been a gift from Zachary. They'd been together four years, sharing an apartment for two. They'd been in law school at Suffolk University at the same time, studied for the bar together, had eaten dinner every Friday night at the same Italian restaurant on Federal Hill when they'd both gotten jobs at different firms in Providence.

It was at this restaurant, not so many Fridays ago, that she'd told him about the internship.

He was halfway through his gnocchi (not just the same restaurant every Friday night, but the same *order*); he paused with a forkful in the air. "But you can't take it. You have a job."

"Not anymore. I quit today."

Zachary had been suffering all week from a cold, one effect of which was that his normally vivid blue eyes had a rheumy opacity.

"You *quit*? Why?" The forkful of gnocchi lowered somberly.

"I don't like it. I don't like being a lawyer."

"But you went to law school."

"I know." She had the loans to prove it. She was good at the things that make good lawyers; she had an analytical brain, and she was a good listener, and a good communicator. But she hadn't thought through enough what the actual *doing* of the job would be like, and now that she'd done it, she knew it didn't suit her. "I'm bored, Zachary. And I don't want to be bored for the rest of my life."

"Bored?"

"Aren't you ever bored?"

He blinked at her. "No?" In high school he'd been a middling backstroker, and he gave off a perpetual vibe of having emerged from the deep end after a relay, shaking water out of his ears.

She tried coming at it from a different angle. "Do you—do you think maybe we act older than we are?"

"Is that a bad thing?"

"I mean, do you ever feel like we act like we're sixty?"

"My parents are sixty."

"Exactly."

"And I think they have a really good life."

She sighed. "Exactly."

He lowered his voice and asked, "Is it the sex?"

Yes, Nicola thought, but didn't say. "No. *No.*" Zachary looked relieved. "I just feel like I need—a change. Something different."

Nicola has friends who are married or engaged to be married; her best friend from University of Rhode Island, Reina, who lives in Brooklyn, already has a toddler and an infant. Two wholly separate lives, two beating hearts, four lungs, twenty fingernails and twenty more on the toes, are dependent on someone who was a champion Flip Cup player until age twenty-five. It's not that Nicola doesn't want to end up there eventually (maybe), it's that she doesn't want to go from one to the other with nothing in between.

When Zachary had helped her carry the last box down to her car he'd cried. She tries not to think about that now.

"Honestly, I'm not even sure she comes to her own parties," says the guy in front of her.

"I don't think she does," says the female. "Or she might make an appearance, sometimes."

"Let me get this straight," Nicola says. "This famous person named Juliana George throws these parties and doesn't even come to them? Why would she do that?" She'll have to move her white noise machine closer to her head. Maybe she'll prop it on her pillow, where a romantic partner might go, if she had one.

"Dunno," says the girl. She takes the guy's hand, the one not holding the vape, and turns to make her way back toward the house, tossing an invitation over her shoulder. "Hey, Polar Bear Girl, you should come in. Get a drink."

"No, thanks," says Nicola. "I have work in the morning." It doesn't matter. The couple is gone before she's finished talking, and her words dissolve into the night air.

THE NEXT EVENING Nicola, tired and cranky, has been invited to have dinner with David and Taylor. She's due at seven, so at six-thirty she hops on her bike to make her way, for the first time, to the Carr-Buchanan home. She can practically see where David and Taylor live by peering across Great Salt Pond, but, not being a fish or a bird, she has to bike out Corn Neck to Beach to Ocean to West Side to Champlin before turning right on a dirt road, rutted and hilly, that leads past a gate from an old horse barn, past meandering stone walls, and finally to the house.

And there, swinging open one of the double dark-wood front doors, cool as a frozen cucumber, is David, her favorite cousin, the brother she never had, her partner in crime on long-ago humid, firefly-laden summer nights at the lake. When David was fifteen and Nicola thirteen they once stole the neighbor's pontoon—"Borrowed," David corrects when they tell the story—went for a moonlit ride, and fell asleep once they'd moored it.

"Hey, Nicky," he says, leaning against the doorjamb, one finger hooked casually in a belt loop, the still-high summer sun illuminating his Hollywood-worthy good looks, those sapphire eyes. "Welcome to my little shack."

"You know I'm rolling my eyes at you, right?" says Nicola, wiping the sweat from her brow. She wheels the bike up close to the house and lays it ever so gently on the grass; the bike is just as borrowed as the cottage and has no kickstand. "We're not in Kansas anymore, are we?"

"Nope. But we never were." He opens his arms, and they embrace, and David says, "Holy hell, you're sweaty. Why didn't you tell me you were biking? I could have sent someone for you."

"Sent someone?" Nicola can't keep a straight face. *"Help me, Officer. My cousin has been kidnapped."*

He waves a hand, dismissing her humor, and says, "Sorry, that made me sound like a jerk. I would have picked you up. You want the tour?"

"Uh, obviously." She punches him in the arm and says, "When'd you get so rich, David?" Brice Buchanan bought this house just under two years ago, when his love affair with Block Island began, and Nicola knows it's just the—*a*—summer residence, one of two or three, and that there's also the home in Boston's Back Bay, the ski condo in Montana, and whatever else the Buchanan family owns around the world.

"September twenty-third, almost four years ago," he said, grinning wickedly. Of course. His wedding day. "Let's see. Follow me. Family room." The family room contains every shade of white you can imagine: white couch, a slightly different shade of white armchairs, a white leather coffee table. The couch is dotted here and there with nautical accent pillows. A massive stone fireplace anchors the room; facing Great Salt Pond is a row of floor-to-ceiling windows, uncurtained, unshaded, the better to let the view in, and beyond, a patio and a giant square raised deck with weathered loungers cushioned in navy blue. "Pool," said David unnecessarily, because that part is obvious, then, turning from the windows and leading Nicola toward the center of the house, "Kitchen." Open-concept, slate-gray cabinets, wide-tiled floor, a woman in pinned-up braids busily chopping at an off-white island. Not Taylor. The woman doesn't look up. Then Nicola hears footsteps clicking along from somewhere, and David calls out, "Come and say hello to Nicola. You know each other, right?"

"Of course," says a voice from a distant, distant hallway. The voice comes closer, and here's Taylor, saying, "The Country Cousin."

Nicola feels her skin warm just as David says, "Jesus, Taylor."

"I'm kidding! Of course I know Nicola. We met at our wedding." She kisses Nicola on the cheek. Taylor's lips are cool against Nicola's hot face, and she wishes she'd rinsed off after the bike ride. "I married him for his looks, not his memory," she says. Nicola laughs uncertainly and looks back and forth between the two.

A moment passes when it seems that the mood could go either way—it puts Nicola in mind of the seconds after a child falls, when he is deciding whether to wail or not—and finally David unleashes his megawatt smile again and says, "And I married Taylor for her money." They all laugh then, and Taylor tells David something about a meeting with a something-or-other guy about a this-or-that permit. Nicola tunes out—she doesn't speak Developer—and takes the opportunity to study Taylor.

She starts with her long, flaxen hair (that shade of gold can't be natural—can it? It looks natural, but that's what money can buy you, a natural version of unnatural). Then she moves on to her full-but-not-too-full lips, her prominent cheekbones. Her clothes—flowing, layered garments—give the impression of being pure silk, but it's possible they are instead a very expensive sort of cotton. If Ivanka

Trump and Blake Lively had a baby, Nicola decides, Taylor Buchanan could be the grown-up version of that baby.

Taylor looks at her watch and says, "Let's eat, okay? I have a meeting."

David grimaces. "Another evening meeting?"

Taylor nods. "This permit thing is no joke. It's turning out to be much harder than Daddy thought it would be, and guess who gets to do the grunt work?" Nobody answers; Nicola figures she and David are both assuming the question is rhetorical. A grown woman calling her father "Daddy" freaks Nicola out a little, but, like so many other things, she attributes this habit of Taylor's to the money. The rules are different for the rich.

"Where's Jack?" asks David. "Does he know we have a dinner guest?"

"Who's Jack?"

"He's our lodger," says Taylor, rolling her eyes. Nicola, still burning from the Country Cousin comment, turns to David for the real explanation.

"My college buddy," corrects David. "You've met him. He was the best man at our wedding!"

Nicola shakes her head and says, "There were so many people at your wedding."

"But he was the *best man*," insists David.

"Well, I have the *worst memory*."

"He's a playboy without a mansion, is what he is," says Taylor. "Jack Baker, the golfer?"

"Am I supposed to know that name?"

"You follow the PGA?" David asks this.

"Nope." If it's not the Twins or the Vikings, she doesn't follow them. The old David would have known that. David lowers his voice and says, "He's sort of a celebrity in the golf world. And he should be on the Tour but he had a thing—well, I won't get into it. An injury of sorts."

"Achilles," says Taylor.

"It's a lot of pressure," says David.

"Pressure," says Taylor, "is dealing with the people on this island who control everything. Pressure is the planning board." She shakes her head and scowls prettily.

Nicola has never understood how people who make millions of dollars feel pressure—real pressure, she thinks, is what people feel who have to decide between turning on the heat and buying insulin for their child. But so much about this world is relative.

"The TV cameras love Jack," says David, not acknowledging Taylor's complaint. "Whether he's playing or not."

More footsteps, another hallway, and then David says in a loud, overly cheerful voice, "There he is! The man himself. Come meet my cousin, you old bastard."

The old bastard comes out, and David introduces Nicola to Jack Baker, who puts out his hand. And Nicola, who tries to avoid clichés, she really does, feels for at least three seconds like her heart stands still.

Jack Baker is hot.

A flop of blond hair, dark brown eyes, suntanned skin, an easy, jaunty smile revealing white, white teeth. He is almost the genetic opposite of Zachary, who is pale of skin, Keto-thin. You have to work to get a smile out of Zachary, not because of his moods, though there are those sometimes too, but also because he is self-conscious about his smile. Nicola found that endearing, until she didn't.

"Pleasure," Jack Baker says, and Nicola says it's a pleasure for her too, trying not to let on just how much of a pleasure it really is.

David says they're going to eat outside, so Nicola follows him to the patio, where two enormous fans usher the air from Great Salt Pond toward them. David and Taylor take the two ends of the table, and Jack and Nicola sit across from each other. A glass of cold white wine to Nicola's right, a tender butter lettuce salad set before her by the woman she'd seen in the kitchen. Then, as soon as they've eaten the salads, plates of poached salmon with a cucumber-dill sauce appear.

She leaves the talking to the others—more about the same permit, or a different permit, something about the wedding of a friend Jack and David and Taylor went to college with, something about a sailing trip to somewhere—and digs into her food with gusto. The salmon is phenomenal, but even so, she isn't sure what lapse of logic causes her to say, "Taylor, this is amazing."

Taylor stares at Nicola for an instant and says, "I'm glad you like it. I'll tell Caroline."

"You didn't think Taylor cooked this, did you?" asks David.

"No, sorry, of course not," Nicola says, flustered. She can't seem to get her footing with her cousin: he's familiar, and also a stranger. David used to eat gherkins right out the jar at the lake and call it dinner. Nicola feels herself blush for a second time.

"You should see your face, Nicola!" David chortles. "Man oh man. Taylor cooking. I'd like to see that."

For an instant Taylor looks like she might be hurt, and Nicola wonders if she, Country Cousin or not, should defend her. Then Taylor says, smiling sweetly as can be, "It would be almost as shocking as seeing you mowing the lawn."

Ah, okay. Taylor can hold her own: she doesn't need Nicola.

Jack's laugh is loud, almost a guffaw. Nicola guesses that if this were a book it might be described as infectious, because hearing it makes her laugh too. They're laughing still when the slider to the house opens and out comes a young woman leading by the hand Taylor and David's three-year-old daughter.

"Felicity!" says David, and Felicity says, "Daddy," and launches herself into his arms so fervently that the uneaten portion of his salmon is at risk. David takes her elbow and moves it gently away from the plate. He kisses her on the back of the head, and a look passes between father and daughter that is so tender, so loving, that tears spring unexpectedly to Nicola's eyes. And she is not, by temperament or habit, a crier. Two of her sisters are, but if you've ever lived in a house with four girls, you'd know that not all can be criers. One house can hold only so many tears.

Felicity is stunning in the way of certain children who have an old-fashioned, timeless beauty, the sort you can imagine in long-ago Hollywood stills or in advertisements, in the *Mad Men* era, for laundry soap or ketchup. Golden ringlets, gigantic blue eyes, cherubic cheeks. She pops a thumb in her mouth and regards Nicola from underneath eyelashes so impossibly long most people can achieve them only from a serum or extensions. Neither of which, Nicola supposes, even someone of Taylor's means is using on a child.

"Say hi to my cousin, sweetie," says David, "this is Nicola," and Felicity says, "Hi."

"Hi, Felicity," says Nicola. "I can't believe I've never met you." At one time it would have been unfathomable, absolutely unfathomable, for Nicola and David not to see each other for years. Now he has a whole entire kid who Nicola is just laying eyes on for the first time. "She's gorgeous," Nicola says. "I mean, obviously."

Taylor, who has stood to plant a kiss on the top of Felicity's head, passes a hand over her daughter's hair and says, "My beautiful little fool."

"My favorite book in high school," says Nicola.

"Mine too," says Taylor, and for a second Nicola feels the beginnings of a tentative solidarity between them.

David grins and says, "I thought it was Taylor Swift who claimed that."

Taylor rolls her eyes and looks like she's about to say something more, but just then her phone, which has been sitting on the table the whole meal, occasionally buzzing with texts, lets out a proper ring, and Taylor looks at the screen and says, "I'm so sorry, I've been waiting all day for this call, I have to take it, sorry, sorry." She grabs the phone and beelines for the slider. Felicity begins to squirm in

David's lap, and, as if equipped with sensors, the nanny reappears, announcing, "Bath time, my girl!" and leads her off.

Caroline comes back out then, bringing shortbread and small bowls of gelato for all of them. She disappears and returns with a bourbon for David and one for Jack. She asks Nicola if she wants anything. Nicola has already had two and a half glasses of wine; she says no, but thank you, then changes her mind and asks for coffee, which appears without delay along with a tiny pitcher of cream and a bowl full of sugar cubes. Wow! thinks Nicola. The good life!

David sips his bourbon and looks out at the water, so Nicola sips her coffee and does the same. At the end of the dock, Nicola can see a green light burning.

"What's that for?" she asks, pointing.

"Keeps the monsters away," says David, and at the same time Jack says, "Lets the ladies know where to find me."

Nicola rolls her eyes. It's impossible to get a straight answer around here. Jack leans back in his chair and closes his eyes. She asks David, "Are you still doing the race car thing?"

"Not so much," says David.

Jack's eyes flip open and he says, "The missus doesn't approve. She thinks it's lowbrow."

"I thought you were into the fancy cars, though," says Nicola.

"I am," says David.

"Was," corrects Jack. "But to Taylor it's all the same."

"Okay," says David. "Okay, okay. Can we change the subject?"

"Sure," says Nicola. Even though she wants to know more, she's sensing something from David, a hurt that's deep enough he doesn't care to have it excavated. After a time he snaps his fingers and says, "You know what you should do, Nicola? You should come to the Vineyard with us. We take *As-Is*. It's a blast."

"A blast," confirms Jack. His eyes are closed again.

"*As-Is?*"

"Our boat. Don't laugh. Real estate term." He shrugs. "I didn't name her. There's space to sleep on her, but sometimes we get rooms at the Winnetu instead."

"David," Nicola says gently (but she's also annoyed). "You know I can't afford to do that."

David takes another slow sip of his bourbon. "It's okay, Taylor has an account at the Winnetu."

"I'm not spending Taylor's money!"

David shrugs. "Spend my money, then. It's all the same money."

Nicola knows from her father that David signed a comprehensive prenup, so it's actually not "all the same money."

"I don't know," she says, and David shrugs and says, "Suit your-self. Or spend Jack's money."

"Sure," says Jack carelessly. "Spend my money. The Tour has been very kind to me." After a beat, "I'm going to head out. I'm sup-posed to meet someone in town. Nicola, can I drop you anywhere?" He stands.

You can drop me into your bed, Nicola wants to say, but of course she doesn't. She says she's going to ride home. She yawns, suddenly exhausted, maybe from the wine or the bike ride there or the pros-pect of the bike ride home or maybe from the sheer effort required not to say the wrong thing in Taylor and David's beautiful home.

David says, "They're working you hard over there at the Insti-tute, huh?"

"They are. I mean, yeah. I'm just a lowly intern. You've heard of the forty-year-old virgin?" She glances at Jack and blushes. Why'd she bring up virgins? "I'm an almost-thirty-year-old intern. But I love it. I'm learning a lot about aquarium maintenance, and I'm going to lead my first dockside exploration soon . . ." She's losing her audi-ence. This stuff is interesting to her—she hasn't even broached the wonders of the squid dissections they do with the kids!—but Jack's shoulders are turning away from the table, and when the shoulders go, knows Nicola, so goes the attention. She switches gears. "Actually, I haven't been sleeping well. There's this house next to me where there's a party every night."

She has him back. "Sounds like my kind of neighbor," says Jack, sitting back down. "Go on!"

"Apparently you don't have to be invited to go. You just . . . show up. It's all courtesy of Juliana George."

David and Jack exchange a look. And it's there—Nicola feels it, as sure as a pinch on her arm—that the night, in fact the entire summer, takes a turn.

"Did you say Juliana George? She's your neighbor?" David is sitting up straight, his hand gripping his bourbon glass.

"Apparently. I haven't met—"

"Here? On Block Island?"

"Yeah. Yup. I guess. That's what someone told me. So what? Who is she?"

"LookBook!" say David and Jack together.

"Sorry?"

"LookBook."

"I don't know what that is."

Jack taps on his phone and holds it up for Nicola to see a website on the screen. "It's an online fashion portal. The Expedia of fashion."

"How do you guys know this stuff?"

"I may look like a golfer," says Jack (actually he looks like an underwear model), "but deep down I'm a business ho."

"He's hot for startups," David concurs. "Company valuations are his porn." Nicola tries not to snicker but snickers anyway. "That, and regular porn."

"Oh, please. I spend more time reading *Businessweek* than you want to know," says Jack.

Without Nicola really noticing, the table has been cleared; her napkin, which had fallen to the ground, is folded neatly in the shape of a swan. Was this what it was to be rich? Invisible people moving quietly around you, tending to things you didn't even realize needed tending? Making birds out of your napkins? Jack rises again, ready to leave for real this time. He kisses Nicola on the cheek, and she's weirdly, irrationally jealous of whoever he's going to meet. *Stay here,* she wants to say. *Right here.* Instead she says, "I should be going too. Do I say goodbye to Taylor?"

"Nah." David waves a hand. "She does a lot of work at night."

"I never even thanked her for letting me use the cottage."

"You'll have plenty of chances for that. She's probably still on the phone." He leads Nicola around the house to the front, where her bike is waiting. "She's on the phone so much if I didn't know any better, I'd think she was stepping out on me." Nicola looks sharply at him, thinking he's joking, because honestly, what person in their early thirties uses a phrase like "stepping out on"? But he's not joking. Nicola has been reading David's expression her whole life; she can see that his smile is a little bit wry but a little sad too.

"Stop it. David. You don't mean that, do you?"

"'Course not." He slips his armor back on so fast. "Don't ride home in the dark, Nicky. I'll get someone to drive you."

Nicola laughs at that. The front yard is illuminated with all sorts of soft yellow lights in the grass, each pointed in its own specific direction. "You sound like a mobster."

"Not some random person." He laughs too. "I meant Joe. The handyman. I'd drive you, but that bourbon hit me. You know how much I like to drive."

"Oh, believe me, I know. But I think they have speed limits here."

"Depends on who you ask."

Nicola guffaws. Same old David. When Nicola was learning to drive, her mother hired David to teach her. He's only two years older, so this plan was possibly more efficient than legal, but they had a blast. (In retrospect, though, maybe don't ask a burgeoning race car driver to teach a newbie.) "Back up, though. You have a handyman who works at night?"

"We don't usually ask him to do stuff at night. But he lives here, on the property, so he's often around, and he doesn't mind running out here or there."

"I'll take my bike," Nicola says, thinking that the night air might revive her. She taps the handlebars. "I have a bike light, a helmet. Legs. I have all the things I need." She pauses. It's a natural time to take her leave, but she can't help but ask, "Do you ever miss the lake in the summer? I mean, it's hard to compete with this . . ." She waves her hand back toward the house, toward Great Salt Pond, toward the intersection of nature and luxury that David and Taylor have somehow figured out how to inhabit.

"It's not hard," he says instantly. "I miss the lake every day."

"The smell of the pine needles," she ventures.

"The roar of the lake trout."

She snorts and climbs on her bike.

THE RIDE HOME, in the dark, with the air lighter and clearer than it had been on the way to David's house, goes by quickly. There's a fingernail of a moon hanging over Great Salt Pond. The tanks at the aquarium are fed directly from the waters of Great Salt, which, if you stop to think about it (and here Nicola does), is quite remarkable. She loves it here! She feels approximately one thousand times more alive than she ever felt at the law firm.

Maybe it was seeing David, or maybe it was something more nebulous that transpired over the course of the dinner, but for the first time since leaving Zachary, Nicola feels like a kid again, coasting along some wide midwestern street, all of her decisions in front of her, yet to be made. No law degree, no breakup.

She dismounts in front of her cottage (Taylor's cottage) and strains to discern what she's hearing. Then she realizes: nothing. She's hearing silence. No party next door. Scarcely a light on. She's surrounded by a quiet so obtrusive it seems almost like its very own noise.

She walks around the back to the little patio, the small table that came with the place, two chairs, none of it fancy, and she sits for a moment, letting the night air settle around her. She sees the green light flickering on the far edge of Great Salt Pond: the end of Taylor and David's dock. Then she notices another light, much closer—a light at the end of the dock at the house next door. Maybe it's a flashlight, maybe it's a cell phone, but either way it's held by a solitary figure whose shape Nicola can just make out, legs hanging over the edge of the dock, facing out into the great, grave darkness.

JULIANA

On the Tuesday of the third week of June, Juliana George wakes at dawn. She usually wakes early, but now, with the IPO looming, she's been rising even earlier. There's so much to do! Rehearsal and prep for the road show. Meetings with analysts. Constant monitoring of the market, and of the value of the companies that are comps for LookBook. Preparation for the S-1 filing.

She brings her coffee to the end of her dock, where her decorator, Zelda, had placed a set of outdoor furniture and a small propane-powered fireplace, and even, because Zelda thinks of *literally everything*, a covered basket of extra-absorbent towels to wipe the dew-kissed cushions. Juliana sits there for a long time, catching up on emails, looking at her calendar for the day ahead. She has a pair of binoculars (Zelda again), and she lifts them to her eyes, watching Payne's Dock wake up for the day: The Cracked Mug opening, the overnight boaters going ashore to use the bathroom or shower or walk their boat dogs.

Each week, she has decided, she'll set aside two hours for some sort of excursion to get to know the island. If she doesn't, she's going to succumb to the pressure of her work. She might actually explode. Today she's going to walk Clayhead Nature Trail.

Block Island is a small island—seven miles around, Juliana's Realtor, Holly, told her when she sold her the house in February. But though small, it has a whole string of beaches on the eastern side, a sandy bounty stretching almost the entire length. Then there's the western side of the island, with unspoiled, rockier beaches. And besides the beaches, there are dozens of hiking trails that lead to stunning ocean views. There are the shops in town. There are the giant clay cliffs at Mohegan Bluffs. There's an exotic animal farm, with a zedonk and kangaroos! Juliana has never seen a kangaroo in person. (In kangaroo.) And she's never even heard of a zedonk. She had to look it up. What a place she's landed in!

The fact that she started where she started and is now *here*— Juliana couldn't have written more of a surprise ending had she been Agatha Christie herself. But she's not a writer. She's a business-woman, a badass, a girl from the streets (quite literally), who, earlier that morning, after brushing her teeth in her marbled bathroom, after rinsing her face with water coming out of the touchless faucet, had looked in the mirror and said, with a mostly straight face, "You live here now. This is yours, motherfucker."

She reads up on the Clayhead Trail online after she finishes her emails and while she drinks her coffee. She leaves ten emails unan-swered, but she started the morning with eighty-two, so that's not bad. She'll complete the rest of them before noon. Juliana has never met a deadline she hasn't kicked in the nuts. She closes her computer, gets in her car, then follows her GPS directions to a small parking area off Corn Neck Road. She parks, locks her car (is there crime on Block Island? She's not sure. But her car, an Audi SQ8, is the first new car she's owned in her entire life, and she doesn't want to take any chances).

It's more walk than hike: a mainly flat, easy, curving path that winds through vegetation, heads delicately uphill, and opens up above a stunning, secluded beach. "Ridiculous," says Juliana out loud when she arrives at the end. "This is just ridiculously beautiful." She'd read online that this trail could get crowded on summer days, but for now she's the only one here. Far below she sees a couple of beachgoers, a surfer, a dog. But here, she's alone. The air is hospitable, the sun is shining, and she sits on the ground and lifts her face to it, soaking in the—

"*Jade!*" Juliana stiffens, and all of the sounds around her seem to pause at one time: the chirping of the birds, the crashing of the waves, the buzzing of an insect that she hadn't even realized she could hear until she hears it no more.

No. Absolutely not. This is a small island, not nearly as well-known or popular as a place like Nant— "Jade!" again, and pair of long, suntanned legs appear in Juliana's line of vision. Her gaze follows the legs up and up, past a pair of shorts, a cropped tank, until she gets to the face of—"Shelly!" says the owner of the legs. "It's me, Shelly Salazar! From Boston College. It's *me*." She points to herself, ostensibly to clarify the "me" she's talking about.

Ho-ly shit. No. *What?* No. But it is, it's Shelly. Juliana scrambles to her feet, scrambles for a foothold, mental or physical or both, scrambles for her composure, wills her heartbeat to settle. "Hey, hi. Wow. Shelly."

"I had a feeling I'd run into you," says Shelly.

"You did?"

"I did! When someone said the founder of LookBook had just bought that big house over by Great Salt, I thought to myself, It's only a matter of time until I run into Jade!"

"Juliana."

"Juliana! I know that, from the articles. I just keep forgetting." Shelly beams so hard Juliana wonders if her jaw hurts. "And look, here we are."

"Here we are," says Juliana. She squints up at Shelly. Shelly is tall, and Juliana is petite, so even though they're on equal footing the setup feels almost purposefully unequal.

"I mean, tbh, I didn't believe it at first," says Shelly. "Why Block Island, of all places, for you to buy a home? It seems so . . . random."

Juliana steels herself. Do not, she tells herself, forget who you are. Do not forget where you came from. "*You're* here," Juliana points out.

Shelly purses her lips and nods. "You're right. I'm here. But that was random too. I was in New York, and a few years ago I got sent up here on an assignment, when I worked in book publicity. I fell in love with it, but of course I was like, Calm down, Shelly, you can't just up and move your whole life to Block Island." She looks at Juliana expectantly, so Juliana says, "Right."

"But then, I was just getting out of this terrible relationship, don't get me started on *that . . .*"

"I won't," says Juliana.

"And I came up here to lick my wounds. I ended up doing a couple of freelance jobs and—well, I never left. So here I am."

"Here you are," says Juliana. "Here you definitely are."

"And here *you* are. I can't believe it. Jade Gordon. Sorry. Juliana."

"Jade was—a nickname. I dropped it when I started my business."

"I didn't know Jade was a nickname for Juliana," Shelly muses.

Funny how you don't know everything, thinks Juliana. Funny how you all thought you knew more than me, and look at us now.

"It's like you fell off the face of the earth!" Shelly continues. "You never come to any of the BC stuff. A bunch of us try to get together every three years or so. We rotate locations, usually over a long weekend. We have a blast. We've done, let's see, Nantucket, and Nashville, and Napa . . . We invited you!"

Yes, Juliana knows this; she's received invitations through her office, but she has never responded. Her scars from BC run deep.

"I never got any of those invitations," she says.

"Well, you were so *busy*. Of course, we knew what you were doing with LookBook." Shelly beams. "I've read all the articles. You're everywhere!"

"Everywhere," agrees Juliana. Damn right she is. *Forbes*'s 30 Under 30. *Fast Company*'s best female entrepreneurs. The *How I Built*

This podcast. The spread in *Vogue*. An article about her foundation in the *New York Times*. And on and on.

"So we figured you were just too occupied, you know, being rich and famous."

"Right." Juliana feels a pinching along her collarbone: this is her anxiety tell. (Who is she going to tell, though?) So far, a lot of her wealth is paper wealth, but there is no way in hell she's going to admit that to Shelly. Fake it until you make it, etc. Juliana's been faking it one way or another her whole life. Now she's making it, and she's not going to kowtow to Shelly or anyone else.

She stretched to buy the Block Island house, and stretched further to decorate it. The car, the clothes, all of it—they are the possessions of the person she will be in October more than the person she is right now. But this is how business works; this the nature of entrepreneurship. You build your life on spec. It's all so close to her now that she can taste it. She can reach out and touch it. She just can't have it quite yet.

"We're so proud of you! Our little Jade, from the dorm!"

"Juliana."

"I heard about the parties at your house, and I thought, That can't be true! Not the Jade *I* know! I mean—"

"I know," says Juliana. It doesn't seem worth it to correct Shelly yet again. "I'm full of surprises."

"We should go out!" cries Shelly. "We should totally go out for a drink. We should go to Poor People's or The Oar. Phenomenal cocktails at both places."

"Now?" asks Juliana dubiously. She glances at her watch. It's 9:22.

"Not now!" chortles Shelly. She gives Juliana a light, jocular punch on the upper arm. "Even *I* don't start drinking at ten in the morning." Juliana tenses her arm, tenses all of her muscles. Shelly is coming really close to crossing Juliana's threshold. Shelly purses her lips. "Eleven, maybe. But I meant some evening. Or afternoon. I'm pretty open. Or maybe I'll come to one of your parties. I can't believe I haven't come to one yet."

"Definitely come," says Juliana insincerely.

"Really?"

"Sure."

"When is the next one?"

"I'm trying to figure that out."

"Well, *here*, let's at least exchange numbers so you can let me know. Right?"

"Right." Juliana hands Shelly her phone and takes Shelly's from her, tapping in her number under the contact Shelly has already created with the name Jade. She changes it to Juliana.

"But right now, if you're free, we should go get a coffee. Have you been to Joy Bombs yet?"

"What's Joy Bombs?"

"Oh, girl. You *have* to go to Joy Bombs! It's one of my favorite places on the island. You ever had a mini whoopie pie?"

"No," says Juliana again. She doesn't want to get a coffee; she doesn't want a mini whoopie pie, whatever that is. She is Juliana George, founder of LookBook, a person who has created something out of nothing. She has to answer to her board, and to her attorneys, and soon she'll have to answer to the stock market, but she no longer has to answer to or worry about or feel naked and exposed in front of Shelly Salazar.

"I'll show you! Are you free now?"

She can easily be not free. She could have a business meeting, a plumber coming, an online therapy appointment. Any of these would do. Or none of them; she doesn't need an excuse. How many times in the past ten years has she reminded herself that *no* is a complete fucking sentence?

But there is a part of Juliana that does want to show Shelly what she's become—a part of her that wants to have the upper hand, and to make a fist with it.

"I have a little time," she says. "I have a call at one, though."

Shelly says, "Great! My treat." She reaches out and impulsively hugs Juliana to her. Shelly smells like the ocean and like sunscreen and, inexplicably, like limes (breakfast margarita?). When she releases Juliana she holds her at arm's length for a moment, considering her proudly, almost like a parent. "You'll love this place, Jade."

Juliana takes a deep breath. "Hey, listen, Shelly. Don't call me that. Like I said, it's Juliana now. Especially here, okay?"

"You got it." Shelly makes a motion like she's zipping up her lips. "If you ask me, Jade was a great name. Why'd you stop using it?"

Juliana will explain herself to nobody. "It's complicated."

"Juliana is pretty too. But your last name—?"

"Long story," said Juliana.

"Got it. If there's more to it than you want to say, girlfriend, you don't have to worry about me. I'm not sure if you remember this about me but I am a total vault." She turns and begins to make her way down the trail, and Juliana, walking the twin tightropes between past and present, present and future, follows. Hopefully they'll at least take separate cars.

They don't take separate cars. Shelly insists on following Juliana home to drop off her car ("So I know where you live for the next party!") and makes room for Juliana in her cluttered Corolla, sweeping a whole collection of items off the passenger seat. A lipstick without a cover, a lipstick with a cover, a Styrofoam takeout container that smells like vinaigrette, three dimes, a pair of tweezers, two empty nip bottles.

Joy Bombs, it turns out, is a cute little café in the center of Block Island's small, bustling downtown. They each order a coffee, and once they're seated at one of the tables Shelly leans in and says, "So, *Juliana George*, tell me *everything* that's been going on with you."

"Since college?" says Juliana. "Everything?" A café worker, a pretty, suntanned teenage girl, is cleaning the table next to her, maybe listening in, maybe not.

"Everything relevant. I gave you my capsule bio. Give me yours!"

Juliana takes a long sip of her drink. She ordered a hot cappuccino, and Shelly has an iced Americano. Adult Shelly, Juliana notices, still chews on the end of her straw the way College Shelly did. Because the straws are paper this habit now results in a shorter, messier chew, but there you are, habits are hard to break.

"Well. Honestly, I've just been working. It's all-consuming, running a company like mine."

Shelly nods sagely and says, "I bet. Never mind spending all the money!" She chortles. (Adult Shelly chortles quite a lot.) "Not married?"

"Nope."

"Too independent for all that, I bet. Or just haven't found the right person?"

Juliana hesitates and looks around the café. There's a line now: teenage girls in tiny shorts and bikini tops, a sandy family already done with the beach, a toddler wiping his eyes and saying, "No no no NO."

"Yeah. I mean, I've dated plenty. Not that much in college, but after, sure."

"Yes, queen," says Shelly supportively.

"Once I found the right person," says Juliana. She can't believe she has just confessed this to Shelly. "But he was taken."

"Oh, that sucks," says Shelly with what seems like genuine feeling. "Was he married? I've been involved with a married man before. Trust me, it's *no bueno*."

"Not then, but he is now. *No bueno*," agrees Juliana. "Definitely *no bueno*."

Shelly's straw is now a lost cause. She removes it altogether, then whisks the plastic top off her cup and begins to drink it that way. "You remember Mary Ann? From BC?"

"Of course I remember her. We were roommates freshman year. That's how I met you, Shelly." Juliana allows herself an internal shudder. Freshman year at BC had been challenging. (All of the years at BC had been challenging.)

"She lives in Greenwich, Connecticut, and has three kids! Can you believe it? Three kids already! I don't think I could even handle a cat."

"Wow." Juliana can believe it, in fact. It seems like exactly what Mary Ann would be doing. Lots of barre classes and competitive healthy eating, a nanny.

That wasn't fair.

Maybe she did yoga instead of barre.

The coffee is gone; the whoopie pies are gone. Juliana begins to do all the little things you do when preparing to leave a table: wiping crumbs with a napkin, stacking her mug on top of her plate. All of this to give the hint that she is ready to go. The pretty teenager swoops by and says, "I can take that."

"Hey, Maggie," says Shelly, and the teenager says, "Hey, Shelly."

"Before we go," says Shelly. "Do you need any help with Look-Book?"

Juliana feels like this emoji: 😊 "What kind of help?"

"Publicity, etcetera. I could help you, you know." Shelly leans conspiratorially over the table. "I've been working as a publicist to the stars."

"Oh, yeah? What stars?"

"Lots of stars."

Juliana considers inserting her own chortle, thinks better of it, and asks, "For example?"

"All kinds. Books, theater. I'm publicity-fluid. I coined that phrase. Do you like it? This summer I'm working for Buchanan Enterprises." Juliana blanches, and Shelly, seeing this, says, "Do you know them?"

Careful, Juliana, careful. "No," she says. "I've heard the name, is all."

"Okay, well, I'll be honest, one of the perks of working for them is spending a lot of time in their house. And that's a perk because there's this guy staying with them, a friend of the Husband Buchanan, and he's *such* a hottie. Jack Baker. He gives major Justin Trudeau vibes."

"Justin Tru*deau*? The world leader Justin Trudeau?"

Shelly blinks at her. "Of course. Don't you think JT is sexy?"

"I've never thought about it."

"Well, think about it. He's a super hottie. Anyway. I am doing actual work for them. I've done book publicity too, like I mentioned. I could do, and don't take this the wrong way, Juliana, but I could do like an image makeover on you."

"Image makeover? You think I need an image makeover. Shelly, do you even know what LookBook does? I practically invented image makeovers."

"Oh, sure! Yeah. I know you did. For clothes. I'm talking more about makeup. Everyone can use a little objective help." Shelly looks carefully at Juliana and purses her lips. "I mean. You're like a whole different person, stylewise, than you were in college. Which is a good thing, no offense. And obviously tracks with your business. But have you ever considered eyelash extensions?"

"No."

"You totally should. Those gorgeous dark eyes of yours . . . a Medium Glam set would really make them sing."

Juliana isn't sure she wants her eyes to sing—but she grants that Shelly's eyelashes are attention-grabbing. The lashes seem to have their own life, their own range of motion. "Is that what you have?"

"I get the Mega Glam." Shelly blinks—oh, how she blinks! "The longest ones they offer. That's how I like to roll. But honestly, you don't need a lot. You've always been Gorgeous with a capital G. You just didn't know it, back in college. I mean, that Thanksgiving at Mary Ann's—" Juliana wants to hold up her hand and say, *Stop*. She doesn't want to think about that Thanksgiving at Mary Ann's. She doesn't want to think about Mary Ann at all.

She's like obsessed *with my mom* is what she thinks about when she thinks about Mary Ann. She remembers Mary Ann saying that, and Shelly laughing.

"And now you do know how gorgeous you are," continues Shelly. "That's it. Same face, different attitude. Different bank account, obviously. Maybe . . . maybe it's more of a touch-up. A touch-up can be for any reason, you know." Shelly pauses, tips her cup back toward her lips one more time. There's no coffee left, so the ice hits against her teeth. "Okay, to be honest, I sort of need the work. I've been piecing things together, but that only goes so far. I don't want to go back to New York. And we're thirty-two now, and I look at you, and I look at Mary Ann, and you guys are cruising, just like all set, doing your thing, living the dream. And I—well, I guess I'm a little bit stuck." Shelly's mouth twists in a sad way.

What makes Juliana say what she says next? Is it again that desire to have the upper hand, to feel like more than that college freshman out in the cold, hands pressed against the metaphorical glass, peering into a place where everyone else is gathered, warm and safe? Or maybe Juliana simply wants a friend, and here is potential friend material, available for purchase. Everything is available for purchase. (Almost everything.)

"Sure, Shelly," Juliana says. "I'm sure I could use you."

Shelly's whole aspect changes. She sits up straighter. Her eyes sparkle. Even her lashes stand at attention. How easy, Juliana thinks, it is to make some people happy. "Really?"

"Really. I could use some extra help, going into a big fall."

"Big fall?" Shelly squeals.

"I'll have my assistant contact you, draw up a contract for some freelance work. There will be a nondisclosure agreement in there, but that's standard."

Shelly holds up a hand like a Girl Scout taking a pledge. "Oh, I told you, I'm a vault."

"Right," says Juliana. "A vault." And finally, on that dubious note, Shelly stands, deposits her cup into the recycling bin, bids goodbye to Maggie. Finally, they are leaving. Finally, Juliana can be alone.

As they walk to Shelly's car, Shelly says, "I'd love to hear more about why you changed your name. Now that I'm on the inside."

What have I done? thinks Juliana. I've put Shelly Salazar *on the inside*. "I already told you," she says, as kindly as she can manage. "I just wanted a fresh start, for the business. There's really nothing more to it than that. People do it all the time."

"Honestly, it doesn't even matter. That's our mantra in PR. All that matters are the parts we show." (Juliana has worked with a lot of publicists over the years, and she's never heard this mantra. But okay.) "It's sort of like when a lawyer for someone accused of murder doesn't want to know if the person actually committed the murder, because that would take away their ability to do the whole innocent-until-proven-guilty thing."

"I didn't kill anyone," says Juliana, and her heart starts to pitter-patter.

"Oh, *I* know that!" Shelly looks closely at Juliana as she unlocks the car. "I mean, I think I do." She stares so long and so hard over the hood of the car at her, really gazing deep into her eyes, that Juliana starts to feel uneasy.

Several wretched seconds pass, until finally Juliana says, "What?"

Shelly bursts out laughing and says, "Nothing! I'm just playing with you! Oh my gosh, your *face*. But nevertheless, the point stands. My job is to worry about your future, not your past. Hop in."

Juliana doesn't exactly hop, but she does at least slide into the car. Is she reverting to her old college self, unsteady and bewildered?

How can she *stop*? Shelly takes the back way, avoiding Water Street, and when they reach the intersection of Old Town, Dodge, and Corn Neck she turns, expertly avoiding a couple of cyclists who have drifted too far from the edge of the road. "Good beach day," Shelly observes. "Still pretty quiet. Wait until you see how absolutely *nuts* it gets here after July Fourth." They pass the Yellow Kittens, Mc-Aloon's, the Beachhead, the pavilion at Fred Benson Town Beach.

When Shelly pulls up the long drive to Juliana's house, Juliana opens the door and gathers her phone, her water bottle, her resolve. Then she sees that Shelly has turned off the ignition and is getting out herself.

"I'll pop in and see the house."

"Oh," says Juliana. "I'd love you to. It's just that I have a call with L.A.—"

"Don't worry about it! I can totally entertain myself."

Juliana draws in her breath. "It's going to be a pretty long call."

"Okay," says Shelly merrily. "Did you say it's at one?"

"Yes. But I have to do some prep first."

"No worries. Let me just—" She sticks her head into the back seat and emerges with a pad of paper and a pen. "Let's just do a super-quick meeting, so I can get started on the PR plan."

In they go through the side entrance, and into the kitchen, with its vast, gleaming countertops, the island that goes on *forever*, the appliances that are too fancy to be shiny so instead are gunmetal, industrial.

"Oh my *God*," says Shelly. "This is yours?"

"Mine," says Juliana. She straightens her spine. Mine, mine, mine. Her assistant, Allison, pokes her head in and says, "Need anything?"

"All good!" says Juliana. "Thank you." She points at Shelly and says, "Ran into an old friend. This is Shelly. Shelly, Allison."

"Hi, Shelly." Allison consults her phone. "You've got L.A. at one. You know that, right?"

"Yup. One. I'll take that in the office." Allison gives a jaunty thumbs-up and disappears. Shelly pulls out a stool at the island, so Juliana does the same. Shelly lays out her phone, face down, her notepad, her pen.

"My wheels are just turning here . . . turning, turning, I've *got* it!" Shelly snaps her fingers. "How do you feel about animals?"

"Fine?" says Juliana. "Do you mean like dogs or cats or—"

"Doesn't have to be pets," interrupts Shelly. "Could be something endangered. Wildlife. Or the environment! How do you feel about the environment?"

"Hopeless," admits Juliana.

"Perfect," says Shelly. On her notepad she writes, *HOPELESS RE: ENVIRONMENT.* "Hopeless we can use." Her phone begins to buzz and she flips it over and frowns at it. "Listen, I have a hundred things to take care of. But this is a great start. I'm going to begin working on this, on putting together a plan. In the meantime, when did you say the next party is?"

"I haven't decided yet."

"How about Friday? Summer solstice party!"

Juliana has to think for only a second. That's an *excellent* idea. She's impressed! "Actually, Shelly, that's a really good idea."

Shelly beams. "Do you have people who can pull it together for you, or should I share some thoughts on the theme?"

"I have people."

"Amazing. I'll come Friday, and after that we'll talk about how we can elaborate on the parties in the future. I'm so glad I ran into you, Jade!"

"Juliana."

NICOLA

On Thursday evening Nicola is in her kitchen, about to FaceTime her parents, when she hears a rapping on the front door of the cottage. She opens the door to find a young woman, maybe college age or maybe slightly older, with glorious eyebrows and pillowy lips. An Instagram face; it looks, even standing in front of Nicola in real life, as if it has been run through a filter to smooth and plump the skin and raise the cheekbones. Her name is Allison, she says, and she's been sent over by her boss, Nicola's neighbor Juliana George, who would be "honored" if Nicola would attend her "little get-together" the following night.

"What's the occasion?" Nicola asks.

Allison blinks, her wide, catlike eyes growing even wider and more catlike. "Summer solstice."

The longest day of the year. This is not something Nicola can remember having specifically celebrated before.

"Wow, okay, thank you very much. If I'm free I'd love to go." Allison cocks her head as if seeing right through Nicola. *You already have plans?* her look seems to say. *You?* "Oh, who am I kidding," Nicola confesses. "I'm very free." Then, because she's from Minnesota and this is how she was brought up, she says, "What can I bring?"

Allison looks startled, as if Nicola has asked if it's all right if she comes mostly nude, but wearing tap shoes. "Just yourself," she says, all business. Maybe Allison's personality has been run through a filter as well.

BY THE TIME the next evening comes Nicola is tired and not feeling festive, summer solstice or not. There has been an emergency at the Institute; a recent high tide has blocked the flow of water leaving one of the tanks, and it's overflowed. Apparently this is a common occurrence, this overflowing, and actually it was a little bit exciting, the way the interns all pulled together to sort it out, but it was also supremely messy, and as a result she smells like algae and plankton.

She considers not going. She won't be missed—she doesn't even know the host. But early evening falls toward late evening and cars begin to pull into the driveway next door. FOMO gets her by its ugly teeth. She showers off the algae; she dons the one nice dress she brought for the summer. She takes a deep breath and tells herself that she can do this, she can go to a party alone. She hasn't been to any parties since Zachary, not real parties anyway. There are a lot of things she hasn't done since Zachary. Sex is another thing. She hasn't done sex since Zachary. It was her decision, to end things, to move here, to start over—but that doesn't make it all a breeze.

The party has the feel of a scene where you might turn around and see, say, an indie movie director or a singer just off a tour, maybe not an outdoor giant stadium tour but one that includes lots of hip, smaller venues. Olivia Rodrigo before the Grammys; Noah Kahan before *Stick Season*. In one corner of the lawn, in a cabana, a DJ in a plain black T-shirt, sunglasses, and giant headphones is frowning at the sky, which is growing dark, with tinges of pink around the edges, and dancing by himself. Which Nicola supposes is what DJs do.

There's a small line at an outdoor bar, and behind the bar the doors to the house are flung wide open. In and out of these doors move a steady stream of partygoers, flitting like moths. Nicola misses Zachary so suddenly and fiercely the missing feels like pain.

The feel of entering a new situation with a hand in hers: she misses that.

Deep breath, girl. Deep breath. She joins the line at the bar.

". . . get you?" says the bartender, the first half of his question lost because just then the DJ turns up the music and a little cry goes up from the dancing crowd and a song Nicola almost knows, rendered nearly unrecognizable by a beat laid underneath it, begins to play.

"I don't know," she says, unsure of what sort of drinks people order at a party like this. Gin and tonic is her go-to summer drink. Can she do better? "What's good?" He holds up one finger and says, "I got you," and before Nicola can think twice she's in possession of an apricot-colored drink.

"A twist on an Aperol Spritz," the bartender says. Nicola takes a sip. She likes it. Another sip, and then, because she drinks too fast when she's anxious, a third one.

"Have you seen Juliana?" demands a woman with streaky hair and long tanned legs. Nicola shakes her head and says that she hasn't even met her; she doesn't know what she looks like. The woman scrutinizes Nicola and says, "Juliana and I went to college together. BC. Go Eagles!" With that pronouncement she's gone, melting into the crowd.

Nicola moves toward the edge of the bar area and almost bumps into a woman with a half-shaved head. The hair on the other half is pink. She's drinking a twist on an Aperol Spritz as well, and smiling at Nicola.

"Melanie," she says, offering the hand not holding a drink.

"Nicola."

"Dog trainer to the rich and famous," she says. Her handshake is firm and she has about her a no-nonsense attitude that Nicola figures goes a long way with a doodle or a corgi. When she releases Nicola her hand hangs for a second in the air, as if at any second it's going to reach for a treat pouch or a clicker.

"What rich and famous?" Nicola is genuinely interested.

The woman makes a motion as if closing a zipper running hor-
izontally across her lips. "Client confidentiality."

Nicola tries not to roll her eyes. "Got it."

Nicola sees someone moving toward her. She glances, then her
eyes come back for a double take. It's none other than Jack Baker.
Jack Baker! A familiar face. A familiar, sexy face.

"Take my arm, I'll rescue you," he says. She takes his arm and he
leads her to the edge of the crowd and says, "That lady is a nutcase.
She had me cornered at another party the other night."

"A party here?"

"No. It was—" He waves a hand in the general direction of town.
"It was somewhere else. I couldn't get away. I don't even have a dog,
Nicola." (He remembers my name! thinks Nicola.) "Do you need
another drink?"

She looks down at her glass: empty. "Yeah," she says. Then, remembering her manners, "Yes, please."

"Wait here."

He returns with fresh drinks and offers Nicola his arm again. He
doesn't have to ask her twice to grasp back onto that smooth, tanned
limb. She walks with Jack Baker inside, through what she imagines
would have been called the ballroom, if this were a Disney movie
and she the misfit in rags. Her dress is hardly rags but everybody else
is wearing something more interesting, more Instagram- or VSCO-
worthy, or at least their eyebrows and jewelry and shoes are more
interesting. The hair on almost all the women, save the Dog Trainer
to the Stars, is preternaturally straight, center-parted, swinging. By
comparison, Nicola feels like a frizz monster, and like the only person who smells like the bottom of the ocean despite the shower.

Anchored together in this way Nicola and Jack move past a long
table with an impressive raw bar and, next to that, an array of tiny
desserts: mini carrot cakes and cheesecakes and exquisite cupcakes
and fruit kebabs, all lined up, soldiers ready for battle.

"Hungry?" asks Jack, and Nicola says that she isn't, even though she sort of is. She berates herself silently for that: this is not the 1950s; women are allowed to have appetites! She casts a regretful look at the kebabs and follows Jack to a corner high-top table. Several clumps of two or three or four party guests are scattered throughout the room; it's a lot of people, but there is space to spare. Long windows, nearly floor to ceiling, line one wall. Through them Nicola can see the dark edges of the sky moving closer toward the center; the sun has set, and, just like that, the longest day of the year has come and gone.

(Later someone will point out to Nicola that this year the solstice had actually occurred on June 20, so the party was off by one day. You can, Nicola will reflect, wait and wait for the longest day of the year, and still you may miss it.)

They rest their drinks on the table and look around. There is a strong feeling—almost an odor, or anyway at least a scent—of money in the air. Perhaps in some cases it's a lack of money, and a corresponding desire for it. Everybody seems to be making a Secret Deal, or taking a photo that might turn out to be Important, if Not Life-Changing, and the promise of Something seems so close, so tantalizing, as if you can reach out and pluck the possibilities like peaches from a tree. "How's she know so many *people*?" Nicola asks Jack.

"Oh, I don't think she knows them all," says Jack, smiling. "They're not all invited. They just come."

"*I* was invited," Nicola says, "not to brag or anything," and he smiles again, that wide, white smile. He taps the tip of Nicola's nose with his finger and says, "Aren't you adorable."

Two girls dressed in yellow (in homage to the solstice? Nicola wonders) come up to them then; they chat with Jack and mostly ignore Nicola. When they're gone Nicola puts her face close to Jack's ear—there are speakers in here to bring the DJ's music closer, and it's loud—and whisper-shouts that she has not yet met Juliana George.

Jack furrows his brow and taps his ear the way you do when you need somebody to repeat something.

"I haven't met the host yet!" she says.

"Ahhhh!" Jack nods. "Let's fix that. Come with me." They leave their empty glasses on the table—three young men in black T-shirts have been clearing glasses and plates—and Nicola follows Jack out of the ballroom to another part of the house, down a wide hallway that leads to a set of stairs. "Front stairs," he says, pointing. "Back stairs are over there. Library," he says, pointing again, and Nicola sees, through the open door, a semicircle of a room with floor-to-ceiling bookshelves. She spends a moment contemplating the feat of architectural design that makes possible built-ins in a rounded wall.

"I feel like I'm in a live game of Clue," she says.

Jack laughs appreciatively at this. "Colonel Mustard did it, if you're wondering."

"I knew it," says Nicola. "The bastard."

"Seems like it's always Colonel Mustard," he says.

"Yesss!" Nicola cries, even though in her experience it's always Professor Plum. She and her sisters used to play a lot of Clue, especially at the lake, where there is only one television and no cable, no Wi-Fi. Sometimes they hated that, and sometimes they tolerated it, but more often they loved it. Especially now that those endless summer days are over—they still go when they can, but never so freely, never so unencumbered, never so *endlessly* as they did in the past—now they really love it.

Jack's phone buzzes, and he glances at it and says, "Sorry, darling, I have to take this." Despite her internal efforts to remain impervious to his charms, the way Jack Baker says *darling* does something naughty to Nicola. "Here, wait for me in there"—he gestures toward the library—"and I'll be right back. Okay, Nicky?"

From where did Jack get permission to use the nickname that only her family is allowed to use? "Okay." She enters the library and stands for at least a full minute, maybe longer, looking at the spectacular shelves, before someone says, "It's something else, isn't it?"

Nicola jumps. There's a person in the room with her, a woman about her age, could be younger, could be older, with shoulder-length dark hair, really curly, those enviable curls that probably drive the owner crazy, and a simple white slip dress. Beautiful skin, darker than Nicola's. That's not saying much; most people have skin darker than Nicola's, Minnesota having originally been settled by pale people. The other woman is upright in one of the three easy chairs that sit, like the three points on a triangle, in the center of the room, around a large round leather table. She's not looking at a phone or at any of the books; she gives the impression of having been recently deep in thought. Her smile is small and cautious, and her eyes are big and brown.

"It's amazing," Nicola says. "I'm pretty sure this is the nicest house I've ever been in." The woman nods, as though this is a test and Nicola has given the right answer. Nicola thinks of the home she grew up in, a home that a real estate listing might describe as *cozy* and *well-loved* but only when using those terms as a collective euphemism for *cramped* and possibly *shabby*. She thinks of her and her sisters sharing the one bathroom on the second floor, the endless stream of female clutter moving across the countertops, bobby pins and scrunchies and bottles of makeup and perfume and mouthwash, one of them always tipped over and leaking resolutely from a cap that hadn't been put on tightly enough. The lake house on Pokegama, the real estate listing would call *rustic* and *full of character from times gone by,* which mostly means that the appliances are all due for replacing.

"Are you trying to escape the party?" ventures Nicola. A fellow introvert?

"A little," says the woman. "I'll go back out soon. I just—" A fraction of a shrug, a pause. "I just needed a break."

"Sure, I get that." Nicola wonders when Jack is coming back to call her *darling* again and to let her lips get close to his ear. What is *taking* him so long? "I just can't believe all this space for one person," Nicola goes on. "For one person! It's almost criminal."

"Almost," the woman agrees.

"I guess that's why she throws the parties," Nicola says. "To fill things up. Otherwise it would be lonely here, right?"

"That's probably one reason." Nicola waits, but the woman doesn't offer an idea of what the other reasons might be. Something about the smooth, eager expression on her face makes Nicola feel like she should keep talking. "It's the first time I've been here," she says. "Even though I live right next door."

"Right next door!"

Nicola nods. "How about you?"

"Oh, I've been here since early May," she says. "I haven't missed a single party."

"Wow. That's commitment."

"I guess you could say that."

"I'm Nicola, by the way." Nicola steps toward her and extends her hand. The woman's fingers are long and slender, ringless, though there is a trio of simple gold bracelets on her wrist. They shake. The timing works out such that she says her name at the same time Allison enters the room and also says the name: "Juliana!"

Nicola looks from one to the other. "*You're* Juliana?"

She smiles and nods. The smile is still small and careful but it has opened a fraction, then opens up more, until it's an actual grin. "I am," she says. Nicola roots around in her recent memory, trying to recall exactly what she said about the house being too big. And had she called the owner lonely? Had she said something worse? "And if you live in the cottage next door, that makes us neighbors."

"I guess it does."

"Juliana," says Allison again. "I think I found the person you were looking for. He's near the bar."

Juliana's face betrays nothing; she turns to Nicola and says genially, maybe just crossing over into formality, "I need to go speak to someone, Nicola. It was so nice to meet you. We should get together in a more intimate setting someday soon, so we can chat."

"We should," Nicola agrees. But she doesn't mean it. She's flustered; she feels tricked, even gaslit. Anyway, this is the sort of thing people say casually to each other all the time and never follow up on. Like the way you promise all your extended family members at a funeral that you'll have to get together in happier times, and you don't see them until you're peering into another casket.

But: "How's Monday?" Juliana turns in the doorway to say this to Nicola.

"Monday?" *Taken aback* is a gentle term for what Nicola feels.

"We'll take the mopeds out. Maybe . . . four P.M.?"

"I work until five."

"You've got meetings on Monday," Allison reminds her. "Until five-thirty."

"Let's make it six, then."

"Okay," Nicola says, too much on her back foot to really consider if she wants to accept or not. She's annoyed at Jack for depositing her in the library and not coming back for her. She's peeved at Juliana for not revealing her identity right away. She doesn't like feeling duped. She's bothered by Allison for being so together.

Allison says, "We should . . ." and looks meaningfully at Juliana.

"Right." They sweep out of the library, leaving Nicola alone. She stands there for a few minutes, looking at the books, wondering if they're real. They're arranged by color, a style she's seen on Instagram, and it looks fantastic, but she wonders how you could ever find anything you're looking for. Nicola pulls out a few, one by one, randomly: a blue, a light pink, a green. She checks them. Real.

Then she decides that if Jack isn't coming back she'll go enjoy the party on her own. Or at least she'll observe the party on her own. The DJ is going strong, and the dancers are still at it, and there's still a line at the bar. She overhears somebody say:

"Ordinance—"

And another person say, "He's a celebrity watcher, which is the same as—"

And another person say, "Fuck if *I* know, Katie—"

A couple is in the middle of a heated argument, whose flames alcohol are definitely fanning. He *never* wanted to go out with her friends even though she went out with *his* asshole friends all the time, even to that stupid hockey . . .

Who hasn't been there? I mean, seriously, *who hasn't been there?* Once Nicola and Zachary got into a fight at the Public Garden in Boston, when they'd gone for an overnight to celebrate their second anniversary. A Public Fight in the Public Garden, which, when she looks back on it, is utterly humiliating. In the moment, though, she remembers the way the rage overtook her, and how she didn't care who in the world was listening. Maybe she was even exhilarated by the sidelong glances of strangers, and the way they both refused to let the fight end. Zachary was a champion one-upper; had it been a D1 sport he'd have gotten a college scholarship.

Now that she's on the other side of it, she can see that it's not a great look, airing your grievances without checking to see who might be around. Nicola wants to take this couple aside and tell them to go to bed and talk about it in the morning. Or maybe don't talk about it! Maybe just forget it, and go out for coffee and bagels to soak up all of the alcohol, and get on with your weekend.

Nicola is feeling her drinks—ho, boy, is she feeling them. She only had two! What was *in* them? She wants to go home. She has work in the morning, even though it's Saturday; they're hosting a dock exploration, and she's in charge. The interns each take a turn with the Saturday shift. She's about to leave when she feels a hand on her arm. She turns. Jack! It's Jack. She pulls her hand away and cries, "Where'd you go for so long?" She actually sputters this; had she been a cartoon there would have been an exaggerated back-and-forth motion of her head, rubbery lips.

"Here and there," he says, looking infuriatingly sexy-chagrined.

She tries her best to ignore the sexy part. She folds her arms, hoping this gesture, pedestrian though it may be, sufficiently conveys the depth of her frustration. "You left me! I was talking to Juliana but I didn't know it was Juliana and you *never came back*, and then she had to go talk to someone, and you never came back!"

"Sorry," he says. "I am sorry, darling Nicky, I am. I got caught up talking to some guys I know." Jack strikes Nicola then—as he will even more later in the summer, after everything—as someone who remains smoothly impassive in the face of others' agitation. Even grief, probably. She'll learn more as time goes on, but she can see already that he's shellacked all over with an impermeable coating that allows nearly every outside influence to slide off him like water from oilcloth. Then he says, "You won't believe the story I just heard."

"Well, what is it?" Nicola tries sticking her lip out like a grumpy toddler, realizes it's not playing the way she wants it to, puts the lip back where it belongs.

"Never mind, I can't tell you all of it right now—but I will eventually."

"Aw, come on! I was waiting all this time and you won't even tell me?"

He shakes his head. "It's a story for another day. But I'll definitely tell you, because it has to do with you."

"With me?"

The music stops, and Jack looks at his watch. "Right on cue. Eleven P.M."

"What's right on cue?"

"The end of the party. Block Island noise ordinance."

Where was this noise ordinance, Nicola asks, last week and the week before? Where was the noise ordinance when she couldn't sleep? Jack tells her that Juliana hadn't followed it, and had been given a warning, and was now compelled to comply. Or else.

"Or else what?"

Jack yawns. "To be honest with you, I don't know. Come on, I'll walk you home." The partygoers begin to leave, calling out to one another, or simply scattering into the darkness, the reverse of the moth-to-the-light actions from earlier. Nicola doesn't see Juliana anywhere. She hears engines start up from the driveway. The DJ has his equipment almost dismantled. It's amazing how quickly the scene goes from a party to a not-party, as though the whole thing had been merely a stage set and has to be taken down to move the production to a new city.

Jack takes Nicola's hand as they cross the lawn toward her cottage.

"How do you know everything about this place?" she asks him, still perturbed. "Noise ordinances and all that. How do you have people to meet in town? Didn't you just *get* here?" Taylor's father had bought the Buchanan house two summers ago, but renovations and decorating had taken a long time, and they'd become official residents only in April. Jack had arrived just a little earlier than Nicola had.

"Sort of. I come and go."

"Blown in by the east wind? Like Mary Poppins?"

Nicola can see the outline of his grin in the lights still blazing from the house next door. "Something like that. I'm a professional chameleon. I learn what I need to fit in wherever I end up."

"I thought you were a professional golfer."

"Ha! That too. Or was. And will be again."

He swings their joined hands between them in a gesture more intimate than Nicola thinks they deserve as two people who have only recently met, but even so there's something sweet about it, something that makes Nicola feel like they're two teenagers headed off to prom. She looks over her shoulder at her neighbor's house and feels her mood begin to shift and lighten. She's been to a real party! She stayed *until the very end* at this party! Laptops and Netflix in Providence, this is not. Look at me now, Zachary, she thinks. Look at me now. She can see shadows moving around the vast lawn, bending over to pick up trash, stacking discarded chairs, clearing the bar.

Over New Harbor hangs a slender moon. Nicola can see the green light at the end of David and Taylor's dock.

"So this is where Nicola lives," says Jack Baker, when they reach the front door of her cottage.

"This is it." She shrugs. "Nothing fancy. I'm just the poor neighbor."

"I bet it's a great little place."

"It's not bad. Perfect for one person."

His teeth are gleaming in the darkness. He leans toward Nicola, placing his palms on the door behind her. She thinks he's going to kiss her, but instead he leans his forehead against hers and stays there for a good long time. Somehow he makes this feel more intimate than a kiss. His breath smells like mint. When did he have time to pop a mint? "Should I come in and see how not bad and how perfect for one person it is?"

Every fiber of her body wants him to come in, and every fiber of her brain is telling her not to listen to her body. She's known guys like Jack Baker—who hasn't? College is full of them. The world is full of them. Jaunty, athletic, careless boys at home in their bodies, sexy boys who know their worth and where to spend it. He moves his face back from Nicola's and put his hands on her waist, tilting his chin down so he's looking up at her.

"*No*," she says finally, reluctantly. "It's late. I have work in the morning." But she's laughing when she says it, half of her wanting him not to listen to her, half of her hoping he's not the type to ignore the words in favor of what he thinks the words are really saying.

"Fair enough," he answers easily. "Could I give you a quick little good night kiss, at least?"

"Okay." She thinks it's sort of adorable that he asked.

"I'll keep it innocent, I promise."

Then his lips are on hers, and it's quick (quicker than she wants, after all) and mostly innocent, until his tongue slips briefly between her lips before he pulls away. Like a promise, that slip.

"Good night, Nicola Carr."

She tries to keep her voice steady and composed. "Good night, Jack Baker."

She goes inside, but from the window she watches him walk down her walkway, heading toward the front of Juliana's house. How is he getting home? How did he get to the party in the first place? She didn't ask. She knows he'll figure it out—he's exactly that type.

What would have been the harm in having him come in? she wonders, when she has tucked herself into bed. Lack of sleep, obviously. She would have paid for it the next day at work. She's already going to pay for the evening, because of the drinks. She gets up and guzzles a glass of water, then goes back to bed, where she lies for a long time, with her chaotic, unfamiliar thoughts, in this unfamiliar home in her small corner of an unfamiliar island, waiting for sleep.

Host: And we're back after a word from our sponsors. Remember to use the code lifeanddeath, no spaces, to get ten percent off at our gold sponsor, Mattress Queen, and our silver sponsor, Buddha Bowls 2 U. Brought to you by All Ears Media, *Life and Death on an Island* is a five-part series looking at one summer on Block Island. This is episode two, "The Town Council." When we left off before the break we were talking with council members about a mysterious death last summer. Some have attributed the death to a "party culture" that reached new levels when a business entrepreneur moved to the island. Betsy, let's start with you. What did you know about the founder of LookBook?

Betsy: Juliana George was definitely involved in something illegal. Anyone who makes that much money is not on the up-and-up. I'm sorry, but it's true. Look at Elizabeth Banks.

Evan: You mean Elizabeth Holmes?

Betsy: Either way.

Kelsey: Aren't we here to talk about the council? Should we maybe like *talk* about the council meetings? I'll start. We meet on the first Wednesday of the month.

Evan: I've got three kids under the age of seven. I look forward to these meetings. Sometimes we go over to Poor People's and get a beer after. Lou over here? That guy can drink.

Lou: I'm not ashamed.

Evan: Last summer the island was considering a proposal by Buchanan Enterprises to tear down a motel on Dodge Street and build a "boutique inn and spa." I know the listeners can't see me but I'm using air quotes because I can't say it with a straight face.

Kelsey: Personally, I think a spa sounds amazing. Can I tell you how many hours a week I spend on my feet?

Betsy: People are real touchy on the subject of hotels since the Harborside burned down two summers ago. I mean, what if these Buchanans were involved? It's not like they'd be the first people on Earth to commit arson.

Lou: Betsy!

Betsy: What? I'm not the one who thought of that. It was Catherine from the bookstore who said it first.

Evan: It was while that proposal was front and center that Instagram account started; @keeptheblock, it was called, and—

Kelsey: Sorry to interrupt. But I think it was @keeptheblockthe block. I don't know who started the Instagram account. Some of those comments were pretty harsh. The whole account is gone now.

Betsy: In retrospect, I wonder if we ganged up on Taylor Buchanan.

Evan: We who?

Betsy: We as a town. As an island.

Lou: We didn't gang up on her.

Kelsey: I definitely didn't. By the way, I would kill for her hair. Sorry. Bad choice of words. She has really pretty hair. No question, she goes off-island for those highlights. Goes? Went? I don't know.

Betsy: You want the real scoop on what's going on in this town, though? Don't go to the town council meetings, or the zoning board meetings, which are even worse. It's a snoozefest at the zoning board meetings.

Lou: I second that.

Betsy: What you want to do is go to the post office in the afternoon, when the locals go pick up the mail that came in on the boat midday. Better yet, better than the post office? Go to the dump.

Lou: Man, I love the dump.

Evan: That's where I first heard about the body. At the dump.

JULIANA

By the time six o'clock on Monday rolls around Juliana no longer feels like going on a moped ride with a stranger. What had she been thinking? She wasn't even drunk when she invited Nicola! She never gets drunk at her own parties. She never has more than two drinks, period. Drunk equals loss of control and loss of control is what causes bad things to happen. She's seen enough of that in her life.

Obviously she knows what she was thinking. She knows exactly why she wants to get to know Nicola. But she's tired. She had a long day of meetings—an investment bank interview, prep for the upcoming board meeting, a check-in with the CFO.

Juliana peeks out the window in her upstairs office and sees her neighbor making her way across the grass between their house; she wills herself into a better mood. She can will herself into anything. She's gone to school hungry; she's gone to bed scared; she's stood before a roomful of investors and conquered her terror only by telling herself that not a single person in the room has overcome what she's overcome to be there. Just keep moving, she'd told herself in every one of these situations. Just. Keep. Moving. A moped ride is nothing.

Anyway, why *shouldn't* she be in a good mood? The day had been cloudy, but an afternoon rain shower took the clouds and some of the humidity with it when it departed, and now the air is clear, the water in Great Salt Pond sparkling. She lives *here*. She owns *this house*. Just keep moving.

Juliana greets Nicola and walks her around to where the two mopeds wait in all their gleaming black sleekness. She's barely used one of them; the other one, she's never used at all.

"Wow!" says Nicola. "These look a little fancier than what they rent down by the ferry. These look like the Cadillacs of the moped world!"

"Actually, they're BMWs." Immediately after the words leave her mouth Juliana chastises herself. Was that an obnoxious thing to say? She can never get this right, the line between being generous and arrogant. With the board? Sure. With potential investment bankers, journalists? No problem. She knows who she is and what she wants and how to get there. But put her with someone close to her own age and her mind goes off the rails, she flounders.

Nicola laughs. "Okay, then," she says merrily. "BMW, Cadillac—honestly, it's all the same to me!"

Juliana suggests they do a partial loop of the island, following West Side to Cooneymous to Lakeside, then take Mohegan Trail to Spring Street into town. They'll end up at Ballard's, where Juliana will treat them to a cocktail and dinner.

"Oh, gosh, you don't need to treat," says Nicola, and in her voice Juliana can hear a touch of Minnesota that makes her think of . . . well, of David. Of course, David. "But I do need a little moped lesson. I've only driven one once, and it was a long time ago."

Juliana shows Nicola the accelerator, and how to brake and steer. She shows her how to balance with her feet on the ground, and where to place her feet on the running boards. Once Nicola has all of this down—she practices on Juliana's driveway, and she's a quick study—off they go.

The island looks spectacular as they cruise around toward the west side. Sunset is still nearly two hours away, but the sky is getting ready, and Golden Hour is almost upon them. The sunsets on this side of the island, off Dorry's Cove and Stevens Cove, are said to be phenomenal, and Juliana makes a mental note to see one sometime this summer. The rolling hills of Mohegan Trail as it eases into Spring Street give her that roller coaster euphoria (a trip to Canobie Lake Park during a YMCA summer camp for underprivileged children unleashes itself from her memory), and, as they coast into town, the thought floats through Juliana's mind, unobtrusive and wispy as a cloud, that she's finally made it.

Ballard's is massive, with a large indoor section and a multitude of blue-umbrellaed outdoor tables. Beyond the tables is a long stretch of beach and two tiki bars. A breakwater juts into the ocean; on the sand, a group of young women photograph each other. And why shouldn't they? This is the literal definition of picture perfect. A ferry moves majestically past. Juliana and Nicola order two Rum Runners.

Nicola gulps her Rum Runner, then says, "Sorry. Sorry! I need to slow down. Had a crazy day." She tells Juliana that she works at the Block Island Maritime Institute; she tells her that she left a career in law to become the Oldest Intern in the World. She tells Juliana she has law school loans that would keep her up at night if she let herself think about them.

"We had a class of six-year-olds in from a day camp in Newport," continues Nicola. "They looked cherubic from the outside, but let me tell you, there was something very different going on inside. A girl named Avery tried to climb in the touch tank."

"Oh, no!" says Juliana dutifully.

"A boy named Smith, who *had a more recent iPhone than I have,* wanted to take a selfie with a shark, which obviously wasn't an option, but he wouldn't stop talking about it." She tells Juliana she's involved in planning the Dolphin Program, a weeklong residential program for groups from schools that traditionally have low college attendance rates.

"Oh my god," says Juliana. "There are *dolphins* here? This island keeps getting better and better!"

Nicola smiles. "I made the same mistake. No, the program is named after a woman with the last name Dolphin."

"Ah! Got it."

"Sorry. I was disappointed too, when I first heard about it."

"There are also," says Juliana, "zero mansions on Mansion Beach."

"Also disappointing," says Nicola. She sits back and adds, "I love it, though. Honestly, I'm complaining, but I'm not really complaining. I'm learning so much already, about coastal exposure, and the effect of rising sea levels on marine life . . . well, I don't want to bore you."

"I'm not bored," says Juliana, though she is, in fact, a tiny bit bored. Nevertheless! She's on a mission. "Let's order," she suggests.

The menu is nearly as vast at the landscape. Lobster thirteen ways. Steamers, sautéed littlenecks. Sushi! Drinks served in whole pineapples. They each order a lobster roll, and while they're waiting they trade backgrounds: schools, previous jobs, and so on. Juliana learns that Nicola recently broke up with a long-term boyfriend, and that she has a lot of sisters. Juliana gives her short version of her education and the beginning of her company. Nicola says Juliana should come snorkeling with her. There's a great spot at Surf Beach, she tells her.

Juliana's heart skips. She hates when this topic comes up, but it's best to get it out of the way and keep it there. She shakes her head. "Can't. I'm sorry, but I can't."

Nicola blinks. "Why not?"

Deep breath. Push down the shame, Juliana. The shame isn't yours anymore. "I'm scared of the water."

Brow furrowed, Nicola asks, "In what way?"

"In the scary way. I can't swim."

Nicola takes several seconds to absorb this and then she says, "Like, at all?"

"At all." Juliana clears her throat. "I never took swimming lessons as a kid."

Nicola's eyes grow wide. Juliana can see what she's thinking: everyone takes swimming lessons as a kid. "You live on the water. Isn't that—dangerous?"

"Not if I don't go in the water."

"But what if you fall in?"

"I won't. I'm careful."

"I could teach you," says Nicola. "I used to teach swimming at the lake. We have a family cottage? On Pokegama? Back home, in Minnesota."

Juliana knows about the lake house; it was described to her only once but she memorized the description so well, and she has thought about it so often, that she could probably draw the place: the screen porch, the dock, the galley kitchen, the picnic table on a blanket of pine needles.

"I don't think so," says Juliana. "Thank you. I appreciate it. But I'll be okay."

Nicola nods, and Juliana watches her cast about for a way to change the subject. Here it comes: "Did you like Boston College?"

What a loaded question, thinks Juliana. What a loaded, loaded question. Not that she hasn't been asked before. She's perfected the art of the *"Loved* it!" before smoothly changing the subject. Their lobster rolls arrive, and for a minute both Nicola and Juliana are busy, each taking a bite, reaching for napkins. Then, surprising herself, Juliana says, "College was hard for me. Not so much academically. Academically, it got me exactly where I needed to be. I never would have started LookBook without the education I got there. I mean more—socially." Wow, this conversation is getting deeper than she'd expected. "I—my mom died when I was thirteen. I never knew my dad."

Juliana waits for the response that all people give when she reveals this part of her history, which she doesn't do very often. The response is typically a widening of the eyes, a tilt of the head, a soft intake of breath, followed by one of three statements: *I'm so sorry to hear that.* Or *I had no idea.* Or *I can't even imagine what that must have been like.* It's an a la carte menu; you can have any combination. Nicola chooses the intake of breath with *I'm so sorry to hear that.* And Juliana says what she always says, which is, "It's okay. It was a long time ago." Even though, yes, it was a long time ago, but no, it's not okay. Then she says what she sometimes says, because the cultural touchstone resonates with enough people: "Before she died, my mom and I were like *Gilmore Girls.* It was the two of us against the world." For a certain type of person—typically a female who was a teen or preteen in the early 2000s—this romantic ideal is almost enough to erase the pity.

"I *love Gilmore Girls,*" says Nicola, right on cue.

Usually Juliana stops there. But there's something about Nicola's warm, open face, her ready smile, that makes Juliana keep talking. (Is it possible that Juliana, in high school too lonely and bewildered, in college too socially marginalized and later too driven, too busy for real female friendships, is making a *new friend?*) "I thought when I got to college I'd finally be on equal ground with everyone else, you know? Because we were *all* there without our parents. We were *all* beginning our adult lives. But it wasn't like that. It wasn't like that at all. I don't think I realized how it all worked . . ."

Nicola is nodding slowly, chewing, nodding some more. It seems like she might actually get it, and she's looking at Juliana with a face so full of *understanding* that it almost makes Juliana want to cry. "Yeah. I totally see what you're saying."

They both let those sentiments lift and settle around them, and then Juliana finds herself saying, "But having acknowledged that, I got a lot out of my education. A lot. I'm the only person from my class with a company about to go public." She pauses, checks herself. What is she *doing?* Has she completely lost her mind? She's not supposed to talk about this with someone she's just met. "That's not public knowledge yet. It's just rumors, for now. So if you don't mind keeping that to yourself . . ."

"Oh, don't worry about me," says Nicola. "I'm not into gossip. Or fashion." She gestures to herself; she's wearing cutoffs and a T-shirt that says SKIP A STRAW, SAVE A TURTLE. "Obviously."

One visit to LookBook and Nicola could change that, if she wanted, thinks Juliana. Maybe she'll offer Nicola a friends and family code. She'd look amazing in a smocked maxi dress, and Juliana would bet she's never even tried one on.

"The way I grew up," continues Nicola, "high fashion was like if you went to Target when they put out a new bathing suit line and you could convince your mom to get you one so you could match with your middle school friends." (Target would have been downright fancy for Juliana in middle school, but she doesn't say that.) "My whole family is low-maintenance like that," Nicola adds. She seems to pause to consider and Juliana waits, metaphorically sitting on her hands so she doesn't raise one out of turn. "Except for one. My cousin David. He married into money. Like, a lot of money. He knows LookBook! In fact, he was shocked when he heard you're my neighbor. He lives here, on the island, in the summer. He's the reason I have use of the cottage. Well, his wife is."

Juliana can feel the blood pulsing to her heart, to her cheeks. She tries not to overreact. She says, "Isn't that funny." Acting like it's no big deal. Lots of people know her company! She can't say anything more. She's already shared too much about herself, more than she meant to share, even if she didn't let Nicola get all the way to the core, where the most naked truths lie. She hadn't expected Nicola to be so nice, so willing to listen, so *interested* in All Things Juliana. She hadn't planned to roll over, reveal her soft and tender underbelly. Usually it took much longer than this for Juliana to trust someone.

The bill comes and they both grab for it. "No! You just had me at your party. It's my turn." Nicola says this sternly, midwesternly, the accent popping through again, the upward tone at the end of the sentence, the emphasis on the *r* in *turn*.

"Absolutely not," says Juliana. "Nope. I told you at the beginning, my treat." Almost, she comes out with the rest of it right then and there, cuts out the middleman. But she's already spoken to Jack; the middleman is in place; she shouldn't muddy the waters by changing the plan.

Deep breath, keep moving, don't stop.

"Anyway," she goes on. "I might need a favor from you someday."

"From me?"

"Yes."

Nicola squints at her and says, "I can't imagine what *I* could do for *you*." Juliana produces what she hopes is a Mona Lisa smile, serene and enigmatic. "But, here, give me your phone. I'll put my number in. Text me with yours."

Juliana does this, and when Nicola hands her back the phone she feels a childlike thrill. She had planned on this trip to take Nicola's measure, to see how Nicola might react when Jack Baker talks to her. But maybe in the process she's done something unexpected: maybe she's made a new friend.

As they wind their way through the tables and out to the mopeds, what Juliana notices more than anything else, what she's really been noticing the whole time, is that Nicola moves through the world like someone who's loved by a lot of people. It would be easy to hate her for that. But if Juliana played by those rules, she'd have so many people to hate.

———

When Jade learned that she was the recipient of a full scholarship to Boston College, the first person she told was her guidance counselor, Ms. Morin, who had shepherded her through the college application process, and who had also found money for the application fees in a mysterious "PTO fund" that Jade suspected was actually Ms. Morin's own bank account. She helped Jade fill out a FAFSA; she helped her set up a Naviance account to track her applications; she showed her how to do virtual tours on the websites of the colleges she couldn't visit in person—which was all the colleges, because how was Jade supposed to get to college visits when there were days she could hardly get to high school? When Jade needed a quiet place to concentrate on her applications—and she wouldn't find this at home, that was for sure, not at foster home number nine—she sometimes sat in Ms. Morin's office, at a small table in the corner, listening to the tap tap tap of Ms. Morin's hands on her own keyboard and occasionally her conversations with her husband or children about what was for dinner or whose turn it was to unload the dishwasher.

I'll unload the dishwasher! Jade wanted to say. *Take me in, I'll unload all the dishwashers forever!*

But of course you can't say that.

One day in late November, staring at the supplemental essays required for her application to the University of Massachusetts, Jade felt a weight on her shoulders and neck so heavy she suddenly could hardly move. Her chest felt tight; her arms were tingling; the words on the screen in front of her began to blur. "I can't do it," she said.

Ms. Morin turned from her own screen, startled. "Why not?"

"It's all impossible. I'm not meant for college."

Ms. Morin set her lips in a tight line. "Trust me. Nobody is more meant for college than you are."

"But there are so many steps." Ms. Morin didn't understand. Jade shook her head. "I mean, so I get in somewhere, right? Then what? I can't pay for it. I know we filled out the forms, but—it's so much money. Those forms don't get you all the money, and I need all the money."

Ms. Morin pushed her chair back from her desk and stood up so fast Jade thought she was going to knock over her computer.

"Uh-uh," said Ms. Morin. "Nope. Absolutely not. I will not hear that from you." Jade had heard her talk this sternly only one time before, when her children called to tell her that they'd broken a vase Ms. Morin and her husband had gotten as a wedding present. "There's scholarship money all over this planet if you look hard enough, if you value yourself enough. Might not be to your first choice. Might be to some school you've never heard of. But you are valedictorian of this class, Jade Gordon, and no valedictorian in *my school*"—she said this as though she personally owned the school, even though it was public and she was not even vice principal, never mind principal—"no valedictorian in *my school* is going to fail to go to college. You hear me?"

I guess this is what they mean when they say tough love, thought Jade. Didn't feel as nice as gentle love probably felt, but given the choice between the tough kind and no love at all she'd take it.

So when she *did* get the money, and when it *was* to a school she had not only heard of but dreamed of attending, her first call was to Ms. Morin. Who was she kidding? Her *only* call was to Ms. Morin. Ms. Morin *screamed*. Jade heard her telling whoever was in the room with her that it was okay, it was happy screaming. Then she returned to the call with Jade and said, "You're going to college, girlfriend. You, Jade Gordon, are going to college."

JADE'S ROOMMATE WAS a randomly assigned girl from Weston, Massachusetts, named Mary Ann. Mary Ann's parents were an ageless, lovely-smelling couple named Bob and Kathleen. They worked with the efficiency of the military to set up Mary Ann's side of the room. Bob used a level from a tool kit he brought to affix four small, square, uniformly framed black-and-white photos of Paris to the wall. Then, while he attached a gray padded headboard to the wall (Headboard? thought Jade. She had no headboard at home, never mind an extra one to bring to college!), Kathleen made Mary Ann's bed with crisp white sheets whose edges were piped in gray, and sent a matching gray comforter billowing over it. When the comforter had settled (with an audible sigh of satisfaction, it seemed to Jade), Kathleen folded a darker gray quilt in thirds and placed it at the foot of the bed. Next came the storage cubes that fit under the bed, the suede hangers for the standing wardrobe, the office supplies to unpack into the desk. Jade tried to make herself appear busy on her side of the room, though truth be told she had already unpacked everything she'd brought and had nothing left to do.

"Lawrence, huh?" said Bob, after grilling Jade politely. "How about that, huh? Jade's from Lawrence!" Jade watched Kathleen rummage through her mental file box, emerging eventually with the pronouncement that she thought she'd once "eaten a First Communion cake from a bakery in Lawrence" and that it had been delicious. Only she didn't say *delicious*, she said *scrumptious*, with a toss of her honey-colored bob, and Jade thought she saw Mary Ann gently cringe.

"Great area," Bob said affably. "Lawrence." Jade said, "Sure," although it really wasn't, in places it was terrible, and Bob added, "Shame they can't do more with those old mill buildings." Jade agreed that yes, it was a shame, not realizing then that this genial, agreeable, ultimately *false* costume she had slipped on for Bob and Kathleen was one that she'd wear for the next four years, and for a long time after that.

Kathleen and Mary Ann had moved on to the dresser, carefully arranging underwear and socks in small white boxes that somehow fit the drawers exactly. How had they known to acquire these?

"I don't know what I would have done if you'd chosen Chapel Hill," said Kathleen. "If we had to say goodbye to you and then get on a plane . . ." Her voice trailed off. Bob squeezed Kathleen's shoulder, as though to shield her from even the thought of a multistate distance between her and her daughter.

The goodbye between daughter and parents, though Mary Ann's house in Weston was only nineteen minutes away, less as the crow flies, was tearful and punctuated by long silent hugs that seemed to have no end in sight. Jade tried to bury herself behind the open door of her own wardrobe, but this was a fruitless endeavor because the door didn't reach all the way to the floor and certainly her feet were visible. After the hugs came admonitions to call or text if Mary Ann had forgotten anything, *anything at all*, and while Jade was marveling over what it must be like to be loved like this, so thoroughly and unconditionally, so, well, so *publicly*, Bob and Kathleen slipped out the door.

At this point Mary Ann, wiping unashamedly at her tear-dampened eyes, turned to Jade and said, "Where's all your *stuff*? Is someone else bringing it?"

THEY GOT ALONG well enough, Jade and Mary Ann. It didn't take long for Mary Ann to unleash her inner party girl, and it took about the same amount of time for Jade to unleash her inner ghost, floating through the dorm, mostly invisible. Soon Mary Ann's attachment to her mother fell somewhat by the wayside, though the same could probably not be said in reverse. After a time, if Mary Ann's phone happened to be face up on her bed, Jade could see a call from Kathleen go ignored, and then two more calls after that, and then a text. The text usually said something like JUST CALLING TO CHECK IN! followed by several cheery emojis. (Emojis were new then, and Kathleen made copious use of them.) Jade couldn't imagine anyone in her life trying to get in touch with her with such vigor and regularity. She couldn't imagine anyone "just checking in."

Jade and Mary Ann were respectful of one another's space. Both tended to do laundry in the hangover quiet of a Sunday afternoon, and sometimes they'd fold together in companionable silence, playing *Gilmore Girls* in the background on Mary Ann's laptop. Both girls could sleep through mostly anything, Jade because she'd been reared in chaos, the ignoring of which was necessary for survival, and Mary Ann because she had both a state-of-the-art noise machine that played soothing waterfall sounds and an expensive pair of noise-canceling headphones that she used when her family traveled to Europe because "overnight flights were brutal."

Not that there was much noise to block from Jade's side of the room. From the first day of matriculation, when the first-year class gathered at the First Night Festival on Stokes Lawns, to graduation in Alumni Stadium, Jade mostly put her head down and she worked. And she worked. And she worked.

It was her shameful, dark secret, that she didn't come from a place of love. Maybe she wasn't the only one on the campus who had that secret—but she felt like she was.

AT BOSTON COLLEGE, Jade studied. Her classmates also studied, but they did other things too. They went to shop on Newbury Street or eat in the North End; they went to a Red Sox game, a Bruins game, a nightclub called Venu. Winter break or spring break rolled around, and off they went, sometimes on trips with their parents (Aspen, St. Barts) or with each other (Cancún, Punta Cana, Miami). They returned tastefully tanned, complaining of lack of sleep and airport delays and the papers they had yet to write for the next day's class.

Lawrence was forty-two miles from campus; fifty-two minutes in average traffic. But it may as well have been another country, because here people spoke an entirely different language. Ski houses. Prep school. Parents who were "helicoptering."

And yet the same students called upon these very same helicoptering parents when the slightest bump appeared in the road: a professor who had graded them unfairly, a credit card that wouldn't work, a simple appointment that needed scheduling.

A partial list of things Mary Ann called her parents about that first year:

1. A broken clasp on her favorite gold bracelet (her mother swung by after work one Wednesday evening to pick up the bracelet; she delivered it, clasp repaired, the following Monday).
2. Help composing an email to her writing seminar professor to challenge a poor grade on the first paper of the semester.
3. Help replacing her iPhone 4, which she had dropped on the way back to the dorms after a night out.
4. An appointment at a day spa on Newbury Street when her "skin was so dried out she couldn't stand it." (There she was the following afternoon, arranging a ride downtown from a sophomore with a car, returning with a damp sheen to her skin, needing a nap because "treatments were exhausting when they were intense.")
5. Advice on what courses to choose for the second semester.
6. More shampoo, which came from a specific hair salon near her home, and which appeared, as if by magic, outside the dorm room thirty-six hours after the request went out.

It went on from there. And on, and on, and on.

One day that freshman fall semester, Jade returned from the library to find Mary Ann lying on her own bed and, on Jade's bed, a girl from down the hall. Jade didn't know this girl's name but she saw her sometimes in the bathroom, brushing her long, wavy hair, or standing as close as she could get to the bathroom mirror, considering herself with a stern, unsparing look. Once she had said out loud, "God, I wish my nose wasn't so pointy."

Jade looked around to see who this girl might be addressing; it turned out it was nobody, or it was Jade.

"Your nose isn't pointy," Jade said after a time, because it seemed like this was what she was supposed to do. "Ohmygod, really?" Jade nodded. "Ohmygod, you're the best. *Thank* you."

"This is Shelly," Mary Ann told Jade, in the dorm room, and Jade said, "Hi," and Shelly said, "I'm *totally* lying on your bed," and smiled but made no move to rectify the situation.

"That's okay," said Jade. "I was just picking something up." (Not true.)

"No, stay!" said Shelly. She sat up, swung her legs to the floor, and patted the spot next to her, to indicate that Jade should feel welcome to sit down on her own bed.

Shelly's phone rang at that point and she glanced at it and said, "Oh boy. Mama Salazar's on the prowl."

"Answer it!" said Mary Ann, laughing. "Put her on speaker!"

Shelly laughed too and explained to Jade, "My mom's prone to day drinking and dialing." She shrugged, and pressed the *ignore call* button, while Jade gathered two books and a notebook she didn't need and slunk out of the room. Make yourself invisible, Jade. Ask nothing of anyone.

NICOLA

Three days after the moped ride Nicola and Jack Baker have drinks at the outside bar at Mahogany Shoals, in New Harbor. The workday is over. Nicola's workday, that is. Jack doesn't have a workday. How's he fill his time? He says he's mostly doing physical therapy to rehab the Achilles. He tells her that he sometimes does odd jobs for David and Taylor in exchange for their hospitality.

"What kind of odd jobs?" Nicola wants to know. (Hadn't David said they had a handyman for odd jobs? Hadn't she made fun of him for having a handyman?)

He walks it back. "Well, maybe not exactly *jobs*," he concedes. "Not jobs so much as keeping them company. I'm *very* entertaining, Nicky."

The night before, Jack texted Nicola and asked her to meet for a drink so he could tell her a story.

WHAT KIND OF STORY? she texted back, then, feeling sassy, she added, A BEDTIME STORY? She added this 😊 emoji, then deleted it. Too far.

NEXT TIME ON THE BEDTIME STORY, came the answer. STORY ABT YOUR NEIGHBOR.

All day an anticipatory sensation had traveled up and down Nicola's spine, keeping her company while she cleaned out the touch

tanks and greeted visitors. Already life on Block Island is more interesting than life in Providence. Earlier in the week a dead humpback
whale washed up on the west side of the island, and tomorrow a
group from the Institute is going out to see it.

Not only that, though. She's been to a party with influencers!
She's having drinks outside! Somebody (somebody hot) is going to
tell her a story!

"It was New York City, almost five years ago—" begins Jack,
when they're settled at the bar. Payne's Dock reaches out into Great
Salt Pond, and along it are dozens of boats.

The bartender approaches, and Jack tells Nicola, "To be continued." The bartender has leathery skin and bright blond hair and a
line of earrings marching up both her ears. "I'll have the usual," Jack
tells the bartender with a wink (he looks like the emoji she didn't
use, but hotter) and she nods and looks at Nicola. Nicola says she
needs a minute.

When the bartender has moved away Nicola says, "You have a
usual drink? So not your first time here?"

"It's not even my first time here *today*," he admits. "I'm trying to
make this my summer version of a local pub."

"Okay," she says. "Living the dream, are you?"

"A version of the dream," he says.

When Nicola looks across the pond she can see Juliana's massive home with her own (Taylor's) small cottage beside it. Her
cottage looks like a toddler sitting next to its mother, waiting for
instruction. When she swivels her head in the other direction she
can see, in the great distance, what she thinks is the dock at David
and Taylor's house, though the house itself is obscured by the curve
of the land. She faces front once again and studies the menu, hanging
over the bar.

The bartender returns and puts a drink in front of Jack. "One
Dark 'N' Stormy for my favorite golfer," she says.

"Why, *thank* you," he says flirtily.

She rolls her eyes at Nicola as if to say, *This guy!* "One for you?"

"What else is good?"

"Get the Mudslide," Jack tells her. "They're famous for their Mudslides here."

"Yeah? Okay. Sure, why not. I'll have a Mudslide." The bartender nods and gets to work. A catalog-ready family with two blond adults and two blond children, one boy and one girl, step off a yacht. Anyway, Nicola thinks it's a yacht. Truly she doesn't know the difference between a yacht and a very big boat. Three young adults dock a motorboat and somebody whoops. A twentysomething in shorts and a bright pink bikini top cheers them on from land, taking pictures with an iPhone. A couple around Nicola's parents' age sit on one of the benches, watching all of this go on. She notices the way their fingers intertwine between them, and the way they aren't talking but they don't seem bored with each other either. She feels a pinprick in her heart, and that pinprick is the loss of Zachary. Is she allowed to feel the pinprick, when it was her decision to go? She hates that thoughts of Zachary have the nerve to pop up like this, unwelcome, *making her feel things.* Interlopers in her mind.

She's got to get out of her own head. So she tilts it toward the boat-maybe-yacht and asks, "Who lives like this?" Rhetorical question mostly, but seriously, *who lives like this?*

"Lots of people." Casually, as though he's petting a dog that happened to sit down near him, Jack traces the inside of Nicola's elbow with his fingers, and the sensation of pleasure she feels is almost violent. She shivers and tries not to look too closely at his lips. He has really good lips: full but not too full. Well moisturized. "Someday I'll buy you one of those, and we'll go off in it together." He says this affably, nonchalantly, like he's saying someday he'll take her to the driving range.

"Stop," she says, when what she really means is *please keep going.*

"Stop talking? Or stop this?" He lifts his finger. She doesn't answer and he continues tracing. Her drink arrives. The Mudslide is perfection in a disposable cup: cold and just sweet enough, with the tang of the vodka hitting the back of her throat. Almost instantly, she feels a little woozy. Lunch was a Clif Bar.

"Okay. Now, the story I'm about to tell you is what Juliana talked to me about the other night at the party."

"The night you deserted me in the library for like an hour?" She's teasing, a little, but she's also still stung by the abandonment, and her third sip of Mudslide has loosened her tongue. What a lightweight she is.

He puts a finger to her lips and holds it there for an instant. (Can he just *do* that? Can he just put his finger on her lips without permission?) "Yes," he says. "And you know it wasn't an hour."

"Fine," she concedes. "Go on."

"It was September, almost five years ago. Tiger Woods was recovering from knee surgery. Justin Thomas won the BMW Championship, but then Rory McIlroy won the Tour Championship in Atlanta. The next month, the Nationals were going to beat the Astros in the World Series."

"That's a lot of sports context," Nicola says. She squints into the middle distance and thinks back to almost five years ago. She was in law school. She knew Zachary, but they weren't dating yet. If she was being honest she'd say she was trying to get his attention, because at the time she thought his opacity was mysterious and sexy.

Jack continues, "LookBook was a few years old then, gaining traction. David and Taylor were engaged. David was living with me in New York City, in an apartment owned but not occupied by my parents."

"Sorry, I have to interrupt," says Nicola. "Your parents just had an extra Manhattan apartment lying around?"

"Well, it wasn't *lying around*. It was sitting. Sitting empty. They bought it as an investment." He smiles. "And they decided to invest in me." He picks up her hand and traces the inside of her palm, delivering a wicked grin at the same time. "You'll see, Nicky. I'm worth investing in."

Flustered, she tries to keep them on track. "David and Taylor didn't live together?" Taylor and David had met freshman year of college, and they'd been almost inseparable since.

"Not yet. They were renovating that brownstone in Back Bay to move into after the wedding. Taylor's dad wanted her in the Boston office, but at that time she was still in New York. She was off and running with her career."

"What about our David?"

Jack shakes his head regretfully. "Our David was at loose ends. His degree was in sociology, but, shocker, nobody was hiring sociologists with no experience."

"Was anyone hiring sociologists *with* experience?" asks Nicola, and Jack hoots.

Even if they were, explains Jack, Taylor and David were soon moving to Boston, so what was the point of trying to get a job?

"What was *your* degree in?" Nicola asks.

"Golf."

"No, seriously."

"I'm being completely serious." Jack grins again, to show her that he really isn't, but he doesn't answer the question.

"My theory," says Jack, maybe reading her mind, drawing out the word *theory* like he's getting paid for extra syllables, "is that everything I'm about to tell you has to do with race cars."

Nicola does a spit take. "*What?*"

"You know about David's race car thing," Jack says. He looks at Nicola sideways, in a way that suggests he's going to share a tremendous secret.

"Of *course*," says Nicola, pinched by the tiniest, most unobtrusive irritation. "Of *course* I know about David's race car thing." They had talked about this at dinner, didn't he remember? "I know David better than you do!"

Jack arches a single sexy eyebrow and says, "Do you?"

"Well, I used to know him better. I used to know him better than anyone did." David was the brother Nicola never had, her teacher, protector, sometimes enabler. You don't spend every holiday, a bunch of weekends, and most of the summer with someone without getting to know them as well as you know your own siblings. David taught her to drive, taught her to drink (not at the same time), taught her how to throw a football and catch a baseball and survive the scary Spanish teacher at the high school who refused to speak in English even to the beginner-level classes.

She slurps down the rest of her Mudslide and doesn't object when Jack orders another round. "So you know about the state fair," says Jack. He presses his elbow to hers, almost indecently.

Nicola reclaims her elbow and says, "Yes, Jack. I know about the fair." In 2002, the day before school started, both families, hers and David's, all eleven of them, took a family trip to the Minnesota State Fair. "I was *at* the fair. I was at the race when Gary St. Amant won the 300 after seventeen years of not winning."

"Look who has the sports knowledge now," says Jack, impressed.

"I have a lot of knowledge," says Nicola, secretly proud of herself. "Want me to tell you about it?"

"Of course I do."

"So we're at the fair, trooping around, doing all the fair things. It started off as just this experience we were going to have as a family, watch a NASCAR race, you know, something different to do before we went off to get the fried dough—"

"But something changed in David when he watched that race," says Jack, and now Nicola is impressed, because that's exactly how she would have put it.

"Exactly. Something changed in David."

"And then it became an obsession."

"Obsession is an understatement," says Nicola. "Like calling a sperm whale a moderate-sized creature." Immediately, an inconvenient, telling warmth floods her cheeks. So many whales to choose from, and she chose the sperm whale. Then: Grow up, she tells herself sternly. You are an almost-thirty-year-old woman, not a fifth-grade boy. You can say *sperm* in the context of a whale. You can say *sperm* in any context! She hurries on with her thoughts, to move the conversation forward. "But if NASCAR opened the door," she says, "sports car racing ushered him over the threshold."

"Gorgeous metaphor," says Jack. "If I were wearing a hat right now, I'd tip it."

After that, David was a lost cause. All his energy went into thinking about cars; every penny he made at their fathers' furniture store went into his car fund, until he had enough to buy an old Mazda Miata. Once he had it, all he did in his free time was tinker with it, modify it, make it into the closest thing to a sports racing car he could.

"When we were in college, he used to talk about missing that Miata like some guys in college talked about missing their high school girlfriends," says Jack.

"He loved that car," says Nicola. "I remember he was always talking about the holy trinity of sports cars. Bigger wheels, bigger engine, closer to the ground."

She heard enough about it back then to know the deal. If NASCAR is the Country Cousin of motorsports, sports car racing is a two-olive martini, elegant, elevated, with turns and curves and straightaways. Racing sports cars became what David thought about, what he wanted to do. *All* he wanted to do. He did a track day with his car when he was seventeen, and after that he was officially a lost cause. He wrote his college essay—this is the one that got him into Yale—on coming from behind in his first race. "It was called 'The Power of the Underdog,' and it was published in some anthology," she tells Jack.

(David going to college on the East Coast, by the way, paved the way for Nicola to make her pitch for attending the University of Rhode Island; she had a visceral desire to put herself near the ocean, even if it took her an undergrad degree in poli-sci, a law school degree, and a failed relationship to allow her to find her path.)

But, but, but. Racing is not like soccer; you don't grab a ball and a pair of cleats and go for it. You need time, and you need money, and in an ideal world you need a parent who's willing to support you in your quest. David didn't have any of these. The Furniture Brothers work at the store on holidays and weekends, even now. There are four girls in Nicola's family and three boys in David's: there was never room for one child out of seven to retain an expensive, time-consuming hobby. When David went east to college, most people assumed his dream had remained behind. Still, the flame burned strong and bright all those years. Nicola knows it did.

"But what," she asks, "does any of this have to do with Juliana?"

"Let's go back to 2019," Jack says. Taylor was going gangbusters working for Brice Buchanan, learning the ropes so fast it was almost like she'd made the ropes herself. Jack was on the Tour and was gone a lot. And David was going any chance he got up to Monticello Motor Club, in the Catskills.

"To drive cars?"

"Noooo," says Jack. "The people who drive cars there are gazillionaires. The Buchanans are mere millionaires. He had a job there."

"A job? Doing what?" How did she not know about this? There was a time when she knew everything about David!

"I don't know, changing tires and stuff. Pit work. Sometimes he got to take a car around the track, to test it or whatever. Basically he did all the work he did for those rare moments of driving. But here's the thing. Taylor had just asked him to stop doing it."

"Why?"

"Depends what you believe. It's far from the city. The trip could take two hours each way. And David didn't have a car. He had to take one of the Buchanans' cars. He wanted them to plan an occasional vacation to a big race. But Taylor didn't want any part of that. It wasn't a shared interest, blah blah."

"What do you mean, 'depends what you believe'? It wasn't that?"

"That's not what I think. What I think is that she didn't want to be engaged to someone who was working as a mechanic. When they first met, she thought it was cute and wholesome. But as time went on, not so much. Taylor felt that every little boy needs to move out of his race car bed and into a real one eventually."

"David never had a race car bed."

Jack laughs. "Metaphorically speaking, then. Anyway. On the day in question, I was home. I wasn't playing again until Sanderson."

"I don't know what that means."

"Doesn't matter. I had just started dating this model"—he says this so casually, like someone like Nicola would say, *I was eating this grilled cheese sandwich*—"and it was Fashion Week, you know, so there were events going on everywhere, not just the shows but all kinds of networking stuff, and parties, and whatever. She got me an invite to one of these parties, and I needed a date, so I brought David as my plus-one."

"What about the model?"

"Oh, we were over by then."

"That was quick."

"Yeah," he says ruefully, rubbing his chin. "Yeah. Short but sweet."

"So how did you get into the party if you and the model were over?"

"I was on the list. And I thought, Why the hell not? Anyway. We go to this party at Chelsea Piers, David and I. Juliana was there too, networking for LookBook. Something to do with her next round of funding. Who knows. The details aren't important. What's important is—" Jack takes a long, dramatic breath. "What's important is, David and Juliana met at that party."

The puzzle pieces begin to slot into place. David hasn't just heard of LookBook—David *knows* Juliana. She remembers Juliana's enigmatic smile, her mention of a favor. David is hiding something from Nicola. What is it?

"When I was ready to go—the party was *so boring*, by the way; Fashion Week is so much hype"—Nicola doesn't try to hide her eye roll—"I went to find David. He was standing where he'd been standing all night, right near the oysters, talking to the same person I'd seen him talking to every time I glanced over. And that person was Juliana."

"So you met her too. You both know her."

Jack tents his fingers. "I met her briefly."

"And what'd you think?"

"What I thought was—well, this is going to sound really weird, but it's the only way I can describe it. What I thought was, This is a big party, but I feel like I just walked in on two people alone in a room."

"So what'd you do?"

"I got out of there. And then, when all the model-y and fashion people went off to do whatever they do, Juliana and David went on a walk." Jack pauses again, as if allowing the import of this to sink in.

"Okay," says Nicola. "A walk. What's the rest of the story?"

"That's it. The walk *is* the story."

David and Juliana talked long into the night, the way you do, Jack explained, when one conversation with one person can make you remember that there's a whole world of people out there you haven't yet met, a buffet of personalities and backstories yet to sample.

"Are you saying David cheated on Taylor?" David had always been, to the dismay of many (just ask the female half of his high school class), hopelessly monogamous.

Jack shakes his head. "I don't think he technically cheated on Taylor." Nicola figures she must look dubious because he says, "I'm not even talking about sex, see." Nicola tries really hard to look away when he says *sex* because she's still feeling his hand tracing her elbow, his finger on her lips. "I'm talking about *talking*, you know? The way you do when you have all the time in the world." For a moment he looks pensive, almost sad, so Nicola doesn't point out that he still very much presents as someone who has all the time in the world. "They had this connection, according to David, this really deep, instant connection."

"From talking one night?"

"From talking *all night*," Jack said. "As in, they walked around the city until dawn. They saw the sunrise from the High Line. They were like Ethan Hawke and that French girl in that movie, you know?"

Nicola does know that movie. She and her roommates watched it one drunken night in college. *"Before Sunrise."*

"Exactly," he says.

Nicola understands that you can have a night like this in New York in a way you cannot have in most parts of Minnesota, because New York is lousy with all-night diners and all-night bars and lights that don't go out. "The city that never sleeps," she says.

"Never sleeps," concurs Jack. "Never ever." His palm is on the back of her neck for an instant, then not.

What transpired between Juliana and David on that one night in New York City? Nobody knows. The machinations of the human heart are mysterious, enigmatic, utterly personal.

"What I gather," he says, "is that David understood parts of Juliana that nobody had bothered to understand before. And vice versa, with David. Especially the race cars, this crucial part of David's DNA that Taylor never cared about."

"And Juliana did? From one night?"

"It only takes one night," says Jack. "In the right circumstances." He fixes her with a gaze. She tries to look away but can't. "Or the wrong circumstances," she says.

A tip of Jack's head concedes this point. "Also that." He goes on: "Juliana could see it coiled inside of him, all that desire. Taylor was dating a Yale graduate, acceptable husband material, not an aspiring race car driver. Definitely not a mechanic. She had other things in mind for David."

"Eye Candy."

"Mr. Mom."

Jack snorts.

"But wait, then what?" Nicola asks. "What happened after that one night?"

"Well, I was a good boy, asleep by midnight. But the next day, when I saw David? I swear I've never seen him that way. It was like he was high, but he wasn't high. David doesn't get high."

"He drinks," Nicola says loyally.

"He *definitely* drinks. But this was not Drunk David. I've seen a lot of Drunk David. He was—I don't know how to describe it. I mean, I guess the easiest way to describe it was he was acting like someone in love."

"And *then* what?"

"And then nothing." He shrugs. "Taylor came home from wherever she was, and life went on, and the next year they got married, and the rest is history."

"But what about Juliana?"

"Well, *nothing*," Jack says slowly, "until the wedding."

"What happened at the wedding?" Taylor and David had been married at OceanCliff, the most spectacular of the spectacular places to get married in Newport. "Besides the fact that my mom almost had a panic attack." While a lot of the world had been canceling weddings that fall, David and Taylor's had managed to go on. Taylor wasn't about to be undone by a pandemic. Aside from that, David's new financial status unnerved Nicola's mom. To see this child whose diapers she'd changed, whose Easter eggs she'd hidden and night terrors she'd banished (their parents traded kids back and forth like baseball cards), surrounded by such opulence—it didn't sit right with her.

(The fact that Taylor's mother was absent for so much of her life didn't sit right with any of the Carrs. Not that that was Taylor's fault. *Of course* it wasn't. But the Minnesota Carrs wondered: Wouldn't a motherless childhood manifest itself in some ways that nobody could predict? The fact that Taylor's mother appeared at the wedding with a man nearly two decades her junior and did not seem even to have the good grace to feel sheepish about it—that must signify something too, although none of the Carrs could say what.)

"Not *at* the wedding. The night before," explains Jack. He relates the rest of the story. He bought a good bottle of bourbon and he brought it to the hotel room after the rehearsal dinner. As David's best man he was going to stay with the groom-to-be, while Taylor and her maid of honor slept in the bridal suite. Taylor wanted the traditional no-seeing-each-other-before-the-ceremony wedding eve. The rest of the wedding party and any guests who had traveled were scattered elsewhere throughout the same hotel or in other hotels in Newport.

"We were at the Howard Johnson," says Nicola. "Most of Newport was beyond our budget."

"Well, no wonder." Jack restarts the infuriatingly hot tracing of her elbow. "I would have remembered you if we'd been at the same hotel."

The idea of bringing back the bourbon was that David and Jack would have a toast, hang out a little, get to bed. David was happy with an early night. He wanted his beauty sleep, he said.

So Jack poured them each a drink and they settled back, David on one of the beds in the suite, Jack stretched out on one of the two couches. It was a big suite. They turned on the TV and watched whatever movie came on. One of the Bourne movies, Jack thought, though he couldn't remember for sure which one. David was half watching and half scrolling through his phone. Mindlessly at first, then suddenly he sat up and made a little strangled noise.

"What's going on, buddy?" Jack asked. "Everything okay?"

David didn't answer; his gaze was glued to the phone. He reached over to the nightstand, where the bottle of bourbon sat. He poured, filling his glass nearly to the brim. He drank.

"Whoa," said Jack. "You've gone beyond fingers now. You're looking at an entire hand. You want to slow down? You've got kind of a big day coming up tomorrow."

David shook his head and drank more, and after a while he said, "I can't do it. We should call someone." His movements had become erratic, unconsidered. He reached for the hotel phone as if to put the receiver to his ear but instead knocked it off its base. "Who should we call?" David asked Jack, the night before his wedding in his suite at the OceanCliff.

"Call someone why?" Jack asked.

"To tell them the wedding is off." David was slurring by then.

"Come on," said Jack. "That's just the alcohol talking. You don't want to do that." He looked carefully at David and watched a variety of emotions cross his face: bewilderment, discord, maybe even a flash of grief. He looked, Jack tells Nicola, like a little boy who'd lost his mother at the shopping mall. Full of consternation and angst.

"Did he show you what was on his phone?" Nicola is trying to square this backstory with the fairy-tale wedding she'd attended the next day.

"He didn't."

"Never?"

"No."

"Then what?" Nicola is nearly breathless. Here are David and Taylor, married all this time, and here is Felicity, proof of their union. Nicola knows the end of the story. But she doesn't know the middle.

Then, Jack tells her, David flopped back against the pillow, his arm covering his eyes, and the next thing Jack knew David was sleeping deeply. Snoring.

"Well, did you look at his phone after he was asleep? To see what was going on?"

"Nicola!" Jack fixes her with a stern look, or maybe a fake-stern look. "Does the word *privacy* mean anything to you?" She's momentarily flustered until he grins and says, "Obviously I tried, but it was passcode protected."

"What do you think it was?"

"The passcode?"

"The thing on his phone!"

"I know what it was, now." He pauses, maybe for dramatic effect. It works. It's very effective.

"Well . . . ?"

"It was an email from Juliana George. She'd seen the announcement somewhere—this is Taylor Buchanan, you know, so this wedding was a Big Deal. The wedding had its own Instagram account."

"And what was in the email?"

"What was in the email was Juliana asking David not to marry Taylor."

Nicola whistles. Well, she can't actually whistle, so she makes sort of a puffing sound, and she says, "This is what she told you at her party?"

He nods. "This is what she told me."

"So what happened between the email and the wedding?"

"Took me a while to get to sleep, is what happened."

She rolls her eyes. "What happened with David?"

Jack put a tall glass of water and four Advil by the bed, and sometime in the night David must have gotten up, because by the time Jack woke the glass was empty and the Advil were gone and David had changed from his rehearsal dinner clothes into an ancient T-shirt that read TOM AND BILL: THE FURNITURE BROTHERS, with cartoon renderings of his dad and Nicola's dad on it.

(Nicola has the same shirt.)

"He was fresh as a daisy," says Jack.

"And did you talk about the night before?"

"I brought it up." He strokes his chin when he says this. Somehow this is at once an old-man gesture and also unbearably attractive.

"But honestly, I'm not sure if he would have, on his own. He was acting like nothing had happened."

"How'd you bring it up?"

"I just asked him. I said, 'Do you love Taylor?'"

"Simple, yet direct," Nicola says. "Approved. What'd he say?"

The bartender comes back and nods at Jack. "Another Dark 'N' Stormy?"

"Why not?" says Jack. "I've got nowhere to be." It was true: he had nowhere to be that day, nor the next one, nor the next one after that.

"You?" she says to Nicola. "Another Mudslide?"

She shakes her head. "Still working on this one." Then, to Jack: "So what'd David say? When you asked him if he loved Taylor?"

"He said, 'Of course I love her, you asshole. I'm marrying her, aren't I?'"

Nicola sits with that for a moment, and then she asks, "Do you think he forgot, about the email and everything? Or do you think he was pretending?"

Jack looks pensive. He narrows his eyes and looks skyward. "I'm not sure," he says slowly. "It was a *lot* of bourbon."

"Well, did you talk about it again?"

"Not a word. Never mentioned it, either of us. We had breakfast with the other groomsmen, as planned. Played nine holes of golf—as planned."

"Did you win?"

"Of course I won."

"And then what?"

"At five that evening, David married Taylor." That part Nicola remembers herself: she was there. "Next thing I knew I was getting a baby announcement for little Felicity there," says Jack. "And I didn't give another thought to any of it until this summer, when I made the connection between *that* person and the person throwing these parties everyone is talking about."

Nicola remarks on the coincidence that Juliana ended up buying a house on the same small island where David and Taylor own a home. Jack nearly does a spit take. "Coincidence?" he said. "It's not a coincidence, my darling Nicky."

Her mind is moving more slowly because of the heat of the late afternoon sun, and because of the liquor, and because of Jack's hand. "Wait. Are you saying Juliana bought a big house and started throwing parties to get David's attention?"

Jack laughs and kisses Nicola on the nose. "You have the cutest nose. No. Juliana bought a big house because she's a badass."

"She *is* a badass," Nicola agrees. She almost spills the beans about the IPO, but she remembers just in time that it's not public knowledge.

"She's throwing these parties for the business," says Jack. "To drum up excitement with influencers and brands. CEOs do that all the time. She thought David would come to at least one. But he hasn't showed. And they haven't casually bumped into each other either, out getting an ice cream cone or, I don't know, sunbathing." Nicola can't picture Juliana doing either of these pedestrian summertime activities. "She's been trying to figure out how to see him. At the party the other night she asked me to ask you if you'll have David over for drinks."

Jack rests his hand on Nicola's thigh. Her shorts are short, more so because she's sitting, so this hand of his, which strokes the edge of the shorts, is pretty far up her leg. Like really far. She's already tingling from the almost-two Mudslides; now, she begins to tingle even more. She tries to focus on the story.

"What would my having David over for drinks do?"

He makes a motion like he's knocking on Nicola's head. "She wants you to invite her too."

"Ohhhh." She takes this in. "But I'm confused. How did she know before I told her that David and I are cousins?"

He shrugs. "I'm assuming she did her research when you moved in. Or someone did it for her. Where there's an assistant there's a way."

Nicola snorts. "Okay. But why didn't she ask me herself, when we went out on the mopeds?"

"She'd already asked me to ask you. She doesn't really know you yet." (Nicola tries not to be offended at this statement; do a moped ride around the island and cocktails at Ballard's mean *nothing?*)

"She hardly knows *you.*"

"True. But she met me at that party, and she must have figured when she sent that email that David would have his best man with him the night before his wedding."

"How'd she know you were David's best man?" Is this how investigative reporters feel? She'll have to ask Reina. Maybe Nicola has chosen the wrong career pivot.

"How's anyone know anything?"

"The assistant again?"

"Instagram. The wedding account."

"Ah."

"I guess she felt she could trust me to tell you the story, that I knew enough of it to do it justice, and then she didn't have to go through it herself with you. Who can say? Maybe she also knows that I'm not Taylor's biggest fan."

"You're not?" Nicola leans in closer, very interested. "Why not?"

He doesn't answer for a minute. "I don't love the way she tries to un-David David. Like, all the things that make him *David*, his midwesternness, and his obsession with car racing, and the way he won't throw away socks with holes in them . . ."

Nicola winces. "I think I'm with Taylor on that last one."

"Okay, fair. But the rest of it, you know, that's *David*. How much he loves his family—" Nicola can't help but interject. "His family *is* pretty amazing."

"I think Juliana really appreciates that part of him, where Taylor wants to strip him down and build him back up as a Buchanan."

Nicola bristles because this hits home. "Criminal," she says. "Do you know the one time they made it to the lake they stayed in a hotel? And Felicity's never even been out there!"

Jack whistles and shakes his head, either appropriately shocked or pretending to be. "And besides all that, I think Juliana talked to me because she's terrified."

Nicola raises her eyebrows. "Of what?"

"Of seeing David." He pauses. "And of not seeing David. She considers me a buffer." He takes a long sip of his drink and then says, "I'm an amazing buffer, Nicola."

Does *this* statement have a sexual connotation too? *Does everything?* Nicola takes a deep breath. She tries to square the person from the party with the person from lunch at Ballard's with the person Jack is describing. The many faces of Juliana George.

"Anyway, it doesn't have to be a big deal. Just keep it simple. Drinks on your patio, that's all she's looking for. To see if the spark is still there, I guess."

"But David is *married*! David and Taylor are your friends!"

"David is my friend," corrects Jack. "Taylor is my friend's wife."

"Even so." However moved Nicola is by the tale of true love between David and Juliana, of that single, romantic, cinematic night walking around the city until the sun rose, she doesn't think she wants to be a party to—nay, an enabler of—infidelity. Especially when there's a *child* involved.

"So what do you say?" prods Jack.

But then Nicola remembers the thing Taylor said about Country Cousins, and the way her lip curled up when she said it. Taylor is a Mean Girl. Worse, she's a rich, privileged Mean Girl, which is deadlier than your garden-variety Mean Girl.

"I don't know . . ." The pendulum swings back again. Felicity is her first cousin once removed! Or her second cousin! She can never remember which is which, but either way, shouldn't she be protecting her? "I'm not a home-wrecker!" she says.

"Nobody's asking *you* to wreck anything."

"You're asking me to be a party to it."

"I'm just the messenger. And anyway, you know that having drinks with someone doesn't constitute infidelity, right?"

"I guess so." She thinks some more. "Well, will you come too? If I do it? As an icebreaker."

"Of course I will." Jack smiled. "My middle name is Icebreaker! I'll even break the actual ice for the drinks, if you want."

"Jack Icebreaker Baker. That has a nice ring to it, especially with the rhyme at the end."

"It's a great touch," he agrees. He drains his glass. "My parents really thought it through. You want another, or should we get out of here?"

"Let's get out of here." Around them there's a steady stream of foot traffic to and from the boats. Everyone here seems content, their worries and cares far from them, mitigated by the beauty of the day.

Jack slides a credit card, a black Amex, to the bartender and unleashes his smile on her. She smiles too, and at the same time she points to the sign above the bar that says CASH ONLY. She slides the card back.

"You only take cash?" he says.

The bartender rolls her eyes. "You know that," she says. "You're here every day." She fixes Jack with a stern look—she's maybe in her late forties or early fifties, so she can pull this off—but there is also the hint of a smile or a twinkle in her eyes. She, like everyone else, is vulnerable to the charms of Jack Baker.

Jack lets a small chagrined puff of air out of his mouth. "I forgot," he says.

"ATM over there." The bartender tips her head in one direction.

"This isn't a debit card," he says. "Credit only."

Nicola sighs, a little exasperated. "I've got cash," she says, rummaging in the pocket of her shorts.

"I'll make it up to you, promise."

"Don't worry about it."

Nicola's father once told her you could divide the very wealthy into two groups: those who are more careful with their money than the poorest, and those who are careless with their own money and by association careless with everyone else's money too. The cost of five cocktails is a lot for Nicola that summer. Jack belongs to the second group.

Jack leans over and rests his head on Nicola's shoulder. She's not quite sure what to do with this. Ignore it? Pat him on the head?

"How about dinner on me?" says Jack.

"Tonight? Or a different night?"

"You pick."

"Different night." She needs to be in early the next day, and the Mudslides have made her tired.

He lifts his head and delivers a look that Nicola figures, if she had been standing, would have made her weak in the knees. "Drive me home?"

She laughs and reminds him that she doesn't have a car.

"Walk me home, then."

"I have my bike!" she protests.

His eyes stay on hers for an indecent amount of time. Then his lips land on her clavicle and an actual jolt goes through her. Against her better judgment she says, "Anyway, shouldn't *you* be walking *me* home?"

"Okay. I'll walk you home, Nicola. Or I'll jog gently beside you while you ride your bike."

"What about your Achilles?"

He brushes that concern away with his hand. "My Achilles will be fine. But you might be sorry you asked. Because if we make it to your place I might never leave." His smile is so wide and so white and so beguiling she can see why the TV cameras love him—she can see why everyone loves him.

He doesn't jog; they both walk, the bike between them like a toddler. And once they get to her house, he doesn't leave until the next morning.

Forbes 30 Under 30 Alumni Profile

Juliana George: The Leader with a Future So Bright

When we included Juliana George in our 30 Under 30 Class of 2020, the founder of online fashion portal LookBook had built the fledgling brand into something to, well, *watch*. Now, with an IPO rumored to be on the horizon, George stands to become a multimillionaire less than a decade after an angel investor helped her get started with $500,000.

LookBook is an online retailer and fashion technology company that aggregates and metasearches discounted items from major fashion brands as well as luxury discount retailers (think Rue La La or Revolve) and sorts curated products into "looks" that customers search for, filtering by specific occasion, geographical region, size, season, and price range—ending up with the perfect outfit for up to 80 percent off retail.

George first envisioned LookBook in use on college campuses after some of her own experiences as a scholarship student at Boston College. "Low-income students can often feel socially excluded when they land at some of these prestigious institutions," she told us in 2020. "Maybe you need a dress or a suit to wear to a social occasion, and you don't know where to start. Maybe you have an interview for an internship, or you're a first-generation student at a school where Greek life is important, and you can't even begin to prepare for rushing." It has since expanded far beyond the campus. "I mean, *resort wear?* What does that mean to someone who's never been to a resort but now has to dress for a work off-site? We take the shame out of not being prepared."

George's entrepreneurial spirit was born out of necessity and fueled by her experiences. Before college, George was shuttled among various foster homes in her native Lawrence, Mass., a city twenty-five miles north of Boston in which residents live below the poverty line at almost twice the national rate. She watched one foster family go through a particularly tough time when both parents lost factory jobs simultaneously during the recession of 2007.

"Not all foster parents are good," she says. "But these people were good people trying to do their best, trying to help me, and others like me, and their lives became more than they could handle. When you have control over your work life, control over your income, you have control over your whole life." At that moment she knew entrepreneurship was the path for her. "People might outsmart me," says George. "People might have better ideas. But nobody—*nobody*—is going to outwork me."

After graduating summa cum laude with a degree from the prestigious Carroll School of Management at Boston College, George had a brief foray into management consulting in New York City. There, working with apparel clients in the operations division, she saw how often major fashion brands discount excess inventory but don't use the power of merchandising they lavish on their full-priced items to make them appealing to potential customers. Soon after launching LookBook, she discovered that customers were clamoring for the service far outside the quad.

Without the full scholarship she received to college, George contends she'd be lucky to have a good job, never mind a thriving business. "That scholarship changed everything for me," she says. The same year *Forbes* chose George as one of its 30 Under 30 awardees she started a foundation, Girl/Power, to help low-income girls like herself. Each year, the foundation fully funds a four-year scholarship to a private or public college or university for a first-generation female college student who is interested in studying business. Along with the cost of tuition and room and board, the scholarship includes a generous stipend for living expenses. Girl/Power does not make this amount public, and according to a foundation spokesperson it varies based on the recipient's particular circumstances. This add-on to tuition money, according to George, is almost as important as the tuition itself, and it serves the same goal as LookBook. "Money for dinner out with friends, Uber fare, a dress to wear to a formal: those things that seem like small extras to some people are a really big deal to others. We want to erase the shame that comes with not having."

In addition, Girl/Power provides ten scholarships of $10,000 for first-generation students in the University of Massachusetts system, earmarked for girls interested in becoming entrepreneurs.

"The thing I'm most proud of is my foundation," says George. "Building a great business, seeing how LookBook has captured so many imaginations, that's amazing. But helping other girls from backgrounds like mine to reach for the stars? That's everything to me."

NICOLA

On the last Saturday in June, Nicola rides her bike by the land that Buchanan Enterprises is developing in the heart of the island, with Great Salt Pond to the north, the airport due east, and undeveloped woods to the west. She did her research online: Buchanan purchased fifteen acres, including a former equestrian facility and a home (demolished to make space for the new construction), for around six million dollars; when finished, each of the four homes the land is now zoned for will sell for at least five million. Each home is going to be 4,500 square feet with the option to add more: finished basement, finished attic, finished bonus room over the garage.

Nicola isn't the only Peeping Tom on location that day, as it turns out. An older gentleman whom she first mistakes for a member of the construction crew pulls up in and heaves himself out of a pickup truck not too far from where she stops her bike. The site is a beehive of activity, with equipment—cranes and bulldozers and, she doesn't know, maybe a backhoe? She's no expert—lined up in an orderly row alongside the driveway. Men (maybe they aren't all men, she can't tell from where she is) in hard hats are calling to each other or standing in line for one of the porta-potties or carrying long pieces of lumber over their shoulders, two men to a piece, like a builder's version of Noah's ark. The four houses are partially framed.

"My buddy used to own this place," the pickup truck guy says. "Fact, I helped build one of those stone walls right over there." He points in a general westerly direction.

"No kidding," she says respectfully, even though whatever stone wall he's referencing is out of her line of sight.

"You shoulda seen this place in its prime," he goes on. "The barn had a tack room, a farrier station, the whole deal."

"What's a farrier?"

"Guy who puts the shoes on the horses." He looks at Nicola, appraising. "Or gal," he adds eventually. "My granddaughters tell me not to assume the gals can't do the same jobs the gents can do these days." Nicola guesses his granddaughters would also tell him to go easy on his use of the words *gals* and *gents*, but he seems like a man who's just trying to get along in a world he finds occasionally bewildering, with new rules and admonitions cropping up every day, so she keeps the thought to herself. He's probably a wonderful grandfather. He probably keeps a cupboard full of packaged snacks he offers on an unlimited basis when the parents aren't looking. "They live in Wellesley, Massachusetts," he says, as though that explains everything.

"Ah," says Nicola, because maybe, in fact, it does.

"I don't know who's going to buy these houses," he says.

"The kind of people who have a lot of money to burn, I guess," she says. "It's not a group of people I'm familiar with." She's not about to mention her connection to David and Taylor, not to this guy!

"Probably for some third house they'll only use two weeks out of the year," he says gloomily. "I grew up here. Married my wife here. Raised my kids here. Ran my business here. But in the last, oh, ten years, seems like every time I turn around this island is changing into something I don't recognize."

Nicola tries to find the bright side, even though, looking at the skeletons of these massive houses on land where horses had once freely grazed, she's having trouble locating it. "Maybe change isn't all bad?" she ventures. "My father always says, 'We can have no progress without change.'"

"No offense, my dear, but that quote's got nothing to do with this." Nicola's companion grimaces and motions toward the not-quite-houses.

"No," she agrees. "No, maybe it doesn't."

"Nothing against your father. I'm sure he's a great man."

"He is," she confirms. "But when he talked about change and progress I'm pretty sure at least fifty percent of the time he's referring to La-Z-Boy's introduction of nanobionic fabric to its recliners."

"I love a La-Z-Boy."

"He sells them more than he sits in them," Nicola says, in case she's giving the wrong impression. "Though he sits in them sometimes too."

"'No progress without change,'" he repeats thoughtfully. "Yeah, I can see where that's sometimes true." He pauses and gives the impression of puffing on a cigar even though his hands and his mouth are all empty. "But that doesn't mean that change is always progress. Sometimes change means you're sliding back."

She thinks about this. "You're probably right."

"Damn straight I am."

The morning is bright and clear. There's humidity on call for later in the day, but it hasn't arrived yet, and even though they're smack in the middle of the island, about as far as you can get from the beaches on either side, and way more than a stone's throw from Great Salt Pond, Nicola can sense the salt in the air; it feels like a chewiness. She imagines what the island might have been like all those years ago, before ice cream cones and espresso shots and weather cams and mopeds, when only the Narragansett tribe inhabited it, before the Dutch came to rename it and take it over. It had once been called Manisses, which translated to "Island of the Little God." She imagines the Narragansett watching these homes rise from their sacred ground, shaking their heads regretfully.

"I can't see much from back here," she says. "It's hard to be a Peeping Tom from a distance. Do you think I'd get in trouble if I went a little closer?"

"I'll do you one better. Stay here." He walks to his truck—he has the very particular walk of a man with a hip replacement in his not-too-distant future—and returns with a pair of binoculars. "The wife got into bird-watching in a big way these last couple of years," he says. "She recently saw a king rail. Pretty rare, she tells me." Nicola makes a noise that she hopes conveys being impressed, even though she wouldn't recognize a king rail if it served her a Mudslide. He hands her the binoculars. "Here, take a look."

She begins by training the binoculars on the houses, but then her eye catches on a midnight-blue Mercedes that has stopped close to the construction vehicles. She recognizes the car, and she recognizes the person who emerges from the driver's seat too. Tall and blond. She sucks in her breath. If this is a beehive of activity, here comes the Queen Bee. Taylor's hair is such a bright, bright blond, and so long, like fairy-tale princess hair, it's unmistakable, especially when coupled with her height and her slim build. Of course it makes sense that she'd be here; this is a Buchanan project, and she is one of the chief Buchanans.

"See it now?" asks Nicola's companion. "The way these houses are going to mar the landscape? How they're set against the tree line there . . ." He cluck-clucks his tongue against the roof of his mouth.

"Terrible," she agrees (and she *does* agree!), but her gaze is still fixed on Taylor. She even feels herself shrinking back a little, as though Taylor has binoculars too, and is looking straight at her. And then something happens that makes her take in her breath even more. Taylor is leaning against her Mercedes, looking at her phone, when a man in a hard hat approaches.

They speak for a minute. Mostly it looks like Taylor is talking, gesturing as she talks, and the man is nodding a lot. Nicola watches as he removes his hard hat and leans against the car next to her, so they're both facing out. It's an odd stance on both of their parts for a work-related conversation; there's something too casual and intimate about the body language. Then she sees him take her hand and squeeze it.

What. Is. Happening.

Then he puts his arm around her, the way you do when you're comforting someone.

And then.

And then!

They turn toward each other, and they *kiss*. Not just a peck either. It's a long, searching, actual kiss—a kiss that makes Nicola feel like she's walked in on a couple in bed. Truly it is *quite a kiss*. She can't help it: she gasps.

"Makes you wonder what's going on with the permit approval," says her buddy, misreading the gasp as a reaction to a closer look at the construction. "All that progress on the houses, and none on the hotel."

"Right?" she says. She lowers the binoculars. She thinks of Taylor getting a phone call at the dinner table; she thinks of Felicity's plump little cheeks. She thinks of Taylor calling her Country Cousin. She thinks of the story Jack Baker told her about David the night before his wedding. She thinks of Juliana sitting alone in the library of her vast house.

She hands the binoculars back to the man, and she thanks him and says goodbye, then she gets on her bike and pedals as fast as she can, all the way home. She doesn't even make it all the way into the house before she pulls out her phone and texts Jack Baker.

I'LL DO IT.

Immediately he texts back: ?

I'LL HOST THE HAPPY HOUR.

The reply comes at once, with this emoji: 🍸
And then: I'LL BRING THE DRINKS.

FEELING VERY CLANDESTINE, Nicola calls David a few hours later to see if he wants to come by for a drink soon.

"Sure," he says. "What's the occasion?"

"No occasion. Casual drink, that's all. You had me over, now I'm having you over."

Nicola is such a terrible liar that even though she's alone in her kitchen she blushes and her palms start to sweat.

"When?"

"How's, let's see—" She makes a big show of checking her busy calendar. "Six o'clock Monday?"

"Drinks on a Monday! You're turning into a summer person."

"But just you, okay? No Taylor."

There's a long, pregnant pause. Not too long: a pause in early pregnancy. Then comes David's voice, smooth and affable.

"Taylor who?" he says.

PARTWAY THROUGH MONDAY morning, it starts to rain. And not a gentle, forgiving rain either: angry dark sheets. After the string of perfect summer days they've had, it feels offensive to Nicola, or at least inauspicious. What is she supposed to do with her star-crossed not-lovers later, plop them on her wet patio furniture? She worries her way through her morning interning. Will Jack remember to show? It's slow at the Institute, because of the rain, but it's also chaotic, because the visitors they do have cram themselves into the inside space. Everything smells a little bit like wet dog, even though there are no dogs present. The rain continues through lunch. At two o'clock she texts Jack to see if they should cancel.

DEFINITELY NOT, he texts back. I WANT TO SEE YOU.

"What's so funny?" asks Liam, a fellow intern. "You're smiling at your phone."

"Nothing," she says, dropping the phone into her pocket. "Just a reel."

An hour later the rain slows, then stops altogether. By the time she bikes home at five, the sun is trying mightily to make a late appearance. The puddles on Beach Avenue send up surfable waves over her tires, and she has to shower when she gets home. At 5:40 she's braiding her hair—no time for a blow-dry—when Jack appears. He knocks once, then comes right in before she tells him to. Is this kind of confidence obnoxious, or sexy? He puts a brown bag down on her kitchen table and kisses her on the lips. He smells like limes. Sexy, she decides.

"I brought craft beer, the makings for two different kinds of spritzes, and a bottle of champagne," he says.

"You think that's enough for four people?" Nicola asks, deadpan. Together they go out the back door and onto the patio. "The good thing about having basic furniture," says Nicola, "is that it dries quickly." She and Jack get to work with two dish towels.

At 5:50 comes another knock, and Nicola opens the door to find Juliana. Gone is the person from the library, the person from Ballard's, the person who gives the fabulous parties and maneuvers around the fancy people, and in her place is a woman who suddenly looks very young and very terrified. She's in a white sundress that makes her skin glow. Her hair is pulled back into a bun and she's wearing lip gloss and no other makeup. But she's almost shaking.

"Thank you for doing this, Nicola," Juliana says. She squeezes Nicola's hand. "Sorry I didn't ask you myself, I just—"

"It's okay," says Nicola. "It's no big deal. It's just a drink."

"Just a drink," Juliana repeats. She follows Nicola through the living room and into the kitchen, her eyes darting around as though David might be hiding somewhere. "He's not coming, is he? I don't think he's coming."

"Chill," says Jack. "He's coming. Can I get you a drink?" Nicola sees that he's set up a makeshift bar on her small counter; she has only four glasses, and they don't match, but he's lined them all up like very good soldiers awaiting orders. Juliana shakes her head.

"Well, don't mind if I get started," says Jack. He cracks open a porter. "Nicola?"

"Not yet, thanks." Then she says, "Wait. Was I supposed to get snacks?"

"I'm not hungry," says Juliana in a strangled voice. "Should I go sit on the patio? I'll sit on the patio."

"Whatever you want," Jack says amiably. "The seats have been professionally dried. Please, take a drink out there. You're making me nervous." He opens the champagne and pours Juliana a glass.

When David arrives Nicola thinks, Third knock's the charm! She opens the door and David says, "Hey, cuz. Sorry if I'm late. Am I late?" She can tell that David has taken care with his appearance; he's wearing a blue polo that brings out the color of his eyes, and his face is scruffy in that carefully scruffy way that requires effort. (Zachary had tried this a few times but never managed to pull it off.)

David has the kind of good looks that require, or at least politely ask for, a second look. There's something perfectly imperfect about his face. It's almost symmetrical, except one eyebrow lifts a tiny bit higher than the other, and only one cheek has a dimple in it. These small asymmetries somehow make him even more beautiful than he would have been without them. If you look at the most famously good-looking people in the world you'll find this to be the truth. Alexander Skarsgård's cleft chin. Nicole Kidman's high forehead.

If David was known for anything in high school, it was for making things look easy that were not easy at all. The fact that he got the grades he got and the SAT scores he got and the admission to Yale he got without seeming like he was trying at all drove a lot of people in their high school crazy. The girls who never went out on the weekends because they were doing their APUSH reading and the boys who didn't have a girlfriend until grad school. The valedictorian rejected from Harvard and Cornell. David was even-tempered and funny and never an asshole to his girlfriends (and there were a *lot* of girlfriends) and as a result there was a constant line of girls waiting in the wings, as it were—though he drew the line at high school theater. He probably would have been good at that too. Actually, he does have a decent singing voice. They used to put on plays when they were kids, that's how Nicola knows, all the cousins with a makeshift stage in one or another of their basements, an old sheet slung across whatever they could find, to approximate a curtain. Their best show was when they performed one of the early scenes in *A Sound of Music* because there were enough of them to pull it off. (Nicola was Marta, if you're wondering.)

Is she supposed to pretend David doesn't know why he's here? Of course Jack has already told him. She jerks her thumb behind her.

"She's on the patio. Jack will get you a drink."

"Cool, cool," says David, and she sees now (because an unruffled David would never say *cool, cool*) that David is just as nervous as Juliana is.

Olivia Rodrigo is 100 percent right. Love *is* embarrassing.

She hears ice crackle into glasses, then stop. When the door to the patio opens and closes again she decides she's ready to brave the kitchen. Jack is alone in there, contemplating the drink choices. "Ready for one now?" he asks. Out the kitchen window, Nicola can see David and Juliana sitting far apart from each other, each holding a drink, each looking toward the water.

"I don't know if I can go sit out there with them," she says. "It feels like, I don't know, like walking in in the middle of someone's dream or something."

In an instant Jack's hand is on the small of her back, his lips on her ear. "Then let's get out of here," he says.

Don't melt, she tells herself sternly, as she starts to melt. "Shouldn't we stay? We're the hosts."

"We *definitely* shouldn't stay. Let's go for a drive."

Jack has David's Tesla; next to it is David's Porsche. In Juliana's driveway Nicola can see the Audi. What the exact hell? she thinks. How am I the only person in this scenario without a luxury car—nay, any car?

"Where to?" Jack asks her.

"Let's go out Corn Neck, all the way to the end."

Nicola loves this drive, past all the best swimming beaches, Crescent and Scotch and Mansion (where there used to be an actual mansion, she has learned), then the entrance to Clayhead, then the hidden gems of houses on their right, beautiful and remote, with Sachem Pond to the left.

They park and walk out on the rocks; Nicola points out where the seals sometimes gather and she tells him about the rescues she's heard about. "Not that I want a seal to need rescuing," she explains. "But if one does, I really hope I get to see it." She goes on about the seals for what might be a few beats too long, so she checks Jack's face for signs of boredom.

"Sorry," she says. "Am I talking too much?"

"Never," says Jack. "I'm hanging on your every word." She can't tell if he's kidding or not. Zachary told her, two years into their relationship, that she was overly chatty in the mornings; he's an only child, and in Nicola's house you basically woke up talking if you wanted your voice to be heard. Ever since then she's been insecure.

She told Jack she'd just come out of a long relationship the night after Payne's, but does he want to know more? Does Jack want to share anything about his romantic past? It must be extensive—he's too hot for it not to be. She turns over the question for a while in her mind, looking out at the water, feeling how the ocean calms her, brings her peace.

"Who was the last person you dated?" she ventures eventually. Probably some beautiful golfer who knows how to pull off wearing a visor and has amazing calves.

His smile is mysterious. "I live in the present, Nicky." He touches her cheek with two fingers and she shivers. "Only in the present."

"Smart," she says, even though she's a little stung by the rebuff. A seal's head appears, then another, then another, and she points them out to Jack. Does he appreciate the seals as much as she does? Does it matter if he doesn't?

After a time Jack peers at the sky, then looks at his watch. "Should we get back before the sun sets?"

"I guess," she says, trying not to sound sulky, though she's feeling it—sulky that he won't tell her more, sulky that he can leave this secluded place so easily, sulky that he has a power over her that he hasn't earned and she hasn't asked for.

By the time they get back it's getting dark, and at first Nicola can't make out the figures on the patio. Then her eyes adjust to the dim light and she sees that David and Juliana have pulled their chairs close together. They're talking intently. Every trace of awkwardness is gone, as though it's been sucked by a giant vacuum into Great Salt Pond. When David and Juliana hear Jack and Nicola approach they look up, startled, and rise from their chairs.

"Oh, hey. We were waiting to say goodbye. I'm going to show David my house," says Juliana. "Thank you for having us over."

David and Jack do a complicated male handshake/fist bump thing, and while they're doing that Juliana leans toward Nicola, hugs her, and repeats, in a whisper, "Thank you."

What have I done? Nicola starts to think as she watches them walk across the grass, now almost obscured by darkness. But then Jack's lips are on hers again, and she forgets to wonder.

JULY

JULIANA

The best part of a party, thinks Juliana, is when it's over—when the quiet is so thick you can take a bite out of it. Everyone is gone now: the caterers, the DJ, the bartender. Even Allison, who got invited to an after-party with a couple of locals. What is the point of an after-party? Juliana has never understood this, just as she's never understood the point of a pre-party or a pre-game. The students at BC loved their pre-gaming! They couldn't get enough of it. You didn't even need a game in order to pre-game. You could pre-game a party, or a dance, or a trip into downtown Boston. You could pre-game a pre-game.

Allison met her new local friends when she went out on July Fourth, the day before. Should Juliana have asked Allison where she was going? No. Juliana is not her mother. She's far too young to be Allison's mother, and probably too old to be her big sister—there are eight years separating them. She's happy that Allison is having fun. Their workdays are stressful and busy. There's so much prep to do for the road show, when Juliana will travel around the country and meet with potential investment banks. She'll visit eight cities in six days, and she'll pitch the story of LookBook again and again and again, while the banks decide if they'll put orders in the books. Before the road show comes the regulatory process, and the valuation, and before *that* comes the constant monitoring of similar public companies, to see how they're faring in the market.

Juliana is tired just thinking about it, but she's energized too. This is the same kind of energy she used to feel at college, especially as a freshman, especially in her Portico class, the first-year multidisciplinary business class, which opened her eyes wider than they'd ever opened in her life. She learned then the connection between doing well and doing good; the philosophical foundations of business; the importance of reflection. She'd worked so hard. She's been working ever since, always grinding, always reaching, never taking a step back. And it's about to pay off. Once LookBook goes public she's going to have access to more financial stability than she's ever dreamed of.

And now there's David. She'd been so scared walking over to Nicola's house. But the world kept turning, as it does, and she just kept moving, as she always did. Eventually the door from the kitchen to the patio opened, and there was David, looking as he'd looked nearly five years ago, with some small additions, like little crinkles around his eyes when he smiled. More substance in the neck, in the shoulders, but also almost exactly the same. Now she knows. She knows that David isn't happy with Taylor. She knows she didn't make any of this up: what they both felt that night was real and true. Taylor doesn't care about David or his thoughts and passions, about his inner life. She never has. Look what she's done to David's dream of race car driving: He'd presented it to her, holding it carefully like it was made of crystal. And she'd knocked it to the floor. Shattered it! She treated David like a bit player in her life. In Juliana's, he'll be a costar.

It's a lot of emotion for four days. Happiness—real, true happiness—is so close she can almost touch it. She has to be patient; she has to be careful. She can do that. She's made it through 100 percent of her bad days so far. Just. Keep. Moving.

Right now, though, for just a moment, she's remembering how

to reflect. The moon is entirely invisible: it's a new moon. The opposite of a full moon. It's a little creepy sitting out here on her dock in total darkness, but not creepy enough that Juliana does anything about it. Where she came from, darkness could be dangerous. Here, as long as she stays away from the water, it's safe. If she needs a light, she can use the flashlight on her phone, or turn on one of the battery-operated lanterns placed (tastefully) around the seating area by the decorator. But she doesn't do that, not yet, because there's also another light she can see: the green light at the end of David's dock.

Someone is coming toward her down her own long, black dock. Juliana sucks in her breath, positive she's about to get murdered. It would be an easy job: all the murderer would have to do would be to push her into the water and step back. One murder, done.

Now she does turn on the flashlight on her phone, angling it toward the murderer, hoping to blind him into submission. Then she hears, "Hey hey!" A familiar voice.

"*Shelly?*" What is Shelly doing here? Juliana sighs and switches on one of the lanterns.

"There you are! I've been looking *everywhere*. I don't even know what happened! I went to the bathroom, and I got *so tired* so I lay down to take a tiny nap in the tub, really just a catnap. I mean, I closed my eyes not even for a second, and when I woke up everyone was all gone."

Juliana rolls her eyes. This means that Shelly ventured to the second floor, or even the third floor; there are no bathtubs on the first floor. She hopes she didn't leave anything personal in easy reach in her bedroom. She wouldn't put a little snoop past Shelly.

"All gone," repeats Shelly. She palms-ups her hands, sounding exactly like a bemused toddler whose ice cream slipped off the cone.

"Right," says Juliana. "Maybe it was a little longer than a catnap. The party's over. There's a noise ordinance, you know. We have to shut things down at eleven P.M."

"I *hate* when parties are over," says Shelly. "It's the worst part of the night." She slumps in the love seat, looking forlorn. Then she perks up and says, "Oh, but guess what? I think I fell in love tonight."

"Yeah?" Not a shock. Shelly fell in and out love with lightning speed in college. It's an irritating habit, but it's also somewhat endearing. Shelly is so—what is it? She's so *open* to the possibilities in the world. She's guileless. She's hopeful.

Because this isn't her first experience with Besotted Shelly, Juliana knows the next line in the script. She asks, "Who'd you fall in love with?" She thinks about turning on another lantern but decides to keep the atmosphere as it is. The waters of Great Salt are still and quiet, and occasionally the cry of a night bird reaches them. Crickets too. There are all kinds of lovely sounds that come out when the lights go off. This is not how it was where she grew up; sirens were the crickets of her childhood summers.

"Jack Baker." Shelly sighs. "The guy I mentioned to you before, who's staying with the Buchanans. Do you know him? I mean, did you invite him? Or is he one of those people who just showed up?"

"Hmm," says Juliana, playing it cool. She's not going to tell Shelly about why she knows Jack Baker, and his connection to David, or, for that matter, Juliana's connection to David, or Jack's connection to Nicola. Shelly claims to be a vault, but what she really is is a sieve. "Isn't he a tennis player or something?" Sure, it's dark, but even in the daylight Juliana's poker face is top-notch.

"Golfer," says Shelly dreamily.

"Oh, right."

"Who knew golfers were so hot?"

"Not me!"

"I just felt like—God, I just felt like our sexual chemistry was *tangible,* you know? Visible. I'm sure it was visible." Shelly might have caught the lantern-lit look of horror on Juliana's face because she hastens to add, "We weren't *doing* anything. We were just talking. But like *very* intimately." After a pause Shelly says, "Is he seeing anyone, do you know?" Shelly shifts her body into prone position, rearranging the pillows so that her head is protected from the love seat's arm.

Juliana coughs, feels around inside the moral quandary—and settles on a nebulous "I'm not sure?"

"Well, if *I* have anything to do with it, the person he'll be seeing is this girl right here." Shelly motions to her chest with both thumbs.

They say that Block Island has no native predators, Juliana thinks, but looking at Shelly now she might disagree.

"Be careful," says Juliana.

Shelly stretches out. "Careful? Why?"

"No reason," says Juliana. "Just—it's always a good idea to be careful."

Shelly unleashes a massive yawn. "Well," she says. "I'll be a tiny bit careful. But not too careful. Careful isn't really my specialty."

Facts, thinks Juliana.

"The last person I thought I was in love with I wasn't," says Shelly to the night sky, to the invisible new moon. "As it turns out, I was in hate. Which is the opposite!"

"Hate isn't the opposite of love."

Shelly pushes herself up on her elbows and peers at Juliana. "It isn't?"

"Of course it isn't." This is a piece of wisdom gleaned from The Lumineers by way of Elie Wiesel. But doesn't everyone know it? "The opposite of love is indifference."

"Ahhhh," says Shelly. She puts her head back down on the pillows. "Indifference. That makes sense. You're so smart, Jade."

"Juliana."

"I like Jade better." Then Shelly's breathing becomes deep and even. She doesn't talk any more. Is Shelly asleep?

"Shelly?" says Juliana.

No answer.

Juliana sighs. She can't *leave* Shelly here. Can she? No. It's too close to the edge of the dock. In just a minute she's going to wake her up and walk her into the house. She'll deposit her in a guest room, and in the morning she'll have Allison drive her home, provided Allison makes it back from her own festivities.

But she won't wake Shelly just yet. For a little longer, she's going to sit in the darkness and look out at the green light at the end of David's dock. She's going to think about the past, and she's also going to think about the future, which feels so close.

The opposite of a new moon is a full moon. The opposite of love is indifference. What is the opposite of Shelly? Maybe, in fact, the opposite of Shelly is Juliana herself.

———————

Thanksgiving loomed that first year, casting a shadow over much of November, as plans started to take shape. Shelly Salazar's mom was on a cruise, and her dad was traveling for work, so Shelly was going home with Mary Ann for the long holiday weekend. Kathleen and Bob, dropping by the dorm room on a November Saturday, pre-tailgating before the Virginia Tech game with their old neighbors, inquired about Jade's plans.

"Heading to Lawrence for the holiday, Jade?" asked Kathleen.

Jade, who was packing her backpack for the library, froze. (She loved the library during football games because everyone on campus was at the game; she practically had the place to herself.) "Maybe," she said.

"There's always a seat at our table." Bob squeezed Jade's arm. He might've done a little pre-pre-tailgating; he seemed a little wobbly. The squeeze was borderline . . . well, it was fine. It was probably fine.

"Oh, I don't know—" said Jade. "My family's not . . . we don't really do Thanksgiving."

"We insist that you join us," said Bob.

"Absolutely," said Kathleen. "Don't we insist, Mary Ann?" Mary

Ann was studying her lip gloss with a critical eye in the makeup mirror on top of her dresser.

"Sure, why not?" said Mary Ann.

Mary Ann's house, obviously, was palatial. All the houses in Weston were palatial, with wide, sloping lawns scraped free from fall foliage. In Mary Ann's backyard was a pool with a dark green cover pulled tight around it. A lustrous golden retriever named Cinnamon greeted them, then repaired to a plush dog bed that looked more comfortable than the beds Jade had had in her last two foster houses.

Mary Ann's bed was king-sized and had a daybed next to it with a matching comforter. What would the sleeping arrangements be? On the one hand, Jade had never slept in a king bed, and it looked amazing. On the other, Shelly and Mary Ann were closer than either of them were to Jade, despite Jade's status as roommate. Jade would offer to take the daybed.

"I'm *so* excited for tonight," Shelly said. She stood in front of Mary Ann's built-in bookcases, studying the framed photos of her high school friends. Tonight? wondered Jade. Nobody had said anything to her about tonight.

"I've been waiting my whole life to be a college kid going out with my high school friends the night before Thanksgiving!" squealed Mary Ann. To Jade she said, "We have to eat pizza with my parents first." She rolled her eyes. "It's our night-before-Thanksgiving tradition. Then we're leaving at seven, k?"

"I cannot believe I finally get to meet Chris," said Shelly. "We're going to his house, right?"

Mary Ann confirmed that, yes, they were going to Chris's house. The thought of this almost gave Jade a panic attack. She didn't know anything about Chris or his house, or these plans, or this world. She took a deep breath.

"Do you mind if I hang here, you guys? I have a headache."

Mary Ann and Shelly turned to her with identically furrowed

brows. "Oh, no!" said Mary Ann. "Is it bad? My mom can get you some Advil."

"Thanks," whispered Jade. "That would be great."

Later, after Advil, after pizza, after Shelly and Mary Ann had tried on multiple combinations of tops and jeans and left Jade, not exactly without a backward glance, but with only a very small backward glance, she tucked herself into the daybed with her accounting textbook. She dozed briefly and when she started awake she found she was thirsty. She crept down the stairs and toward the kitchen for a glass of water. She could hear unfamiliar voices coming from the living room: Bob and Kathleen had friends over. Everyone was with friends except Jade! Should she have gone to Chris's with the girls? Who was Chris? It would have been fine, probably, except if it wasn't, and then it would have been terrible.

The lights in the kitchen were turned down low. There was a bottle of red wine open on the giant square island, and two wineglasses, their bowls almost as big and as round as globes, were set beside them. Jade opened a kitchen cabinet, taking care to be quiet— but no need, because the cabinet closed with a sigh so soft it sounded almost regretful. Jade couldn't have slammed it if she'd wanted to. She filled her water glass from the little spout on the outside of the refrigerator door and was turning to make her way upstairs when she heard the murmur from the living room resolve into a voice, Kathleen's, and the words resolve into something recognizable:

". . . seems like someone who doesn't want to take up too much space." Murmur murmur murmur. ". . . heart is sort of breaking for her."

Then the lilt of a question from another female voice, and after that this:

"I think she was in the system . . . or maybe sometimes lives with a relative or something? She doesn't seem to have family . . ."

Jade froze. They were talking about her. The heat of a deep, deep shame started in Jade's feet and made its way up her legs, through her torso and arms, all the way to her face. Her cheek, when she put her hand to it, was hot to the touch.

". . . goodness she has you all . . . so generous to include her in your—" Murmur murmur.

"Oh, well. It's nothing, really," said Kathleen. "I couldn't bear for her to be left all alone; you know what an empath I am." Her voice was louder now, too loud; it was impossible *not* to eavesdrop. Jade held tight to her glass of water (chilled, it should be noted, to the perfect temperature) and slunk out of the room and up the stairs.

Though that humiliation had been grave enough, the next day, Thanksgiving morning, a graver one developed. The girls woke and ate breakfast together in the kitchen; Shelly and Mary Ann, clearly hungover, dissected the events of the evening before. (Max had been *out of control*, ohmygod, *so funny* Shelly *couldn't even believe it* and Jade *should have been there*.) Breakfast was a platter of bagels with three different kinds of cream cheese plus a fruit salad, and as they ate, Jade wondered why there seemed to be no meal preparations afoot. No turkey roasting since 5 A.M., no potatoes in a colander in the sink, ready for peeling. Maybe rich people simply ate Thanksgiving dinner later in the day.

The answer became clear soon enough, when Mary Ann broke from her repast to walk to the bottom of the stairs and call, "Mom! What time are we leaving?"

Leaving?

Two forty-five, came the answer. Cocktails at three, dinner at four.

"Leaving to go where?"

Both Mary Ann and Shelly stared at her and said in unison, "The club." *What club?* "Did I forget to tell you? We always eat Thanksgiving dinner at the club." Mary Ann shrugged and rolled her eyes and said, "Honestly, it gets old, but what are we going to do, start cooking turkeys all of a sudden? That's not really my mom's MO."

"Ah," said Jade, in a voice that she hoped conveyed, *Oh, yes, the club.* "Am I supposed to wear—is there like a dress code or something?" She'd never been to "the club"—to any club. She took a panicked mental walk through her suitcase: sweats, jeans, a nice-enough sweater she thought she could wear for the holiday meal. "I didn't bring anything to wear out to dinner," she added. Her palms started to sweat.

Kathleen swept through the kitchen just then, refilling her coffee mug and dropping a "Hey, girls!" like a DJ dropping a beat.

"Just, like, whatever, a dress or a skirt or something. It's pretty casual."

"Okay," said Jade.

Upstairs, not so long after this, Jade emerged from the shower in the bathroom that attached to Mary Ann's bedroom to find a dress laid out on the daybed. It was a wrap dress, hunter green, with a high-low hemline and a band of silk along each side of the V-neck. It was a beautiful dress. Next to the dress, on the floor, was a pair of black wedge ankle boots that looked brand-new. Jade approached the outfit cautiously, like it might bite her.

"Where'd this come from?"

Mary Ann, entranced by her face in the makeup mirror on her vanity, looked over causally and said, "My mom. I told her you didn't bring stuff for the club." Then she walked over, fingered the dress fondly, and said, "I used to love this dress, in high school. I thought she put it in the giveaway bin."

High school had been not even a year ago for either of them, but never mind. Jade thought she'd remember forever the flood of warmth to her cheeks when Mary Ann said *giveaway bin*. Mary Ann didn't mean anything by it, unless she did.

Maybe in fact she did.

Probably she did.

She definitely did. If it wasn't enough that she said it once, when they trooped downstairs, the three of them, dressed for Thanksgiving dinner at the club, Mary Ann said it again: "I thought you put that dress in the giveaway bin, Mom!" For extra, unnecessary emphasis, she pointed at Jade.

Kathleen's face softened when she looked at Jade; she said, "Don't you look lovely in that dress, Jade. Doesn't that color just make her skin glow? I swear, at this time of year I'm about as pasty as a dinner roll. How I envy you your skin tone."

Mary Ann and Shelly agreed that yes, Jade looked wonderful, and no, Kathleen did not look like a dinner roll, and then Mary Ann uttered the phrase *giveaway bin* for an unfathomable third time, in this context: "If it was in the giveaway bin she should just keep it, right, Mom?"

"Of course," agreed Kathleen, who was already distracted, looking through her handbag for something. "Jade. By all means, keep the dress."

Never again, thought Jade at the end of the long weekend (emphasis on *long*) as they packed to return to campus, and she folded the green dress *ever so neatly* and left it on the pillow of the daybed. Never again would she be at someone else's mercy like this, wearing cast-off clothes, trotted out like a charity project. Before she was thirty, in ten years, she vowed, *she* would own the home. *She* would dictate the guest list, buy the bagels, have the dresses. She would take up all the space she wanted, wherever she felt like it. Nobody would ever speak about her in soft, fake-empathetic voices. Nobody would feel bad for Jade Gordon, for anything, ever again.

The remnants of fall faded; winter arrived. Shorter days, the buzz of midterm studying, final papers. Football ended, and the winter sports began in earnest: hockey, basketball, indoor track. An early snow fell, melted, another snow came. Students from warmer climes may have wondered why they turned down that acceptance to William and Mary, to UC–Santa Barbara, to Clemson or the University of Virginia. But for Jade, who'd been living through a much drearier version of New England winters her whole life—the snow in Lawrence sometimes seemed to fall from the sky in shades of gray—there was nothing so beautiful as a light snowfall over the quad, students bundled against the cold and darkness, moving from the warmth of the dining hall to the warmth of the library to the warmth of the residence halls with the bright squares of light set against the darkening sky. Everywhere was warmth, to someone who had come from such cold. The food in the dining hall that students complained about was an unfathomable feast to Jade; the library where they didn't feel like going to study was a bastion of safety and reliability.

Once, Jade came back to the dorm on a Saturday afternoon to find Mary Ann stretched out on her bed, on the phone with her mother. Shelly was there too, lying in the space at the end of the bed not taken up by Mary Ann, scrolling through her own phone, her feet pressed against the wall and her head hanging over the edge of the bed. "What? Oh, nothing. Jade just came in . . . yeah, I'll tell her. Okay. Sure, I'll tell her now." She made a show of removing her phone from her ear. "My mom says hi," she said. "Apparently she needs me to say it *right now*." She rolled her eyes.

"Tell her I said hi back," said Jade. She hoped she didn't sound too eager. "Tell her thank you for the cookies." Because the week before Mary Ann's mother had dropped off a dozen cookies from a bakery near her office in Boston, and on the box she'd written *Mary Ann and Jade*. Jade was embarrassed by how happy it made her to see her name written on this box—on any box! She'd never received so much as a card in her post office box. Mary Ann had rolled her eyes at the cookies and said, "These things have like a trillion calories," before leaving the box on Jade's desk. (Jade ate all of them, one by one, always when she was alone in the room.) "They were so good," she added now, and she could tell by the shift in Mary Ann's expression that she'd gone a bridge too far.

She made herself busy at her desk while Mary Ann finished her phone call, then grabbed her stuff to leave with Shelly. They couldn't have known that the door hadn't closed all the way when Mary Ann said, "She's like *obsessed* with my mom." She didn't mean for Jade to hear her, but knowing that made it actually worse. Jade remained motionless in her desk chair for a good five minutes, the shame pooling around her feet like hot lava. She tried to forget it—in that moment, the next day, in the days and weeks that followed—but the memory lodged in the back of her mind, and she couldn't pry it free. It popped up at the oddest times, beyond Jade's control. In the dining hall, maybe, or in the middle of her first-year writing seminar. *She's like* obsessed *with my mom.*

AFTER DINNER ONE evening, Jade was heading back to her room to gather her books for a study session when she saw a person near the entrance to her dorm who looked like he didn't belong. He was older than the student population, for one thing, and he was dressed differently, in an old denim jacket, not warm enough for the weather. He looked, in fact, at lot like . . .

"No," she said aloud, though she was walking alone. "No no no no . . ."

Her uncle. He was pacing back and forth in a way that suggested something more than impatience—it suggested that he was drinking, or using, or something.

"Hey, princess."

"Don't call me that," she hissed. And: "What are you *doing* here?"

"What? An uncle can't visit his favorite niece?" Jade looked up at the window that was her room—hers and Mary Ann's, fourth floor, third from the left. She knew that anyone looking out from her room wouldn't be able to see them because of the angle, but what about people in the dorm across the way? What about people coming in and out of the dorm? She'd eaten with a few people from her class, but had Mary Ann and Shelly and the rest of the crew been at the dining hall at the same time? What if they were on their way back?

"No," she said. "You can't visit me here. I don't know how you found me, but you have to leave."

He held his hands out, supplicating. "I need money, Jade."

"I don't have money," she said. Her spending money was carefully calculated to last from now until the end of the year. She didn't have extra.

"Just let me come up. We can talk about it."

"*No*. You can't come up. No. My roommate's sleeping. You definitely can't come up." The thought of her uncle in hers and Mary Ann's carefully organized room, the thought of him sitting on her comforter, looking in derision at Mary Ann's quadrant of prints of Paris in the rain—no. "Visitors aren't allowed."

"Which is it, princess? Your roommate is sleeping, or visitors aren't allowed?"

"Both."

"Just a little bit of money. Just to get me through to my next paycheck."

"I told you, I don't have any money."

He snorted and gestured—at the dorm, at the campus as a whole, at the first few brave stars in the newly darkened sky. At the students walking around her, each of their vests, one of their boots, worth more, probably, than the amount of money Jade's uncle was seeking.

"Bullshit. Look at this place. You're here, ain't you?"

"I'm on a full scholarship."

"Exactly." He rubbed frantically at his chin and blinked rapidly. Using, she thought. Not drinking. "That's what I mean. That's why I know you got some to spare."

"They don't give me *cash*. The scholarship covers my fees."

"No other money?"

She shook her head. "No other money."

"Talia needs things."

Talia was Jade's cousin. "Talia doesn't live with you anymore How do you know what she needs?"

"She called me."

Now she could see that people walking by were beginning to do double takes. It was *so clear* that her uncle didn't belong on the Boston College campus. She wanted to sink into the frozen ground. "She called you? From her foster home? I don't think that's possible."

"Well, she did."

"And what'd she say?"

"Said she needs things. School supplies and shit. New sneakers. Hers don't fit."

The thought of Talia, with her curly black hair and her crooked smile, walking around in shoes that didn't fit was almost enough to make Jade bend. She remembered that when Talia was really small she had a pair of sneakers she loved, little pastel SKECHERS with light-up hearts along the sides. Talia had loved those shoes so much she wouldn't even take them off to go to sleep. Jade remembered sharing a bed with Talia when she was wearing a Tinker Bell nightgown and the sneakers. Those were the days when Talia would start off in her own bed but sometime in the middle of the night she'd migrate to Jade's bed, pressing her skinny little body against Jade's back and issuing her warm breath into Jade's neck.

She shook her head, ridding herself of the memory. Talia was safe where she was now, and Jade was 96 percent sure her uncle was lying. She'd call his bluff.

"Well, okay, then. Let's go buy her some things. I can put school supplies and maybe a pair of sneakers on my credit card. Where's your car?"

Her uncle shifted, wouldn't meet her eyes. He kicked at the ground, shoved his hands in the pockets of his jacket, and said, "Naw, Jade. You just give me the cash. I'll do the shopping."

Bluff called. By now more people were starting to cast surreptitious glances their way, sensing something off. A boy in a flannel shirt and a vest (the uniform of a BC student) approached and said, "Everything okay here?"

"Everything's good, man. Just talking to my niece here." Her uncle stepped between Flannel Boy and Jade, his back to FB.

"Yeah?" Flannel Boy stepped around the uncle and looked at Jade for confirmation. "This your uncle?"

Jade nodded mutely. She imagined Flannel Boy in some well-appointed two-parent home, gathered with flanneled siblings around a dinner table while one parent delivered a lesson on Why You Need to Intervene When You See a Girl in Trouble. Or maybe it wasn't a parent at a dinner table—maybe it was a Boy Scout troop leader or the coach of a rich-person sport, like lacrosse or downhill skiing. Somebody intent on teaching the future leaders of America how to Do the Right Thing. And even though she knew that if it really came to blows Flannel Boy wouldn't stand a chance—he probably wasn't reared on street fighting, and she wouldn't be surprised if her uncle had a switchblade or even a gun somewhere on his person—she still appreciated that he was trying.

"I told you already that's my niece. Why you need to ask her too?"

FB held up his hands, palms out; his hands were saying, *Hey hey hey, don't overreact.* To Jade he said, "You need me to get campus security?"

She started to shake her head, then she reconsidered, looked her uncle directly in his wicked, bloodshot eyes, and said, "Yes, please. I'd like you to call campus security."

Her uncle whistled and said, "Ho-lee shit, princess. You kidding me with this?"

"No." She folded her arms. "I'm not kidding even a little bit." She turned to FB. "Thanks so much," she said. "I think there's a campus security phone right over there." She pointed. She did not, in fact, know where the nearest campus security phone was.

"You think you're better than me, princess. But you ain't. You came from the same damn place."

I may have come from the same place, she thought. But I am a million times better than you.

"I'll go call," said FB.

"Never mind," said her uncle. "Don't worry about it. I'm going. You can't help your little cousin out, that's okay, princess." He turned and walked away. "Stuck-up little—" Something took the rest of his sentence, the wind or the night, but it was pretty clear what word came next.

"You okay?" FB was looking at her with a furrowed brow. He made Jade think of a shar-pei.

"Yeah." She nodded, forced a smile. "Yeah, I'm okay." It was important to act like this wasn't a big deal, like her legs weren't shaking, like her heart wasn't beating so fast that the heartbeat felt almost visible, even bundled as she was against the cold. It was important to act like she belonged where she was.

"You sure? What if he comes back?"

"He won't come back."

The brow furrowed even more. "How do you know?"

"I just know," she said. "That was the end of it."

"I know it's none of my business, but—the end of what?"

She couldn't really explain it to Flannel Boy, nor, she was sure, did he actually want to hear. He didn't have the context to understand that her two different worlds had just collided, right there in front of her dorm, and that her uncle walking away the way he was doing now: that was her past moving away from her future, she hoped for the last time.

Sophomore year Shelly and Mary Ann decided to room together. Jade became an RA and remained one for each of the remaining three years. And so college went by. From the outside, Jade learned to fit in. Hair: straighter and smoother. Clothing: more casual—anything other than sweats and you looked like you were trying too hard. Makeup: minimal, tasteful. Voice: modulated. In this way, while most people grow outward during their college years, Jade drew inward.

She played the part. Sometimes she even enjoyed the part. She never missed a class, a paper, an exam, an opportunity. She upheld the Jesuit traditions espoused by the school; she volunteered at food pantries, at fundraisers. She could handle herself in the bro culture of the business school; academically, she thrived. But underneath it all—or maybe more accurately, running through it, like a current through a river—was the deep, deep shame of not having.

She couldn't believe how supported her fellow students were: by their parents, their extended family, even by their former teachers at their prestigious prep schools. Mary Ann, rolling her eyes because her mother was calling her again, was not the exception. Mary Ann was the rule, and Jade and other students like her, students in the shadows, were the exception.

Family Weekend was an exquisite form of torture. Parents filled the quad, the football stadium, the hallways of the residence halls. Everyone seemed to have a parent, or an uncle, or a sibling, who had graduated in an earlier year. Jade couldn't *believe* how many families came—families with two parents, families with rental cars full of siblings, families who dropped hundreds of dollars in the bookstore for sweatshirts and hats and collars for their purebred dogs. She couldn't believe how much the word *legacy* meant in a place like this. Everyone knew the rules, where to go, what to wear, how to be.

When Jade graduated, when she gave the commencement speech for the business school, she was debt-free, with exactly the education she needed. But she was *tired*. She was twenty-two, but she'd been grinding so long and so hard she felt like she was forty.

The only person from Lawrence who was there to see Jade give her speech was Ms. Morin, who somehow found her in the immense crowds of happy families and gave her a bouquet of white roses tied with a maroon-and-gold ribbon. Ms. Morin hugged Jade; they both cried. Ms. Morin wished she could take Jade out to lunch, she really did, but her daughter had a dance recital that she couldn't miss, and there was something with her costume that took a long time to—

"That's okay," Jade interrupted, to save them both the humiliation. "That's totally fine! I have plans anyway. I'm so glad you could come." Smile, Jade. Smile harder, so that nobody knows you're lying.

NICOLA

Felicity's nanny comes down with strep throat on Saturday and has to stay isolated for twenty-four hours while the antibiotics do their work.

"I'm so sorry," David says when he calls Nicola to ask if she can babysit. Taylor had to go to Boston for a meeting, and he has a commitment he can't change at the last minute, he explains. "If I had anyone else to ask, I would," he says. He doesn't want to take advantage of Nicola, especially on a Saturday, her day off.

"Are you done with your extended apology and speech?" Nicola asks.

David snorts. "I think so."

"Okay. I'm in. And I don't need all of the reasons behind it. I'd be mad if you *didn't* ask me."

"Are you really sure? And if you're really sure, bring a bathing suit."

"If you ask me again, I'm telling your mom about the rum you stole from the house where you were dog-sitting the summer you were fifteen. I'll see you in forty-five minutes."

David says, "Do you want me to—" and at the same time Nicola says, "Don't you dare send a car or driver for me."

"What about a helicopter?"

WHEN NICOLA ARRIVES on her bike, only moderately sweaty (she's getting better at the hills!), she very carefully does not look around for Jack Baker. David opens the door, and attached to his leg, looking at Nicola from underneath her ridiculous lashes, is Felicity. Jack doesn't appear from any of the places where Nicola's carefully not looking, and she doesn't ask David where he is. She hasn't seen Jack since Monday.

"You look fancy," she says. "Where are you headed?" David steps aside to let her in and gently detaches Felicity from his leg. He's wearing a long-sleeve button up in white linen, the sleeves rolled up halfway, and faded dark red shorts like you see on wealthy men of all ages on Nantucket. Well, like Nicola imagines you see. She's never been to Nantucket, but she's read a lot of summer novels set there. His skin has an even, golden tan, and Nicola can smell a subtle cologne when he bends to hug her. His teeth gleam. He's like an advertisement for what money can add to what are already really fortunate genetics. But, she knows, he also looks right on a creeper (terrible name) under a car, or at a Minnesota lake house.

"Oh, to meet a friend. It's more like a lunch appointment." He doesn't allow his eyes to meet Nicola's.

Nicola darts her eyes toward Felicity, to see if she's listening. Felicity is fully absorbed in a bracelet on her wrist. "Is the friend Juliana?" Nicola asks softly. David looks like he's going to answer, but in the end he just turns toward Felicity and says, "Bye, sweetheart. I'll be back in a little while, okay?"

Felicity looks up briefly. "Bye, Daddy."

"Maybe an hour and a half, or two?"

Felicity lifts one of her hands in a gesture that seems fascinatingly adult, even dismissive. "Bye, Daddy," she repeats. "I'm playing with Nicola now."

"Well, there you have it," says David. "I guess I'll see myself out."

"Come on." Felicity takes Nicola by the hand and something in Nicola's heart shifts with the sensation of Felicity's warm little fingers tucked into her palm. It's almost a jolt. Is this what a biological clock feels like, when it starts ticking?

She follows Felicity down a hallway; her first tour with David didn't include the bedroom wing (it is really and truly *a wing*). Many of the doors are closed (she's *dying* to get a look at Taylor and David's room!) but one is open. She can't help it, she pauses for a peek.

"What's this?" she asks Felicity.

"Daddy's office." And then, with more authority than a three-year-old should have, "You can go in."

Nobody has to ask Nicola twice. She pushes the door open wider. It is, maybe, a little bit funny that a person with no job has an office this nice, but okay, whatever, this is how the wealthy roll. The office has obviously been touched by the wand of the same interior designer responsible for the rest of the house—sleek, minimalist, a long low couch, a desk made of reclaimed wood with impossibly slender legs, an assertive chair in a deep orange that matches the small square pillows on the couch—but it does retain a few touches that seem very specifically David. On the desk, a coffee mug with an inch of coffee in it alongside an open can of Narragansett Fresh Catch. A tiny pile of clutter—sunglasses, mail, a bottle of vitamins. A pair of running shoes, laces akimbo, in the corner. And above the desk, incongruous with the decor in the rest of the room, is a framed poster, wildly neon, that makes Nicola smile.

"The Minnesota State Fair!" she says. She can't tell if it's beautiful or garish; probably, like the state fair itself, it's a little bit of both. It makes her feel nostalgic.

"Mommy hates that poster," Felicity says pensively.

"She does? Why?" Not that Nicola really has to ask. It's the antithesis of the rest of the office, the rest of the house.

Felicity shrugs.

"Have you ever been to a fair?"

Felicity shakes her head and says, "What's a fair?"

Oh, this poor kid. *What's a fair?* Nicola tells her all about it. Rides, and bunnies, and llamas and alpacas. Music shows all day and night. Dock-diving dogs, and a lumberjack show where real lumberjacks with arms the size of Felicity's whole body chop wood as fast as they can. And the food! Cotton candy, and key lime pie on a stick dipped in chocolate, and foot-long hot dogs, and mini doughnuts so small you can eat twelve of them, and pizza on a stick. Also corn dogs on a stick, and pork belly on a stick, and cheesecake on a stick (so many foods on so many sticks!).

"*Twelve* doughnuts," says Felicity incredulously. "Don't you get a bellyache?"

"Of course you do," says Nicola. "But it wouldn't be the state fair if it didn't give you a bellyache. All of the food tastes so good, but none of it is good for you."

Felicity nods solemnly, taking this in. They both stare at the poster, the vivid colors (the phrase CHEESE CURDS in bright yellow somehow jumping out of the bottom left, and suddenly nothing sounds as good to Nicola as a red-and-white-checked paper basket full of them). Felicity stares for so long it seems as if the molecules have reordered themselves. It seems as if now that she understands the poster the world has new meaning.

"Okay," says Nicola finally, feeling a twinge of guilt that they're in here at all. "We need to make sure we play enough. Your daddy won't be gone that long."

Wrong. It isn't an hour and a half, and it isn't two—it's more like three and a half hours, but Nicola doesn't mind. She loves this day. They play for a really long time in Felicity's room, where she has rows and rows of dress-up clothes. Dolls and books galore. When they're finished there, they change into bathing suits and go out to the pool. Felicity digs in a wicker bin and pulls out a contraption that she begins strapping around herself.

Felicity calls this contraption her "bubble" even though to Nicola's eye there's nothing bubble-like about it; it's three rectangles of foam that land on Felicity's mid-back like a skydiving parachute pack. It keeps her safe, though; in the pool she bobs around like a cork, while Nicola stretches out on one of the foam floats, listening to Felicity's voice, high and bright, singing some song about a turtle and a frog.

She's got two eyes on Felicity, and then she's got one eye, and then, for just a slice of a fraction of a second the sun gets to her, and the light motion of the float gets to her, and, really, it's hardly any time at all that her eyelids flutter and she's got no eyes on Felicity, because then the song about the turtle and the frog stops, and she opens her eyes, and the bubble is floating all on its own.

Nicola is off that float *so fast*, every lifeguarding lesson, every day swimming on the lake coming back to her, and she's underwater, grabbing Felicity and bringing her to the edge of the pool, holding fast and tight to her little body, saying, "Ohmygod ohmygod ohmygod, what *happened*, Felicity?"

Felicity's big blue eyes are brimming over. "I took off my bubble."

Deep breath. It's okay, everyone is okay. "Why'd you take off your bubble?"

"I wanted to see if I could swim yet."

"Oh, sweetie." She tries to keep her voice steady, but she can hear it wavering.

"Don't tell Daddy I took it off," whispers Felicity. "I'm sorry." She looks so bereft, and so fragile, and so huggable. Ergo, Nicola hugs her.

"It's okay. It's okay. I won't tell. But don't do that again, all right? Don't take off your bubble again unless a grown-up is right there, and a grown-up says it's okay."

Nicola doesn't let herself think about it, doesn't allow her mind to go *there*. But later, at the end of the summer, when she isn't there to do any saving, she does remember this day, the way they dodged a bullet. She thinks about how you can be above water one second and underneath it the next.

Once Nicola's blood pressure lowers to a reasonable level, they dry off with fluffy pool towels, change back into their clothes, visit the bathroom, find a carton of organic strawberries in the refrigerator. "Cut off the green part," Felicity instructs, climbing on a small step stool to bring herself up to counter level, so Nicola does, she cuts off the green part, because what can she say, for a three-year-old Felicity presents as quite the girl boss, and Nicola doesn't feel qualified to disobey. After the snack comes a brief lull. Is David ever coming back?

"Let's play a game," she suggests. "Do you have any games?"

"Playroom," Felicity says, pointing down one of the endless wide hallways. Nicola didn't even know about the playroom! She follows Felicity into a white, white room with acres of cubbies. In the cubbies are pastel baskets, and inside Nicola sees art supplies, many of them not opened, and board books, and a tiny globe whose continents light up in different colors when you touch it. Nicola wants to trade places with Felicity, like immediately. She's about to set up Chutes and Ladders when suddenly David is there, leaning against the doorjamb, arms folded, watching them and smiling.

"Hey!" says Nicola. "I didn't hear you come in."

"I'm sneaky."

"Daddy!" Felicity runs to him and hugs his leg.

"How was your appointment?" Nicola asks. She puts extra weight on the word *appointment*.

"What?" He looks startled. "Oh, good. It was good. Fine, you know. Good."

"Where'd you go?"

"Spring House. You been there yet?" (Is he slurring?)

She shakes her head. "Out of my price range."

"Have Jack take you." She winces. That's humiliating. (But also, she wants Jack to take her.) "And get the Point Judith calamari appetizer and a Mudslide. You won't be sorry."

"Copy that," she says. She uncrosses her legs and stands, reluctant to leave and go back to her own cottage, where there's no pool, no strawberries, no dress-up clothes. She stalls a little, angling for more time, maybe an invitation to stay.

"*Come on*, Daddy." Felicity pulls his arm. Nicola sighs. How quickly she's been replaced.

"Just a sec, sweetie. I need to find money for Nicola." He pats the pockets of his red shorts. "Sorry, I don't—I just . . . my wallet." He looks perplexed, a little emotionally rumpled. "I wonder if I left it . . . it's probably in the . . . Do you have Venmo?"

"Venmo?" Of course she has Venmo; everyone has Venmo. But does David think she expects to be *paid*? They're each other's favorite cousin! Cousins do each other favors. Especially cousins from Minnesota. "I'm happy to spend time with Felicity anytime. Please don't pay me."

"You sure?"

"One hundred percent." It all feels a little cheap, suddenly, and she's irritated with David. The long absence, the slurring, the caginess. He can tell he's offended her, and he unleashes one of his winning smiles.

"In that case," he says, "I'll see you Monday at eight sharp. The nanny costs a fortune."

It's a decent recovery, and she gives him credit for it. "Eight sharp it is," she says. Then Felicity announces, "Bathroom!" and disappears. "Listen, David," she hisses, once Felicity is out of sight. "What are you doing?"

"What do you mean?"

"What are you doing with Juliana? What are you doing to Taylor?"

His eyebrows shoot up. "What am *I* doing to *Taylor*?"

"I mean, what are you doing in general?"

He clears his throat. "Am I obligated to explain all of that to you?"

Coming from David, this smarts; wow, it *really* smarts. She blinks hard, wondering if she might cry. Then she rebounds and says, "No. Of course not. But there was a time when you would have wanted to."

"Yeah, well." He rubs his temples.

Just like that, Felicity is back.

"Listen, Nic—"

She bends down and opens her arms for a hug. Felicity dives right in, and Nicola says, "Bye, Felicity. I had a great time today."

"Tell my favorite cousin thank you for hanging out with you," David says. He's trying to make it up to her, but Nicola keeps her eyes on Felicity, who says, "Thank you for hanging out with you."

BY THE SECOND week in July, Nicola has led two dock expeditions and five tank explorations at BIMI (pronounced "bimmy," which she always finds funny). She has prepped for and attended two of the weekly talks. She's going to be in charge of her own Creature Feature; she's going to focus on starfish, which she knows will be a hit with the younger visitors. She's hard at work getting ready for the impending arrival of the College Crusade students who will come for a week in August. (The College Crusade helps underrepresented youth get on a college track.) She's tested water; she's collected plankton; she's cleaned tanks. She's gone along on one harbor cruise.

They celebrate the birth of a baby seahorse. By now most people have read the Eric Carle book *Mister Seahorse,* so people are typically not surprised by the fact that the female seahorse lays her eggs in the male's pouch, but it still makes Nicola smile to think about it. She pictures laying her eggs in Zachary's pouch. She imagines telling him that he is to be responsible for toting the eggs around, and that when the time comes to give birth his body will undergo contractions that straddle the line between vehement and violent. Zachary would 100 percent never go for it. He's way too finicky for all of that; pregnancy would complicate his career trajectory. He'd never want to wear maternity clothes to the firm.

But she can't imagine Jack toting around the eggs either. What male that she knows *would* tote the eggs?

David! David would tote the eggs.

She's never been happier, and even though she worked hard in her previous life, there are days when she feels like she's never worked harder. As a proud millennial—she barely squeaked in, born on the very tail end of the generation—she's determined to show the Gen Zers what hard work is all about. If there's something to volunteer for, she'll raise her hand. If there's a tank to clean, she'll clean it. A Tuesday Talk to set up for? She'll Tuesday it until the cows come home.

And then there's Juliana. Nicola has never been friends with a famous entrepreneur before. It's exciting! But also, it's like making any new friends, because except for the giant house she's a regular person; she puts her pants on one leg at a time, etc., even if those pants are typically part of a curated, occasion-appropriate look.

Sometimes Juliana will text Nicola during the workday, and Nicola will text back, maybe sending a photo of the touch tank or the dock. If they happen to be outside their homes at the same time they'll have a chat, like two dads in the fifties bonding over a garden hedge after mowing the lawn.

Nicola didn't go to Juliana's last party, although Juliana had sent a text inviting her (with three emojis—clearly their relationship has reached a new level!) because that night the bimmy interns who are old enough to drink went out to Captain Nick's. At the bar, one intern, Cherry, a local, told Nicola about the hundreds of glass floats made by a glassblower named Eben Horton on the mainland. The floats, the size of an orange, are hidden around the island at the beginning of each summer, and people go crazy looking for them. Nicola is instantly determined to find one. She'll look first on Mansion Beach, because, why not?

"You have to be open to it, without looking too hard," Cherry told Nicola. "Just like love."

And then, of course, there's Jack, whose unpredictability stands in direct opposition to Zachary's unvariedness. Jack (and Taylor too) ping-pong on and off the island like it's nothing; Taylor for business, and Jack for—who knows what. He has friends to see on Nantucket; he has a party in Boston. Sometimes he texts before he shows up after being away but sometimes he just appears at her door, grinning. She's on her back foot a lot, but after years of distributing her weight evenly she sort of likes it.

He drives David's silver metallic Tesla that Nicola rolled her eyes at until she first climbed inside, at which point, she admits, she marveled. There's a reason why people with money pay a lot for their cars. Their cars are nicer than the Pontiacs and Hondas the rest of the driving world has. With Taylor's midnight-blue Mercedes, their driveway looks like the valet section of a hotel in the French Riviera. Not that Nicola would know. But she has an imagination.

"This isn't the fancy car," Jack tells her. "This is the kick-around car. David would never let me near his Porsche."

"Why not?"

"It's a 911 GT3," he says, as if that explains everything. And maybe it does, what does Nicola know about cars?

"A *Tesla* is the kick-around car?" she says.

Sometimes, Nicola thinks about what Taylor called him at that first dinner in June—a playboy without a mansion. He might not have a mansion, but he has a credit card. He takes Nicola to places she never would have gone on her own: out to dinner at Kimberly's, to Eli's, and finally, yes, to Spring House. They bike out to Settler's Rock one evening and pick their way over the rocks toward North Light. The museum is closed for the day, nobody around but the seals swimming close to the shore, so Jack leans Nicola up against the rocky wall and kisses her so intently, so urgently, so *indecently* that when a party of three shows up just behind them they scurry back to their bikes and pedal as fast as they can, back to Nicola's place.

Once he materializes at the Institute while she's running a squid dissection. She looks up from her magnifying glass to see him leaning against a pole behind the table. "Sorry," she tells him. "Reservations are required, and we're fully booked. You can sign up online for a spot next week." Jack lingers while she crouches between a couple of ten-year-old girls, showing them the three-chambered heart and explaining to them that squids have blue blood because of a copper-based pigment.

"The way you say *dorsal aspect* makes me so hot," he says later that night in bed.

"Oh, stop it."

"For real," he says. He puts his lips close to her ear and says, "Talk to me about the three chambers of the heart."

"I can never tell if you're kidding or not."

"Me either," he says. Then, "What should we do tomorrow?"

"Do? I have to go to work."

"Silly Nicky," he says. He kisses her on the forehead. It's a kiss that should have felt merely endearing but somehow manages to feel sexy. "Play hooky with me."

In the world Nicola comes from, people work. If they are lucky they enjoy their work, but it's still *work*, and you go because you have an obligation and you need the money and people are counting on you but besides all that, if you don't go to work, what are you supposed to do with yourself all day?

But here's Jack, who talks like money is the very last reason to return to his job. ("How's your Achilles?" she asks him every now and then. "Better every day," he says, grinning. "Better and better and better.")

THERE'S A TUESDAY Talk this very night. The speaker is the head of animal rescue at Mystic Aquarium, and Nicola knows this will attract a crowd. Who doesn't want to hear about animals being rescued? Who isn't looking for a feel-good moment in a feel-bad world? After lunch she and Cherry are going to set up the folding chairs. It's

Cherry's turn to have dinner with the speaker, at Dead Eye Dick's, before the talk. They each get a turn once in the summer. Nicola is holding out for the white shark expert, but aren't they all?

Nicola hops on her bike and cycles toward town. She stops at Three Sisters, the pocket-sized sandwich shop on Old Town Road. She chooses the Twisted Sister sandwich, although it's a tough call between that and the Celeb Sister. Then, back on her bike, she cycles to Fred Benson Town Beach, where there is a bike rack and a bathroom, and where she can be alone with her thoughts. What thoughts does she want to be alone with? She's not sure. But she's feeling jumbled—too jumbled to eat with the other interns.

She locks her bike at the rack—it's so crowded, she almost doesn't find a spot—and, once she's clear of the parking lot and through the pavilion, she crouches down and removes her sneakers and her socks, which she immediately regrets because the sand is hot hot hot.

She's not, of course, alone at the beach. It's a postcard-ready day on the Block, and the beach is jammed with families and gaggles of teenage girls in bikinis and pods of teenage boys playing Frisbee with no shirts, their bodies so effortless and lean and muscled in a way that they probably think will last forever. But she doesn't know any of these people, so she sort of feels like she's alone. She sits well back from the ocean, on the other side of the pavilion from the chair and umbrella rentals. She's in her blue Institute polo shirt, which feels a little weird at the beach, but so be it. She unwraps her sandwich.

She tries to put her metaphorical finger on what's bothering her. It's the thoughts of Zachary that surfaced earlier in the day, as she was thinking about the seahorses. It's the troubled way the thoughts made her feel. It's the realization that she's so much older than everyone else doing her job. Usually she's okay with that—she even finds it a little funny, like she can be the cool aunt of the Institute, the one who takes the Institute interns out for their first pedicures. But geez, many of the interns will vote in their first presidential election this fall. They are *really young!*

Maybe she does miss Zachary. They lived together for two years; it would have been strange if she didn't miss him! She misses having someone who knew her coffee order (Nicola is the only person left on the planet who still drinks regular milk, no almond or oat, and she almost always gets an extra shot of espresso in her cappuccino) and who will watch six episodes of *Succession* on a rainy Sunday. She misses planning Halloween costumes with him; last year, when everybody was dressing up as Barbie and Ken the first Halloween after the movie came out, they went to a party as Siegfried and Roy and won first prize in the costume contest. They had big white stuffed tigers they carried around all night, and even though the tigers were awkward they really sealed the win.

At the same time, she's mad at herself for missing him, so in her head she lists the things she does not miss. She does not miss the way it was okay for her to know things, but only if he knew more things, or had just a different angle on one of her things. She does not miss the way he sighed audibly when she stopped to meet dogs in the street, even if the dogs very clearly wanted to be greeted. She does not miss the way he had to send a steak back to be cooked "a smidge more" every time he ordered one and yet refused to change his order from medium rare to just plain medium. She did not like that he used the word *smidge*.

She pulls out her phone from her backpack and calls her best friend from college, Reina. Due to Reina's current circumstances as a full-time mother (current but *temporary*, Reina would hasten to add), she's sometimes available to talk at odd times of the day. Because Nicola has kept Reina updated on Jack through text, and because they lived together for so long—holding each other's hair back during the Jägermeister vomiting incident of sophomore year, sharing clothes and makeup, and twice, albeit accidentally, a toothbrush—they typically forgo niceties and formalities.

"I don't know what any of this means," Nicola says. "This Jack Baker stuff." She glances at her watch; it's almost time to head back to work. In the background, on Reina's end, she can hear Mia jabbering, Cooper making new baby noises.

"Hang on, okay? I've just got to get Cooper to latch on." There are some muffled sounds, and then she says, "Okay! I'm back. Sorry, what was the question again? My brain is mush."

"No specific question. I just don't know what this all means." Reina and Hunter had gotten married and had two children within the space of three years. They had been on parallel tracks once, Reina and Nicola, ten years ago, in that double dorm room, with their fairy lights and their complementary comforters and their mini fridge full of vitaminwater, but somewhere along the way Reina zigged when Nicola zagged. Now Reina has Cooper and Mia and Hunter, and Nicola has—what, exactly? The squid and the plankton.

"Who *cares* what it means! Are you having fun?"

Nicola looks down at her bare feet. She digs her toes into the hot sand and then squints out at the ocean. The sun shimmering on the water gives the beach a wavy, fun-house vibe. "Yes."

"How's the sex?"

Even though nobody is looking at her, and of course nobody can hear the question, Nicola flushes. "Pretty good."

"That's it?" Reina sounds doubtful. "No kids, you're riding around an island in a Tesla, and sex that's 'pretty good' is all you can manage? Honey, I thought I raised you better than that."

"Okay," Nicola admits. She thinks of Jack's long, cool fingers on her ribs, his lips on her neck, and elsewhere. She thinks of kissing at North Light, and how they could barely get back to the cottage and take their clothes off fast enough. "Better than pretty good."

Sex with Jack is so different from sex with Zachary: more urgent, more unpredictable, more frequent. More confusing? Sure. That too. "Would you go so far as to say *amazing*?" asks Reina.

"I would go that far," Nicola concedes. "I might go further."

She hears Reina suck in her breath. "Yesssss, queen. That's more like it."

Then Reina asks, "Did you google Jack? You should google him."

"Of course I googled him!"

"And?"

"Lots of pictures of him playing golf in a visor."

"But did you deep-dive google him, to find the skeletons?" Reina has a degree in journalism. She's really good. Before she had Mia she was working at the *Wall Street Journal*, and she's going to go back, she reminds Nicola often, as soon as Cooper is a little older.

"No."

"Want me to do it for you?"

"No," Nicola says. Then, immediately, "Sure. Okay."

"A caper!" Reina says.

"I don't think this qualifies as a caper."

"A project!" she says, in the exact same manner.

"But don't tell me if you find anything really bad."

"I most certainly *will* tell you if I find something really bad," says Reina.

But Nicola feels suddenly uneasy. "You know what? Never mind."

"Never mind what?"

"Don't do the deep dive. I'm going to stick with the shallow one."

"Yeah?" Reina sounds doubtful. "You sure?"

"I'm sure." Is she sure? No. "I'm sure," she says again, as much to convince herself as to convince Reina.

"Okay. In that case, don't overthink it. You don't want to get yourself in another Zachary situation."

"I definitely don't want to do that."

"I'm trying not to be jealous. Here's me, leaking through my bra, sixteen pounds overweight, and there *you* are, fabulous as ever in a bikini, those killer abs, sex—"

"Stop," says Nicola. "I'm currently in a polo." (She does have killer abs, though; it's genetic. Her sisters have them too. No boobs.

That's their trade-off.) "You wouldn't give up that for this, Reina. Are you forgetting that I am broke and technically single?"

She laughs. "Most days, I concede that," she says. "But every now and then . . ."

Mia's bright, clear voice slices the conversation in two. "Mommy! Mommymommymommy. There's *sticky juice* on the iPad."

"I have to go," Reina says as Cooper, maybe prematurely disengaged from his meal, begins to wail. "I think we're entering a Code Red. Remember what I said, though, okay? Don't overthink things."

"Okay," Nicola says. "I'll try not to."

She thinks too much about everything. She always has.

An errant Frisbee lands near her, and one of the cute high school boys runs over—actually, even though the sand is hot and hard to run in, he *floats*, the way only a teenage boy can do—and says, "Sorry, ma'am." She tries not to mind this. She's 93 percent sure she got *ma'am*ed because of the polo. If she were in her bikini that wouldn't have happened. Reina's absolutely right. She *does* have killer abs. And she has to get back to work.

Riding back by Beach Ave., she returns to the question that has been nibbling at the edge of her conscience. Who is she to say love doesn't matter? What does she know of love? Has she ever *been* in love? Does she want to be?

She knows two things about love. One. It's not as common as people think it is. Two. She saw it between David and Juliana, when she and Jack returned to the happy hour on Nicola's patio. She felt it; it was almost palpable.

What's that worth, to be in love with an unavailable person? Is it worth everything, or is it worth nothing?

What exactly constitutes *unavailable*?

LIAM HELPS HER set up the chairs for the Tuesday Talk. They make sure that the screen is working, and Liam, whose work-study job at college is in the media services department, checks the connections. When they're finished they step outside, onto the deck attached to the Institute.

If they were young urban office workers in, say, the eighties, this is the point where they would shoot the shit over a cigarette. But since they're wholesome marine interns in the 2020s who would rather die than pollute the ocean or their own lungs, they carry their refillable, environmentally responsible water bottles and do what Americans between the ages of two and thirty-five do better than anyone: they hydrate.

Liam, sipping exuberantly, says, "I had a dream I was drowning last night. I fell right off the harbor tour boat and sank straight to the bottom! It was insane."

"Jesus, Liam." Nicola shudders. "You know how to swim, right?"

"Of course I do. Doesn't everyone know how to swim?"

She thinks about Juliana. "Well, no."

"Everyone in America, though."

Is this what they're teaching this kid at his progressive college? "Still no," she says. "Not everyone has the privilege of swimming lessons."

Liam reflects on this, then says, "True. I did. In my youth. But you're right, that was a privilege. Hey, is this your guy again?" Jack is walking (sauntering) up the sidewalk, not a care on him, no compunction about appearing at her work so soon after the last time.

In the time it would have taken to say *starfish* Nicola finds herself in the passenger seat of the Tesla, driving too fast down Ocean Ave. He glances over at her. "Where do you want to go? Your place?"

"What? *No!* I have a Tuesday Talk. I can't go back all . . . disheveled."

Jack grins. "You sure? I'd love to dishevel you." Nicola crosses her legs primly and tries to scowl.

"Well, you can't. You can dishevel me another time. How about we just take a drive? I really can't be late getting back."

"Sure." Jack lowers the windows, turns up the music—Jack Johnson singing "Better Together," so many Jacks, all in one place—and they cruise, following an oval in the center of the island. Nicola closes her eyes, letting the summer air fly over her face. Jack reaches for her hand, and for just a moment she thinks, Why worry about anything? Just enjoy.

Then, turning left to head back to the Institute, he whips the car so hard into the turn that Nicola's eyes fly open. A car coming toward them with the right of way screeches to a halt, and the driver honks.

"Jesus, Jack," says Nicola.

"What?" He glances over at her; he seems legitimately confused.

"You almost got us in an accident. Be a little careful, would you?"

He shrugs and doesn't look a bit concerned. "I'm careful enough. I had plenty of time."

She snorts. "Not really."

"Doesn't matter anyway, if other people are careful. It takes two to make an accident."

She won't really think about this until later, but that about sums up a lot of the summer right there: these careless people with their money and their drama and their disregard for the basic rules. "Uh," she says. "I'm pretty sure it just takes one." No wonder David doesn't let him near his Porsche.

Host: And we're back with *Life and Death on an Island*, where all politics is local but death is universal. In this episode we're speaking with four members of Block Island's town council. I'd like to dig into the hotel plan Evan brought up before we had a word from our sponsors. Evan, can you fill the listeners in on exactly what's involved in a proposal like the one Buchanan Enterprises brought before you last summer?

Evan: Okay, sure. Technically, it wasn't brought before us first, but it did end up in front of us eventually. To tear down an existing structure like the motel Buchanan had bought, the owner would first put a proposal before the Historic Commission. If Historic denied some part of the project, for whatever reason, and the owner wanted to fight it, the appeal would go to Zoning. If Zoning denied, they could kick to us for a reversal. That's what happened.

Lou (whistles): Historic can be tough, but Zoning can be tougher.

Betsy: You can say that again. My ex-brother-in-law is on Zoning.

Kelsey: Remember when they first proposed the bathrooms at Mansion Beach? That was some *drama*.

Lou: That's how it should be. You don't want to let people build willy-nilly all over the island. There's only so much land.

Kelsey: Taylor Buchanan must have felt like the whole town was against her when she was trying to get that proposal through. Did you read that opinion piece in the paper?

Host: Can you elaborate on that?

Lou: Yeah, sure. I'll take that. Somebody wrote an opinion piece against the hotel proposal, unsigned. The piece itself was okay, fair enough, I'd say, but online, in the comments section? Sheesh. They got rough. They got personal about the Buchanans. You'd have to be pretty thick-skinned to let that roll over you.

Betsy: I can't imagine what would have happened if we ever got to the public hearing. I don't think people would have held back. Henry, though? My grandson? Like I said earlier in the episode he was GC on the four homes Buchanan had under construction. He spoke *very* highly of Taylor Buchanan.

Kelsey: But we never got to the public hearing. They pulled the proposal.

Evan: Because of the death.

Lou: Well, come on now. Those two things aren't necessarily related.

Kelsey: It's all related. Trust me. Everything's related.

JULIANA

July is more than half over already, the date of the IPO approaching faster and faster. Not quite three months to go. There are days when Juliana is busy all the time, from dawn to dusk, and Allison basically runs the rest of her life while she works. Then there are days when she has only one meeting in the morning and nothing in the afternoon. There are days when she needs to put out three or four fires, and other days when not so much as an ember burns. There is a two-day period where she has to fly to New York to meet with research analysts. It surprises her, when she comes back, how much returning to the island feels like coming home. Is she *acclimating* to the Block? Does she, a woman so long without a country, finally have an island?

The week after she returns, a journalist from *Bloomberg Businessweek* is coming to the island to do a piece on Juliana. Her name is Caitlin O'Donnell, and she's written profiles on Sara Blakely of Spanx; on the duo who founded Away suitcases; on Tory Burch; on the founder of a hands-free breast pump.

This isn't the first journalist who has done a piece on Juliana, and in fact not by a long shot is it the biggest publication that's covered LookBook, but she's atypically unnerved by the whole thing. The closer she gets to the IPO, the more important it is that everything go well, that all the press be positive, that everything she does casts the company in the very, very best light. She needs the level of excitement about the company to be at its very highest right before the valuation is complete. The most delicate days are ahead of her, and she must tiptoe through them like a maiden through the dew.

No, not like a maiden through the dew. Come on, Juliana. She must be much more forceful than a tiptoeing maiden. She must be like—oh, never mind. The metaphor isn't important. The end result is.

Juliana debates over whether to take the journalist to Joy Bombs, the coffee shop where she and Shelly went that day they saw each other on Clayhead Trail. Appropriate, or is it too cute, too folksy?

(Later, when people pick over the events of the summer, they might come to think of the Clayhead meetup as "that fateful day.")

"Meet her at the Joy Bombs," Allison tells her, full of confidence. "And then bring her back here. You don't want your photographs done at a coffee shop. You probably want them by the water."

"I forgot all about photographs!" Juliana recalculates. Will she be able to show anyone around her house without her eyes darting across the pond to where, when it's dark, she can always see the green light at the end of the dock? Will she be able to (will she even need to?) justify her choice of location for a summer home?

"Wear your white jeans with the frayed hem," instructs Allison. "The Moussy Vintage ones? And your silk tank top in baby blue. The blue is going to pick up the undertones of your skin."

"Blazer?" asks Juliana.

Allison considers this question. She lets out a little puff of air, and she clicks her tongue on the roof of her mouth. "Yes," she says finally. "Also white, but one shade off from the jeans."

Allison is Juliana's own personal LookBook. "Got it."

When the IPO goes through, thinks Juliana, Allison is getting a bonus so big it will make her eyes pop. Shelly might get a bonus too! Despite what Juliana is beginning to suspect is a Very Messy

Personal Life, Shelly is, surprisingly, *very* good at PR. It was Shelly's idea to create VIP areas at the parties for meetups and subgroups, and Shelly's idea to have gift bags with curated accessories from the website featuring a variety of brands. It was also her idea to have a step and repeat at the last party, and to create a hashtag to go with it! The step and repeat was a giant hit.

JULIANA GETS TO Joy Bombs first and scans it for a potential New York reporter and photographer. She sees a sandy family, two teenage girls in tiny shirts, one man in a gray T-shirt with a laptop and a worried expression. She chooses a table, considers, chooses a different table. She opens her laptop, closes it, scrolls through her emails on her phone.

And then. The door to Joy Bombs opens, and who walks in but Taylor and David. Juliana's heart jackhammers. She's most likely going to have a heart attack. She's never met Taylor, but of course she knows what she looks like from years of online observing, from the wedding announcements, from frequent visits to the website of Buchanan Enterprises. She's just as beautiful, just as elegant, just as *tall* in person as she is in photos. She's wearing a pink-and-white embroidered sundress that manages to be both fitted and full-skirted without looking frumpy, and contemporary while also looking timeless. Juliana is too short to pull off a dress of that length.

She decides she might have a stroke instead of a heart attack. She looks down at her phone, pretending to be busy, and also wondering: Can you have a stroke *and* a heart attack at the same time?

Out of the corner of her eye she sees Taylor get in line to order, and David turns to come over to her.

"Hey," he says softly, and her heart flips three times, then does a back handspring, then settles enough so that she can say, "Hey," right back.

"In a minute, I'm going to introduce you to Taylor," he says. How is he playing it so cool? Juliana is actually dying. She's *dying*. She takes a deep breath. Meeting Taylor is going to be like meeting the sun. She calls upon the reserves of calm and badassery she employs when meeting with investors, when going before the board. "Okay?"

"Okay," she answers. What else is she supposed to say? She looks down at her hands, and by the time she looks up David is back at Taylor's side. She watches as they get their drinks, and as he takes the route from counter to door that leads by her table. She rolls her eyes a little as he feigns a surprised double take (Robert De Niro he is not) and says, "Juliana?"

So she looks up and says, with equally fake surprise, "Hey! David!"

Taylor's head whips around so fast it looks like it's on a swizzle stick. She gives David a quizzical look, and he says, "Taylor, this is Juliana George." To Juliana he says, "Nice to see you again," but he says it so formally that Juliana cringes.

"You too," chokes out Juliana.

"Wait," Taylor says. "'Again'? You two know each other? You're the LookBook person, right? With all the parties?" she asks. Juliana nods, suddenly mute. She's *so warm*. She's never regretted a blazer quite this much. She thinks about taking it off, but what if she has sweat through her blue tank top? Better to keep it on, and to suffer in silence.

"I met Juliana in New York, when LookBook was starting to take off." There's such a heat coming off David, off both of them. Juliana simply cannot take it. She's going to melt.

Taylor looks back and forth between them. "You never told me that."

"I'm sure I did. You were in Europe with your dad. You were in a whole different time zone; you probably forgot."

Taylor is confused. She shakes her head slowly. "I don't think so. I think I would have remembered."

Juliana says, "I'm here to meet a reporter. Then we're going back to my house, for photos." She feels like she has to explain the blazer.

Taylor turns from David to Juliana and says, "I know your house.

It's just on the other side of Great Salt, right?" Juliana nods, not trusting herself to talk any more than she has; she's sure that if she opens her mouth again her voice will crack like a fault line. *Get ahold of yourself,* she wants to scream. *You have been through so many things harder than this.* Has she, though? "We own the cottage right next to it. David's cousin is living there for the summer."

"Nicola," says Juliana. "Sure, we've become friends. She's great."

Taylor narrows her eyes at Juliana and says, "I'd love to see your place sometime. My company is investing a lot in island real estate, and I like to get a look at the comps whenever I can."

"Of course. Anytime." Juliana resists the urge to put her hand on her heart, to make sure it stays in her chest. Instead, she reaches into her bag and pulls out a card. "This has the number of my assistant, Allison. Just check in with her before you come, in case I'm in meetings." Because you are a badass, she tells herself, you may very well be in meetings. Involuntarily her eyes flick over to David, but he has put on his sunglasses, so his expression is inscrutable.

"Will do," says Taylor crisply. "Will definitely do."

Three days after graduation Jade moved to New York City for a paid internship at McKinsey. She lived in a minuscule sublet that belonged to an actor who had gone on tour with *Kinky Boots.* All of her itty-bitty paycheck went to paying rent and subway fare to get from West Forty-Fourth Street to Lower Manhattan.

It was the summer of the Ice Bucket Challenge, the World Cup in Brazil, and the death of Eric Garner. Ebola was ravaging Africa. Cronuts turned one that summer, and the Backstreet Boys toured with Avril Lavigne. Lauren Bacall and Robin Williams died, and Taylor Swift threw her second Fourth of July party. Blogs were in; the neon of 2013 was out.

Jade *worked her ass off* at McKinsey. By rights, she should have no backside left at all. She was the only intern who both came in the earliest and stayed the latest. She was definitely the only one who needed a second job to get by. She gathered from context clues that everyone else had parents paying their rent, their cell phone bills, their health insurance premiums, their *health club fees*, the bills for the credit cards with which they purchased the clothes they wore to the job they didn't have to work as hard at because if this didn't lead to a full-time job, something else would.

If the working world was easier than college in some ways—no projects or papers, no round social structure where she, a square peg, struggled to fit—it was harder in others. No matter how carefully she observed the other interns or young working women on the subway, on the street, and tried to put together similar outfits by combing the racks at Marshalls or T.J. Maxx, she never felt quite right. Something was always a little bit off: the shoes or the belt, the earrings. She was haunted by her ghosts from that pivotal freshman year.

I thought you put that in the giveaway bin.

She's like obsessed with my mom.

Her second job was as a receptionist for a therapist in Chelsea who had evening hours three days a week. Fourth floor. There was an elevator, but sometimes Jade took the stairs—this free workout was her own personal health club. Jade met George Halsey on a stair day. She was panting when she got to the fourth floor, gently sweating, searching her bag in vain for a tissue or a napkin. Outside the office, in one of the two swivel barrel chairs where patients who were early waited, was an older gentleman. Older than what? Older than the hills. He wore a bow tie and bowler hat, which you would think made him look like Charlie Chaplin but somehow didn't.

"Well, aren't you a sight for sore eyes," said the man. Just as the hat should have made him look like Chaplin but didn't, this statement should have made him sound pervy but didn't. Jade smiled and sweated some more. "My children are always telling me I need to stop saying things like this. I suppose I should just say good evening."

"It's okay," said Jade. "Good evening." She pulled open the door to the office and went inside. Amanda, a dancer who did nighttime insurance billing for the dentist in the adjoining office—they shared the common space—looked up from her computer and said, "Did he tell you you're a sight for sore eyes?"

"He did," said Jade, only slightly disappointed that the compliment wasn't unique to her. "Who is he?"

"George Halsey. He owns the building. He stops by sometimes to check on things. Drives Dr. Pratt crazy."

"Why's it drive Dr. Pratt crazy? He seems harmless enough."

Amanda snorted. "That's just it. Harmless people drive Dr. Pratt crazy."

"Got it," said Jade.

"He's filthy rich," Amanda offered. "He owns buildings all around here, apparently. I think he's bored. Once he told me that his wife is dead and his kids barely talk to him." Amanda made a fake gun with her thumb and forefinger and pointed it at her temple. "Shoot me if my life ever gets that sad, okay?"

"Will do," said Jade.

The second time George Halsey was sitting in one of the barrel chairs, Jade decided to sit down in the other one—she was fifteen minutes early, so why not?—and talk to him. She told him about her internship, and he told her about how he'd gone to Harvard, graduating in 1956, and how he'd made his fortune buying distressed properties around the city, fixing them up, and reselling them. Amanda, she realized, was wrong: George wasn't a sad, doddering old man. He was a whip-smart success story. He was a big deal. "I'll tell you something, Jade," he said. "Never underestimate the value of something nobody wants. That's where the gold is."

At McKinsey Jade worked on supply chain operations with a few different fashion brands: Ralph Lauren, J.Crew, Banana Republic. Looking at these companies from the inside out, she realized how little of their merchandise they sold for full price. The rest got discounted and relegated to the nether regions of the websites, or sold to discount resellers. There, a bargain shopper like Jade might find the clothing, but might just as likely never find it. Or someone like Jade might find a top, but no bottoms to pair it with; a dress, but no jacket or shoes. Because, while full-price apparel was always merchandised together in a look book to see how outfits coordinate, discounted items were often grouped only by category and by price.

"What I wouldn't do," she muttered to herself one day, perusing the companies' websites for a report she was working on, "for someone to put together all of this sales stuff from all these different places and make me an outfit, like they do with their full-price products." Somehow Expedia had done this for travel; Expedia didn't buy and sell plane tickets and hotel rooms, they simply scraped the web for them, put them all in one place, and collected a fee from their sale. Why couldn't this be done for fashion? And why couldn't she develop the technology to merchandise outfits by occasion or price? Why couldn't Jade create a fully customizable online look book?

I'll tell you something, Jade. Never underestimate the value of something nobody wants.

She hurried to Chelsea that night, hoping George was there, hoping he had time to listen. He was; he did. He listened, and she talked, and the more she talked the more she realized she was onto something real. If she could create a company that pulled together, say, a top from one brand, a bottom from another, shoes from yet another, she could collect a fee from the companies because she'd be getting volume on pieces they were hardly selling. Customers, in turn, could purchase a complete outfit at the same discount they'd get cobbling together individual pieces—without the work, and the uncertainty.

"This is brilliant, Jade. This is really brilliant."

She took maybe the deepest breath she'd taken in her life, then let it out. "Thanks for letting me talk it out," she said. "It's good practice. I'm thinking of taking it to my bosses."

"Don't take it to them." He shook his head. "No. Definitely not."

"Don't?" Her face felt warm: stupid idea, Jade.

"*You* need to build this business," he said. "All on your own, you need to do this. Do you have a name?"

"LookBook," she said. It slid out of her mouth like it had always been there, waiting.

"LookBook," he repeated. "Yes. Yes, Jade. LookBook." And it seemed almost possible.

"What was that all about?" asked Amanda when Jade entered the office.

"He's just lonely." Let Amanda think George was a has-been in a bowler hat. Jade saw him now as a secret weapon.

Amanda snorted. "Yeah. Lonely for your tits." She turned back to her computer.

The next time Jade saw George Halsey he wasn't wearing a bowler hat, and she was lying on the sidewalk on West Nineteenth Street, right outside the building. George was bending over her, holding out a hand.

"My dear. You just took quite a spill. I saw the whole thing. Your feet went right out from under you. I'm afraid you hit your head."

"I'm okay," said Jade immediately, even though she wasn't, because she was used to telling people she was okay when she wasn't. She didn't remember falling. In fact, she didn't know if she was coming from the office or going to it—she'd lost time. She was probably hungry: without the college dining hall, she was often hungry. When she sat up, she heard a ringing in her ears. She allowed George Halsey to help her. He pointed to an uneven part of the sidewalk, a lip she'd caught her foot on.

"Do you have someone to call?" George said. "You really whacked your head."

"Yes," said Jade.

He looked at her closely and called her bluff: "Do you really have someone to call?"

Softly, truthfully: "No."

"Well, then. You're coming home with me. My driver is just around the corner."

Later, days later, when her head was clear enough to wonder this, she wondered, Was it weird that she went with him so willingly? Was it another symptom of the disease of growing up without anyone caring for her the way children should be cared for that she accepted any kindness without question, slurped it up greedily in case it disappeared?

She's like obsessed *with my mom.*

Was there something particular about George that allowed her to trust him, or would she have gone with anyone who showed her kindness, the way a baby duck imprints on a human if no duck is available?

It might have just been because of the concussion—because as it turned out, she had a concussion.

The first day, she sent a message to one of the other interns, Olivia, to ask her to pass the message on to the appropriate channels.

OMG, Olivia texted back. THAT'S INSANE. FEEL BETTER, OK?

I'LL TRY.

In some ways, Jade reflected, she had never felt this good in her life. For four days and four nights she lay in the bed in George Halsey's guest room. In this room she felt cocooned, cared for, safe. Outside, Manhattan was in the middle of a heat wave—the sidewalks were burning, the subways were hell on Earth, the garbage began to smell the instant it was placed outside. But Jade was in George Halsey's guest room, air-conditioned to a perfect sixty-seven degrees, under the weight of an unbelievable comforter, and the sheets were so thick and at the same time so soft, and who would have thought that such thickness and such softness could coexist? But they did. And Jade, who sometimes felt like she had never rested a day in her life, rested. She wore a pair of cotton pajamas that had been laid out for her in the attached marble bathroom on the first day, along with a new toothbrush and a basket of toiletries, all brand-new, all quietly luxurious.

She drifted in and out of sleep; with the heavy blinds closed against the sun, day was nearly indistinguishable from night. Three times a day George Halsey's housekeeper, Mrs. Sanchez, came into the room with a tray of food for Jade—homemade breads or muffins, sometimes, or chicken noodle soup from Zabar's, or soft pillows of ravioli with a homemade marinara sauce. Mrs. Sanchez was mostly hurried, seemingly consumed with many other tasks (What tasks? wondered Jade), but every so often she lingered by the side of the bed and asked Jade how she felt.

"Better than yesterday," Jade said, even on the first full day there, when it wasn't really true, because she didn't want to be a bother, and once her head cleared she began to realize what a very odd situation she was in. "A little better every day," she said, hopefully, optimistically. By the third day this was the case.

"Do you need me to call someone for you?" Mrs. Sanchez asked. "Let someone know where you are?"

"No," said Jade, and that vicious, sneaking shame returned. "Thank you. You don't need to call anyone."

Mrs. Sanchez laid the back of her hand against Jade's forehead. Jade knew from books and movies that this was a gesture indicative of care, even, in some circumstances, though obviously not this one, of love. Don't read too much into this, she told herself. This housekeeper doesn't love you; she doesn't even know you. She's probably wondering why you're in her house, making extra work for her. When Jade got up to take a shower in the attached bathroom she hung her towel carefully back up, just as she'd found it, to indicate she could use it again and again and again, but each day Mrs. Sanchez swept in with a clean one and whisked the used one away.

Sometimes, in her haze, she imagined Mrs. Sanchez to be like a nurse from old photos of World War II, with a loving bedside manner and a jaunty striped cap.

She's like obsessed *with my mom.* Snorts of laughter.

Twice a day, once in the midmorning and once in the midafternoon, George Halsey himself would knock softly at the door, and after Jade called out, *yes?* he'd enter and inquire whether he might sit with her, always leaving the door open "to avoid the appearance of impropriety," as he put it. Of course she always said that he could. For one thing, how strange it would have been to deny him this permission, in his very own guest room, but for another, she was really beginning to enjoy his company.

AT LAST, ON the morning of the fifth day, the blinds were raised, and Jade got up, still wobbly, but much less wobbly. She saw that she was not, as she guessed, *near* the park, but actually *on* the park, high up on Fifth Avenue, where, out the window, she could see the Egypt-inspired play structures at the Ancient Playground, Manhattan's finest coming and going and going, parents and children and nannies.

Now, she knew, it was time to return to her own life. She dressed in the clothes she'd been wearing on the day she fell (these had been professionally dry-cleaned, an embarrassment, considering the tags that made it clear they had come from Zara).

"I'm not sure how to pay you back for all of this," she told George. "For this kindness and generosity."

The courteous little nod again. "I didn't do it so you'd pay me back," he said. "I did it because I've been fortunate in my life and I want to help where I can help."

"But there must be something—?"

He cleared his throat and said, "There's one thing."

She waited.

"I wonder if you'd consider having lunch with me once a week for the remainder of the summer. My treat. I'd like to act as a sort of mentor to you, as you develop your business idea. I've been thinking more about LookBook. I think this idea has real potential. I'd like you to talk out your plans with me, as they develop. I'd like to be of assistance."

It didn't matter if the idea had potential. She had no way to get from here to there. She couldn't afford the loans to get an MBA; she couldn't stop working long enough to pitch her idea to VCs, never mind develop the technology. She'd gotten a great education for free and had already come further than she'd ever thought she would. When she was done with her internship she could apply for a permanent job, at a regular company.

But she said that she would like that, she would like to have lunch with George.

He said, "I'll leave you to your packing. Give Mrs. Sanchez a fifteen-minute warning, and the driver will be ready."

What packing? She had nothing to pack. Could she take all of the partially used toiletries?

"He asked me to have lunch with him once a week," she told Mrs. Sanchez, who was folding towels in the laundry room. (This was Jade's first look at the laundry room, in which she would have happily lived for the rest of the summer. It was so big, and so bright, and so airy and well organized.) "That's not weird, right?" She watched Mrs. Sanchez's long, capable fingers at work, mesmerized by the perfect rectangles she was creating from the towels.

"His wife is gone. His children are assholes," she said. She looked up briefly, locked eyes with Jade for a second. "Pardon my French. If a dying man wants to have lunch with you and you can spare the time, I say do it."

Jade thought, How does such a nice man have assholes for children?

Then her mind snagged on the last thing Mrs. Sanchez had said. *Dying?*

THERE WAS ALWAYS something off about Jade, when people were nice to her. She had enough self-awareness to know this but not enough wherewithal to do anything about it.

She attached herself to people who showed her the smallest acts of kindness—Ms. Morin the guidance counselor, her roommate's mother, and now a gentle old man. There were other people too. There was the lady in the registrar's office at college, who had also come from Lawrence but who had married a man from Newton and had two kids at Newton North High School. There was her high school basketball coach, who, the one season she played (she hated it and was terrible, too small to score, too clumsy to bob and weave), waived the cost of the uniform and, Juliana knew, must have paid her team fees out of his own pocket.

There had been nothing reciprocal about these situations, nothing she could give back. These people had helped Jade out of a general bigheartedness or a well-developed charitable muscle or maybe something as basic as old-fashioned pity. All Jade could offer in return was her gratitude, and even that she had to be careful with. She was constantly calculating and recalculating the doses in which the gratitude should be meted out so she didn't come off as too grateful, which in turn came off as needy. Not grateful enough, and she wouldn't be eligible for anything more. It was a tightrope walk, and she was constantly teetering, worried about falling off. It was *exhausting*.

But here was George, who actively sought her company! They had four lunches over four Wednesdays, from the beginning of July through the beginning of August, while Jade completed her internship. They always ate at the same restaurant, the Landmark Tavern on Eleventh Ave., which had been around for billions of years. It was dark wood and brick, with an old-fashioned cash register behind the bar and signs written in Gaelic. George always got the shepherd's pie; Jade, the chicken Caesar salad. Neither of them saw anyone they knew there.

Each lunch George started out by asking how things were going at work and then by asking her more about LookBook. They talked about funding: "You've got to reach out to the VCs, Jade. This is the kind of thing they'd eat up." And they talked about the development of the technology: "I know a guy who can find the right people to help you with that." They talked about George's children—"I know they mean well but they just get so busy"—and about his beloved wife, dead now ten years: "Absolute love of my life."

After the fourth lunch, George asked, "Would you consider dining at my home? Monday? My housekeeper is away, and I suppose I get lonely." Would she? Sure. What else was she doing on a Monday evening? "I'll send my driver."

"Oh, you don't have to do that! I'll take the subway."

"He'll be there at seven."

When she arrived at George's building, when she disembarked from the car, when she glided past the doorman and through the door, she imagined she was someone else entirely.

"Mr. Halsey is expecting me," she said to the concierge, who had cornrows wound into a bun, a furrow between her brows.

"Let me call up," she said. Her expression conveyed skepticism.

"He's definitely expecting me," Jade said.

They ate sushi, and they drank white wine. George wanted to look at her numbers, to help her figure out how much of an investment she'd need to get started. He scribbled some figures on a pad of paper with a fountain pen (a fountain pen!). Half a million dollars, he decided. With half a million, she could build out the website, nail the algorithm, hire two people, rent office space.

"Well, forget that," she said. "I don't have half a million dollars."

"That's what investors are there for, my dear. That's what they do."

"I don't know how to find an investor. I'm not ready yet."

He put his hand over hers, there at the table: hers palm up, his palm down. "It's not as hard as it seems," he said. "There are people all over this city with money to burn. You're ready."

Was she ready? She whispered, "Thank you."

"It is I who should thank you, my dear," he said. His voice caught. "I who should thank you."

Jade looked at George; she looked into his watery brown eyes. She looked down and studied their hands together on the table, his spotted one over her open palm. George, who looked at her like she was an angel sent straight from heaven, just for him. Nobody had ever looked at Jade like that, not once, not ever. Everybody thought she needed to be saved, never that she could do the saving.

WHEN THE END came it came quickly, but the dying had happened more slowly, under the surface, the way much dying does. After the sushi night they resumed their weekly lunches, and Jade watched George carefully for signs that he wasn't feeling well. What she observed was mostly subtle. Partway through the month George began to stand up more slowly from the table, gripping the edges of it. By the end of the month she noted a decrease in his appetite. His had never been enormous, especially not compared to hers (she had read somewhere that a person who grew up without enough food would forever approach each meal as though it were their last one on Earth), but the ratio of what he ate compared to what he left behind shifted in the wrong direction.

After their last meal together (she didn't know it would be their last), he took her hand as they left the restaurant. She couldn't tell if he meant anything by it, but she didn't pull away. Who was she to school a dying man—a kind, courteous, sad, generous dying man—in the rules of modern-day civility? Let him take her hand! She wrapped her fingers around his, held them tight.

A week after that, George failed to show up at the Landmark. She sat for twenty-two minutes at the table, not ordering, feeling a knot of dread develop. The knot grew larger and warmer in her gut until it took up so much space it was hard to breathe. She kept her eyes fixed on the entrance of the restaurant in the same way a dog tied to a lamppost outside a store into which his owner has disappeared might keep his gaze, unwavering, on the door.

When her phone buzzed she turned it over, hoping for it to be George with an apology, an excuse, a request to reschedule. His kids were in town! His driver was ill! And old Harvard friend had shown up out of the blue! But it was a number not associated with a contact.

THIS IS VALENTINA SANCHEZ. (Mrs. Sanchez had a first name?) PLEASE CALL ME AT THIS NUMBER.

Fingers trembling, Jade dialed. "I saw in his calendar that he had lunch with you. He asked that I see if you could come to him."

"Is he . . . okay?"

"No."

"No, like—how much not okay?"

"His children are on the way. But he wants to see you, as soon as possible."

"I'll come now."

Jade never took cabs. She couldn't spare the money; she barely knew how to hail one. But she was worried that the subway would take too long.

Mrs. Sanchez was waiting for Jade in the lobby. Mrs. Sanchez in the lobby was as unexpected as the revelation of a first name. Jade had never seen Mrs. Sanchez outside the apartment.

"I wanted to ride up with you," she explained, nodding at the concierge as they passed. "To tell you a couple of important things." She pressed the button, and the elevator doors yawned open. They stepped inside. "First. He's on a low dose of morphine, for the pain.

So if he seems not quite like himself, that's why. Second, his daughter will be here in twenty minutes. If I were you, I'd be gone before she arrives. Say your goodbyes, and be on your way."

"Morphine," said Jade. "Daughter. Got it." Then she said, "I knew he was dying. But I thought he was dying slowly."

"We're all dying slowly," said Mrs. Sanchez.

NICOLA

After work on the third Tuesday in July, Nicola is sitting on her patio with her phone, watching an Instagram reel of a lost border collie being reunited with its owner, when she hears the purr of mopeds. She looks over and sees three of them moving up Juliana's driveway. Has Juliana been out for a ride? Has she found company she prefers to Nicola's?

Her phone buzzes, a text from Juliana: CAN YOU COME OVER? NEED BACKUP.

Nicola thinks for a moment, and then texts back: ?

TAYLOR IS HERE

            WITH DAVID?

NO

Then an emoji, this one: 😬.
Then one more word: HURRY.
Nicola's a rule follower at heart—you'll find that many who end up at law school are (though certainly not all), and besides that she tries to do what's asked of her, for a friend, even (especially?) a new friend. She hurries.
Allison meets Nicola at the front door and tells her everyone

is on the back patio; she says Nicola can go around or through the house. Nicola chooses the former, and as she nears the patio she spies a party of three arranged on the furniture: Taylor and another woman about her age, with dark hair, on one of the love seats, and a redheaded male, practically an Ed Sheeran lookalike, same carefully tousled look and alabaster skin, in a chair. Juliana, in denim shorts and a white tank top, messy bun—Nicola knows these to be her working clothes, when she doesn't have video calls—is hovering on the outskirts, and beyond her, also hovering but much less desperately, is Allison, who, having taken the through-the-house route, arrived before Nicola.

"Lemonade?" Juliana is asking. "No? Does anyone want a *drink* drink? Champagne or a glass of rosé? How about at least a seltzer—"

"I'm fine," says Taylor coolly, then adds, "Thank you." Ed Sheeran's lookalike asks for a beer, maybe a lager, and the other woman says she'd love a seltzer *if it is naturally flavored*, and otherwise just water, thank you. No ice. "Actually, never mind all that. Did you say you have champagne? I feel like we're getting into champagne hour—does anyone else?"

"Of course. I'll have that too." This seems too eager of Juliana; she isn't someone who starts drinking before the day is done. She hardly drinks at all. Juliana signals to Allison, who hurries toward the house.

Juliana sees Nicola and says, "Nicola! Hey!" The relief in her voice is so thick you could have stood a spoon up in it. "What a nice surprise. I'm so glad you stopped by."

"Yeah, I just . . ." Nicola tries to figure out the best way to play along. "Sorry, I just came to say hi. I didn't know you had company."

"That's okay!" says Juliana with an unfamiliar brightness that feels forced. "The more the merrier."

Taylor says, "Oh, hello there, Nicola. I forgot you lived right next door." No way, thinks Nicola, has Taylor forgotten. Taylor is not a person who forgets things. Nicola tries not to think again of the

Country Cousin comment, she really should let it go, but she can't help it, it still rankles.

Taylor introduces her companions, Michael and Mo, the two Ms, if she prefers. (Nicola doesn't prefer.) Both Ms half stand, offer their hands. Old friends from her high school days, Taylor says. "This is David's cousin," she tells them. "And Jack Baker's—" She clears her throat. "Friend." She looks at Nicola questioningly. "Summer friend?"

"Sure," says Nicola, blushing a little. "Summer friend." Imagine, she wonders, if she said out loud that she'd seen Taylor with her own "summer friend"?

"I *love* Jack Baker!" says Mo, suddenly coming alive. She looks Nicola up and down and Nicola is pretty sure she finds her lacking. Michael hits Mo lightly on the leg and says, "I'm *right here.*"

"No, I just mean from like a distance," clarifies Mo. "He's just so—he's adorable, that's all." And Michael says, "Oh, from a *distance,* then I guess that's fine," and Mo smirks.

"We were just out for a moped ride," Taylor says. Her voice is so smooth and cool—can a voice be blond? "And we thought we'd come and check things out here. We obviously weren't going to invite ourselves *in*, but Juliana happened to be outside—"

"My cell connection sometimes drops upstairs," explains Juliana. "So I was walking around in the front, trying to get a signal . . ."

"And Mo is a *huge* LookBook fan," adds Taylor.

"I'm on that site all the time!" cries Mo. "I *love* a bargain."

"She really does," confirms Michael.

"Well, thank you. Thank you for being a fan. And I'm so glad you all stopped by," says Juliana, although she doesn't look at all glad. She looks awkward and stressed. Nicola heard the mopeds, of course, so she knows that's how they'd come, but something about the general demeanor of these three gives the impression that they have recently dismounted from a trio of horses, which are now being sponged down and given water by the stable hands.

Nicola can't remember where Taylor went to high school—one of the well-known New England boarding schools, the kind with classes in Mandarin and hard-core ceramics and with gorgeous students who, in mystery novels, are always murdering each other and not getting caught for twenty years, when new information comes to light. Both Ms have the same breezy, slightly bored way of looking at their surroundings, like maybe they think Juliana's house is nice but not as nice as their uncle's place in St. Lucia, or maybe Block Island is a cute island but wouldn't it be cuter if it were annexed to the Vineyard?

What is Taylor playing at? And why does Nicola care? None of this affects Nicola, not directly anyway. She's involved tangentially through Jack, tangentially through David, so why can't she leave it in the tangents? She doesn't know; she answered Juliana's summons; she's drawn in. She studies Taylor, trying to figure it out. Either she knows about her husband and Juliana and has come to confront her, or she knows about them and has come to engage in some mindfuck game without confronting her. A third option: she doesn't know, but is somehow, at this awkward visit, about to find out.

"Who kayaks?" asks Taylor, nodding at the pair of paddles down on the dock.

"Oh, nobody. I mean, I keep them for guests. I don't go in the water. I don't like to swim."

"You don't like to swim?" asks Mo. She gazes at Juliana like she's an exotic creature recently brought over on the ferry, the way the island's first deer were in the late sixties.

Allison brings out the drinks and asks Nicola if she wants anything. No, thank you, she doesn't. She notices that Juliana's hands are shaking, and she sees her grip one hand over the other to try to hold them both still. By the time she takes she champagne flute from Allison she has them under control. There's one unoccupied love seat in the circle. Juliana perches on the edge of it and signals for Nicola to sit beside her, which she does. Continuing the charade that this drop-by falls closer to normal on the spectrum of normal to bizarre than it actually does, Nicola asks, "What are you guys up to after this?"

Mo says, "A little more exploring, I think. It's our first time here, me and Michael. Ever since Taylor got the house she's been promising to let us visit . . ." Taylor rolls her eyes and says they haven't had it that long. "Then we're going for drinks at . . . what's it called, Tay?" Mo looks at Taylor expectantly.

Tay. Hearing a nickname, meeting two of her high school friends, Nicola is able to see in this haughty version of Taylor a younger version—less ice queen, more teenager. Because the fact is that tall, willowy women like Taylor are often gawky and graceless in high school: legs too long, feet too big, breasts too small to fit the idealized version of a high school girl. Then around college they hit some sort of Gisele Bündchen level of beauty and nobody can believe that they ever did anything but glide effortlessly through life in extra-long size zeros.

"The Oar," says Taylor. She points across Great Salt Pond in the general direction of the place.

What Nicola is trying to articulate is that for an instant, she can see a vulnerability in Taylor, an openness that many of us have when we are our teenage selves. Nicola supposes this is because that's when we form truly intimate friendships for the first time, peeling ourselves away from our families layer by layer and giving our minds, our bodies, our hearts to others.

"Love The Oar," Nicola says because she feels like she should say something. And also because she did love The Oar, the one time she went there.

Mo is sipping her champagne, but when Nicola glances at Juliana's glass there's only a quarter remaining. Ed Sheeran has barely touched his beer. Taylor's hair glows even more goldenly as the late afternoon light turns to early evening light.

"We should come to one of your parties!" cries Mo.

"Absolutely," says Juliana smoothly, glancing at Taylor. "Come on Friday."

"Yeah? Really?" Mo sits forward eagerly.

"We're leaving Thursday," Michael reminds her.

"We don't have to, though," says Mo. "We can leave on Sunday instead. Right?"

"I don't think so. My parents are expecting us in Bar Harbor on Friday."

"What are these parties all about?" asks Taylor. The aggressiveness of her question, the suddenness of it, makes it seem like she's interrupting but actually nobody else is talking at the time.

"About?" asks Juliana.

"I mean, what's the point? Big parties are so much *work*."

"I'm not doing the work," says Juliana. "I'm paying oth—"

"Well, no, of course not, obviously. But what do you get out of throwing them?"

"Oh," says Juliana. Nicola watches her wrestle with herself. "It's good for the brand. Free publicity, you know." She can't say anything about the IPO, and Nicola can see how badly she wants to.

"I wouldn't call it free," snorts Taylor.

"Well, no. Not exactly. But the idea is that with a pretty small investment we can increase the attention on the brand by a lot. The more influencers are promoting LookBook, you know, the hotter it's going to be . . ."

"Maybe I'll come see for myself," says Taylor. "If Mo and Michael are invited, I'm sure I'm invited, right?"

"Of *course*," says Juliana. "Please come." She hesitates so briefly that Nicola may be the only one who notices it before adding, "Bring your husband." Nicola tries to catch Juliana's eye but Juliana is looking at Taylor.

"Maybe I will," says Taylor.

Michael says, "You guys should come to The Oar with us. We might grab dinner after."

Juliana says, "Oh, yeah?" She drains her glass, sits up straighter, looks at Nicola and says, "That sounds like fun."

"Oh, I'm sorry, I can't, I have plans," says Nicola.

"You can't?" Juliana sends a pleading glance Nicola's way.

"Jack's in the Hamptons," says Taylor, as though that leaves no other options for plans, and Nicola resents this.

"That's such a bummer!" says Mo. "I was hoping to get a glimpse of him." And Michael again says, "I'm *right here*," and suddenly Nicola really wants to get away from all of them.

"My plans are with other people," Nicola says jokingly (but also sort of seriously). "I'm allowed to have other people!"

"Who?" challenges Juliana.

"Work people," Nicola says. "I have a work thing. It's a Tuesday Talk."

"What's a Tuesday Talk?" Mo sounds skeptical.

Nicola explains that on several Tuesdays throughout the summer they bring in experts from the scientific community to talk about topics of interest. "You could come to that," she suggests. "It's for the public." She doesn't really mean it.

"What's the topic?" Michael asks. "If it's great white sharks I'm *one hundred percent in*."

The Institute does bring in a great white shark expert, and it's the most popular program of the summer, but that isn't happening until August. Nicola clears her throat and says, "Tonight's talk is on the benefits and progress of seaweed aquaculture in New England." To a person, they wince. "It's more interesting than it sounds," she says. "All of our speakers are fantastic."

"I'm going to pass on the seaweed," Michael says, and Nicola thinks that if she got to know him better she might actually hate him. "Well, then, *you* come out with us," says Michael to Juliana. Once he started drinking he took his lager down in about three gulps. It seems to have enlivened him.

Taylor shoots Michael a look. Nicola doesn't see how any of this can be anything but a terrible idea. She asks where David is, and Taylor tells her he's out on Johnny O'Neill's boat for the whole day. She says that like Nicola knows who Johnny O'Neill is.

"Johnny O'Neill's boat is *insane*," says Mo. "I hope he's here when we come back in August."

"I can come!" says Juliana. "Sure, why not? That'll be fun." She looks down at her shorts. "I might just change."

Taylor's lips are pressed close together and she's squinting out at the water. She opens her mouth enough to say, "You don't need to change. It's just The Oar."

Allison reappears and quietly tells Juliana that Asia is on the phone.

"*All* of Asia?" says Mo. Her champagne flute is empty.

"Excuse me, please," says Juliana. "I'm so sorry, please excuse me, I've been waiting for this call. I'll be right back, and I'll be ready to go. Ten minutes, max."

She follows Allison toward the house, and Nicola, thinking about it for only an instant, excuses herself from the group and catches up with Juliana.

"Hey!" she says. "What are you *doing*?"

Juliana turns toward her, confused. "I'm going inside to take a call," she says.

"Not that. Going to The Oar. Aren't you playing with fire? Are you really looking to hang out with Taylor?"

Juliana tucks her hair behind her ears and straightens her spine. "These are the kind of people, Taylor included, who would never have given the old me a second glance, coming from where I came from. Now look. They invited *me*. They want to come to *my* party."

"So what?" Nicola is exasperated.

"I don't expect you to understand. But I need to go. Tell them I'll be right back, okay?"

"You told them."

"If they forget."

When Nicola gets back to the group Mo is whispering something to Michael. He communicates to her with a shrug that whatever she is saying is of no consequence. Nicola doesn't like any of what's going on. She doesn't like the whispering. She doesn't like the version of Juliana that emerged in front of Taylor. She's physically smaller in size, yes, they all are, both Ms included, because Taylor is so tall, but Juliana has made herself emotionally smaller too, and Nicola doesn't like that. She doesn't like how eager she is, how desperate to be included, like a middle schooler on the outskirts of a friend group. *Act like who you are!* Nicola wants to say. *You're Juliana Fucking George! Flex a little.*

Taylor stands up, turns to Michael and hisses, "What did you *do?*"

"What?"

"You can't just . . . I mean, we were going to hang *out,* the three of us, you can't just invite an outsider without completely changing the vibe."

Michael holds up his hands in the defensive posture, palms out, and says, "We're at her house! And you're the one who wanted to come here."

Taylor starts to answer, then she must remember Nicola, and maybe remembers that she's not sure where Nicola's loyalties lie, so she clamps her mouth shut.

Several awkward seconds pass, then Nicola can hear her say, "I'm not waiting more than ten minutes. And it's already been four."

Michael says, "But who's counting."

"You know what?" says Taylor. "There's no such thing as a ten-minute call with Asia. I take calls like that too."

"This could be just a quick check-in," Michael tries.

Nicola can see Mo wavering, then, deciding to come to Taylor's defense, she says, "Come on, guys. Let's stick to the original plan. Cocktails await."

Michael says to Nicola, "Tell her we couldn't wait, would you?"

"But—"

They're off the dock and walking around the side of the house before Nicola can figure out how to keep them there.

The mopeds start up just as Juliana flies out of the double back doors, in flared black stretch pants, perfect for The Oar, holding a cardigan in one hand.

THURSDAY OF THAT week Nicola's phone pings, late.

U UP? Jack is away through the weekend, but here he is anyway, on her phone.

She checks the time: 1:23. She'd been fast asleep. Nicola remembers when she was just a preteen, her oldest sister, who had experience in such things, told her that nothing good happens after midnight. Many nights in her life have borne this out—college nights, messy post-college nights, even a night or two during law school—and they are words she now, on the cusp of thirty, tries to abide by.

But she taps back with a thumbs-up. The day before, she'd had one of the most exciting workdays she'd had all summer. Scratch that! One of the most exciting workdays she'd had *ever*. She and two of the interns had assisted in the rescue of a seal, along with the animal rescue people from Mystic Aquarium. They'd been out by the North Light, doing a seal count. It had been foggy, so it had taken a while to figure out that one of the seals had a fishing line wrapped around its neck, and that it needed human intervention.

Does Jack, perchance, want to hear about the rescue of this seal, which weighs as much as five Bernese mountain dogs?

No, Jack does not. She knows that without asking.

WHAT R U WEARING? comes the next text.

She turns on the lamp on the night table and looks down. She's wearing her *EVERYTHING WHALE BE OK* T-shirt, a gift from her mom.

SOMETHING SUPERHOT, she texts back. She doesn't tell him she means rising-sea-temperature hot. He'll see it if he FaceTimes her.

Which he does. He's lying in a bed in somebody's summer home, looking rumpled and sleepy and gorgeous.

They stay on for a long, long time, and when he asks her to take off the whale T-shirt she does, and eventually she goes to sleep with her phone next to her on the pillow, thinking that maybe sometimes whatever happens after midnight isn't all bad.

"You have to come tonight," Juliana tells Nicola the next day. "You *have to*. It's going to be the best party of all of them. Who cares if Jack isn't here." Nicola has said no: some of the people from the Institute are going to a house party off Lakeside Drive. She's promised that she'll go. But then Vanessa, one of the interns, who was going to drive her, comes down with food poisoning, and Ricky, another intern, decides to go visit a friend in Newport, and suddenly nobody she knows is going to the house party after all. So against her better judgment Nicola puts on a new dress she bought on sale at one of the shops on Water Street (she should have ordered from LookBook, she realizes too late), gathers her resolve and her phone, and makes her way across the grass, a moth, as always, drawn to the lights.

But she won't stay long! She'll stay half an hour, or maybe forty-five minutes. Her eyes feel scratchy from not enough sleep the night before. She'll have one drink, and then she'll leave.

On the face of it, the party feels like the first party. The DJ is there, giant headphones, black T-shirt, dance moves. The influencers are there. There are photos galore, and people bent over their phones, tagging and posting and reposting. Word is there's a yacht down from Camden and a party of six in from the Vineyard. Four young women are artfully arranging themselves on the patio furniture and photographing each other in different configurations.

But something is different. *Something feels different.* Nicola can't put her finger on what the difference is. But it's there.

The signature cocktail is a twist on a highball. Nicola's never had an actual highball so she's not sure where the twist comes in. She sips hers slowly, not wanting a hangover the next day, wanting, for some reason she can't exactly name, to keep her wits about her. She scans the scene. A couple is having a massive fight near one of the outside gas fireplaces. Two girls who look underage, and commensurately excited to be there, are drinking too fast and laughing too hard. People are dancing, then not dancing, then dancing again. There's too much food. There's too much of everything.

It isn't until later—much later, maybe even the final days of summer—that Nicola puts her finger on it. They're still in July, albeit late July, but the party has the feeling of an end-of-summer bash. The first party she went to was pure jubilance; this one is tempered with some sort of gravity, diluted, like a whiskey on the rocks whose ice has begun to melt.

She texts Jack. Maybe he came back early; maybe he'll stop by. Jack's travel plans are always fluid. Is this a desperate move? Is she showing her hand? (What *is* her hand?) He doesn't text back. She wanders into the house, pokes her head into the library, where she first met Juliana—empty. She takes a spot in the bathroom line, more for something to do than because she really needs to go. The woman in front of her—red streaks in her hair, dangly gold earrings—asks if Nicola has a tampon. "I can't believe my luck!" she says. "Of all the nights."

Nicola doesn't, but says she can run and get one from her house because she only lives next door. The woman says, "Oh, don't do that! I'm sure I can find one here. Maybe I'll sneak around, see what Jade is hiding."

Nicola asks, "Who's Jade?" and the woman claps her hand to her mouth, spreads her fingers out to talk through them, and says, "You didn't hear me say that."

"Okay." Nicola doesn't wonder for too long because someone comes up to the woman and squeals, "Shelly! *Girl!* You will not. Be-lieve. Who I just saw . . ." and Shelly says, "Who?" She turns away from Nicola and Nicola busies herself with her phone, looking to see if Jack texted back. Negative.

It doesn't matter! She doesn't care. Anyway, this party feels weird. The vibe of the night is *weird*. She finishes her highball in the bathroom line. Maybe she'll limit herself to two. Two is very reasonable.

Nicola powers her phone all the way off so she won't be tempted to look any longer. That little fucker, she thinks; he has her falling for him; he has her joining the long line of women who, from the beginning of time, have sat by the phone (or in this case held a phone), waiting for a man to call.

Anyway, who cares. She and Jack aren't exclusive. She can sleep with anyone at the party that night—any night! Any party!—without a speck of guilt.

After the bathroom, she joins the line at the outside bar. It's then, just as the bartender hands her a second drink, that she figures it out, why the night feels so unsteady, its potential chaos just beneath the surface. She spots Taylor's golden hair, and David beside her, coming from the wide-open patio doors.

Oh boy, thinks Nicola. This night could go any number of ways from here, and none of them are good. Just as Nicola sees David and Taylor, she sees that Juliana does too. She takes a healthy sip of her drink and follows behind as Juliana emerges from a small clump of people at the edge of the patio.

"You're *here!*" Juliana says, looking from one to the other. "David, hello." She puts out her hand and they shake, formally and absurdly. "Taylor, how nice to see you again so soon."

David turns to Taylor and says, "So soon?"

Taylor smiles an icy smile at David. "Didn't I tell you? I stopped in here the other day. I was out on the mopeds with Mo and Michael. They'd heard about Juliana being here, you know how Mo is about clothes." She rolls her eyes. "And she wanted to see if she could meet Queen LookBook here."

"I was so happy they came by," says Juliana, looking the opposite. "Are Mo and Michael here too?"

"They couldn't stay after all."

"Oh, that's too bad." Juliana doesn't sound like it's too bad at all. "But they'll be back in a few weeks."

Right, thinks Nicola. Johnny O'Neill's boat. Nicola feels disengaged from her own body, like her mind is a balloon, bobbing high above the party on a string. "Well," Juliana goes on. "I'd love to show you both around." She may as well have been saying, *I'd love to slice my tongue in two and throw half of it in the ocean.*

"That," says Taylor, "would be spectacular." She takes David's hand. The result of this is that to move through patio crowds, Juliana can't walk beside them; she has to lead, tossing her words awkwardly over her shoulder as David and Taylor follow behind.

Nicola stays where she is. She has the feeling that if she stood over *here*, in one place, the ground might be solid enough, but if she goes over *there*, to that other place, maybe the ground will move beneath her feet. Is it a full moon? She looks up but can see no moon whatsoever. It's hiding from her. She tries not to take it personally. She powers her phone back on, ostensibly to pull up a lunar calendar, but maybe also to see if Jack has texted back.

Not far from her, a girl says to her friend, "You *always do this*, Harriet, and you never say why. I'm seriously so fucking sick of it!" See? Things are so off-kilter tonight!

Jack hasn't texted. And the moon doesn't even have the courtesy to be full; the full moon, she sees, was the week before. She takes a lap. Takes another lap. Talks to someone whose niece works at the Institute with her. She's itching to leave; she's so tired. She checks her phone. Nothing. She should just go home, right? She should go home. Nobody will miss her.

It's after some time that she hears her name, an urgent whisper from the shadows at the edge of the patio. Taylor. She's sitting on one of the many outdoor couches—who can keep track? There are so many places to sit out here.

"Taylor!"

"I lost David."

"David?" Nicola's not sure what to do, so she feigns confusion, as though there are a lot of Davids, and they are often disappearing.

"My husband. Your cousin. David."

"Ah. That David. I thought I saw him by the outdoor bar, but that was maybe fifteen minutes ago . . . I was talking to these other people for a while . . . or maybe could he be in the bathroom line? The bathroom line has been long all night."

Taylor says, "I hate this party. Who are these people? I don't know anyone here."

"Yeah." It's maybe the first time Nicola has completely agreed with Taylor on anything. "I don't know anyone either. I kind of hate it too."

"I mean, who even *is* this person, this Juliana?" (Does she really want Nicola to answer this?) "I know *who* she is, obviously, but like, why is she here? It's so random." She takes a breath and then says, "If you see David, please tell him I'm looking for him. I've got work tomorrow." She holds up a hand as though to stop Nicola, but she hasn't said anything. "Yes, I know, it's Saturday, but still, I've got work. I'd really like to get the hell out of here."

"If I see him I'll tell him."

"Thank you." Then Taylor says, "Nicola?" Nicola turns back. "I want to ask you something. Here, sit down." She knows, is what Nicola thinks. She knows, and she's going to ask me, and I'm a terrible liar, and I don't know what I'm going to say. Taylor pats the cushion next to her, and Nicola, who wants to run in the other direction, sits. And waits. She sits perfectly still, as though any movement may loosen the question from Taylor. The illumination offered by the lanterns and the twinkly lights crisscrossing above them is incomplete, so part of Taylor's face moves in and out of the shadows as she speaks. And somehow, even here, even now, her hair glows. It glows as if it's lit from within.

When the question comes, it's not the one Nicola is expecting. And she's fine with that.

"Did I ever tell you about when I met David?" Taylor leans toward Nicola. But she's not just leaning; she's swaying a little bit. Taylor, Nicola realizes, is *drunk*! Nicola has yet to see Taylor in any state other than perfect composure. This is a true plot twist.

"At Yale, right?"

"In the mailroom," says Taylor dreamily, swaying a bit more. "I had to pick up a package, and I only had ten minutes before my next class, no time for lunch, so I had grabbed some fries at the Elm"— (Taylor says this as though Nicola has any idea what the Elm is, but okay, she nods and goes with it.)—"and I put the fries down on the counter to balance the package after I got it, and somebody else in line bumped into me and the whole thing of fries just went all over the floor."

"Oof," says Nicola dutifully. As far as tragedies go, this is not a big one, but she waits to see what Taylor will follow it with.

"It was such a dumb thing to get upset about. Not a lot of things unnerved me, even as a little baby freshman. I had my shit together. I've always had my shit together; that's what I do. I came out of the womb with my shit together. But for some reason this one thing, these fries . . ." Her voice trails off for a minute, then she regains it. "For some reason this one thing got to me, and I started *crying*. In the mailroom. And this guy came up—"

"And picked them all up for you!" says Nicola triumphantly.

Taylor turns to her in wonder. "So he *has* told you?"

"No." Nicola tries to keep the note of light exasperation out of her voice: where this story is going, after all, is pretty obvious. "It's just what David would do."

"Oh." Taylor looks momentarily confused, then she picks up the thread of the narrative. "Well, yes. He said, 'Hey, hey, it's not so bad, let me help you.' And he got on the ground and started picking up the fries, one by one, until they were all back in the container, and then he found a trash can, and when he got back from the trash can he asked what residence hall I lived in, and somehow he figured out what room, and later that afternoon there was a knock on the door and there he was, with a new container of fries. So hot and salty, little packets of ketchup on the side . . ." Her voice trails off. "And that was David."

Of course that was David, thinks Nicola. That whole move is *so* David. Nicola can totally see it. Because it wasn't a move, the way it would be with some guys. It was genuine kindness.

It was, by the way, *such a big deal* when David got into Yale. For their family, sure. But for their high school too, and for the town. But Nicola, who knew him so well before he went, does not know so much about his life there, only that he came out of it with a degree, and with Taylor.

Taylor goes on: "Oh, but there's one other thing. Back in the mailroom, after he threw away the fries, he took the hem of his shirt and wiped my tears away. It was so silly. I mean, that's like straight out of a rom-com, right? I hate rom-coms. They don't make any sense."

"They don't," agrees Nicola.

"It was just so kind. It was so *kind*. Nobody had ever been kind to me in that way. Because, and I hope this doesn't make me sound like an asshole, but when you have a lot of money, and you look a certain way, nobody thinks you need kindness too. But I did. I do. And this is going to sound crazy, but I said to myself right then, all those years ago, I've got to marry this man."

Despite herself, Nicola is getting caught up in the story. There's something so unexpectedly simple about it. So random. But aren't so many of our meetings that lead to big changes in our lives random? A mailroom, some French fries, then, boom, here you are, fourteen years later, with a child and a house (multiple houses, in Taylor and David's case, fair enough), and a shared history, a shared future. "So you did."

"I did. Because I get what I want. All of the Buchanans do. And now I've messed it all up. I think I can fix it, I *want* to fix it, but I'm worried that I've ruined it."

Of course she must be talking about the man at the construction site. But Nicola isn't supposed to know about him, so she asks, "Ruined it how?"

This questions snaps Taylor out of what almost seems—for someone so controlled—a fugue state. She says, "Oh, never mind. Forget I said anything. I'm sorry to bother you with all of this, okay, Nicola? I'm just tired, that's all. I'm so tired, and I want to go home, and kiss my daughter while she's sleeping, and go to bed."

Nothing about Taylor's posture suggests she's looking for a hug, but Nicola has to stop herself from offering one anyway. She tries to remember the things she doesn't like about Taylor—the way she put the Carrs at such a faraway table at the wedding, the way she wouldn't let David persue his race car dream, the Country Cousin comment, even, perhaps unfairly, her Elsa-from-*Frozen* beauty—but she doesn't see that Taylor now. "Why don't I take a look around for David? Will you be here?"

"I won't move a muscle," says Taylor, resting her head against the back of the couch.

Nicola weaves through the crowd, looking for David. He's so tall, she's surprised she can't find him immediately. Then, on the far side of the patio, she spots him. He's with Juliana. They're standing close together, almost touching but not quite.

"Where *were* you guys?" she hisses at them.

"We went over and sat on your stoop for a few minutes. To talk," says David.

"On *my* stoop?"

"Sorry, we didn't think you'd mind." This is Juliana. It's not lost on Nicola that it's more David's stoop than it is hers. It's actually Taylor's stoop, so to David it's a stoop-by-marriage. Something in her smarts at this realization. Even if she did mind, she's not allowed to.

"Of course I don't mind," snaps Nicola.

The mood of the night is pulling Nicola down. Jack not answering the texts. Taylor showing her vulnerable side. Nicola herself, wondering what kind of a hand she's had in someone else's madness. "Of course I don't mind," Nicola says again, untruthfully. "Sit wherever you want. My stoop, your stoop. But David, Taylor is looking for you. She's over there, sitting down." She points. "I told her I'd send you over. And I'm calling it a night. Thank you, Juliana." *Thank you for inviting me to your weird party.* "Good night, all."

"Well, I guess this is good night, then," says David. Nicola looks away—if there's physical contact between Juliana and David, or even a smoldering glance, she doesn't want to see it, not after her conversation with Taylor.

When David is gone, Juliana looks to Nicola, stricken. "Oh! I was hoping you'd stay until the end with me!"

"The . . . like the very end?"

"Please. Please. It won't be much longer. Please please?"

Nicola sighs. She's never been able to resist a double *please.* "Fine," she says. "Okay."

Juliana's right; it isn't much longer. Nicola finds a corner to study her phone to see if Jack has texted (no). By then the music has stopped and the DJ is packing up and the bartender is racking the glasses, and in no time at all everybody is gone except for Juliana, and except for Nicola. Juliana motions Nicola to follow her into the kitchen. The caterers have made short work of everything there, leaving the lights turned low. Juliana switches on the pendant lights above the island and motions for Nicola to sit in one of the upholstered stools pulled up to the island. Upholstered stools! In a kitchen! Nicola's mother, Linda, who every ten years or so replaces their kitchen stools with a new set from the store—a discount on top of a discount—would have been shocked by this. Food and upholstery, her mother would say, do not belong in the same room. They barely belong in the same house.

The cabinets are gray, and the island is a grayer gray (gray is the new white, supposes Nicola) and the countertops are gleaming white marble. Juliana pours them each a tall glass of water, which Nicola needs desperately, then sits at the far end of the island.

Juliana says, "I don't think he liked the party."

"Who?" Of course she knows who.

"David. He looked miserable. I thought if he came here during one of the . . . I thought if he saw . . . I thought." She takes a deep breath, lets it out.

"You thought what?"

Juliana looks thoughtful. She taps her fingertips on the island top and sucks in her bottom lip. "I don't know. Who knows. Who knows about anything." Then she says, "Nicola, do you want to stay up with me?"

"I *am* staying up with you." Nicola gestures to herself, then to the water glasses, the kitchen as a whole, Juliana.

"I mean all night. Do you want to stay up all night? We could watch a movie. I could make popcorn! We could watch the sunrise. What kind of movies do you like?"

"I can't. I have to go to sleep. I'm falling over."

Juliana doesn't acknowledge this. "Do you think you can get me invited to dinner?"

"To dinner?"

"At David's house." Nicola stares at her, trying to find the best, most polite way to say, *Are you out of your freaking mind?* "I'm ready to make plans . . ."

"Plans?"

"For the future. Future plans."

"For . . . what future?"

"For mine and David's," she says. "For *our* future, Nicola. David is ready too. We talked about it tonight." She goes on, "As soon as the IPO is done."

"Oh, Juliana," says Nicola.

"What?"

"You can't redo the past," she says, as gently as she can.

Juliana looks absolutely stricken. "Of course you can!"

"Juliana! Stop. Get ahold of yourself. You're not thinking straight. You're not making sense."

She blinks slowly, then squints at Nicola as though she's said something in a foreign language. "But he doesn't love her," she said.

Nicola is so exasperated she can no longer pretend to be anything else. "How do you know?"

"He told me. He told me that tonight. And she doesn't love him! Do you know . . ." She lowers her voice, although they are the only two people in the kitchen. "Do you know she's having an *affair*?"

"How do you know that?"

"David told me."

"David knows?"

"Please, Nicola? Just get me invited to dinner. I'll take care of the rest."

Again Nicola has the floating balloon feeling. She wants out of the conversation, out of the party, out of all of the situations in which she's become entangled this summer.

She says, "I can't do that, Juliana."

The clock strikes midnight.

Okay, nothing strikes. But the numbers on Nicolas's phone, glowing next to her on the island, gleam. She says her goodbyes and goes home.

But. Not before she sees, as she's about to cross the lawn, that not everybody has left the party after all—there's a couple sitting *very close together* on the same couch where she'd sat with Taylor not so long ago. The man is facing away from her, and he's in the shadows, but she recognizes the woman, from the bathroom line.

The one with the streaky hair, the one who needed a tampon. Just My Luck.

Nicola tries to skulk past them—she's not about to interrupt a canoodling couple. But she trips on the lip of the patio and puts a hand out to steady herself on a nearby table.

Which wobbles enough to make a noise.

Which causes both parts of the couple to look at her.

Which is how she knows that the other half of the couple is Jack Baker.

She says, "Jack?"

"Hey, Nicola," says Jack easily.

"I thought you weren't coming back tonight." She hates how she sounds, shrewish and demanding. But he said! And she kept checking her phone like an idiot!

"Got back early," he says. "Decided to pop over."

"Jack? Who's this?" says Just My Luck. She sounds the way Nicola feels, which isn't a great sign. She sounds self-righteous and put-upon and a little tipsy and a little possessive too.

"Nicola, Shelly. Shelly, Nicola." Jack Baker smiles. He might have been introducing two business associates at a lunch, so unbothered does he seem by the situation.

They stare at each other, Just My Luck and Nicola, until Just My Luck says, "*This* is the girl you've been seeing?"

God, Nicola feels stupid. Stupid as she walks as fast as she can across the grass to the safety of her cottage. Stupid as she brushes her teeth in the almost-dark, not wanting to turn on the bathroom lights fully so she can spare herself the shame on her own face. Stupid as she crawls into bed, pointedly choosing a T-shirt other than the whale, and stupid as she lies awake for longer than she wants to, wishing, not in a serious way, of course, but still in a way that will haunt her later, that something tragic will befall the whole bunch of them, everyone at that party, those who are rich or want to be rich

and those who are in love with themselves at the expense of everyone else and also in love with chaos, but most of all those who are
careless, careless, careless.

Host: Welcome back to *Life and Death on an Island*, episode two.
Listeners, if you're enjoying this podcast, please remember to
rate it, or, better yet, leave us a review. And remember, order
today from our gold sponsor, Mattress Queen, and our silver
sponsor, Buddha Bowls 2 U, Buddha bowls delivered fresh right
to your door, ready to eat or freeze.

Lou: Can I ask you something? What's a Buddha bowl, anyway?

Kelsey: Not relevant, Lou.

Host (chuckles): Let's make sure anyone who's just tuning in to
the episode is caught up. We're talking to four members of the
Block Island Town Council about some startling events that took
place last summer. In June and July last year Block Island was the
scene of some pretty wild parties, right?

Kelsey: *Very* wild.

Host: And at the same time Buchanan Enterprises was trying to
get a proposal passed to tear down an old motel and build a boutique hotel and spa. And then what?

Betsy: At the beginning of August, all of a sudden the parties
stopped. That was it. You didn't hear anything more about parties at the house on Great Salt for the rest of the summer. I don't
know what the people who always called in about the noise ordinance did with themselves, without that to complain about.

Lou: August is when the you-know-what really hit the fan.

Kelsey: I was super bummed. I was planning on going to another
one. All my friends from nursing school are living in big cities,

like Boston or Seattle or Chicago, and I finally had some nightlife to tell them about. I was going to post! I didn't post the first time, and I really regretted it. I heard there was a Kardashian at one of those parties.

Evan: Yeah?

Kelsey: Not like Kim. But maybe one of the lesser Kardashians. I heard Gertie Sanger was there too. She's like Hollywood royalty!

Betsy: I'm with Lou. I'd say the beginning of August is when things really fell apart. In my house, at least. One day in the beginning of August, Henry came home from work and sobbed in his truck. My Henry never cries. He didn't cry when the basketball team lost in the playoffs his junior year. Didn't cry when that surfboard fin sliced his calf when he was fourteen and he needed eleven stitches. But that day in August, he cried. Something had changed. He wouldn't even talk to me about it—and Henry *always* talks to me. He doesn't always talk to his mother but he always *always* talks to me.

(*Pause.*)

Nobody likes to see their loved ones gutted.

Evan: A lot of what was going on behind the scenes was lost on me. We had our busiest summer since the pandemic at the Hangry Angler. Between that and the kids and these town council meetings, I was straight out. I barely knew my own name. Until the very end. Until the death. That snapped everyone to attention.

AUGUST

NICOLA

David calls on the first Saturday in August and says, without pre-amble, "Taylor wants you to come to dinner tomorrow night. Six o'clock." Nicola is sitting on her patio in her bikini, wondering if she can get rid of the tan lines she's acquired from spending too much time in her BIMI polo.

She almost laughs. Has David dialed the wrong number? "*Me? Are you sure?*"

"Of course I'm sure. She said she enjoyed talking to you at the party. She wants to get to know you better." (Nicola wonders if the unspoken sentiment is: *she thinks she underestimated you.*) David goes on: "She wanted to do more entertaining this summer, but, I don't know, time got away from everyone. It's already August!"

"It is," confirms Nicola.

"So she settled on dinner tomorrow. Sundays are pretty chill for us. I think she's doing some sort of a cocktail party too, in a week or two. That one's more for the locals." (Nicola wonders if the unspoken sentiment here is: *you won't be invited to that one.*)

"The locals? Taylor hangs with the locals?"

"Well, no. But she's trying to win over the planning board, to get this hotel approved. And I guess the way to the planning board—"

"Is through its stomach?"

David snort-laughs. "No. Through town council."

"Ah," says Nicola. "All politics really *are* local, I guess."

"So you'll come tomorrow?"

"Sure. Sundays are chill for me too." Monday, she is leading a field trip to Andy's Way, where the kids are going to try their hands at clamming. They'll also find horseshoe crabs and hermit crabs, and even though you get to Andy's Way by following a dirt road off Corn Neck, so it's not so far from anything, they'll feel like they're a million miles away from the hustle and bustle of downtown. She's excited for the field trip, possibly more excited than the kids are. She wants to re-remember what it is she's come to love about this island: not the giant houses and the showy parties and the cocktails (okay, sometimes those things are nice, especially the cocktails) but the pleasure in unadulterated nature, in the simplicity of a clam—to be fair, though, clams have the most sophisticated heart of all the mollusks.

"I'll send Jack to pick you up."

Nicola's stomach drops. She hasn't spoken to Jack since the last party. He didn't apologize, but he did send her a meme of a humpback whale breaching with the words WHALE HELLO THERE. She left the text on *read*. In moments of strength, she's completely fine with the dearth of real communication: they were never exclusive; they owe each other nothing; he can kiss whomever he wants. But in moments of weakness she simmers in disappointment, nay, anger. She'd thought at least he was *honest*, thought he'd at least *tell her when he was back on the island*. It stings that he wasn't, that he didn't. No, it more than stings: it burns. She hates when she allows herself to think better of people than they deserve.

To ease the burn, she's kept herself busy at work and hanging out with the interns. Wednesday they hit Poor People's after work, and Thursday they went horseback riding at Rustic Rides. On Sunday, they have plans to hear some musician at Mahogany Shoals who apparently could pass for the love child of Ray LaMontagne and

Shakey Graves. If she goes to Taylor's dinner she'll have to miss this, even though she loves Shakey Graves. She tries to sound chill but her words come out in a yelp. "Jack's going to be there? At dinner?"

"Why wouldn't he be? He's living here."

"You know what, David? I don't think I can come. I just remembered plans I have with the work peop—"

David cuts her off. "No retractions. You already said yes." He sounds like he's sort of joking, but also sort of not.

"I can retract if I want," she bristles. "I am my own person, David."

There's a beat of silence where she can feel him figuring out which fork in the road to take. "You are," he says. "You are your own person. But I really want you to be there. Okay? It's important to me. After all . . ."

She wonders if he's going to say, *After all, you wouldn't even be living here if not for me.*

But he says, "After all, you're my favorite cousin."

Damn it. It gets her, the pull of the past, the nod to nostalgia. "Six," she says, making her voice crisp and unemotional. "See you then. But I don't need a ride from Jack. I'll ride my bike."

Ten minutes later David calls back and says, "I have a better plan than Jack or your bike. You can get a ride with Juliana."

"*David!* You invited Juliana? *What* are you doing?" She whispers this, as though someone might hear her, even though she's completely alone, it's just her and Great Salt stretching out in front of her, ponding for all it's worth.

His voice changes, becomes sharper, even clipped. "Wasn't my idea. It was Taylor's."

SHE DOESN'T ASK Juliana for a ride. She'll stick to her plan: She'll take her bike. She'll owe nothing to Jack, nothing to Juliana. Still, she can't sleep Saturday night, thinking about it, twisting the different threads around and around to see what kind of knot they make. Is Taylor planning some sort of a showdown, and, if so, will Nicola be implicated as the link between David and Juliana? And how did she become some pawn, stuck in the middle of all of it? She flips her body over, flips her pillow over, flips them both back so that she's right back where she started.

The thought she's left with as she finally drifts off to sleep, way later than she meant to, is about another Taylor, Taylor Swift, who, she read somewhere, is still and *will always be* the girl whose friends once lied and said they weren't free to go to the mall and then went to the mall, together, without her. Taylor saw them there—she was with her mom. Deep down, Nicola thinks, we're all still walking around with our earliest wounds just under the surface, scared of being re-cut at any time. What are Taylor Buchanan's wounds? What are Juliana's?

The best part of the night, Nicola discovers upon her arrival, is that David and Taylor are serving gin and tonics, and they're strong, and they come fast. She hasn't been to David and Taylor's since she babysat for Felicity. Cocktail hour takes place on the patio where they ate the first night Nicola was there. Caroline, with the same pinned-up braids, the same no-nonsense attitude, brings out a charcuterie board. Nicola tries to catch Caroline's eye, desperate for some sort of connection, a hook onto which she can hang her discomfort. She wants to say, *It's me! Hi! I'm the normal one!*

Caroline, intent on her tasks, doesn't look up.

If the best part is the gin and tonics, the worst part is that besides David, Taylor, Juliana, and Jack—already enough to make the Cup of Awkward runneth over—there is a fifth guest, and that guest is the woman from the bathroom line at the last party, who is also the woman Nicola saw with Jack at the end of the party.

That's right, it's Just My Luck, in the flesh.

Oh, come *on*, thinks Nicola. *Seriously?* She glances at Jack and, reflecting on the fact the bike ride was not a great idea, grabs a cocktail napkin and tries surreptitiously to wipe at the sweat that has collected around her collarbone. Even being quite generous with the euphemism, she's not glowing. Jack smiles at Nicola. She looks away. How dare he. She looks back. He smiles again, even more charmingly. She grimaces and turns steadfastly, finally, in the other direction. No.

David introduces Just My Luck; her name is Shelly Salazar, and she's doing some PR for Buchanan Enterprises.

"We've met," says Nicola.

"She's doing PR for me too," Juliana says hastily, and Nicola watches as Taylor arches an eyebrow. Nobody, she will reflect later in life, when she's seen all kinds of eyebrows arched in all kinds of ways, can quite arch an eyebrow the way Taylor did that night in her beautiful home on Block Island, on what was up to that point one of the last unsullied nights of the summer.

"Juliana and I went to college together," says Shelly. "Go Eagles!" Then, "Till the echoes ring again!" which Nicola supposes is code for something. Nicola turns to Juliana, surprised she never mentioned that she had a college friend on the island. "We just ran into each other one day, back in June," says Shelly. "It was crazy!"

"We weren't really close friends in college," Juliana hastens to explain. "More like acquaintances." She looks beseechingly at Nicola.

"We lived on the same hall freshman year!" says Shelly. "I'd say we were pretty close." Shelly seems like the type of person who drinks too fast at the beginning of a party. And also at the end of a party, and probably in the middle too. Nicola glances again at Jack, and feels her face grow warm with the humiliation of remembering Jack and Shelly on the couch at Juliana's. It's extra humiliating that Jack doesn't seem to think there's anything strange about any of this.

Juliana says, "It's more that you were friends with my roommate." She looks more and more miserable as every second ticks by. *Be careful what you wish for*, Nicola wants to tell her. *You asked for this dinner, remember? You wanted it! And now here you are. Here you are, and what the hell, Juliana, are you going to do with it?*

"Same difference," says Shelly. Is she staring longingly at Jack, or does she just have the sort of eyes that always look like they're longing?

The seating arrangements don't help, or maybe they do. David and Taylor each at an end of the table. Juliana and Shelly on one side, and Jack and Nicola on the other side. Juliana and Shelly get the water view; Nicola and Jack are facing the house, their backs to the water. In the pool, a giant swan float glides majestically by, urged on by a very slight breeze.

The salad course is a twist on a Greek salad. Why, Nicola wonders, must everything in this world be a twist on something else? Why can't anything just *be*?

"What sort of PR have you been doing for LookBook?" Nicola asks Shelly. She feels as unhappy as Juliana looks, but she's excellent at small talk, and she tells herself to buck up and small talk the hell out of everyone else.

(The twist, it turns out, is that the salad is served on oblong slices of whipped-feta toast.)

Juliana answers for Shelly. "So many things! She really elevated the last few parties."

"The step and repeat was my idea," Shelly says modestly. "It really helped our efforts on social. And the goodie bags!"

"I never got a goodie bag," says Nicola. "What was in them?" She's picturing the birthday parties of her youth, with Dum Dums and small plastic games that broke during first use.

"Curated accessories from a few of our brands," says Juliana.

"They were for VIPs," says Shelly regretfully.

"I'll get you one!" says Juliana. "I'll have Allison bring one over tomorrow."

"That's okay. I'm okay, thanks." Nicola wonders how "curated accessories" would look with her BIMI polo.

"I've really been on the ground this summer," says Shelly. Is it Nicola's imagination, or does Jack clear his throat at this? "I still have a few more ideas, you know."

Here Taylor breaks in. "That's great." She looks at Juliana and says, "But our public relations situation is quite delicate on the island currently. We really can't spare too much more of Shelly this summer." Shelly looks enormously pleased with this vote of confidence; she celebrates by draining her gin and tonic glass, just in time for the arrival of the wine. "She committed to us first, you know. Shelly, it's my turn for a party, and I want you to help me. I need to figure out how to get to these locals."

"You got it!" says Shelly. "I'm all yours."

The wine is a cold, welcome Sancerre. David pours generously, and Nicola tries hard not to gulp it. Shelly has no such compunction, and she's on her second glass by the time Caroline brings out the main course: rib eye steak with potatoes and green beans. Nicola hardly ever eats meat, but she does that night, and it's heavenly.

But she can't enjoy it fully, because of Jack, and because of Shelly, and because of the love triangle with Taylor, Juliana, and David at each of the points.

To take her mind off the awkwardness of the present she lets it wander into the past, landing on Zachary. Was she ever in love with Zachary? Love makes a person do crazy things—reckless things, like hijacking a dinner, maybe even a marriage and a life. She tries to imagine a world where she loves Zachary so much—where she loves *anyone* so much—that she'd sit through a meal like this, gulping expensive wine the way she and David as children guzzled lemonade on July afternoons on Pokegama Lake, just to be near the person, just to exchange the looks David and Juliana are exchanging right now.

What is going through David's mind? she wonders. Through Taylor's? Does Taylor know about Juliana and David, or does she merely suspect?

Is anyone else seeing these looks between Juliana and David? To Nicola they seem as hard to miss as a total solar eclipse, and yet on and on goes the conversation around them, Jack telling a story Nicola has already heard about the Tiburon Golf Club in Naples ("Florida, not Italy," he says to Shelly the same way he once said it to her), Shelly reaching over for the wine bottle.

When she misses Zachary, Nicola realizes, it's never for the smoldering emotion that she can see on David's face, on Juliana's. What she misses is her cold feet pressed against his warm ones in bed, or the way his mother always bought her a high-quality scented candle for Christmas. She never even lit those candles, and now she feels nostalgic for them, and guilty too. She didn't take them with her when she left. Are they still there? Has Zachary ever lit them? Is some other woman enjoying the SANTAL 26 in medium concrete?

She suddenly feels, much to her horror, like she's going to cry, and the more she concentrates on not crying the more she feels the tears build up behind her eyeballs, or wherever tears build up. What will she *say* if these tears come out? Will she tell Taylor, *I'm crying because I've never experienced a love as real as the one your husband feels for my neighbor?* Obviously not. She blinks and allows herself a deep inhale, a slightly less deep exhale.

She wishes that she had gone to Mahogany Shoals with the people from work. Just as she's thinking that, and wondering if she can go after dinner, Jack takes her hand under the table, resting both of their hands together on Nicola's knee. What the actual hell? When she looks over at him, startled, he gives her one of his infuriatingly charming smiles.

Nicola cannot *wait* for this dinner to be over. She wants to peek under the table—does he have his foot tucked in between Shelly's at the same time he has his hand on Nicola's knee?—but she doesn't have the stomach for a full investigation. She removes Jack's hand from her knee and puts it back in his own lap. She can't. She just simply cannot.

"—you guys know you were both here?" Taylor is asking Shelly when Nicola returns her attention to the conversation.

"Funny story!" says Shelly. "We were both on Clayhead Trail at the same time. I was just walking along, minding my own business, and I sensed someone beside me. I turned around, and there was Jade!"

"Jade?" says Taylor, and Nicola flashes back to Shelly clapping her hand over her mouth in the bathroom line.

Juliana shakes her head with perfect equanimity—Nicola doesn't realize until later how much composure this takes—and says, "Shelly, they don't know the backstory of that silly joke."

Shelly says, "You're right!" and grabs the wine bottle, empties it into her glass. As if by magic, a fresh bottle appears, slid onto the table by Caroline's hand.

"I'd love to hear it," says Taylor smoothly.

"They called me Jewel in college,' says Juliana. "As a nickname. Juliana, Jewel. But then, because Jade is a stone used in jewelry, and I used to wear a lot of jade, it evolved." She shrugs. "I know, it's really dumb."

"That's not what I rem—" says Shelly.

"College!" Nicola breaks in. She doesn't know what's going on with this name thing, but she's desperate to make the situation better for someone, even if she's not sure for whom. (Definitely not for Shelly.) *They were for VIPs.* "Didn't we all do the dumbest things?"

"I sure did!" says Shelly, merry as can be.

Taylor, Nicola notices, has eaten only half her dinner, and had no more than two sips of her wine. Jack and David are talking about something else, not paying attention to the women. Taylor smooths her hair, which is already perfectly smooth, and says, "There are a lot of coincidences in this group."

"Oh, yeah?" says Shelly. "What else?"

Maybe she gives off an invisible signal, a stop-what-you're-doing-and-listen sign, because at this point Jack and David pause their conversation and look at Taylor; everyone looks at Taylor. Under the table Nicola squeezes her hands together, as if she can halt time by squeezing.

"Well," says Taylor. "As it turns out, Juliana and my husband met long ago. Isn't that right, Juliana? You met my husband?" She leans so hard on the word *husband* each time she says it that had the word been a tree branch it would have snapped in half.

Juliana's glance skitters around the table before landing on Nicola, who she might see as a safe island in this potentially hostile ocean. "That's right. I met David at a party a long time ago," she says. "During New York Fashion Week. When LookBook was going through a third round of funding." There's something in Juliana's eyes Nicola doesn't trust: a dangerous gleam. And she's slurring a little. Nicola has been so intent on watching Shelly's drinking that she hasn't even paid attention to Juliana's. "You remember, right, David?"

David scrunches his eyes together and looks like he's giving his memory a good, thorough scrub, to see what comes up. "I think so," he says finally.

"My husband has a terrible memory for unimportant details," says Taylor. Has the word *husband* ever been employed so many times inside of ninety seconds?

Nicola sees now what Taylor is doing, why she invited Juliana here; not because she's trying to figure out if there's anything between David and Juliana (she knows) but because she's made a decision about what to fight for, and she's ready to show Juliana what's hers.

"That party is one of the reasons LookBook took off," Juliana says. "That's when we really started to get the attention of the high-end designers." She reaches for her wineglass and Nicola wants, like a mother stopping a toddler from drinking his juice too fast, to put her hand over Juliana's. Juliana says, to the table as a whole, "I couldn't have asked for a better night."

"Early publicity is everything," says Shelly, nodding sagely.

Taylor arches an eyebrow. "You couldn't have asked for a better night?"

Juliana says, "Life-changing."

"When was this again?" asks Taylor.

"September 2019." Nicola winces at how Juliana has the date immediately at hand.

"*That's* funny," says Taylor. "Huh. That's right when we were planning our wedding. We got married the following autumn. You were there, Nicola. You were there too, Jack."

"It was a beautiful wedding," murmurs Nicola to her wineglass. She doesn't want to look up because she's not sure whose eyes to meet and what to do once she's met them.

David attempts, "Taylor—"

"Stop," says Taylor. Can a voice be colder than ice? If so, Taylor's is, by triple-digit degrees. "Just don't." Nicola becomes enormously interested in the crumbs on her place mat, the design they make that looks almost like the Big Dipper.

David pushes his chair away from the table and stands suddenly. "Excuse me," he says. What is he *doing*? wonders Nicola. Is he reacting to Taylor telling him to stop? Is he hoping that if he leaves, the tension hanging over the table like a dark cloud will diffuse?

David walks to the grassy area beside the pool, and then—No! thinks Nicola. No no *no!*—Juliana follows him. Taylor takes another sip of her wine. Her expression is sphinxlike, but when she lifts her wineglass her hands tremble, betraying, Nicola figures, bigger emotions roiling on the inside.

"I *love* Fashion Week," cries Shelly. Nicola can't decide if she's enormously clueless or if she's actually quite masterful. "It's one of my favorite weeks of the year!" She looks around. "September is better than February, if anyone is wondering."

Nobody, it's clear, is wondering.

This whole time Caroline has been moving stealthily behind them, clearing plates, and then, in the pause they've all created, announces dessert is coming. Chocolate mousse, she tells them, unless anyone has something against cream.

"Cream has something against me," says Shelly. "But it's not mutual." Jack snickers, and Nicola rolls her eyes.

"Caroline, thank you so much, you're free to go. David and I will serve the dessert and clean up," says Taylor. Her eyes haven't left the grassy area.

A silence falls, and into the silence pours Juliana's voice. "When are you going to tell her?" David's answer, if there is one, is quieter, then comes Juliana's voice again, which is strident in a way that Nicola has never heard it: "When are you going to tell her that you love *me*?"

It is a cliché to say that time stands still, or that everything moves in slow motion at a certain point, but in fact both of these things happen, one after the other, and after time starts moving again everyone left at the table whips their heads toward Taylor. Has she heard? How could she not have? Juliana's voice was so loud and clear it seems like the moon itself must have heard. What will happen now?

What happens now is that the color drains from Taylor's face, leaving her blue eyes shining like cold jewels. She stands.

"If you'll excuse me," Taylor says, looking every inch the dignified one in the situation—looking, in fact, like royalty, standing so tall and straight and composed. But there's no way she isn't dying on the inside. Whatever intentions she had for the dinner—to show Juliana that Taylor has the upper hand, to spread out her home and family like a picnic for Juliana to admire *but not to touch*—have just vanished. She clears her throat, and in the only concession to the pain she must be going through, the chaos roiling internally, she repeats herself: "If you'll excuse me. I'm going to go say good night to my daughter."

"Ho, boy," says Shelly.

Jack's eyes go to Nicola, then to Shelly. "You want to get out of here?"

Nicola says, "Both of us?" at the exact same time that Shelly says, "Hell, *yes*."

"I want to go home," says Nicola. "If you could give me a ride." She has to work not to say *please*. She's had too much to drink to deal with her bike.

"No problem." They all turn to find their hosts, but there's nobody to find. Taylor is gone, and David and Juliana have moved into the shadows, and if they're speaking it's no longer possible to hear them.

At Jack's car (well, David's), Nicola hesitates, not sure who will take the passenger seat. All she wants is to get out of there. It's early; maybe she won't go home after all. Maybe she'll meet up with the other interns.

The problem is settled when Shelly says (slurs), "Can you drop me in town? I'm supposed to meet someone." She slides into the back seat.

"Sure," says Jack, opening the passenger door for Nicola, even giving a funny little bow, like he's a hired chauffeur. "Whereabouts?"

"Oh, just in town," says Shelly vaguely. She pulls her phone out of her handbag and keeps her eyes on it for the whole ride, until Jack says, "Here?" pulling up outside Poor People's.

Shelly looks up from her phone, confused.

"Is this where you're meeting someone?" Nicola prompts. "Or should we bring you somewhere else?"

"This works," says Shelly finally, after looking down at her phone, then back up again. "Yeah, this works. Thanks, babe." *Babe?* thinks Nicola. Ew.

Jack's window is rolled down, and Shelly leans in and tousles his hair, then kisses him noisily on the cheek. Nicola looks out her own window and cringes.

Once Shelly has walked off—*walk* is perhaps too generous a

word, and *stumbled* too mean, so maybe it falls somewhere in the middle—Jack looks at Nicola and murmurs, "Why don't we catch the sunset?"

Is he *serious right now*? Has he not felt the ice daggers coming from her all night? Is he not even going to *ask* what's wrong?

"I don't think so," she says. She won't dignify him with an explanation if he's not going to ask for one.

"I think we have enough time to get to Dorry's Cove."

Someone told Nicola when she first got to the island that Dorry's Cove is where you can see the best sunsets, and she can't believe she hasn't watched one yet. There's one long log on the beach practically built for viewing, and if you get there first, you get to sit on it.

"Come on, Nicky," he says. "Watch the sunset with me. We can go see that dead whale."

"You can't see the whale from Dorry's," she says frostily. "It's between Dorry's and Grace's." When the BIMI people had gone to see the whale, they had done it as *scientists*, not as curiosity seekers. Jack doesn't care about marine mammals; Jack doesn't deserve to see the whale.

"Fair enough," he says. "The sunset it is, then!"

She considers this. It's a long bike ride from her place out to Dorry's, and she's probably never going to watch a sunset and then ride all that way home in the dark. Should she take advantage of the ride as well as the chance to give Jack, as her mother would say, a piece of her mind? Okay, fine.

Fine!

"I want to sit on that famous log," she says grudgingly.

"Life goals," he said. "Let's do it." Nicola checks her phone. Sunset is just before eight o'clock, and they have to get over to the west side of the island. It's now twenty-six minutes past seven—not even ninety minutes since she arrived at David and Taylor's. Wow. A lot can happen in less than ninety minutes.

"Let's do it," she echoes, keeping her voice even.

"Pedal to the metal, then," says Jack. "Should we pick up something to drink before we leave town?"

What is the kindest way to say, *Are you fucking kidding me?* She settles for, "Probably not. I had enough at dinner—and you're driving."

"Fair enough," he says effortlessly, and he takes her hand and presses it to his lips, and that's when she makes the decision that once they get to Dorry's, once they're sitting on the log, she's going to tell him exactly what she thinks of him. Before the sun sets, she'll tell him.

Because even though she's repulsed by his behavior she could see herself getting caught back up, obsessing, even, always wondering, always worrying that there's a Shelly Salazar around the corner. She could see Jack Baker, with his unconcern, with his sexy forearms and perfect abs and beautiful hair, turning her into just the kind of person she doesn't want to be, the kind of person who puts her hands on her hips and cries, *Where have you been?* maybe while wearing some sort of a kerchief, maybe holding a broom or a vegetable peeler.

In the meantime, though, is one of them going to address the elephant in the car? She sets aside her ire for a moment and ventures: "Was that not the most awkward dinner you've ever been to?"

Jack glances over at her. "Which?"

"Which *dinner?* The one we just came from! The one where we all heard Juliana say out loud that she expects David to leave Taylor for her!"

"Oh, yeah. Sure, I guess." He shrugs. "It was going to happen, though, wasn't it? I mean, at some point."

W, thinks Nicola. T. F. She opens her mouth, wondering what words will come out of it, but she's too stunned to think of any, so she closes it again.

They take West Side Road, and they pass the turnoff to the homes Buchanan Enterprises is building, and Nicola wonders about the man she saw Taylor with—where he is, what happened. Jack turns too fast off the main road and onto the dirt road that leads toward the cove. There's a yellow Jeep coming out, and the driver, a woman with curly dark hair, glares at them. There's a teenage girl in the passenger seat and she glares at them too.

"Slow down, Jack," says Nicola. She thinks of one of her first drives with him, earlier in the summer. It takes two to make an accident, he'd said. That wasn't true then, and it isn't true now. It takes exactly one to make an accident.

There comes a point where you can't drive down the road any farther, so Jack pulls over to the side and parks and they walk down the dirt path that leads to the beach. Jack bounces on his toes, takes Nicola's hand, and swings both of their hands between them, so at home in that athletic, jaunty body of his. She pulls away.

The beach is deserted; the log is available. Just after they settle themselves a family comes flying down the path: parents, three kids in varying stages of tweenhood. Nicola starts to move over closer to Jack, thinking they can make room for the new additions, and then she sees that Jack is doing the opposite, sliding away from Nicola. Marking his territory. She rolls her eyes.

A big rock rises out of the water like a humpback whale. One of the tweens has gone into the water and is shouting for the others to join. To the left of them the beach is covered with small rocks, and just ahead the sand is smooth. The sun moves down and down and the sky becomes bruised by reds and purples, with tangerine streaks at the highest point, where there is a little blue left.

Nicola takes a deep breath, readies herself. Now is the time.

But before she can speak: "I'm leaving soon," Jack says, casually as you please.

Nicola starts. "For good?"

"Week, week and a half. Not sure yet. The Achilles is healed. Heading out to Illinois for the BMW Championship. Your neck of the woods!"

"Illinois doesn't border Minnesota," Nicola says shortly. He doesn't even know where she's from.

"Close enough." He flicks his fingers at the log, maybe at a bug. "But I'll be busy wrapping things up before I go. So I guess this is adios, then."

Nicola stares at the bruise of a sky. She won't meet his eyes. She suddenly feels very busy, busy with the humiliation of almost breaking up with someone she'd never been dating, of almost telling someone off who doesn't care.

And just like that, it's dark. It happens so fast, every damn day, and yet it's always a bit of a surprise. The moon is suddenly visible, as though it has just bustled over from stage left and found its mark.

"Okay," she says finally. The unconcern she fakes is the greatest acting she's ever done—she, who had one role in one middle school play and then gave it all up for soccer. There was the cousin production of *The Sound of Music,* of course.

There's a smile in Jack's voice when he says, "Are you going to miss me?"

"No," she says, wanting to hurt him, even though hurting him seems sort of like trying to hurt a pillow. "It's not like I'm staying here forever."

"Liar," he says, taking her hand. "Tell the truth, now. Are you going to miss me?"

"No," she says again, pulling her hand away.

"I don't believe you," he says. Nicola refuses to look at him but she can tell by his voice that he's still smiling. He's always smiling! "You know," he said, "you got me, Nicky. You got me right here." He makes a fist with his right hand and taps his heart twice.

Bullshit, is what she wants to say. But she doesn't say anything. That's when she realizes something about Jack. He's not intentionally cruel, or even truly unkind; both of those characteristics require an element of purpose, and she sees now that, save the effort and thought he must put into his golf game, nothing about Jack is purposeful. That's where they're opposites. Nicola is all purpose. Jack is bobbing along, a stick caught in a river's current. He'll probably bob along forever like that.

"But you know, if we ever find ourselves in the same place again . . . ?"

"Yeah, then what?" She tries to sound carefree but she knows it has come out snarky.

"Then maybe we can . . . reconnect. You know?" A euphemism if Nicola has ever heard one.

She lets a long, long time go by before she says, "Maybe."

She's quiet on the way home.

"You mad?" asks Jack once.

"No," Nicola snarls. "What would I be mad about?"

Jack says, "Whoa, okay."

Okay, sure, yeah. She's mad at Jack because he made her feel foolish. And because now she knows that what she'd taken to be depth behind those liquid brown eyes is simply layer upon layer of emptiness that, taken together, gives the impression of depth.

But she's also angry at *all* of the wealthy for their ability to move through the world—no, not move through, more like *skate over*—without having to look beneath the surface at everyone struggling below.

They pass once again by the road that leads to the Buchanan construction site, but it's too dark to see anything. Nicola imagines what the island might have looked like hundreds of years ago, before Adrian Block discovered it for the second time, before the first families from Massachusetts settled there, before privateers invaded, before the lighthouses were built, and the construction of the breakwater created Old Harbor, and and and. She tries to think about how small her existence and the existence of everyone from the summer is in comparison to the trees on either side of them that have been witness to it all.

It helps, but only sort of. Anyway, she still has her tanks and her squid and her Tuesday Talks—there are two left—and, somewhere in the background, her incomplete plans for the future, which, after these weeks of concentrated outdoor work, the sun and the salt air and the quality sleep, she not only believes she can but will figure out.

Someday soon this whole summer will seem like nothing but a fever dream.

Jack pulls up to Nicola's cottage.

"Goodbye, Jack," she says. Almost, *almost*, she allows herself to see this as a romantic scene from a movie. Or at least from a Hulu limited series. Two lovers from different backgrounds and circumstances, with two different futures ahead of them, saying goodbye. She imagines that the stars in the sky might weep, watching them.

The stars don't weep; the stars don't even tear up. "Bye, darling," he says. "What a summer, right?" He kisses her on the cheek, and though the kiss itself is innocuous he lets his lips linger above her jawbone, and she knows if she were only to turn her face their lips would meet and they'd be right back where they'd started at the beginning of the summer. Nicola would invite him in, and he'd take off her clothes in that languid way he had that was just careless enough to drive her crazy.

He doesn't get out. She doesn't expect him to stay, but he doesn't even walk her to the door. This is the way they want it, she knows, young women like her, in the latest wave of feminism. And yet! It still would have been nice if he'd gotten out. Not because he is a man and Nicola is a woman, but because they are both people, and deserving of each other's respect.

THE NEXT DAY, she calls Reina. It's unnervingly quiet in the background. She says, "Oh my god, Reina, are you okay? Have your children been kidnapped?"

"Hang on, let me put in my AirPods. Can you hear me? Okay, good. Yes, they've been kidnapped, it's all very sad. I told the kidnapper that I'd pay ransom for *him* to keep them."

"Twist," says Nicola.

"I'm full of surprises. Actually, I'm taking a walk with the dog, my most well-behaved child. The children are at the park with their father, if you can believe it. He took a half day."

"I believe it." Hunter *is* a really good father. He just works a lot, and his job gives him almost no paternity leave. But he's a really good father.

"Which means there are probably hotties falling all over him, telling him how a-maaaaaazing it is that he's taking care of the kids."

"Ugh," says Nicola loyally.

"Do you know how many hotties have told me it's amazing when *I'm* at the park with the kids, which I am literally every day but today?"

"None?"

"Exactly none. Zero hotties."

"It's over with Jack."

"Oh! Sweetie! I'm sorry. Wait, am I sorry?"

Nicola hesitates. "I don't know. Maybe you're a little sorry?"

"Tell me." So Nicola tells her, and she can imagine her nodding sympathetically, walking Rosie (that's the dog). Every now and then Reina makes a little noise, a *hmm* or a *tsk*, and when Nicola's done talking she says, "Well, honey, I'm sad if you're sad. But it sounds like he wasn't your person."

"Yeah, he wasn't my person." Who *is* Nicola's person? Does she have one? If so, *where is he*? "It's just, it was fun, Reina. I'm usually the pursuer, not the pursued. It was fun to be pursued. It was *exciting*, you know?"

"I know," Reina says, then, "Okay, so now I can tell you."

"Tell me what?"

"You know how you asked me not to do a deep dive on him?" Nicola nods. Then, realizing Reina can't see her, she says, "I remember."

"Hang on, Rosie's doing her business. I need to pick it up . . . Okay, done. We're moving again. So you told me not to do a deep dive."

"But you dove anyway?"

"I dove anyway. I'm sorry, Nic! I couldn't help it. My brain was *starved* for a project. And I would have told you if I'd found something truly terrible, if I was *worried* about you, but I wanted you to have a fun summer, and what I found was really just more in the unsavory category. Not the dangerous category. I would have told you if anything fell into the dangerous category."

"Reina! Tell me. What was it? Is he not really a golfer?" But she knows he's a golfer. She's seen the photos, the visors, the tournament entries.

"He's really a golfer. But it's not his Achilles that's hurt."

"What is it?"

"It's his reputation." In the dramatic pause that ensues Nicola imagines all sorts of things. A cryptocurrency company gone bad? Public election denial? Racist remarks? Sexual harassment? "There was a cheating charge at a tournament last fall."

Nicola waits.

"By that I mean *Jack* was accused of cheating."

"Really? Wouldn't that have been a big deal, like something that would have come up when *I* googled?"

"Not necessarily. I mean at the US Open, sure. One of the majors. There's like, I don't know, thirty-nine tournaments on the Tour or something, the big ones you've heard of, and then a bunch of smaller ones, but still part of the Tour, and this was at one of the smaller ones. He was accused of removing a leaf from his ball."

"I'm sorry?" Nicola says. "Did you say *a leaf*?"

"Yeah. Apparently you can't remove something that isn't a loose impediment. And the leaf in question was rooted."

"Rooted?"

"Yup. And the charge wasn't proven, but the player who ac-cused him definitely talked like it wasn't the first time your boy Jack had been suspected of cheating. His people covered up LeafGate, claimed an Achilles injury, and whipped him off the Tour before you could say fooooooorrrreeee."

"Ah," says Nicola. She takes a minute to absorb this.

"See what I mean? Not dangerous, but definitely unsavory."

"Yeah," says Nicola. "That actually all makes sense. I never really heard about him rehabbing that Achilles. I mean, he mentioned it a couple of times, but it's not like he was always running off to PT."

"Right," says Reina.

"I never saw him limp."

"I'm sure you didn't."

You got me, Nicky, he had said. *You got me right here.*

TAYLOR'S VERSION

If you really want to get at the heart of this story, you have to understand a few things about Taylor Buchanan. What you have to understand is that Taylor's got an old-fashioned heart trapped in a modern-day body and a contemporary career. You have to understand how high her father's expectations were for her, always. Brice Buchanan wanted a son to take over the business for him one day; at the first sign of his wife's pregnancy, he began to think about when to transition the name to "Buchanan and Sons." He was like an old English king from the Tudor era, spending all of his wishes for a male heir.

He got a daughter instead. His wife nearly bled out during the delivery; doctors told her that another pregnancy would put her in grave danger. So what did Old Man Buchanan do? He gave his newborn daughter a name that could be male or female.

Brice and Taylor's mother, always on two opposite sides of a bitter, contentious relationship, divorced when Taylor was five. In those first years they shared custody, technically and logistically. But Brice gave himself custody of his daughter's future, and by the time Taylor was twelve her mother had decided to live in Europe, handing over most of Taylor's care to Brice.

This delighted him to no end! Brice had Taylor all to himself.

He had her in boardrooms before all of her adult teeth were in. He had boarding school secured, applications ready for the best colleges, business track, please, before she had a chance to think about what else she might want to study. Employment right out of college. Did she need an MBA? Taylor wanted to know. No, said Brice. She'd learn on the job.

And you know what? She did. She was good. Sharp as a (insert your favorite simile here . . . whip? tack? pin?). She was good at all of it. She was every bit as good at the negotiating and the spotting of a deal and the walking away when necessary as her father was. In some ways she was better. She had, for example, a way with people he didn't have, a politician's ability to remember spouses' names and children's sports and, oh, hey, how was that trip to Scotland and is the seventeenth hole at St. Andrews really as tricky as they say? (Yes, it is!)

But inside, curled up like a shrimp, was this other part of her, the part that still wanted the great love, the fairy tale. The happy ending. The prince.

You have to understand that Taylor wasn't allowed to watch Disney movies when she was growing up. The ones that were available when she was a little girl were unacceptable to her father, the stories where the princess is inevitably saved by the prince. "You do your own saving," is what her father told her. *Frozen*, sure, that would have been better. *Moana*. Stronger females, relationships not defined by marriage or sexual attraction. But Taylor was in college when *Frozen* came out; by the time the world was going crazy over *Moana* she was already working for Buchanan Enterprises.

You have to understand that Taylor wasn't permitted dress-up clothes. If she had been, they would have been tiny business suits. A pint-sized briefcase, a mini travel coffee mug. Her mother would have gotten the dresses for her, but her father was Very Firm on this, and so Taylor's mother complied with his wishes. (The alimony and child support were Significant; Taylor's mother complied with nearly all of Taylor's father's wishes.)

That's why Felicity has *so much* of everything. Every princess dress Disney made, the expensive, official, heavy-material ones from the actual Disney Store. Sometimes when she comes home late and Felicity is already asleep (Felicity is almost always asleep when Taylor arrives home in the evening, a fact that breaks Taylor's heart over and over and over again, even though it's expected, even though it's inevitable), Taylor will pull up a chair next to her bed and watch her and wonder what her future holds. Taylor wants to set out all the dreams for Felicity: the dresses and the crowns but also the toy calculator and the soccer ball and the child-appropriate medical kit. The American Girl doll that goes hiking but also the one that bakes. Taylor wants Felicity to have choices.

You have to understand this too. Taylor had been told she could be all of it: wife, mother, businessperson, friend. She grew up with that as the message. But the people who delivered the message weren't always clear. What they really meant when they said that was you could be one of those things at a time, and yes, maybe over the course of a lifetime you could be all of them. But at any given time, you couldn't be all of them. At any given time, you had to pick.

You have to understand that when Nicola came to dinner early in the summer and Taylor made the Country Cousin comment, she meant it as a joke. She flubbed it, and she came off like a bitch. How she agonized over this! She knew Nicola was David's favorite cousin, and in going for a laugh she'd landed on an insult. (She was good with people except for the times when she wasn't, and then she *really* wasn't.)

David was different from Taylor. David was funny and charming and everybody loved him; David was so comfortable in his skin that he made everyone around him comfortable too. He was a balm to Taylor's anxieties, a cool hand on the warm forehead of her stress. Even Brice, whose standards were skyscraper-high for Taylor, loved David. He loved that he had a wholesome middle-class background but that he'd married it to an Ivy League degree.

David could navigate so many different worlds while Taylor could navigate only one. She felt terrible about calling Nicola the Country Cousin. But Brice had raised her in the "never apologize, never explain" school of thought. She didn't know how to walk her comment back without looking weak.

You have to understand that small things like these ate at Taylor and that she had to push them aside and keep going, because that's what she was supposed to do. That's what she's always done. She's always kept going.

Taylor's father wanted her on Block Island that summer to manage what, in his mind, were two fairly easy projects in the Buchanan portfolio: the construction of the four homes off Beacon Hill Road, and the building of the new hotel in the downtown section. The hotel was going to have a full-service spa; a restaurant to which they were close to wooing a chef who'd earned his previous restaurant a Michelin star; oversized luxury rooms with top-of-the-line bathrooms, each with its own infrared sauna for two. Luxury shuttle service around the island. It was going to be beautiful! It was going to attract people to the island, to eat in its restaurants and hike on its trails and spend money on its nightlife.

But while she was managing all of this, her father said, it was supposed to be a "summer off." Family time! said Brice. Go to the beach! Have barbecues! Make friends! Make another baby, you and David! As if it were that easy.

As if it were that easy.

The reality of the business was that there were no summers off; there were hardly any days off. Her father wanted a bigger hotel than originally planned, and that was on Taylor, because it wasn't like on an island such as this you could just snap your fingers and make that happen. There was a sticky approval process to go through, and a lot of locals who didn't want it. If she were being honest with herself Taylor understood how they might feel that way. But she wasn't allowed to say that. Her job was to execute for the company, not to have opinions on what her father wanted her to execute. Navigating that channel between her father and the locals was on Taylor. Everything was on Taylor.

One time Taylor came home from work crying. It was as simple as that, and it was as complicated as that. This was in June. She'd had a terrible day. Somebody had started an Instagram account called @keeptheblocktheblock to protest the hotel. Normally Taylor's skin was thick enough that something as tame as an Instagram account wouldn't get to her. After all, she'd been raised by a man who bulldozed (sometimes literally) over anyone in his path. If Brice Buchanan wanted something, and if he believed he was correct to want it, he didn't worry about the guys on the other side of the table. He wasn't going to let himself get worked up if something he was tearing down or building up made somebody *sad*. It was the nature of the business. He was *improving* the land/building/town/city. Progress was moving forward, not looking back. That's how he trained his daughter too. That's usually what she believed.

But for some reason—oh, who knows what the reason was?—this Instagram thing really got to Taylor. She hadn't slept well the night before, always a trigger for her. David had gone out drinking with Jack Baker. She'd stayed home, hoping for an early night, but she really didn't settle until the boys were back, after midnight. When David drank hard liquor he snored and moved around in his sleep, and when David moved around in his sleep Taylor's sleep suffered. She'd set her alarm for 6 A.M., and when it went off she was already awake, which meant she'd probably slept three hours at the most.

She was answering emails by seven, and on the worksite by eight for a meeting with the foreman, Henry. Her phone kept pinging with messages from her father, who needed her to get in touch with New York, call the Boston office, maybe schedule a trip to Atlanta to look at a building he was interested in. He needed her to kick the tires, look in the horse's mouth, make sure the building was sound. Could he maybe send someone else? Taylor wanted to know. (She was so tired!) There was nobody else he trusted, he told her. Her opinion was everything.

Okay, so now she had to figure out when to get to Atlanta. Taylor was holding so many details in her head, in so many different compartments, that if one compartment spilled over into the one beside it she knew she was going to be in real trouble. She hadn't seen her husband or her daughter for more than a few minutes at a time over the past forty-eight hours—the previous night she'd gotten home right before Felicity's bedtime. She got to kiss her, read her one story, but that was it. She felt disengaged from her family, a ship at sea without its anchor. She worried all the time that she might be a bad mother; it chewed at her, the fear that growing up without a maternal example meant that she was missing some innate understanding of how to mother.

So when she saw the Instagram post around 3 P.M., instead of ignoring it as she normally would, she followed the "link in bio" to an opinion piece in the *Block Island Times*, written by an anonymous local whose opinion it was that the Buchanans should not develop the land they had bought (and paid over market value for, the article *didn't* say) but should *gift* it back to the island to become conservation land. Below the article there was space for comments. Here, people who registered to comment did not need to use their own name, did not need to include a profile photo, did not need to identify themselves in any real way—and therefore they could unleash their vitriol with no fear of repercussions.

Greed is the only thing motivating these people.

Go home Buchanans

And the worst: *Stupid bitch daughter needs to find someone else's island to ruin.*

Where was the line between expressing one's opinion on a topic and hate speech? She supposed that privileged white property developers were not a marginalized group, so the label of hate speech didn't apply—but it all felt *so very hateful*. It felt so personal! *Stupid bitch daughter.* She wasn't stupid (she had a degree from Yale!), and she wasn't a bitch. She was a daughter, yes. She was a daughter.

Did she agree with the sentiment behind what these people were saying, if not their methods? Maybe. But it wasn't up to her. She was at the mercy of her father's wishes. Their whole lives were built around Buchanan Enterprises. She couldn't walk away from her father—where would she go? Buchanan was her job, and her family's livelihood, and the livelihood of all the people who worked for her too. Certainly they couldn't subsist on David's impossible dreams.

The first thing Taylor did after she saw the account and read the article was call her dad. Brice Buchanan was vacationing in Malaysia. It was 4 A.M. in Malaysia, and Brice Buchanan was asleep with his *Do Not Disturb* enabled.

The second thing she did was call Shelly Salazar to see how she could sprinkle some PR fairy dust on the situation. When Taylor looked next, the most vitriolic of the comments were gone (although a few others, not kind but ever so slightly kinder, had tiptoed in to take their place). But they weren't gone from her mind. They burrowed right in there, making a home.

She made phone calls in her home office until 6 P.M., by which time her father was awake and calling, so she spent another ninety minutes on the phone with him. The whole time she was talking to Brice she was watching the clock. She missed dinner. Felicity's bedtime was getting closer and closer.

At seven forty-five she hung up with her father. All she wanted by that time was to talk to David and hug Felicity. She wanted someone to pour her an oversized glass of Sauv Blanc and rub her feet and tell her that everything was going to be okay. She closed the door to her home office behind her and looked for David in the living room, on the back patio, in the kitchen. No David. She checked his location on her phone and saw that he was at Poor People's Pub.

Okay. She could join him . . . maybe? But she didn't want to. She crept by Felicity's bedroom, where the nanny was reading Felicity the book about the bear who has come to visit and won't leave. Every time the nanny read a direct quote from the bear or the mouse—*Perhaps we could have just a spot of tea?*—she did it in a perfect British accent. Taylor knew that if she had been reading the book she wouldn't have been able to do the British accent. She was a terrible mother. She could tell by the way Felicity's arm was hanging over the side of the bed, motionless, that she was already asleep.

The next day she was still upset. She woke before David or Felicity were up, and she headed to the site. The foreman, Henry, who was earnest and handsome and *just so nice*, asked her if anything was bothering her. Yes, she said, everything was bothering her. Everything.

And then she started crying. Crying! On the job site. Mortifying! And what did Henry do? He took one of his thumbs and he wiped away her tears, and then he opened his arms and invited her in. It was so similar, eerily similar, to how she'd met David. Maybe she was only attractive to men when she was vulnerable and teary.

That's how it started. With a hug. She was so tired. And here was a person opening his arms to her, offering her a place to lean. So she leaned. And over the course of the summer, when she didn't know what else to do, she leaned again and again and again. She and David, she realized, had forgotten how to do this; they'd forgotten how to be kind to each other.

Taylor didn't want to be having an affair! She didn't want to be fighting over a man, especially if the man was her husband! That was counter to everything she believed in; it implied, of course, that a man was a prize, and women merely contestants. But also, she wanted to stay married. Yes, she very much wanted to stay married. She wanted to grow old and gray with David. Well, okay, not gray. She would certainly color any grays that crept in, but old, yes. She wanted to grow old with David.

So the day after the party at Juliana's, she broke things off with Henry. She wanted to make her marriage work: for Felicity, of course.

She'd grown up a child of divorce and no part of her thought that was okay to do to a child. For the sake of the business too. She knew her father (though he had been through one himself) would frown on a divorce, on the negative publicity it might bring, on the behind-the-scenes disorder it would imply to potential business associates. Taylor's father wanted everything squeaky clean on the outside and the inside. Besides that, Brice adored David.

But most of all, she wanted to make the marriage work for herself.

You have to remember, all Taylor Buchanan ever wanted was the fairy tale, the pretty dress, the happy ending. The prince. And also the business suit.

NICOLA

For days after the dinner at the Buchanans, Nicola tries to pretend that none of them exist. She doesn't go over to Juliana's. She doesn't call David. She *definitely* doesn't call or text Jack. The kids arrive for the Dolphin Program, and they're all so busy that the days fly by. Anytime she's out on the island, she keeps her eyes peeled for one of Eben Horton's glass floats.

One of the local interns, Madison, throws a party when her parents go to Boston for a night (Madison is young enough that these things matter) and Nicola stays until the very end. *On a Wednesday!* There's no celebrity DJ, no signature cocktail, no raw bar, and yet Nicola has as much fun as she's had all summer. More, maybe! When her mother calls to check in, they barely talk about David. As small as Block Island is, Nicola is living in a whole different world.

Then, the next Sunday, a week after the dinner, she gets a text from David that says GO FOR A WALK WITH ME? At first, she thinks it's a joke. David wants to go for a walk? David has never chosen to walk when he can drive, and drive fast. She texts back, asking him what bar he wants to meet at. Poor People's Pub? Ballard's? Keep it closer to home and go to The Oar?

NOT A BAR, he replies. I WANT TO GO FOR A WALK. SRSLY.

She thinks about it. OK. NATHAN MOTT PARK? Nathan Mott Park

is a series of trails that connects to the Greenway trails and the Enchanted Forest. Madison has told her that in mid to late summer you
can sometimes find blackberries growing on the trails.

WANT ME TO PICK YOU UP?

She answers that it's okay, she'll take her bike. It's about three
miles from where Nicola lives to the entrance of the park, and she
wants the exercise. She begins to regret her decision as soon as
she turns onto Center Road, though. The hill is absolutely vicious,
and each muscle in both quads stands on high alert as she fights
every urge to get off and walk.

A man in his sixties walking a doodle tells her encouragingly,
"You'll get there!" Easy for him to say, he's walking, and downhill,
but she presses on, oddly buoyed by his belief in her.

David is standing near the sign at the entrance. She can't read
his expression; are they going to talk about the dinner? Are they
going to talk about Juliana? Nicola joins him and they read silently,
learning that the park was the gift of Lucretia Mott Ball, and that
she was responsible for the statue of Rebecca at the Well in the center of town, erected by the Women's Christian Temperance Union.
David points to that part and says, "Didn't take, did it? The whole
temperance thing."

Okay. They're not going to talk about it.

"A thousand bachelorette parties would agree with you."

Thirsty from the bike ride, Nicola downs at least half her water bottle. Another car pulls up, and out jump two young women.
Nicola drinks more water while the two young women gaze at
David while trying to look like they aren't gazing—he does, she
forgets sometimes, give off the vibe of an Almost Famous Person, so
tall and model-ish. The women finish gazing and go on ahead, and
Nicola and David start down the path after them.

"So what's *up*?" she says. "Why the sudden interest in nature?"

"I've always been interested in nature."

She snorts. "No, you haven't." To the left of them are open fields bordered by stone walls, once used by farmers. The trail leads first into a set of dense shrubs. The scientist in Nicola wants to be aware of her surroundings, trying to identify shad and arrowwood and bayberry. (She's an aspiring marine biologist first, yes, but she also picked up a weird amount about botany.)

There's a long pause, and then here it comes. "I want to talk about Juliana." He takes a deep breath. "No joking around, okay? I really want to talk."

"Go ahead," she prompts. "I'm all ears, no jokes."

They come out of the shrubby part of the walk and into an open field. In front of them flits a little orange butterfly, an American copper. It stays just ahead of them as they cross the trail, as though it's showing them the way, which Nicola thinks is very hospitable of it. Nicola waits for David to say something.

They cross the open field and start on a gentle uphill. David sees something on the ground, a funny-shaped, sharp-looking thing. "What is that?"

"Oh, that's a deer husk." Nicola explains that the husks come from the oriental chestnut, left by deer in the fall, who break them open to eat the sweet meat inside.

"Encyclopedia Nicola," he says, and then they're both quiet for a little longer. Then David finally begins. It's the same story Jack told her early in the summer, but from a different point of view—and as anyone knows, point of view is *everything*.

The party at Fashion Week, LookBook's round of fundraising. Taylor in Europe with her father, the all-night walk around the city. When David met Juliana, when he fell in love with her, she was smart and she was ambitious and she had a work ethic that you can't make up.

"Aren't all of those things true of Taylor too?" Nicola says judiciously.

"Yes," he acknowledges. "Yes. On paper." But, he explains, *something different* sparked during that night. Not only did David think

Juliana was fascinating—where she'd started and where she was headed, and the grit it took to get from one place to the other, the almost impossibly tall hill she'd climbed—but instantly David was struck by how Juliana valued him, David, as his own person, his own entity, with his own past that was worthy of value. He told her about the race cars right away. It didn't feel embarrassing to share his passion with Juliana, it felt—normal. It felt exciting.

"That's not the way it was with Taylor. Which I didn't even notice in college, you know? I couldn't believe someone like Taylor was interested in someone like me, so I didn't let myself think too much about it."

"Someone like *you*? You're a catch, David. You must know that. It was a match made in New Haven."

He snorts, then turns serious, shaking his head. "I didn't feel like a catch at Yale. I always felt like an imposter there. Everybody I knew was so polished. So bred for it. Juliana felt like an imposter in her life too. We connected on that right away." He gazes into the middle distance. "With Taylor, in the beginning, all the way through college even, I felt like I gave her just as much as she gave me. But by the time I met Juliana that had changed."

"What'd you give her?" Nicola is genuinely interested in the answer to this question.

"I felt like I could soften her hard edges, you know? She had this *barrier* around her, and I was the one who could break it down. I think part of it is her mom leaving and never really coming back, and part of it is the money, and part of it is just how she looks—"

"Like a supermodel."

"And part of it comes from growing up as her dad's right-hand man."

"So what changed?"

"Sometime after college it seemed like she didn't need that from me any longer. She needed . . . I don't know. She needed something different. And I became the tail to her comet." (What a poetic visual, thinks Nicola.) "Time went on, and life was good enough. I mean, it was *good*, of course it was good, I'm not insane, but every time I brought up any of my own plans or dreams, like the race cars, it was like Taylor couldn't comprehend it. It was a real dream, though, Nicola. It was *my* dream." His voice cracks.

"I know it was," she says softly. "I know."

David always seemed so perfectly *David*—so at ease in the world, with the beautiful family and all the money and not a care on him, that she too has forgotten that all this time he's had desire vibrating inside him.

"Well, it doesn't matter anymore. Now I am finally, officially too old to be a race car driver." He smiles shakily as they pick their way over tree roots. Then he stops. "It's not about the money, this story," he says. "Okay, Nicola?"

"Of course not." But also, she realizes, it's very much about the money. To the son of a Furniture Brother, Taylor's wealth must have seemed bottomless, unfathomable. It would be impossible for it not to be a little seductive, to a midwestern guy with simple tastes.

Once they were engaged, she wanted him to find a cause to take up. Something he could be a spokesperson for. He looked good on-stage! Good in a tux at a charity event. "It was like she wanted me to be First Gentleman to her president," he says. There were so many places where he could be useful. Food insecurity or children with cancer. He had carte blanche to find something close to his heart.

"What about the race car thing?" David ventured. He'd been talking about this for years—since college! She knew that this was his passion. "*That's* close to my heart." If only she'd known him when he had the Miata he was always tinkering with—or further back, when he was ten, when he saw that first race at the Minnesota State Fair.

"That's not a *cause*," said Taylor. "That's a . . . hobby. Nobody actually *becomes* a race car driver. That dream is so . . . *middle America*."

"Ouch," says Nicola.

"Yeah. I know." She wanted him to quit going up to Monticello. It didn't make sense! What was the endgame? To Taylor things mattered only when there was an endgame.

Sometimes David thought about what it would have been like if he'd broken up with Taylor after he met Juliana, when she returned from Europe. Even on the eve of his wedding, when he got the email from Juliana, he thought about it. Especially then.

But he didn't. He didn't break up with Taylor during their engagement, and he certainly didn't do it on the night before the wedding, after Juliana sent him the email. On the day of the wedding there were 250 people gathered in Newport. He wasn't about to *ruin* Taylor. He loved Taylor. He really did. He just loved Juliana . . .

"More?" offers Nicola.

"Differently. More equally."

He moved with Taylor to Boston, into the brownstone in the Back Bay, right after the wedding. And in a few months, Taylor was pregnant.

"Were you in touch with Juliana at all?"

He hesitates. "Before the wedding, yes. And—a few times after."

"David!"

"I know. I know! Phone calls. A few emails. We didn't see each other." Of course Juliana had dated people before and after she met David; she wasn't a *nun*, David explained. But she felt the same thing for David he felt for her.

As soon as Taylor got pregnant, David told Juliana he couldn't be in touch with her anymore.

"And you kept to that?"

"Absolutely. When Felicity was born, everything changed. For a while, life was perfect."

"For how long?"

"Two weeks."

Nicola clears her throat. "That's not very long."

"No." David stops walking for a minute and considers the sky, as if there's additional information to be found in one of the scudding clouds. "No, it was brief."

They had a night nurse, so they actually slept like, well, pardon the expression, but they slept like babies. Taylor's father promised, for the first two weeks, to call Taylor only once a day with an update on the business, not two zillion times the way he typically did. For two weeks, they were a family, a cocoon of love and nursing and lying together watching Felicity's eyelids move while she slept.

It was the first and last time Taylor didn't put her work, and by extension herself, first. Then she started interviewing for a day nanny to go along with the night nurse and announced that she was going to begin weaning Felicity so she could go back to the office.

"Wean her?" asked David. "Already?"

If David could have grown breasts and filled them with milk he would have done it.

"I'm glad you didn't," says Nicola. "But I get what you're saying."

"We don't need the nanny every day," David says he told Taylor. "I'm right here! I know how to hold a bottle!"

"I know you do, darling. But it's hard to get anyone good if you can't offer full-time hours."

The nanny was hired, and after that, well, David grew bored. He missed the little triumvirate they'd briefly been. He had no real skills, no true experience, nowhere to put his energy. They lived far from Monticello now; even if Taylor had been okay with his returning, it no longer made sense.

Time went on: one month, two, a year, a year and half, two. David didn't want a sugar mama. He wanted a partner. He wanted to talk to Taylor about the funny things Felicity had said that day, but instead he found himself telling the nanny. He should have thought more about what he wanted to do with his life earlier, in the years after college, but somehow time had gotten away from him, and now the idea of a whole lifetime of leisure was terrifying. He'd tucked his racing dream away and now, if ever it emerged, it did so only to announce that he was too old, his time had passed.

Almost two years ago, Taylor told David about an investment property her father had bought on Block Island. He was going to renovate over the next year and a half, and then he wanted Taylor, David, and Felicity to summer there. He'd give them a budget for decorating. They could return every summer, until Buchanan Enterprises decided to sell. But that wouldn't be for a while. Property values on the island were only going up and up and up. He wanted Taylor to oversee a couple of projects. Brice would be mainly in Boston for the summer; ground was breaking on a skyscraper. And he had a trip to Malaysia planned. Taylor would be his boots on the ground on the Block.

The house on Block Island was a chance at something different; David saw it as an opportunity to reconnect. But on the island, Taylor was busier than ever. Her dad was all over her to make sure the new homes off Beacon Hill Road were on track. They were trying to get approval for the hotel and spa. Many locals were against the hotel plan, so there was a lot of diplomacy involved. There were meetings, and when those meetings were done there were more meetings. She was home less than ever.

"Can I help?" David asked her once.

She was putting lip gloss on in the mirror. It often fascinated him, how much attention she gave a small task like that, how much there seemed to be to it, because there wasn't just gloss but there was apparently a primer to go under the gloss and some sort of a sealant to go over. And when it came to other tasks, tasks having to do with him or Felicity, she seemed to have no time at all. Not that spending time with her husband and daughter was technically *a task*. But sometimes, from this end of things, it felt like it.

"With what I'm doing now? My lips?"

"*No!* With the work stuff. The approval process."

She turned to him in amazement and said, "You?"

"Sure. Why not?"

"Well. Mostly why not because last I checked you weren't an expert on approval processes." She snapped the top on the gloss and told him she had to go; she was late for a meeting.

Sometimes David thought about calling his father and asking if he could be trained to run Furniture Brothers. He thought a lot about Minnesota, about returning to his roots, about raising Felicity with the solid midwestern values he himself had been raised with. The streets with cul-de-sacs, summers at Pokegama. He knew, obviously, that Taylor would never go for this. Taylor couldn't do her job from Minnesota, and even if she could, she wouldn't want to. She had been to the lake only one time. But he couldn't stop thinking about it. It was always humming in the background, this desire for something different.

Once, getting Felicity dressed for the day before the nanny arrived, he reached for a dress in the back of the closet, a little orange sundress she'd never worn. Still with the tags on it. Three hundred dollars. Felicity was going to outgrow the dress in about thirty seconds, and yet Taylor had spent *three hundred dollars* on it. This kind of wealth disgusted him, but it fascinated him too, just as it had for years, how *easy* everything seemed for people with money, how the wheels were greased before they even knew that the wheels existed. Even though he was now part of it, he was still awestruck and repulsed by it.

Here Nicola interjects, "David. I looked up your Porsche. Those cars cost almost two hundred thousand dollars."

She watched the tips of his ears turn red, then redder still, as he says, "Well, now. To be fair. It's a 2021. So, less." Nicola rolls her eyes so hard she almost strains a muscle. More softly, David continues: "It doesn't even have the control-arm front suspension of the newest model."

"I'm sorry you have to suffer like that."

He grins then, and he's the same old David he always was, the kid at the lake who swam farther than everyone else, the teenager who drove faster, the guy who made all the hard stuff look easy. Then he says, "I could live without any of the material things, really I could."

Nicola feels like she has to call BS on that. "I feel like the only people who say that are people who will never actually have to live without any of the stuff they have."

David thinks about this—really thinks about it, letting a big chunk of time and a lot of stepping over roots pass before he answers. "Maybe," he says finally.

In June, two months after they'd moved in, he learned from Nicola that Juliana lived on the other side of the pond. Nicola had them over for drinks, and he remembered what it was like to listen to another person, and to be listened to. He felt all the same things he had felt all those years ago in New York, that night they walked to Battery Park, but stronger now. He didn't want to feel those things. He didn't! But they were there. It was all still there. Something that had been sleeping inside him woke up.

Juliana cared about David, and she let him care about her. She told him things that scared her or worried her; she was vulnerable. She needed him in a way that Taylor never did—never would. And the more time he spent with Juliana the more David began to suspect that this was what might bring him down. This was what might ruin his marriage: his need to be needed.

He had his suspicions that something was going on with Taylor, eventually confirmed. Jack, ever the player (Nicola cringes), was out and about in town, here and there and everywhere, and he heard something about Taylor and this guy Henry, the foreman on the four houses Buchanan Enterprises was building.

Understandably, this broke David's heart. Taylor had made him into the kind of man he was, a playboy without skills, without a career path, *literally loafing around in loafers*, and now, apparently, she wanted a different kind of man, the kind who wore hard hats and worked with his hands and could command a construction crew.

"*I* could have been a man in a hard hat!" he says. "I could have worked with my hands! But Taylor didn't want that."

"Yeah?" Nicola isn't sure about this, David in a hard hat.

"Okay, maybe not a hard hat," he concedes. "But like some kind of hat."

The summer went on. In some ways, it was the first time in a long time their marriage had felt equitable, because they were both looking for something else. In some ways, he said, the month of July felt like a long goodbye to their marriage, a slow burn of the inevitable.

Then, Juliana ended up at their house for dinner, and David expected a scene. Why else would Taylor invite her? But Taylor caused no scene. The opposite. Taylor was the consummate hostess, more present at the table, maybe, than she'd been all summer. She asked Juliana questions about her company—insightful, sharp questions that David wouldn't have thought to ask, had never asked. There were so many things about business that Taylor understood and he didn't.

David thought Taylor wanted to bring things to a head, to hasten the inevitable. He thought she wanted to skip to the last page in the book. In a way, he was relieved by this prospect. Terrified, but relieved. There was so much pressure building inside that house all summer, and if someone didn't stick a pin in it and let some air out the whole place was going to burst. He thought Taylor was the pin.

But he understands now that it was more complicated than that. When Juliana came to dinner, David realized that Taylor had changed course. She didn't want to confront David with what she suspected. She wanted to show Juliana that David was hers. She'd made a decision, and the decision was to do what it took to keep her marriage.

In the end, of course, Juliana was the pin.

Juliana left soon after Jack and Shelly and Nicola. And with Caroline gone too, and Felicity by that time sound asleep, David and Taylor were alone. Taylor cleared the table, loaded the dishwasher, washed by hand the delicate wineglasses. She was calm at first, stacking, carrying.

David began to help her. He shook out the place mats and napkins and carried them to the laundry room. There was a smear of Juliana's lipstick on one of the napkins, and David noted that. Taylor put some music on, country ballads. Taylor *never* listened to country, but there was something about the mournful music, the simple, tragic lyrics, that fit the situation. Then, when the cleanup was done, Taylor put her hands on the edges of the sink, and David noticed that her shoulders were shaking. Taylor was crying. Taylor *never* cried. In fact, since the day they'd met at Yale, he had not seen her cry.

"Hey," said David. "Hey, hey, come here. Turn around." He said this gently, and he touched her on the shoulder, not sure how she would react to his touch. He thought she'd flinch and push him away. But she didn't; she collapsed into David, sobbing. She got her mascara all over his white shirt.

Nicola has stopped walking, trying to square this image of Taylor with the Taylor she knows. "What'd she say?"

"She said, 'Why don't you like me best, David? I like you best. Why don't you like me best?'"

"Wow." Nicola breathes the word out softly; more a sound that an actual word. "That's heartbreaking."

"*Heartbreaking*," David agrees, and his voice cracks.

"So what'd *you* say?"

"What could I say?" He looks up at the sky for a long, long moment. He's not, Nicola realizes, going to tell her any more than that. She waits and waits, but that's all there is.

She holds up her finger and David says, "What are you doing?"

"Listening for frogs."

"Why?"

"Because behind those shrubs," she says, "is a vernal pool."

"A *what*?"

"Vernal pool. Sorry, has the walk become too educational?" She's trying to make him smile.

He shakes his head and, yes, he smiles. "Okay, I can't stand the suspense. Please enlighten me. What is a vernal pool?"

"I'm glad you asked! A vernal pool is a seasonally wet body of water."

"That's good to know. I'm sure that will come in handy in my life as a . . ." He paused and seemed to be searching for the right word. "As a—oh, geez, Nicola. I don't know what to call myself."

"As a philanderer?" she suggests.

He punches her on the arm, but only lightly.

"Sorry," she says. "I couldn't help it." When they were kids it would have been a real punch. David and his brothers didn't believe in treating Nicola and her sisters any differently because they were girls. "Very funny," he says. Then he says, "I'm so jealous of you, you know."

"Of *me*?"

"Yeah. You've got a plan."

"Uh, incorrect. My 'job' is over in a few weeks. I'm only living where I'm living because of you. If I go back to school, I'm accruing more debt while simultaneously avoiding paying off the rest of my law school loans."

"You're living where you are because of Taylor and her father," he corrects. "But you have something you're passionate about, something you're pursuing." He waits a beat and says, "You serve a *porpoise*."

Nicola guffaws. "Have you been waiting all summer to use that one?"

"Just since early July."

He's right. When she leaves this place, and leaves behind all these unstable, unhappy people, she does have something else to think about. She has work to do that she believes is important and necessary.

"Listen, David—" She wants to say something here about him and the cars, about that day at the state fair, about the fact that nobody's dreams are worthless.

"Yeah?"

But she can't really say any of that; it doesn't feel like the right time to strike an emotional chord that deep. So she settles for this: "I'm no expert, believe me. But I bet your Porsche goes pretty fast, almost as fast as a race car."

He's quiet for a long time and she worries that she's tried too hard to make light. But then he cracks a smile, a real one this time, not at all shaky, and he says, "It does. It goes pretty fast. It really does." He points at a log just off the trail covered in leathery orange layers.

"What's that, professor?"

She peers at the log. "Looks like a fungus."

"Ew."

She rolls her eyes. "Calm down. It's part of the ecosystem. It has a job to do, like anything else."

"Rub it in, why don't you," says David. "Even the fungus has a job."

They walk on a bit longer. Nicola consults her map. "This is the Enchanted Forest," she says.

David looks around. "This? Are you sure?"

"That's what the map says. And also this." She points at the sign ahead of them, wooden with white letters spelling out ENCHANTED FOREST.

"Is that a trick? The fact that the arrows are pointing in both directions? Do you think the sign was put here by a hobbled old woman with crooked teeth and a basket of apples over her arm?"

"Kind of feels that way." She suspects that in fact it was courtesy of the Block Island Nature Conservancy.

David seems disappointed. "I thought an enchanted forest would feel much more magical than this. I thought there would be more trees."

Nicola pulls out her phone, checks for a signal, taps a query into google. "Here's the explanation." She reads from the website: "'The Enchanted Forest was a grove of trees planted by the Nathan Mott Park Corporation in the 1940s. It was one of the only large stands of trees on the island and provided excellent habitat for nesting and roosting birds, particularly owls. In the early 2000s, the Enchanted Forest was cut down because the trees were causing a navigational hazard for planes landing at the nearby airport.'"

"*That's* a downer," says David.

"You can say that again." It's the oldest story in the modern world, though, isn't it? The crossroads of nature and progress, the ebb versus the flow. They are always coming up against that crossroads in the marine world. Just ask any right whale scarred by a propeller blade, ask any dolphin with plastic trash caught around its beak.

They start on the steepest part of the hike, which is not very steep, but for a few minutes they do need to concentrate on their footing, making sure their feet don't catch on the tree roots.

David breaks the silence first. "I remember when we were little and we used to think the grown-ups had it all figured out. Right? Don't you remember that feeling?"

"Yeah." Here comes a memory. There's a float about one hundred meters out in the lake, and every summer morning, right after breakfast, the kids would swim out there, the group of them, a great posse. They were all strong swimmers, and nobody had ever had any trouble making it to the float.

But something happened to Nicola one day. Maybe she'd had too much breakfast—David's mom had made her famous blueberry pancakes—and she couldn't make it to the float. For years she'd been making this swim, and all of a sudden, out of nowhere, she began to struggle. Then a pair of strong arms lifted her up, then another pair, and another, until they were all at the float, and these sets of hands collectively got Nicola onto it. She lay there for a few minutes, heaving, spitting out water. She closed her eyes, and when she opened them she saw the eyes of her sisters and her cousins all looking at her with a concern that was almost panic.

Nicola's mom came running out of the house. She had seen a commotion from the screened-in porch. She was wearing a bathrobe, not a bathing suit, and they were all out on the float, so she stood on the dock, waving her arms, calling out to see what had happened. Soon after came David's mom, and David gave them a thumbs-up. Nicola remembers she turned her head and she saw the two of them at the shoreline and she thought, Oh, good. The adults are here. Everything is okay now.

But it hadn't been the adults who saved her. She didn't know then that the grown-ups were just guessing about everything, about the world, about how to live in it, same as Nicola and David are now.

"Yeah," she says again. "I remember that feeling."

"I think the dirty little secret of the world is that the adults never had it figured out."

"They never did. I feel tricked."

"Totally," he says. "I want my money back."

They bear right to get to the very top of the trail. The view is pretty spectacular: to the north they can see all the way to Clayhead, with the water beyond it, then town to the east. Nicola wonders if this all feels the same as it had in Lucretia Mott's day. She wonders what Lucretia would think of Snapchat and Instagram, of Bumble and Tinder and swiping right. She wonders what she would think of Taylor and David and Juliana and LookBook. She's pretty sure she knows what she would think of the houses the Buchanans are building. Nicola closes her eyes and puts herself back in Lucretia's time. She has read that when Lucretia left this land to be converted into a public park, she was the first on the island to do something like that. Without her, there'd be no present-day conservation efforts on the island. "Thank you, Lucretia," she whispers.

She opens her eyes, and David is pointing to something over to the right.

"What's *that*?" he asks.

"What?"

"Over there." There is something, glinting in the sunlight.

"It can't be."

"What?"

"I don't believe it!"

"*What?*"

She says, "Shhh," as though it's alive and might run away. Cherry had been right, at that barbecue back in early summer. *You have to be open to it, without looking too hard.* Nicola takes a couple of steps off the trail and picks it up, holds it in her hands like it's something rare and beautiful, which of course it is.

It's one of Eben Horton's glass floats, with the number written on it. Thirty. Almost Nicola's age. "I can't believe it," she whispers. "I can't believe we found one. David! You found it." She feels like Charlie Bucket, discovering one of the five Wonka Bars with the golden ticket.

"What is it?"

She tells David the whole story. She tells him how some people plan their whole summers around finding one of these. Some people bring entire crews of friends and family out to search. They flood small holes where the floats might be hidden, to bring them to the surface. They search far and wide. And here David has found one without even looking. It feels momentous.

"I don't understand," says David. "What do you do when you find one?"

"You *rejoice*. You celebrate. Also, I think there's some place online that you register it."

"But do you bring it somewhere?"

"Where would you bring it?"

"Like, do you trade it in for something?"

"*No.* What would you trade it in for?"

"I don't know. A reward?"

"It's the thing itself that's the reward. The finding of it." David takes the orb from Nicola and examines it, turning it this way and that. She can see him work his way through this concept, eventually coming out on the other end. He hands the orb back to Nicola with a mournful sigh. He's off the orb, and back on the disorder of his personal life.

"It's going to be okay," she tells him gently.

"I've made a mess of everything, Nicola," he says. She's never seen him so dejected. This version of David makes her sad. She wants the other version, the laughing, carefree version, even the version from fifteen minutes ago who told her her life has porpoise. She wants the version who swings Felicity up in the air until she squeals and begs to be put down, then, as soon as she's been put down, begs to be picked up again.

"It's going to be okay. But things are broken, David, and you have to fix them."

"I don't know how. I don't know what to do." He looks at Nicola, his eyes pleading. "Tell me what to do."

She shakes her head. "I can't. I can tell you about log fungus, but this you have to figure out on your own." She looks around; there are several trails jutting off from the top, more than one way to get down. "Which way should we go?"

"You pick, Nicola, and I'll follow. That butterfly is gone and without him I'm not sure where to go."

"It was a girl," she says.

"Oh, come *on*," says David. "There's no way you could tell that."

She shrugs. "Larger spots in the forewing."

"I thought you were a *marine* biologist."

"Aspiring. But I have a thing about butterflies too. I have a thing about all of nature. The natural world makes a lot more sense than all the rest of it."

"You can say that again."

There are so many loops and trails to choose from up here. She wants someone else to make the decision. She wants both her and David to be kids again, swimming out into the center of the lake, secure in the belief that inside the house the adults have everything under control.

Host: You know the drill. This is *Life and Death on an Island*, episode two, "The Town Council." Remember the code lifeanddeath gets you ten percent off at any of our sponsors. Kelsey, you mentioned that something happened at a party at Taylor Buchanan's house that you thought was relevant.

Kelsey: Yeah. Why Shelly Salazar and Taylor had a very public heart-to-heart at Taylor Buchanan's party, nobody was sure. People were drinking a lot. Did that have something to do with what happened later? It's impossible to say. Summer and alcohol make strange bedfellows, as the saying goes.

Betsy: That's not how the saying goes.

Lou: We were all invited. Town council, planning board, the whole kit and kaboodle. Clearly she was trying to do something. Win us over. But I didn't go. I can't be bought.

Betsy: Even Zoning was invited.

Evan: And nobody *ever* invites Zoning to anything. Don't tell them I said that.

Lou: I actually can be bought. But my granddaughters were in from Newport. I chose them. I'll always pick my granddaughters, if it's a choice between them and someone else.

Betsy: I didn't go out of principle. There's something I don't trust about those Buchanans. I still come upon Henry at the oddest moments when he looks like he's been crying. Blames it on allergies, but I've known him since he was a baby and he's not allergic to anything. Something or someone did a real number on my Henry.

Kelsey: I go to every party I'm invited to. I'm twenty-seven years old and I live on an island that basically shuts down in the winter. I'm not going to miss a party.

Evan: There was a signature cocktail. I've never been anywhere where there's a signature cocktail. My wife had three of them. We had a sitter for only the second time all summer.

Kelsey: In case you're wondering it was Prosecco with a locally made mint blueberry syrup.

Evan: Went down like Gatorade after the Shad Bloom trail run. Which is to say, fast and easy.

Kelsey: I saw them talking. But I wasn't close enough to hear everything. So this is like thirdhand. But my sources are pretty reliable.

THE TOWN

Some people were on the patio outside, where the bar was set up. Others were in the living room. (People marveled at the *white furniture*: Didn't Taylor and David have a *small child*?) The kitchen, of course, was a popular spot, as it is at every party, and what a kitchen this was! Top-of-the-line everything, as you'd expect. Somebody pulled out a drawer to find that it was a warming drawer; another, an extra-cold drawer to supplement the refrigerator. Another, a stand-alone ice machine like you'd find behind a bar. At an actual bar.

Someone saw Shelly and Taylor deep in conversation on that long, white couch. Dangerous, when you consider the potential spilling of the blueberry cocktail, but there you have it. We've all been there, haven't we? A deep conversation with a relative stranger at a party. Sometimes in these conversations we find ourselves going deeper than we do with our closest friends. We put everything on the table. Not on *that* table, though, because it was also white, and made of a nubbly texture. There was nowhere to rest a glass. Who buys a nubbly table? Only people, we supposed, who had so many other kinds of tables to choose from that it didn't matter if one was purely for decorative purposes.

Shelly Salazar was, to put it delicately, wasted. She had eaten only one meal that day (the Shoreline Toast from The Cracked Mug, highly recommended, and try it with an oat milk cappuccino) but that was hours and hours ago. Then she'd ridden her bike out to Cooneymus, just for the heck of it. The day had been hot; the ride was hilly; she'd forgotten to bring a water bottle. Quick shower before the party, and here she was, lightheaded, underfed, really quite drunk from one drink.

Not long after they started talking, Taylor swung the conversation around to Juliana. Taylor had learned about Shelly's connection to Juliana at the dinner at her house, and now she wanted to mine that connection for gold. "Tell me again when you guys graduated from college?" Taylor asked.

"Twenty fourteen," said Shelly. She pumped her fist in the air. "Go Eagles!"

Taylor put on her interested face, the one she used in client meetings. She said, "What was Juliana like in college?" She paused and gathered herself. "I'm always so interested in women entrepreneurs, you know, being a woman in business myself. And she's so successful!"

"Sure," said Shelly. "I get that." For a moment, she seemed to disengage from the conversation, looking off into the middle distance.

Taylor said, "So . . . ?" and eventually Shelly came back to Planet Earth.

"To be honest, I really only knew her freshman year. I was good friends with her roommate, Mary Ann. She was around, but she wasn't like *around* around, you know? She was pretty shy. She didn't really fit in."

Taylor made herself look concerned and said, "Oh, no. Why's that?"

"I don't know?" said Shelly. "She just wasn't all *rah rah rah, BC,* you know. I'm not sure I ever saw her at football games. She was on scholarship. She studied a lot. She had some internship. She couldn't afford to fall behind. And to see the business she's in now? Fashion? We never would have imagined it. Her clothes back then were *very* uninteresting." Then, musingly, like she was talking about a dream she'd had the night before, Shelly said, "Of course, she wasn't Juliana George back then."

"Well no, of course not," said Taylor. "She didn't *become* Juliana George until she started LookBook. In the same way Phil Knight wasn't Phil Knight until he started Nike."

Shelly giggled. "No, I mean she really wasn't Juliana George then. She had a different name."

"Whoa," said Taylor. "Wait. *What* did you just say?"

Shelly clapped a hand over her mouth and said, "Ohmygod, I wasn't supposed to say anything." She looked a little panicked. "I forgot."

"You don't have to worry about *me*," said Taylor. She oozed succor. "I promise. I can keep a secret. Anyway, that's so interesting. So, just out of curiosity, what was her name in college? Was it like same first name, different last name? Or different first name, same last name?"

"Both," said Shelly. "Both were different. Her name when *I* first met her was Jade Gordon."

"How fascinating!" said Taylor. She was still playing it cucumber-cool, though she remembered the weird story at dinner at her house, something about Juliana, about jewels, about Jade. "Why'd she change it?"

"I don't know!" cried Shelly. "Why does anyone do anything?" She swung her cocktail glass, and Taylor tried not to notice when a drop flew out and came *so close* to hitting the white couch, but missed it, and instead landed on the living room rug, which, alas, alas, was also white.

Betsy: Less than a week after that the woman walking her dog found the body, at Dinghy Beach.

Evan: It was a weird time on the island. A weird, weird time.

Lou: It was a westerly wind, you know. That's why the body washed up at Dinghy. Southerly, and it would have been the clam flats.

Kelsey: I don't like to think about that. I don't like to think about any of it.

Lou: Did she have it coming to her? No.

Betsy: Lou!

Lou: What? I said she *didn't* have it coming to her. But looking back, could someone have seen it coming? Maybe.

Evan: Yeah. Maybe.

Kelsey: Well, maybe not *exactly* that. But you could have seen something coming. Possibly something.

CATHERINE

On the third Tuesday in August, Catherine McKee's dog, Myrtle, wakes her at one minute past six, which, Catherine knows, is precisely the time of that day's sunrise. (She checked yesterday.) Myrtle's sense for this is uncanny, her method of waking Catherine always the same. She puts her two front paws on the bed and presses her wet black nose into the side of Catherine's neck.

There are worse ways to be awoken, Catherine supposes, but why must Myrtle come always to her side, never to Amber's? She slides out of bed, grabs her phone from her nightstand, and makes her way downstairs, careful not to wake the couple's two daughters (Sophie and Charlotte, eight and ten), fast asleep in their bunk beds.

"Coffee first, then walk," Catherine tells Myrtle. "Also, Advil." The night before, the girls' favorite babysitter, Maggie Sousa, came, and Amber and Catherine enjoyed a much-needed night out on the town. They've been so busy this summer—Amber manages the front of house at Spring House and Catherine works at Island Bound Bookstore—and usually on such opposite schedules that they've been like ships in the night.

They started with cocktails at The Oar, then moved on to a sumptuous dinner at Eli's. Amber's friend Kip bartends at Eli's and he made their second round extra strong. They split a bottle of Château de Sancerre, so crisp and refreshing it practically drank itself. They had dessert too—both the baklava and the Black Forest mousse cake. Then, as if all of that weren't enough (it was, in retrospect, enough!), they'd made their way to the outdoor bar at Spring House for nightcaps. Baileys over ice for Catherine, and a bourbon (Jefferson's, neat) for Amber. It was when Amber ordered the bourbon that Catherine realized neither of them would be driving home, so they left the car at Spring House and begged a ride home with Back of the House Bobby. No biggie, they'd said at the time; one of them could bike back for the car in the morning.

But currently the abandoned car presents a problem, Catherine realizes. She'd planned on driving Myrtle to Mohegan Bluffs, where they could walk down the steps (good exercise for Myrtle) and clamber among the rocks. Now they must stay closer to home. She could take her to Mansion or Scotch, but those are likely to be more crowded, and her head is pounding so zealously that she doesn't feel like making idle conversation should she run into anyone she knows.

"Dinghy Beach it is," she says. Myrtle regards Catherine with her dark, dark eyes, so dark sometimes they don't show up against the black of her coat, and lets out a soft belch. "Excuse you," says Catherine, and Myrtle looks at her beseechingly. She tries not to look too closely at Myrtle's graying muzzle, because it makes her sad. The thought of Myrtle ever—well, no. She can't think about it.

Making it out the door is no problem, it turns out. Neither is making it down the path that leads to the beach; they are the only two creatures there, and the fresh morning air begins to revive Catherine. Ah. Inhale, exhale.

What is a problem is what happens after Catherine leans down and unhooks Myrtle's leash and lets her run along the crescent of sand. Myrtle runs at a very un-Myrtle-like pace to the water. You might, if you were being generous, call it a sprint.

Myrtle won't stop barking and backing away; the relentless noise is hurting Catherine's already aching head.

Catherine thinks what Myrtle is barking at is eelgrass, at first, and she wonders why Myrtle is making such a fuss about it. This dog has seen eelgrass before! Then she gets closer, and closer, and she sees that it's not eelgrass at all.

It's hair.

Last night's halibut turns over and over in her stomach, and she retches in the sand. As she's fumbling for the phone in her pocket, Catherine screams and she screams and she screams.

JADE

Twenty minutes, Mrs. Sanchez had said. Jade stood outside the door Mrs. Sanchez pointed to, wondering if she should knock or go in or run away. A woman in green scrubs with a stethoscope around her neck, peeling off a pair of latex gloves, came out.

Would he recognize her? Would he talk to her? Would he even be awake?

"You the daughter?" she asked.

"Friend," said Jade. She looked nothing like George, and was too young to be his daughter.

"Go on in. He's sleeping."

George's bedroom was on the same side of the building as the one Jade had spent four nights in, so it shared the same view across Fifth Avenue and down onto Central Park. The same sets of children and nannies were still walking around.

It was warm in the room, almost as warm as it had been outside. George's eyes were closed and Jade watched him, wondering if he was thinking or dreaming. He was wearing navy-blue striped pajamas and his hair, thin enough to reveal the age spots along his hairline, had been dampened and parted neatly on the side: he was part decaying body, part patient, but also part the spit-shined schoolboy he must have once been.

"George," she whispered. He didn't stir.

It was *so* hot in the room. Jade was wearing a pink tank top under the blouse she'd worn to work so she removed the blouse and laid it across her lap. She watched George's eyes move back and forth under his eyelids.

George, who had listened and encouraged and fed her when she was hungry and cared for her when she was hurt. George, the only person in the world who thought Jade was capable of all the things she herself thought (knew) she was capable of. George, who'd made her promise she'd start LookBook, no matter the risk, even though she believed risks were for people with safety nets, not for people like her.

After a time his eyelids fluttered. "Jade?" The eyes closed, then opened again. "I knew you'd come."

"Of course I came," she said. "I'm here, George."

He nodded, and his eyes stayed open. He watched her, considering. "You're so beautiful," he said. His voice was low, no more than a dry whisper, really, and she had to lean closer to him to hear it. "A real and true beauty. Your youth . . ." He trailed off.

His hand was lying on top of the bedsheet; she placed hers on top of his and squeezed it. This is a dying man, she thought. This is a kind, dying man.

She took her hand from his and held it against his cheek, and then, without thinking twice about it, she kissed him, her full, young lips against his old, papery cheek. She leaned her forehead against his, pouring out her respect and her sadness and, yes, her fear—fear of death, fear of mortality, fear of being left alone again. She poured gratitude for his real, pure love, the purest love she'd felt up to this point in her life.

The affection cost her nothing; it was a punctuation, a grace note.

It cost her nothing until an unfamiliar voice said, "Dad? What. The Fuck. Is going on in here."

And then it almost cost her everything.

In the doorway stood a woman; behind her was Mrs. Sanchez with an expression on her face that said, very clearly, that Jade's twenty minutes had come and gone. Jade had never put a blouse on so fast in her life.

"This is Mr. Halsey's daughter," said Mrs. Sanchez.

"I was just leaving," said Jade.

"I should hope *so*," said the daughter. Then she said, "Jesus, Dad. Really?"

Jade wouldn't learn the daughter's name until three days later, when the *Times* ran George's obituary. She looked like a Cleo, a short name with a hard edge, a name that brooked no contradictions. Smooth hair, simple gold jewelry, tailored pants that most definitely did not come from Zara. A slender leather belt around a slender waist. But in fact her name was Serena, which had a softer sound; which implied a calmness and an amicability that this woman did not exhibit. The son was named Edward.

Jade went to the funeral. It was Catholic. Catholic! This surprised her, especially considering what she'd gathered of the Upper East Side. Jade had received her First Communion, and after that, nothing. But now, in the back of the church on Eighty-Third Street, some sort of sorrow and familiarity clutched at her heart: the priest's words, the responsorial psalm, the intercessions, these all rang a bell in her distant memory. When, at the end of the service, the choir sang "Be Not Afraid," Jade cried, and her tears were genuine. The only person who had believed in her was gone.

(That wasn't in the court filings; wasn't in the deposition, the way Jade felt at the funeral.)

After the funeral Jade introduced herself to the daughter. (She knew she'd made a mistake in the bedroom, but she didn't know yet, of course, what was coming.) Serena smelled like jasmine and she had a chestnut bob that was so sleek, so bluntly cut, that Jade wanted to reach out and stroke it. She had one of those upturned noses, small and perfect. Eyelashes that could have been real or could have been subtle extensions.

"I'm Jade," she said. She put out her hand, and the daughter, looking Jade up and down, ignored it. A familiar sense of shame and dismissal enveloped Jade.

"You're the one from his bedroom."

Jade nodded and said, "Your father was very kind to me."

"Well, he never mentioned you," Serena said. Her voice was cool and low, like it had just emerged from an ice cave. This casual cruelty—it seemed so practiced; it seemed like it came so *easily*—loosened something in Jade. She thought for a fraction of a second about holding back, about disappearing, about *taking the high road*, but she didn't.

"Oh?" she said. "Did you talk to him enough that he would have mentioned a new friend? I didn't get the impression that you were close."

Serena's shoulders, already set back (Pilates, Jade guessed), moved back even more. Her chest rose a fraction of an inch; her chin lifted. Everything about her said, *Who do you think you are?*

"Of course we were close. He was my *father.*"

"Huh," said Jade, still stung by the way Serena was looking at her, so, in return, putting out her own stinger. "That is not the picture he painted for me."

There was a barely perceptible flinch behind those cool gray eyes.

George had told her about Serena and Edward. He'd been in his late forties when he married for the first time, a woman twelve years younger, and he was nearly fifty when Serena was born. The marriage was rocky, the wife, by George's account, prone to theatrics and instability ("I should have known when I married a Broadway actress") but it endured for a decade ("There was straying," George said, without elaborating). By the time of the divorce George had fallen in love with another woman, who eventually became his second wife and the true love of his life. The second wife was stable and loving; the second wife was a rock and this allowed George to be a rock for her too. Zero drama.

Serena never forgave him for the divorce and the remarrying; she wouldn't hear that there was another side to the story aside from her mother's. Five years ago, the second wife died. George tried to reconnect with his children at that point, but by then the harm was done. The myelin that covered the fibers of their relationship had been irrevocably damaged. They would accept his money, it turned out, if not his love. But he was still their father, and a very wealthy man, and when he died, they each received a massive inheritance.

Minus the half a million dollars he left to Jade, with the stipulation that she use it for "expenses directly and indirectly related to the creation of her business."

George's children came at her like vipers. Well, Serena did. Edward was a playboy living in South Beach with strategic stubble and a year-round tan, too oblivious to be a viper. Serena contested the will on the grounds that Jade had seduced an old, dying man to get his money. Into the public record went the story of Serena walking in on Jade with her forehead pressed against George's, her hand on his face, her blouse off. Into the record went an affidavit from Mrs. Sanchez, who said that in the month before her employer's death she had gone to visit her family in Mexico for one week. When she returned, her employer had "a spring in his step" that had not been there before. Mrs. Sanchez, who had once seemed like an ally, shifted her wheel hard to the left when money was involved. (I'm sorry, thought Juliana, is having a spring in one's step *illegal?*)

Nowhere in the record did it say how lonely George had been in the final years of his life. Nowhere did it note the absence of his children and the fact that the only person he saw on a daily basis, the only person who truly had an idea of the quotidian details of his life, was on his payroll. Nowhere did it say how all the way to the end George retained an unguarded sweetness, his eyes like those of a Labrador, warm and eager to please.

You know what else wasn't in the court filings? What a bitch the daughter was.

After a time, Serena understood that she didn't have the grounds to keep the money from Jade. She could continue trying, if she chose to. But she'd be looking at a pretrial date more than eight months out; a trial could take years, and during all that time Serena's money would be held up too. Serena didn't want her money held up (shocker); she dropped the contestation, and Jade's money came through.

Jade hadn't done anything wrong. Nothing illegal. Nothing immoral, even. There was nothing she needed to hide from. But it could be a stain on her name, all of those public records of this messy business, and she wanted to start fresh and clean. She wanted to leave behind the girl from Lawrence, the girl from George's bedroom. She wanted to honor her benefactor. People change their names all the time. You don't need to explain it to anyone.

Later, in interviews, or when she spoke to business school classes, or when she was invited to join onstage panels with large audiences at conferences for business entrepreneurs, or when she gave her TED Talk, she spoke of the money from an angel that helped get her started.

Friendship, love, money—all of these were vast, complex landscapes that could not be excavated in the course of a single talk or interview. People always assumed that she'd left off a word; of course she must have meant angel *investor*. But she didn't. She just meant *angel*.

With the money George left her, Juliana worked full-time on LookBook. She hired three people: a technology developer, a stylist, and a marketer. Anyone else she needed she hired on a contract basis. She rented space in the WeWork building near Rockefeller

Center. Five hundred thousand dollars sounded bottomless to someone who had grown up the way Jade had grown up, but it wasn't bottomless. She had to husband her resources.

(What a strange phrase that was. Why not *wife* your resources?)

Just keep moving, she told herself when she felt unsteady or uncertain or unworthy or scared. Just. Keep. Moving. She looked in the mirror and sometimes she saw Juliana George, but sometimes she saw the girl from Lawrence, the foster kid, the scholarship student, the outsider, always looking in.

Just keep moving.

A year after she got George's money, LookBook launched. Then they turned a profit. Then the profit got bigger. The company kept working, kept improving the technology, tweaking the algorithm. They had the college students, then they had the post-college crowd, then they had the suburban moms, and, once they had the suburban moms, it felt like they had the world.

But they didn't have the world yet, not until five years ago, when the luxury brands started coming to *her*. Everybody had pieces they couldn't sell! Nobody wanted to liquidate! More negotiations, more meetings. If she got luxury brands on board, she could reach an entirely new consumer. At Fashion Week she had invites to all the shows. She went to as many as possible, to see what the designers were doing. Her wheels were turning. She could feel the momentum building. She networked whoever she could, wherever she could.

Sunday came, the third full day of Fashion Week. Juliana was tired! She'd started at Tory Burch at 10 A.M.; by 8 P.M. she was toast. But also, she would have killed for some toast. Nobody ate at Fashion Week. At a networking party at Chelsea Piers she leaned against the wall and closed her eyes. When she opened them, a man who looked like a model but as it turned out later wasn't a model remarked to her that the hors d'oeuvres were so small he could hardly see them.

She laughed. "They really are very small." Then, because she was there to network, she stuck out her hand and said, "Juliana George."

"David Carr. Nice to meet you."

Can you fall in love with one handshake? Of course not! That's absurd. But, maybe. She *felt* something. He felt something too. What was it? It was indefinable. They moved to a corner of the room; they talked a bit more. He was there with a friend, a pro golfer, who had already disappeared.

Then Juliana, who had by then learned not to let an opportunity go by, who had learned that fortune favors the bold, gathered her considerable courage, said, "I'm so hungry. Do you want to get some food? Some real food? Like . . . a burger, or a fourteen-egg omelet?"

She watched him consider this and then watched him say yes. She'd play that over and over again in her mind over the next few years, the indecision, then the moment of decision. Her heart was beating so fast.

"I would *love* to get some real food," he said.

Maybe you can't fall in love with one handshake, but what about one evening? What about a night? What if you eat at an all-night diner on Sixth Avenue, then walk from Fifty-Fourth Street all the way down to Battery Park, then back again (eight miles in total), talking the whole time, compressing the normal first weeks or even months of a new relationship into a few hours? What if you tell this brand-new-to-you person stories about your childhood you've never told anyone? What if he tells you his stories, which are tamer than yours, but to you so interesting simply because they are so *normal*? A midwestern upbringing, a father and uncle and mother and aunt and cousins galore. Summers at a lake, weekends at high school parties, the kind you see in the movies, an old Miata that became the gateway to his passion?

What if he doesn't touch you after that first handshake until, oh, around 2 A.M., when he takes your hand so casually, as though you are a couple, as though you always walk around linked together like this? And what if he rubs the knuckle of your right forefinger with the thumb of his left hand and you think you might actually melt into the sidewalk?

What if you don't even kiss until you watch the sun rise from a bench on the High Line? What if you kiss for a second time outside your apartment, and what if you are completely serious when you label this the kiss you will be trying to find again for the rest of your life?

What if you come up for air and you say, "My roommate—" at the same time that he says, "I shouldn't—I can't—" And then he touches your temple, and you don't think you've ever felt anything so erotic in your life?

What if he says, "I have to tell you something. I've been trying to figure out how to say it. I can't—I'm engaged, Juliana. I'm engaged to be married."

What if the bottom drops out then, and you spend years wishing you could reclaim it.

She knew they both felt the same thing. That's the key to this entire story: *they both felt the same thing.*

She saw him again, three weeks later, in Central Park. He was with a tall, beautiful blonde. If you looked quickly you might have thought you were seeing the ghosts of John-John and Carolyn Bessette. Juliana was walking, trying to clear her head from a stressful day. The couple was sitting on one of the wood-and-concrete benches along the perimeter.

Juliana and David saw each other at the same instant, just when Carolyn Bessette stood up to take a phone call. When she raised the phone to her ear Juliana saw the diamond winking on her ring finger. The woman walked away, out of earshot. David said Juliana's name, and she moved closer to him. He said, "Listen, I—"

"It's okay," she said. There was that shame again, the shame she'd never fully gotten rid of. "It's fine," she repeated. She'd come to realize, playing the night over and over again in her mind, that she had misread the situation. Again.

She's like obsessed *with my mom.*

She wasn't normal, like everyone else. She wanted to say, *I have never felt this way about anyone.* She wanted to say, *I know you felt it too.* And she wanted to say, *You're making a huge mistake.* But that was desperate, and desperation was Jade Gordon's weakness, not Juliana George's. So what she said was: "It's okay. We hardly know each other. You don't have to explain yourself to me."

She walked away, exited the park as fast as she could, not realizing until she was out how close she was to George's old building. She made sure she was far enough away before she let herself start crying.

She had thought that love, once she found it, would win out over everything else. But what did she know of love, really? Remember, she'd been raised without it.

Taylor was an Important Person whose father ran a Big Company; it wasn't hard to track the details online. Nearly a year later Juliana made one last effort, writing that email on the eve of the wedding. When David didn't answer, and when she saw the wedding announcement in the *Times*, she told herself to give up. It's over, it's done! Walk away! Wash your hands of all of it. Look at all you've achieved. Look at LookBook! Your company needs you. The last thing *you* need is a complicated personal life.

But oh, even so. Emily Dickinson had it right. The heart wants what it wants. Boy, does it want what it wants.

Time marched on, and on. Series B investing was happening, people were vying to invest. LookBook's cash position swelled; so did the board. Some were partners, and some were critics, but she had a *board*! She had a *company*! She had *money*! By the time Juliana was ready to think about taking LookBook public, she'd been making a good salary for seven years. Market standard, this was called. Can you imagine what market standard felt like to someone like Juliana? She, who had learned to live on nothing, who had no time to spend money even if she wanted to? She'd moved into a slightly bigger apartment in New York, with no roommate, and her clothes were better, obviously, but other than that she lived much the same way she always had, which was running like the wolves were chasing her.

She tried, she really did. She continued to date. She had relationships. Some lasted weeks; one lasted a few months. But LookBook always came first, and she never felt the same way with another person as she had with David.

This past winter, her financial advisor told her she needed to diversify. She had too much in cash. She should buy property now, with a small down payment, and when the IPO came, when *the windfall came*, she could pay it off.

It was a problem she never in a hundred million years thought she'd have—the problem of too much cash. She thought of telling her old Boston College roommate *whose dress she'd once had to borrow for Thanksgiving* that she had too much cash. "The money will be safer in real estate," her advisor said. "Away from the vagaries of the market. Plus, then you get to enjoy it."

She almost asked what enjoyment was, as a joke, but not really as a joke. Sure. She would put something into real estate.

"Where?" she asked him. "Where should I put something into real estate?"

He folded his hands and looked at her across his desk. He blinked from behind his big brown glasses and said, "That's up to you. Where have you always wanted to own a home?"

She still googled Buchanan Enterprises. She knew that Brice Buchanan had bought land on Block Island, and also a home that had undergone extensive renovations. She'd come across an interior design blog with a feature on the house; she knew from this that David and Taylor would become summer residents. She'd read everything she could about the island. Seven miles long and three miles wide. Shaped like a pork chop. Three hundred and sixty-five freshwater ponds, one for every day of the year. Migratory songbirds traveled there, and bachelorette parties traveled there, and a reclusive Hollywood actor owned a home there.

"Block Island," she told her advisor. "I loved it when I used to go there as a kid." This, of course, wasn't true. It wasn't a bad idea, she went on, to have a home base where she could throw parties to put more eyes on LookBook ahead of a potential IPO, to get the social influencers more involved. To get people talking. When you raise the profile you raise the value.

"Makes sense," agreed her advisor. "And once the IPO goes through, the sky is the limit."

Next steps. Find a Realtor. Buy a house. Sign the papers. Hire a decorator. Throw a party, then another, then another, to introduce yourself to the island, to promote the brand, to raise excitement before the IPO. A wise investment will pay back in spades.

Lots of people came to Juliana's parties. It was a small island, and when word got around, people showed up: locals, and social media influencers from the mainland, and rich people whose boats were docked for the night or the weekend at Payne's or Champlin's. But David Buchanan didn't come, and he didn't come, and he didn't come, until one night she heard about the golfer Jack Baker, who not only knew David Buchanan but who was living with him. *Living with him!* Recovering from an Achilles injury, stepping off the Tour, staying with his old college friend, because, why not? They had plenty of room.

And it got even better. The young woman in the small cottage next door, the one she could send her assistant, Allison, over to invite to a party? That was David's cousin.

JULIANA

Juliana gets a text from an unknown number at eleven-thirty on the third Monday in August. The text says: PLEASE MEET ME AT THE BOTTOM OF MOHEGAN STEPS. 4 P.M.

Who is the text from? Someone who wants to murder her for all of the money she doesn't yet have? (But the text says "please"—would a murderer be so polite?)

She puts Allison to work tracing the number. Allison has all sorts of powers that border on the magical—she can get a caterer who claimed to be committed elsewhere to make seventy-five mini lobster rolls; she can procure tickets to sold-out Broadway musicals. Seven minutes after receiving the assignment Allison taps on Juliana's office door and says, "That number belongs to Taylor Buchanan."

Taylor Buchanan.

Taylor Buchanan wants to meet Juliana.

Deep breath.

(Why wouldn't Taylor identify herself outright? What kind of game is she playing?)

At the bottom of Mohegan Steps.

Better than the top, if Juliana is looking for a silver lining.

Juliana is restless for the next three and a half hours. She makes a couple of phone calls and answers some emails. She drinks a coffee, then wishes she hadn't; the coffee makes her jumpy. She works on the board deck for the next meeting. She can't concentrate. She sits out on the dock for a little while. She tries to rest in one of the chaise lounges, but she can't stay still. It starts to rain; she goes back inside; it stops raining.

The weather forecast is all over the place: rain, sun, chance of a thunderstorm later. After the rain, the sun comes out, and with it the humidity. Finally, finally, it's almost time to drive to Mohegan Steps. She leaves earlier than she needs to. She takes the long way around, to chew up some extra time, but also to avoid the crowds in town.

Out by the airport, Center Road to Lakeside, past the Painted Rock, down Mohegan Trail. She arrives at 3:50. There are no other cars in the parking lot, so she takes a deep breath and tries to relax. She's there before Taylor. And there's that; at least she has first arrival advantage.

Three fifty-five. She starts to play psych-up music, then stops. She isn't sure what she's psyching herself up for.

Three fifty-six.

She gets out of the car.

She takes the steps down as quickly as she can, wondering if the exercise might help her shake her nerves. But with the rapid pace and the late afternoon August humidity she's breathing too hard when she gets to the bottom. She doesn't like that; it makes her look weak. She tries to slow her breathing the way a meditation instructor once taught her. She thinks more about that meditation teacher, puts two fingers of her right hand on her forehead, and tries to open her third eye chakra. She can't tell if it's open or not. (How do people tell? Are third eyes for real?)

Just. Keep. Moving.

She opens her actual two eyes.

She takes in the scene: the enormous, looming clay cliffs, the water crashing against the rocks, the wind turbines in the distance, gamely turning, turning. Okay, she can take a moment now, gather her thoughts, calm her heartbeat and maybe even pre—

"Hello, Juliana."

"Jesus *Christ*." Talk about jumping out of your skin. Taylor has appeared literally *out of nowhere*. Juliana had taken her eyes off the steps for only a minute; there wouldn't have been enough time for Taylor to descend. She must have been there already. "Holy shit, you scared me."

"I didn't mean to." Taylor smiles thinly at Juliana. "I try to be six minutes early to every meeting." Her eyes are inscrutable. No sunglasses, which is surprising, and somehow badass. "I find it puts the other person on their back foot."

I'll say, thinks Juliana. "Not me," she says untruthfully. "I just didn't see any other cars—"

"I didn't drive," says Taylor, offering no further explanation. Had she gotten dropped off? Had she cycled? No, she's wearing a pretty sundress, not cycling clothes. Juliana can't imagine Taylor cycling anyway. She supposes Taylor could have dropped from a hovering helicopter, rappelled down the clay cliffs like a superhero. "Now let's get to business. Shall we?" Taylor gestures to one of the wide flat rocks along the beach, against which, Juliana now sees, a straw bag is reclining. What's in the bag? (A weapon?)

"Business?"

"So to speak," says Taylor. "We're certainly not getting down to pleasure."

Juliana kicks off her shoes, holds them in one hand, and follows Taylor to the rock. Taylor takes a minute to remove a blanket from the straw bag and toss it over the rock. Then she takes another minute smoothing out the blanket.

Taylor sits first, and Juliana chooses a spot on the rock as far away as she can get. In the light of the late afternoon sun, Taylor's hair, loose around her face, seems to be shimmering. She really does have beautiful hair. Taylor reaches for the straw bag and Juliana startles.

"Relax," says Taylor. "I'm not going to kill you." Mind reader, thinks Juliana. Almost as an afterthought Taylor adds, "Yet."

Juliana laughs uncertainly. She forces herself to maintain her composure; she doesn't let the laugh become maniacal. She's been in high-pressure situations how many times over the past decade? Too many to count. She can get through this one. Just keep moving.

"Kidding!" says Taylor. "I'm definitely mostly kidding. The only kind of bullet I have is right here." From the bag she draws out a bottle of Bulleit Bourbon and two rocks glasses. "I figure if we're going to handle this like a couple of men then we should really handle it like a couple of men. I figured I'd go all *Yellowstone* on you." Juliana doesn't know what it means to "go all *Yellowstone* on you" (this is a TV reference, but who has time for shows?), and as she's wondering, Taylor pours a healthy amount into each glass—more hand than finger—and passes one to Juliana. Taylor's grip is steady: no wobbles, no spills. "Drink," she says.

"Oh, I don't really want—"

"*Drink,*" says Taylor again. Juliana drinks, and as the bourbon goes down, smooth, warm, she thinks, What is happening now? What is *going* to happen? "It's good, right?"

Juliana nods; *Yes, it's good.*

"I know what you did," says Taylor. No more preamble. She fixes Juliana with an unwavering gaze.

Like the businesswoman she is, Juliana counters. "I know what *you* did," she says to Taylor. "I know what you've been doing."

Taylor looks at her quizzically: "I'm sorry?"

"With that guy who works for your dad—"

"Ohhhh," says Taylor. "Oh." She tosses her head back and laughs so long and so hard that the laugh seems to travel along the beach, bouncing here and there atop the rocks before heading out to sea.

"Oh, *Henry*. Okay, let's get a couple of things straight. First of all, he works for me, not my dad. Second, I'm not talking about you and David. We'll get to that, of course, that's part of this conversation, and it's not like that's some fucking secret anymore, obviously, but that's not what I'm leading with."

"What are you leading with?" whispers Juliana.

"I know how you got the money to start your business."

Oh, no. Not that. Notthatnotthatnotthat. Not Serena. Not Mrs. Sanchez. Not *George*.

Juliana drains her glass and holds it out to Taylor. "May I have another, please?"

"Of course," says Taylor, nice as can be. Juliana has to fight the urge to rip the bottle out of her hands and dump as much as she can directly down her throat. She satisfies herself with what Taylor pours her, and she listens as Taylor begins to talk. Taylor tells Juliana about a party she and David threw not long ago. "You weren't on the guest list. I wasn't crazy about your manners last time you were at our house. No offense."

"None taken."

"One person who was there," says Taylor, "was Shelly Salazar."

Juliana's stomach drops, and her hands feel like they're going to float away from her body. Shelly, who's been calling her Jade all summer. Shelly, who can't hold her liquor.

"Up until this party we hadn't talked socially that much. She's a hoot!"

No, thinks Juliana. "She is," she says.

"We got to talking about all sorts of things, like where we lived in our twenties, and who we might know in common. Shelly knew someone from my class at Yale. Everyone knows someone who went to Yale, you know."

"Sure," says Juliana. On the outside, she's tough as nails. Inside, she's shriveling.

"So while we were talking about college it was an easy segue to get to you. Shelly had mentioned that she was friends with your freshman-year roommate? Someone named Ann Marie?"

Juliana squeezes her eyes shut, holds her breath. When she releases the breath she says, "Mary Ann."

"Right. Sorry. Anyway, Shelly said, 'She wasn't Juliana George then. She was . . .'" Taylor pauses. Juliana's eyes fly open and she doesn't meet Taylor's gaze. Above them a lone gull squawks; the waves crash; far down the beach to the right, two figures are walking. To the left, nobody. Take me away, thinks Juliana. Take me away from here. "Juliana." Taylor's voice is sharp. "I feel like you're not giving me your full attention."

Juliana fixes her eyes back on Taylor. Taylor says, "Shelly said, 'She wasn't Juliana George then. She was Jade Gordon.' I remembered that she'd called you Jade at dinner, right? But then you made it into a joke . . . what was that joke, Jade? Something about jewelry?"

"Stop," says Juliana. She gets up from the rock and stands facing Taylor. "Just *stop*. Stop drawing it out. Just skip to the end."

"I don't want to skip to the end, though. It's such a good story! These are the kinds of stories the press loves, right? I read your *Forbes* 30 Under 30 profile. *Forbes* couldn't get enough of your Cinderella story. A young woman pulling herself up by her bootstraps, from what was it, Lowell?"

Cinderella married a prince and lived happily ever after; Cinderella did not start a company. "Lawrence."

"Lawrence! Yes. A young woman from Lawrence, pulling herself up by her bootstraps, using nothing but her smarts and her ingenuity . . . the American Dream, alive and well, right here in front of me! Amazing, Juliana. Really impressive. From scholarship student to business owner. But there was this question of the name change, you know? I got a little curious. I put some of my people in the New York office on the research. People in New York are *very good* at research, you know."

"I know," says Juliana sharply. "I have people in New York too."

Taylor nods. "I bet you do. *Any*who. Something else that's interesting is how much information is out there that's public record. Most people don't know that, you know. Most people don't know that all you have to do is ask for public information. Ask and ye shall receive, am I right?" Juliana says nothing. "Juliana? Am I right?"

"Yes." She won't bend; she won't say more than she needs to. She's made it through 100 percent of her bad days.

"So. The first thing I did was have my people in New York fact-check this name change thing." She offers Juliana a conspiratorial smile. "I mean, Shelly is good entertainment, I'm sure you know that, having gone to college with her. I can only imagine what she was like back in those days. Part of me was wondering if she'd make something like that up, just for fun. She had a lot of those blueberry cocktails at my house." She looks expectantly at Juliana.

"I bet she did," says Juliana.

"So off they skipped to the courthouse, my people, to confirm the date of the name change. December 2014. After a little more digging, they learned that a person named Jade Gordon had been named in a will contestation case in October 2014, regarding the will of a man named George Halsey. I can see by your face that you know what will I'm talking about."

Juliana chokes out a single, gutting word: "Yes."

"And, guess what? Once that will contestation was filed, all of that was a matter of public record too! The children, talking about how you'd swindled their father out of five hundred thousand dollars. The concierge from the old man's building answering questions about when and how often you visited him. The affidavit from the housekeeper detailing her observation of your relationship *with an old man*. Eighty, was it?"

"He was seventy-nine," says Juliana.

Taylor hoots. "Ohhh! Okay, Anna Nicole Smith. That's much better. And you were . . . twenty-one?"

"Twenty-two."

"Ah. Much *much* better. So you were twenty-two, and you met an old, rich man, and you *dated* him, and conveniently he died and left you money, and now you're about to become a multimillionaire. Oh, I know about the IPO rumors too, by the way. I know a lot."

"It wasn't like that," says Juliana. "It wasn't like what you're saying. He was an advisor. He was a sounding board. I talked out my ideas with him. He gave me feedback."

"I *bet* he gave you feedback," says Taylor. She snorts. "If 'feedback'"—she makes air quotes with two fingers on each hand—"is what we're calling it these days."

"There was never sex involved!"

"I wasn't born yesterday, Juliana. There's *always* sex involved when there's money like that involved. He didn't leave you five hundred thousand for like bringing him vanilla wafers and milk. It's all over the court documents. His daughter walked in on you kissing him."

"I wasn't kissing him," says Juliana. "Not like you think."

"You were a swindler, Juliana."

"I was a *friend*."

Taylor snorts. "Escort."

"Companion."

"So you never slept with him."

"That's none of your business."

"That's a yes."

"That's an *It's none of your business*. That's twice now. Do you want me to say it a third time?" Juliana's heart is beating rapidly but she ignores it and crosses her arms and fixes Taylor with a death stare. The fact that anyone is talking this way about George, *her* George, with his dapper little hats and his habit of standing up from a table at a restaurant if she had to go to the bathroom—and also the fact that he never called it *the bathroom,* he called it *the powder room*—

makes her feel sick to her stomach. George, who had an elevator that opened right into his living room. George, whose children rarely called, never visited, until he died, and then they couldn't stay away.

"It was five hundred thousand dollars. He left it to me, fair and square. I didn't ask for it. It was a gift. He had millions. It wasn't so much to him. It was a drop in the bucket. It was an investment in me, in LookBook."

"It was enough that his children contested the will."

"Let me tell you something. His children are assholes."

"Let me tell *you* something, Juliana. I've been around rich people my entire life. Rich people don't get rich by thinking of five hundred thousand dollars as a drop in the bucket, no matter how much they have. There's a reason he left you that money, and it's all in those court papers."

"He believed in me. It's as simple as that. People are allowed to leave money to whomever they want. There's nothing illegal about that. The contestation of the will didn't make it past pretrial."

"All of that may be true," says Taylor. "Or none of it may be true. But here's the thing. Here's the dirty little secret. It doesn't matter if it's true or not. *It only matters what it looks like.* You're—how many weeks from your IPO?"

"Nine."

"Nine." Taylor smiles. "So it's a delicate time. The business press is all over you. The board is up your ass, am I right?"

Juliana winces at the crudeness of the description; a nicer way to put it would be that the board *is watching things closely.* But yes, it's true.

"Especially that one guy, let me think, the lead director, right? Daniel Scott?"

"How do you know who's on my board? The company isn't public yet."

"Crunchbase," Taylor says. "You know Crunchbase, right?"

Of course Juliana knows Crunchbase.

"It's amazing what you can find out there. Anyway. Scott especially. I did some reading on him. Politically conservative. Socially conservative. A whiff of impropriety would really turn him off, wouldn't it? Like, if it got out that the company's founder got her seed money by sleeping with some dying old man . . ."

"No," says Juliana.

"Yes!" says Taylor. "This stuff happens all the time. I mean, maybe not *this* specific situation. But I can see it. I can practically write the press release from the board. *We lost confidence in our founder. We're canceling our IPO and we're reevaluating our options.* Something like that. Then, the next thing you know, you're out. They bring in another CEO. You still own—what?"

"Thirty percent."

"Thirty percent. Okay. Not bad. But that thirty percent is just paper. And what if they put off the IPO for a year? Now you've got no job, so you've got no paycheck. I'm not sure what you put down on your house here, but it wouldn't take me long to find out. I'm guessing you're mortgaged to the hilt. The decorating, all those parties . . . I'm speculating here, Juliana. Or Jade. Or whoever you are. Maybe you stretched yourself a little thin this summer, knowing you had a big payday coming. You wouldn't be the first founder who spent money before they had it."

This time Juliana keeps her face impassive, neither confirming nor denying. Taylor has hit the nail exactly, precisely, on the head.

"And what do you do with the rest of your life? You can't get another job at the CEO level. Who wants to hire a leader who was removed from her own company? You can't get a job at a lower level, because now you're overqualified. After all, you've been a CEO. You founded your own company!"

Juliana will give Taylor credit for being sharp.

Taylor the Mind Reader leaps on Juliana's next thought before she even has time to formulate it. "And what's the name of your foundation? I'm sorry, I can't remember. Keeping so many things in my head, you know."

"Girl/Power."

"Right. Girl/Power. Decent name. And it does what again?"

Juliana has said this so many times it comes out like memorized lines of poetry in a high school English class. "We empower lower-income first-generation female college students to become business entrepreneurs."

"I love that," says Taylor. "I really do."

"Thank you," says Juliana, before she can catch herself. "We've done a lot of amaz—"

Taylor cuts her off. "But what happens to the foundation when it comes out that *this particular* lower-income female entrepreneur slept her way to the seed money?"

"I didn't—"

"I mean, you did. But. Again, it doesn't matter what you did or didn't do. It matters what the perception of what you did is. There goes the reputation of your foundation. There go the donations. There go the girls you want to help. I guess they'll have to figure things out on their own."

That's it. Juliana stands and walks away from Taylor, parallel to the water's edge, picking out spots where her feet can find smooth sand between the rocks. The waves come in choppily. Everything feels like it's on fire: her heart, her brain, her hands and feet. The sky over the wind turbines has grown dark, but above the beach it's still clear. The air is heavy—portentous.

She hears Taylor calling her name and she turns. "No," she says, as Taylor moves closer. "No. You can't do this. You can't take everything away from me."

"Well, *you*," says Taylor, "can't take everything away from me."

"You just work for your dad. I created something out of nothing.

I've been fighting every day since I was seven years old. You don't understand."

"Oh, I understand," says Taylor. "I understand perfectly. I understand that it's hard to be a woman in a man's world. Believe me, I understand that. I can see where it might have been hard to get the funding you needed to start your business, a girl like Jade Gordon, no connections, not the slightest idea about how to get the attention of the VCs. No income while you got your business off the ground."

"No rich daddy to lean on," spits Juliana. "You might have done the same thing."

"Ho, no. No. I wouldn't have prostituted myself."

"I didn't *prostitute myself.*" But Taylor's right: it's the perception that matters as much as the reality. She wants to pick up one of the rocks by her feet and hurl it at Taylor's head. "You don't know what you would have done if you had to."

"I know where I would have drawn the line."

The dark clouds are moving closer now, racing across the sky. "Maybe you wouldn't have done what I did as *you*, Taylor. But you have no idea what you would done as me. You don't know what you would do as someone who has to work for everything."

"Whoa, easy there, girlfriend," says Taylor. Juliana wonders if Taylor would have the strength to push her into the water, hold her head down until she couldn't breathe. The water is cold on this side of the island, and Taylor is tough as nails. There's real vitriol in Taylor's voice when she says, "You think I don't work? You think my father just hands me everything for free?" She leans in so close that Juliana can smell the bourbon on her breath.

Juliana tries to pull herself straighter but she's no match for Taylor's height. You can teach a lot of things, and if it can be taught Juliana has learned it, but you can't teach tall. If anything happens to her, will anybody know? Allison would remember that Juliana had asked her to trace a number, and she would remember whose number it was. But Juliana hadn't told Allison when she was leaving or where she was going. She could trace the location on her phone—but not if Taylor destroys her phone.

"I think he hands you a lot," she says.

"I've got news for you. He doesn't."

Juliana, who can count on the fingers of one hand the times she's cried in front of another person, can hold it in no longer. She starts to cry. "I worked so hard for what I have."

Taylor's eyes blaze. *"I worked for my shit too!* I work harder than most people you know. I work and I work and I work. People think I'm putting myself first, but you know what? I was bred to put the business first, and that's what I do. I was taught loyalty before I was taught math." Now she actually looks like *she's* going to cry. Does Taylor cry? "And guess what, as a result my husband is the one my daughter calls for in the middle of the night." She is. She's *crying.* Juliana watches, amazed, as Taylor swipes at the tears that have escaped. "And that fucking *sucks,* Juliana, but there's nothing I can do about it, because that road got paved years and years ago. I was left without any choices."

Juliana stares at her.

"You think my dad's money means freedom, but it doesn't. It's a trap," Taylor goes on.

Juliana snorts. Does Taylor honestly believe this? "I'm sorry," she says. *"Wealth* is a trap? Try poverty. Poverty is a real trap." Taylor has been born above the hot struggles of the poor. And above them, she will remain, no matter what happens. *No matter what happens.* "And you got a head start."

More tears have leaked out, and Taylor swipes at those too. "And that's my fault, right? I guess I personally owe you something because I grew up with money and you didn't?"

"Well, no, but—" (But yes. Sort of.)

"I'm sorry. But that's not how the world works."

"It should," spits Juliana.

"Unfortunately, changing the way the world works is above my pay grade." Taylor stops crying—Juliana can almost see her will herself to do that, to tell the tears, *That's enough. Go back where you came from.* She sets her lips together. The wind is lifting her hair but instead of doing anything rude with it, it settles it back down. Taylor's hair still looks perfect. Everything about Taylor looks perfect. "Skip right to the end, is that what you wanted to do? Well, we're here now. We're at the end."

"What happens at the end?"

"What happens is, you make a choice. Choice number one: You keep everything you worked for, your company, your reputation. Your IPO goes forward. You get all that money you've been dreaming about. And I don't say anything to anyone about what I found out."

"What's choice number two?"

"Choice number two is I tell everyone, and you lose everything."

"So, ah, why would I not choose number one?"

"Because number one has a condition."

Juliana's heartbeat picks up. The spot behind her right knee begins to pulse. "Which is what?"

"Which is, you leave Block Island. You don't talk to David anymore. Like not at all. No Instagram DMs, no secret texts, no carrier pigeons. Nothing. Ever. After we finish here, you contact a Realtor, and you put your house on the market, at a price I will dictate. I have a feeling you're going to find a buyer pretty quickly."

Juliana nods slowly and says, "I think I know where I'm going to find that buyer."

"Damn straight you know," says Taylor. "Damn straight."

"I love my house."

"I love my husband."

"No, you *don't*," says Juliana. "No, you don't."

"Careful," said Taylor. "Careful. You don't know what you don't know about someone else's marriage. You don't know what goes on."

"But you—"

Taylor speaks over her. "Trust me. You don't know. Which do you love more, my husband or your business?"

Juliana blinks at Taylor—this must be a rhetorical question, right?

Right?

But, no . . . Taylor's eyes are wide and expectant. She's waiting. She folds her arms and doesn't let her gaze leave Juliana's; she looks like someone who could wait all day. Juliana thinks back to her younger self, to all the versions of her younger self. The girl in that dirty apartment in Lawrence, always looking for a way out. The foster kid, shuttled from place to place. The scholarship student at Boston College, often alone, but not really lonely, because she always had her ideas. She always had her focus. The girl who thought of LookBook. It really was like a light bulb turning on in her brain, a single, beautiful idea, pure and ready. The building of it, the working, always working, always striving and climbing. The grind, and the joy. Just keep moving, the past so dark but the future so bright.

"Which one, Juliana?" prompts Taylor. "I don't have all day."

Then she thinks about David, and what she's yearned for since meeting him, and what it's been like to be with him this summer. She'll never connect on that level with anyone in her life. She knows that. You don't get that chance twice; a lot of people would give up everything for it.

But a lot of people would give up everything for their brainchild too—Juliana already has. She's given a whole decade of her life, and her energy, and her heart. She has hundreds of people counting on her.

"My business," Juliana says finally. "I've given all of me to my business. If I lose it, I'll have nothing."

"I thought so," says Taylor. "So that's settled, then." She looks at her watch and says, "Well, that all went faster than I expected. I think I'm going to make it back to the building site after all." She folds up the blanket and puts it into the straw bag, then picks up the rocks glasses and packs them into the bag. "I'd give you a card, but you don't need to worry about getting in touch with me. I'll have my office get in touch with you, once your house is listed."

Without another word Taylor turns and picks her way easily back over the sand. The rocks between the beach and the sand are treacherous, they look almost like an intentional barrier, but Taylor seems to take these with no problem too, and Juliana remembers that she read somewhere that Taylor had been a track athlete—a hurdler—and she retains a hurdler's grace and agility.

The figures on the beach are gone; it's only Juliana, the waves, the rocks, and the vast clay cliffs rising above her. Long ago, she learned earlier in the summer, the Niantic and the Mohegan battled over supremacy of the island, until the native Niantic forced the invading Mohegan over the cliffs to their death. This was five centuries ago, and here humans still are, battling, struggling, seeking.

Nothing, it seems, is going to change that. Alone on the beach Juliana turns toward the water and unleashes the most primal of all screams. She screams and screams until she can feel her face turning red, her throat growing sore, the small vein in her temple pulsing. She screams until she is all screamed out; until there's nothing left inside.

NICOLA

Juliana texts Nicola at 10:02 P.M. Monday night, asking if she'll come over. Nicola thinks she means the next day, and she answers that she'll be home after work. Juliana replies: Now? With this emoji: 🙏.

Nicola is ready for bed, with a mug of tea steeping on her night table, like a proper grandmother. She grumbles a little, and very quietly, as she changes from her pajamas back into shorts and a sweatshirt. She crosses the lawn between her cottage and Juliana's house, heading for the back door, the way she has gotten used to doing, when she hears Juliana calling her from the dock.

"Check out this moon," says Juliana dreamily once Nicola has made her way down the dock. "It's a seasonal blue moon, did you know that?"

Nicola peers up at the sky. The moon is certainly full, almost obnoxiously so. It makes her think of Eben Horton's floats; she feels as though she could reach up and pluck it right out of the sky, check its back for a number.

Juliana is sitting at the end of the dock, the way Nicola had seen her the first night, looking out at the green light across the way, the light at the end of David's dock. Behind them the house is almost completely dark, save two circles of light Nicola can see through the glass doors and knows to be the pendants that hang above the kitchen island. Even when Nicola turns to face the water she can feel the house behind her, the great brooding hulk of it.

"Is there anyone home?" Nicola asks. "Where's Allison?"

"I gave her a few days off. We have some crazy times ahead with the IPO. I need her to recharge."

"Where'd she go?"

"She went home. To L.A."

"Ah." L.A. That tracks, thinks Nicola. Allison has a certain West Coast confidence, a way of moving through time and space that they don't cultivate in Minnesota. Something about the long winters, the endless frozen lakes, disallows that.

Next to Juliana on the dock sits a bottle of champagne and an empty flute. She's drinking from a flute, and without asking she fills the empty one and hands it to Nicola, then, before Nicola has even taken a sip, she says, "Do you want something else? I'm sorry, I didn't even ask. I can run inside if you want something different. The bar is fully stocked. We have a bunch of seltzer—"

"*No!* Geez, please don't. I don't need anything." For some reason Juliana's offer makes Nicola sad but it also irritates her. She's tired of all of it: the drinking, the desperate hostessing, the treating, the constant offering of things. It sounds like a stupid thing to complain about, because after all Juliana has been generous to her. But it's all made her *so tired.* Everything feels easier at the Institute, with the tanks and the sea creatures, and suddenly she wishes she was living with the other interns, away from this craziness. Who cares if she has a decade on some of them. She could have been like the cool aunt who poured them drinks and looked the other way when their boyfriends slept over.

"I'm not a fool, you know, Nicola," Juliana says suddenly.

Nicola is, in a word, startled. In two words, she's taken aback. "I know you're not. I never thought you were."

"I know I did some stupid things this summer—"

"Well, not stupid—" she begins, but Juliana cuts her off.

"Yes, stupid," she says sharply. "But they were my own choices. I just thought . . ."

There's such a long pause then that Nicola thinks she might have forgotten she hadn't finished the sentence, so she prompts, "Just thought what? Juliana, what is it?"

Juliana drains her flute and pours herself more. "Do you need a refill?"

"No, thank you." Nicola has only had a sip. She'd brushed her teeth before she decided to make tea, and the taste of the champagne mixed with mint made her shudder. She waits a minute to see if Juliana will pick up the train of her unfinished sentence, which is currently dragging on the ground, and when she doesn't Nicola says again, "Juliana, what is it?"

"My heart is broken,'" she says. "That's all. My heart is broken." Her voice cracks.

"Oh, honey," she says. "Juliana. What happened?"

She swipes at her eyes and clears her throat. "It's such a long story."

Nicola tries not to peek at her watch. "That's okay," she says. "I have as long as you need."

"Really?"

"Really."

"Okay. Okay, thank you." She takes a deep breath. "The first thing I should tell you is that I'm not really Juliana George."

It's true what Juliana first told Nicola. Jade Gordon never knew her father. But Jade Gordon's mother didn't die when she was thirteen. There was no *Gilmore Girls* vibe, no mother-daughter bonding. Jade's mother died when she was seven. A drug overdose. Jade doesn't remember much about her. Jade's uncle, who she was sent to live with after, was an on-and-off-again addict.

That's not right. There is no such thing as an on-and-off-again addict. There is only clearing yourself of the addiction or feeding it. Her uncle was an on-and-off-again feeder of his addiction.

Jade was nine years old when Talia came to live with them; Talia was three. She was the daughter of a girlfriend of her uncle, who also lived with them for a time. Was her uncle Talia's father? This was never clarified for Jade, but probably, yes. Because her uncle and Talia's mother were often out, Talia's care often fell to Jade. Eventually Talia's mother disappeared, yet Talia remained.

"I realize, by the way," says Juliana at this point, "that all of this sounds like a far-fetched plot for a network television drama that would never get picked up because it's too hard to believe. But this time, everything I'm saying is true. This is the real story."

In the sky, night clouds race by, covering the moon, then uncovering it once again. A small breeze comes off the water. Not enough to require a blanket, though Nicola knows there's a basket of them near the furniture, behind them.

"I don't believe you," Nicola says. "Go on. Please."

Jade didn't mind caring for Talia. In fact she loved it. She felt like Talia was a doll that had been given to her as a gift: someone to dress up and play with, someone to keep her company. She loved Talia.

Time passed. Jade turned ten and Talia turned four. Jade went to school every day and Talia went to the subsidized preschool attached to the same school. They took the bus there and back home at the end of the day, sitting together always, even though other siblings split up to sit with friends on the bus. They were not really siblings, but it felt like they were.

When they were home, Jade spent hours braiding Talia's hair, painting her tiny fingernails, reading to her. When the TV worked, which it didn't always, they watched cartoons and shows on the Disney Channel. Jade knew the Disney Channel shows were meant for kids older than Talia, but still, this is something the two girls bonded over. The kids on Disney shows typically had stable families and social structures and tiny, easily surmountable problems within those families or social structures. Neither girl could get enough of those story arcs wherein things mostly turned out okay for everyone. Jade taught Talia the few life skills she herself had learned up until that point: How to call 911 in an emergency. How to cut an apple, peel an orange, recite your address to an adult at school. How to see if someone was following you without turning around.

One night, sometime after 11 P.M., Jade was making macaroni and cheese from a box. Why were they doing this so late? The girls were home alone, and they had nobody to tell them to go to bed, nobody to feed them at a normal time. Where was the uncle? Who knows. He never told them when he was leaving, and he never said where he'd been when he came back. Jade had climbed on the counter, the way she often did, to reach a cupboard shelf high above her head. But the hinge to the cupboard door was broken, so when she opened it the whole door came off in her hand, and she fell off the counter, hitting her head on the corner on the way down.

She was fine, as it ended up. Eventually. But there was a lot of blood; even minor head wounds can bleed profusely. A *lot* of blood. Talia screamed when she saw it, then she called 911, just as Jade had taught her. Life skills!

The EMTs who came, winding themselves up the narrow staircase with the gurney, took care of the head wound first. They loaded Jade on the backboard, and then they turned their attention to the situation at hand. Two kids of those ages, alone, fending for themselves so late at night? One of them hurt, bleeding from a head wound with only a four-year-old to call for help? No. Not okay. The EMTs reported the situation at the hospital, and someone at the hospital called social services. After that things happened quickly. Jade was treated for her wound, and Jade and Talia were both removed from the care of Jade's uncle and placed in foster homes. *Separate* foster homes.

Now Nicola isn't looking at her watch anymore. She's riveted by the story, which is giving off Dickensian vibes: Juliana (Jade) as Oliver Twist or Pip, dressed in rags, holding an empty bowl out to someone.

Please, sir, may I have some more mac and cheese?

She looks up and sees again the night-shining clouds—those thin clouds high up above Earth's atmosphere. Scientists think these are created from ice crystals that form on fine dust particles from meteors, which, if you think about it, is pretty astonishing. It's rare to see them too. It feels portentous.

Between the night she hit her head and the day she left for Boston College, Jade lived in nine different foster homes. The American foster system, she told Nicola, like so many American systems, is broken.

"*Nine?*" Nicola says. "In eight years?" She thinks about the time her parents got rid of their ugly brown couch and replaced it with a new piece from the store, which was easier on the eyes but far less comfortable. Nicola and her sisters lost their *minds* over the loss of that couch. Change agents, they were not. And here was Juliana, moving from place to place, all of her things thrown in a black garbage bag.

(Nicola adds the garbage bag to the scene for dramatic effect; maybe Jade had a suitcase or a duffle, she doesn't ask.)

Nine places, Juliana confirms. The place with the cats. The one with the twin babies. The super-Christian one, the dirty one, the clean one. The really dirty one. And so on. The one where the dad sat too close on the couch during TV time. The one with no dad; the one with two dads.

In some of these homes she was welcomed; in others she was barely tolerated. In one she was the only foster kid. In another she was one of five.

Her time in the foster system was a turning point for Jade academically. Previously she'd been a careless student, sometimes doing what she needed to get by, sometimes not even that much. She was bright, and she understood the concepts being taught almost immediately, but she was that kid who was constantly not working to her full potential. Who was anyone at the school going to tell? Nobody came to her parent-teacher conferences. Nobody answered the phone if a teacher called home. Eventually, overwhelmed by how many other students they had who needed help, how many other calls there were to make, the teachers stopped calling.

In the foster homes, that all turned around. Jade's goal was to take up the smallest amount of space possible in any given situation, and to be the best version of herself she could be. She wasn't optimistic enough to think she could attract praise, but she wanted to avoid attracting negative attention. Often this meant that when other members of the family were doing whatever they were doing, Jade found a corner (not always literally a corner, but often enough, yes, a corner) and pulled out her books and her homework and got to work. By sixth grade she was winning spelling bees. By eighth, placing into algebra so that in high school she could double up math classes sophomore year and get to AP Calc by the time she was a senior. In tenth grade she began prepping for the PSAT; when she took the test her scores were high enough to net her consideration as a National Merit Scholar, which she then became.

"It was like a drug for me," Juliana tells Nicola. "Achievement. I'd get some, and all I could think about was how I was going to get my next bump."

On and on goes the story: the guidance counselor, the scholarship. The college part. The early time in New York, where Jade met George and later David. The will, the children, the affidavit, the name change, the business. The paper millions, which, in just over two months, after the IPO, will be real, actual millions, an amount of money that Nicola simply can't fathom. All of this brings Juliana around to where she started the story, with Taylor texting to meet her at the bottom of Mohegan Steps. Because Taylor, as it turned out, had excavated the land where Juliana thought she had buried the past. Taylor had brought a backhoe to the cemetery, and she was ready to bring up the bodies.

Enough of the metaphors. You get the picture.

Nicola can't remember the last time she stayed up talking and listening like this. College, probably, when sleeping until early afternoon the following day was an easy option. It was long enough ago that she's forgotten how at one crucial point fatigue overtakes you—for Nicola this happens around 1 A.M.—but if you push through, what happens is that the fatigue is replaced by a surge of energy, an exhilaration of sorts. The next day, of course, brings the real fatigue, the scratchy-eye, scratchy-skin feeling, and she knows that's what she's in for at work. But Juliana wants to talk, and Nicola has the only set of ears around. She takes a blanket after all.

"How'd she *know* all that?"

"Ohhh," said Juliana. "I left that part out. Shelly Salazar told Taylor my old name and she ran with it."

"Makes sense. She used to be a track athlete." Nicola remembers someone telling a story about that at the wedding. She can see it: the blond ponytail, the long legs and little shorts, the determined set of Taylor's mouth. She can see her arms pumping and her feet kicking up behind her. She can see her winning. (But is this the time for a joke? Probably not.)

Still visible, in the distance, is that green light at the end of Taylor and David's dock. Green for money. Green for envy. Green for *go*.

"What are you going to do?" she asks.

"I don't have a choice. Taylor has me. I can't have anything happen right now that would make the investment bank or the board skittish. I can't risk my business."

"No," Nicola agrees, even though really, what she knows about investment banks and boards and IPOs would fit on a baby's pinky nail. "No, you don't want to make anyone skittish." She waits some more and then she says, "Still. Your heart must be breaking."

"You have no idea."

Nicola is offended by this at first—who is Juliana to say if she's ever had a broken heart?—until she keeps talking. "You have no idea, Nicola, what it's like to be loved by only two people in your life, and only briefly, and not to have them. George loved me, and David loves me. That's it, for my whole life. That's not how it's been for you." She pauses, and Nicola knows Juliana has more to say, so she doesn't fill in the pause. "I can tell how many different people love you. People move differently in the world when they're loved by a lot of people. You have parents, friends, cousins, Jack Baker—"

"*Not* Jack Baker," Nicola breaks in. "That wasn't love." Nicola hates Jack Baker so much right then. She hates his breezy, athletic, careless way of moving, and she hates the way he made her pay for five cocktails when she could barely afford one, and especially, *especially* she hates the way she's still so attracted to him that if he were to show up right now and hold out his hand and walk her across the grass to her cottage she'd probably go with him. "That was just a stupid fling," she says.

(She consoles herself with the thought that if her heart is big enough to hold all that hate for Jack, it's big enough to hold plenty of love too. Maybe not all of it right now. But in the future, for someone else.)

"Fair enough. Okay. But lots of others. You just . . . well, you have no idea. That's one thing I love about David, you know. All those family traditions and values, all that warmth and love. It just oozes out of both of you. You don't know how foreign that is to me, how *exotic*."

Nicola doesn't know what to say. Juliana is exactly right. Nicola has been loved unconditionally by her immediate family, by David and his family, by too many friends to list at the moment. By Zachary, at one time. She's given that same love back to all of those people without thinking twice about it. It was easy, because the supply was replenishable.

"I mean, if you look at where you started, and where you are now . . ." Nicola gestures back toward the giant dark house behind them, then to Juliana, the girl reaching for the mac and cheese in that Lawrence two-family. "You've made it. You've made the quintessential American leap, from one social class to another. There are countries all over the world where that's not an option. There are so many people in *this* country for whom that's not an option."

Juliana is silent for so long that Nicola wonders if she's heard her. She pulls the blanket tight around her, and she waits, and finally Juliana speaks.

"There is no American Dream," she says.

"Oh, come on now," says Nicola. "That's like telling a six-year-old that there's no Santa Claus."

"You know there isn't one of those either, right?" They're both staring straight ahead, and it's pretty dark still. Then Juliana's voice turns serious. "I always thought it's terrible that as a group, as a *society*, we let children believe in this thing knowing that one day they'll find out that they've been tricked."

"Do you feel like *you've* been tricked?"

"About Santa Claus?"

"No. I mean, do you feel like you've been tricked about the American Dream?"

"Not tricked, exactly. It's more that . . . I can't figure out how to say this the right way. Hang on, let me think about it." Nicola hears Juliana inhale, exhale, keeping her eyes fixed on the green light. "It's more that they don't tell you that someone has to be a bridge between classes. You can't skip that step—you can't go right from one class to another and be comfortable there."

Nicola sits with this for a second.

"The money is so confusing," Juliana adds.

"What's confusing about it?"

Juliana lets out a puff of air—more than a breath, but not quite a sigh. "I don't know what to do with it. I don't know what's the right way to spend it, or not spend it. I don't have a healthy relationship with it. So I buy this house and throw these parties. But I throw them for the brand, not for myself. I don't even like parties that much." She shakes her head. "I can't find the middle ground—I can't just enjoy it, like a normal person who grew up around it would be able to. Like Taylor can. I either throw it around, or I hoard it . . . when I don't spend it, I feel guilty. And when I do spend it, I feel guilty."

"So you're the bridge?"

"I'm the bridge. I'm *a* bridge. No matter how successful this IPO is, or what I accomplish, or how many whatever-under-whatever lists I'm on, I can only ever be the bridge. I'll never be the one who walks over it." She pauses. "At least I helped Talia. Besides my foundation, that's the thing I did that I'm most proud of. She works for me now. She runs the New York office. She's amazing—she works so hard. She has shares, and I hope this IPO makes her really fucking rich. But she won't know what to do with it either. She'll be a bridge too."

Nicola thinks hard about this, trying to understand. "And who's going to walk on your backs?"

"Our kids."

This is the first time Nicola has heard Juliana mention children. She'd assumed that she didn't want them—that she'd find child-rearing incompatible with her career. Which isn't fair of her, because a person of Juliana's means can afford to rear children in any way she wants, buying either the time to do it herself or the people to do it for her. "Do you *want* kids?"

"I don't know."

"Maybe you could start with a dog," Nicola suggests. "A little rescue. Then you can get one of those bumper stickers that says something like *Adopt Don't Shop* or *My Dog Thinks I Rescued Him but Really He Rescued Me.*" She's trying to lighten the mood, and she waits to see if it takes.

Juliana snorts. "I've never seen that second one."

"It's a good one."

Nicola feels a shift in the air. It's the first time she's sensed that they're turning a corner toward fall—there's momentarily a briskness, a hint of what is to come. Then the briskness disappears and the air feels just as it has all night: a little heavy, very August-y. This is the kind of night when they would have caught fireflies as kids. Nicola doesn't know if there were ever fireflies on Block Island but she knows they're disappearing from many of their native habitats, victims of climate shifts and light pollution. Another vestige of childhood gone.

Then something happens. As the two of them sit there, both training their eyes across the water, the green light at the end of David's dock goes out. They both start, as though the light's disappearance had been accompanied by a loud noise. Nicola waits to see if Juliana will say something, acknowledge it in some way. Finally, after a yawning pause, she does.

She says, "Well. I guess that's that."

And before Nicola can stop her, she stands at the very edge of the dock, and she jumps off.

———————

Lou: There's three kinds of money on this island. Old money, new money, and no money.

Kelsey: No offense, Lou, but that is *such* a Boomer thing to say.

Evan: I heard Buchanan Enterprises is abandoning plans for the hotel altogether.

Betsy: They still own a home here, so I'm not betting on that. And they bought that big house out by Great Salt. The one with all the parties.

Lou: Are we going to talk more about what happened the week after that party at Taylor Buchanan's?

Kelsey: Do we have to?

Evan: I mean, yeah. Isn't that what we're here to talk about?

Kelsey: Even this long after, I can't shake the image. I've seen dead bodies before, obviously. But a body that's been in the water for hours? That's a whole different story.

SHELLY

Shelly's in the mood for a cocktail. Bikini under her dress, a spring in her step. Why not? To be fair, it's only four-thirty, and it's only Monday. But there are just two Mondays left in August, and then there's Labor Day, and then life around the island will start to slow down, and, who knows, maybe a Monday cocktail won't even be a possibility for much longer. Gather ye rosebuds and all of that.

Something she loves about Poor People's Pub is that no matter how hot and bright the day it's always cool and dark inside, just as a bar should be. Today there was rain, then sun—it's hot now, and Shelly is thirsty.

"Mudslide, please," she says as she slides onto a barstool. She smiles outrageously at the bartender—he's younger than Shelly, but not illegally so—and tries not to take it to heart when he doesn't give her much of a smile back. He's busy.

She wonders if Jack Baker might join her. Why not?

It can't hurt to ask.

She texts him.

Her Mudslide arrives, and she sucks down a third of it right away. Man oh man, whoever invented the Mudslide deserves a prize of some sort. What's the equivalent of a Nobel Prize for cocktails?

Shelly should invent it, and assign herself the job of publicizing it. She would slay that job.

Still no answer from Jack. She texts him again. Should she call him?

She probably shouldn't.

But she does.

No answer.

The past sneaks in, as it has a wicked tendency to do. Many summers ago Shelly sat right at this very bar and had a drink with Anthony Puckett, the local writer who is the reason she came to the island in the first place. She'd been chasing a PR opportunity, trying to get Anthony and his father photographed by Annie Leibovitz. Never panned out, then the father died, and obviously after that it was too late. But, hey, Shelly found herself a new home. There had been an older man in Manhattan at that time, and Shelly was in the process of leaving him. What better way to leave someone than to move yourself to an island?

She orders a second Mudslide and checks her phone again. Jack Baker owes her nothing—not a call back, not a text. Intellectually, she knows this. She knows that in their relationship she was the pursuer, not the pursued. She also knows that calling whatever went on between them a "relationship" is a fairly generous term.

She's known all summer that he was also seeing Juliana's neighbor Nicola, who is pretty in a fresh, unassuming way, which is exactly the opposite of the way Shelly is pretty. Shelly is pretty in a processed, Instagram-ready way. She can't settle on a hair color. She has eyelash extensions—the longer the better—and henna brows. If she didn't tan so well naturally (thank god she does) that would be fake too, and as the winter approaches certainly it will be. She can't stand the way she looks with no color. But even acknowledging this, and even somewhat liking Nicola, she can't get her mind off Jack. What if he's The One? If he's The One for Shelly but not The One for

Nicola (and, seriously, there's almost no way he's really into someone who spends her days with her hands in a fish tank)? Thus Shelly has a right—nay, a *duty!*—to wrench him away from Nicola.

Sure, it would be better if the act were less forceful than *wrenching*, but.

Shelly could call someone else, but who? Juliana? Taylor? One of her local island friends? (She does have them, though this summer she's been distracted with her work for Buchanan, and for Juliana, and of course with Jack.) On a Monday, people are probably working. She feels a little bad—she does! She really does!—that she told Taylor about Juliana's name having been Jade in college at the party over the weekend. It just slipped out while she was drinking. But Taylor had said she could keep a secret, hadn't she? Surely she's not going to say anything. Shelly doesn't even know why it matters, but it seems important to Jade that nobody find out.

Oops, Juliana.

I Don't Like Mondays by The Boomtown Rats is playing. Shelly's brother used to play this song.

"Sweet sixteen, ain't that peachy keen?" sings the bartender under his breath as he racks dirty glasses.

"You know this song is about a suicide, right?" Shelly tells him. *This* gets his attention. He looks up, startled. Good.

"Whoa. Mood shift. I thought it was about, like, not liking Mondays."

"Well, it's not," says Shelly. Her voice sounds more shrill than she means it to.

The bartender tells another customer he has to change the keg on the Captain's Daughter Double IPA. (This beer, Shelly has heard, is so strong that there are some places that won't serve a customer more than two.)

When he comes back, she decides, she'll have one more Mudslide. Just one. They're on the smaller side, after all.

"Can I have another, please?" She taps the edge of her glass with a turquoise nail. (These too are completely unnatural: acrylics. Nicola's are cut as short as they go, probably so she doesn't get like crab poop caught in them. Do crabs poop? There's so much about the world Shelly still doesn't know.)

The bartender looks at her carefully. Okay, has he finally noticed that she's *pretty*?

"You driving?"

She sighs. Is Shelly losing her touch?

Did Shelly ever *have* a touch?

"No," she says untruthfully—her car is parked across the street. "I'd like one more, please, and then I'm going to walk to another establishment."

Shelly's college boyfriend, a lacrosse player from Maryland named Ryan Griffin, broke up with her at the beginning of the season senior year, fourteen months into their relationship. It was his last year of college lacrosse, and he wanted to give it his all. No distractions.

"Fair enough," said Shelly, playing it cool. Inside, though, she was dying. (She was a *distraction*? This whole time, she had considered herself an *asset*.) "I totally get it."

"I'm impressed by how you're handling this," said Ryan. He gave her a friendly arm tap that had a definite guys-in-the-locker-room vibe. "I'll be honest, it's not what I was predicting."

When he was leaving she couldn't resist, though. She grabbed his sleeve and pulled him back. "But we had fun, right?" She could hear the note of pleading in her voice and she hated herself for it.

"Sure," he said. "Lots of fun."

Could she help it that she called him a couple of times after nights out? Okay, more than a couple. Among her many traits, some good and some bad, is the fact that Shelly Salazar is an incurable drunk dialer.

It was after one of these calls that he hit her with a whopper so hard it still stings when she lets herself think about it, which she doesn't do often. "Your problem, Shelly, is that you don't know when things are over. You never pick up on the end of the party." He said this to her gently, and that's what gutted her. He wasn't trying to wound her. He was trying to educate her.

Shelly was, in a word, bewildered. How did other people know when things were over? What was she missing? She's bewildered by this still.

The third Mudslide goes down like water. It's practically evil, how good these things are. She pays then heads toward the door. Though she's been in Poor People's many times, she's never before noticed that the floors are uneven. They must be, because she stumbles a bit on the way out the door.

There's a twentysomething couple on their way in, the guy in a Sox cap and a T-shirt, the woman in a pretty pink beach cover-up and flip-flops.

"Whoa, hey, you okay?" says the guy. He catches her by the elbow.

"Fine," she says breezily.

"You're not driving, are you?"

"*No,*" says Shelly. Why do people keep asking her this? She can feel the couple's eyes on her as she crosses the street, so she gets out her phone and studies it while she waits for their attention to shift back to their own day.

It's just after 6 P.M. There's still a lot of the evening to fill.

This is why I don't like Mondays, she thinks. This, right here. This is exactly why I don't like Mondays.

When she gets in her car, she points it toward Spring Street and drives as slowly as a great-great-grandmother. The sidewalks in town are teeming. She slows down so much that the car behind her honks. Two mopeds by the statue of Rebecca almost throw her off her game, but they swerve just in time.

In her mid-twenties, when she was first living in New York City and working for a small PR firm, Shelly Salazar briefly saw a therapist named Eleanor. Eleanor was the first person Shelly ever talked to—*really* talked to—about her family.

Shelly's father left when Shelly was ten years old and her brother, Tyler, was fifteen. At the time she remembered everyone talking about what a devastating event this was for Tyler. Such a precarious age for a boy! Just entering the most difficult of the teenage years, and having to navigate them without a father present!

"Meanwhile I was like, *hello?*" Shelly told Eleanor. "It was not a great situation for a ten-year-old girl either. Let me tell you. But nobody cared." All people could focus on was the fact that Tyler had made the varsity football team as a sophomore and his father, who'd moved from the family's home on Long Island to McLean, Virginia, would not be able to attend his games.

Her fingers hover over her phone screen. Should she text Jack Baker?

Your problem, Shelly, is that you don't know when things are over. You never pick up on the end of the party. She sees now that this is—has always been—her Achilles' heel. If you please, Jack Baker isn't the only one with an Achilles problem.

What did she expect, anyway? That he'd want to take Shelly on the PGA Tour with him? Obviously not, although she did think she'd be pretty good at coming up with spectating outfits. White denim skirt, pastel top (sleeveless?), cute white sneakers.

She pulls into the small parking lot at Mohegan Bluffs. She gets out, takes her phone and her keys, locks the car, starts down the stairs. It's 6:43. Sunset is—what? Maybe an hour away. The day is waning, and summer itself is waning too. She'll go down to the beach, and she'll engage in something that is not always her forte. That thing is Introspection.

Finally she reaches the bottom of the stairs. The beach is completely deserted. The sight of so much water, the rocky, unpeopled sand, fills Shelly with a sudden, piercing loneliness.

When Shelly's parents divorced, Tyler, Shelly, and their mother stayed on in the family home in Plainview; it was the only place Shelly and her brother had ever lived. It emerged sometime later—when Shelly was entering her own precarious teenage years!—that Shelly's mother had had an affair with a client at the real estate office where she worked. She'd sold this man a three-bedroom, two-and-a-half-bath house with an "exquisite gas fireplace" and a "generous backyard, perfect for weekend barbecues with the family." And then she'd slept with him.

This was why Shelly's father left, you understand. But nobody told Shelly for three years. When she confronted Tyler about it—by then he was a senior, a veritable giant in shoulder pads with eye black perpetually smeared along his orbital bones—he shrugged and said, yeah, he'd always known but they'd asked him not to tell Shelly. She'd been so young, and had so many more years to live under their mother's roof.

"Can you freaking believe that?" Shelly told Eleanor.

It was Eleanor who helped Shelly understand that by trying to shield her from the truth her parents damaged her in an irrevocable way.

Soon after what Eleanor called Shelly's "significant progress," Shelly changed jobs, which necessitated changing health coverage, and Eleanor was no longer part of her network. Shelly could have found another therapist, but the thought of starting all over again with someone else was *exhausting*. How was she supposed to re-excavate the past when the shovel was so heavy the first time around?

Why is she thinking about all of this now? Eleanor hasn't crossed her mind in years.

Then, miraculously, her phone pings with a text. It's Jack. It's Jack! He's on a boat moored out in Great Salt. Johnny O'Neill's boat.

(Is she supposed to know who Johnny O'Neill is?)

People are hanging out. She should stop by.

She waits a few beats, not wanting to appear too eager, then texts back, K. She wants to say something more, but she forces herself to exercise restraint. *You never pick up on the end of the party.*

IT'S AN AZIMUT. GORGEOUS BOAT.

Okay. Shelly is not exactly sure what that means, but ooookay. Why not? She taps her acrylics on the phone screen, thinking, then types:

HOW DO I FIND U?

TEXT WHEN YOU GET TO PAYNES. She gives this the thumbs-up. SOMEONE WILL GET YOU. BAD INTENTIONS
She texts back, ?

NAME OF THE BOAT. BAD INTENTIONS.

Well, okay, then. As she makes her way back up the stairs she observes that she's more sober than she was going down them, which is a good thing for getting herself to Payne's but not promising for the rest of the night. She'll catch back up when she gets on the boat.

BY THE TIME Shelly makes it onto the boat—true to Jack's word, someone picked her up at the dock in an inflatable—it's almost sunset. She clambers up on the platform and follows the noise to whatever the living room on a yacht is called (the salon, she learns). A rough count of the people comes in at about twenty—some in little pockets on the crescent couch, others out by the railings. There must be bedrooms below, Shelly surmises, and who knows who's hiding out there.

She sees Jack nowhere. (Could he be in one of the bedrooms? Her stomach curdles as she considers this possibility.) A man in uniform offers her a drink. A crew member! This boat has a crew. Wow. Shelly has finally arrived at the Big Time.

"Thank you," she says, when the crew member returns with an elegant blond drink in a martini glass. "What is it?"

"A Limoncello Lemon Drop," he says. "It's a nod to the boat's Italian heritage."

"Well, then," answers Shelly. *"Ciao."* It's the only Italian she knows. Where is Jack? She doesn't know, and nobody else on the boat has acknowledged her or tried to welcome her. That's okay. She'll take herself on a tour. In the galley (she knows enough not to call it a kitchen), she waits until nobody is looking and pulls open a drawer. Each glass and cup has its own wooden cutout in exactly the right size and shape. It's enchanting. This setup reminds Shelly of a dollhouse she once had as a child. There's a row of bar glasses, and another of wineglasses, and a row of espresso cups.

"The richer the person, the smaller the coffee," she observes. The only person to hear her is a crew member, who chuckles. The same crew member as before? A different one? Shelly's not sure. She requests another Lemon Drop, and in no time at all it's delivered back to her. Service with a smile.

When drink number two is half gone, she finally spies Jack, out on the deck. Has he been there the whole time? He's leaning over the railing, talking to a pretty brunette in a red dress.

"Rude," she says under her breath. He invited her, and here she is, and he's not even looking around for her! Should she approach, or should she wait until he sees her? She stands for a minute, contemplating. She feels very alone. She can't gain a foothold at this party. She can't get any traction.

But just as she's deciding whether to stay or go, the fun begins.

Okay, now this party is speaking Shelly's language. A few people begin jumping off the bow into Great Salt Pond, landing with whoops in the dark water below. Should Shelly? Why not? She knew she wore this bikini for a reason. She shimmies out of her dress and stands on the bow. There are lights on the boat, and lights under the boat too. She sways for a moment, then a guy behind her says, "You okay?"

Seriously. Why do people keep asking Shelly this?

"I'm chill," she says. She thinks about her best childhood friend, Caitlin, whose family had a pool with a diving board. This is where Shelly perfected her famous swan dive. "Ready, set, execute," she says to herself. This is what she and Caitlin used to say from the diving board. After each dive, they'd rate each other.

In she goes.

She gives herself an eight, maybe an eight and a half. Slight bend in the knees; she could feel it. Still, not bad.

Wow. The water is a little colder than she imagined it would be. She feels like the dive has propelled her all the way to the bottom of the pond. It hasn't, of course, and she pops up not far from the boat. It's all good.

When is the last time Shelly swam at night? She can't remember. It's *invigorating*. Exhilarating. She's never felt more alive.

The other jumpers have all climbed back onto the boat, where the crew members are probably wrapping them in like the plushest of the plush towels. But not Shelly. No. She'll stay in. She floats on her back, staring up at the starry sky, at the plump, bright moon. How come she never noticed how many stars are visible here on Block Island? She flips over on her stomach: dead man's float. Then she strokes out, swimming among the other moored boats. Shelly is a strong swimmer, owing to the lessons she took as a child. The hours she and Caitlin spent in Caitlin's pool, racing up and down the length, holding somersault contests.

How much time passes? She doesn't know. Should she find her way back to the boat? Maybe. She will soon. She will now. She can still see the lights, shining like beacons, though admittedly the boat is farther away than she realized. And there's more than one boat with lights, so how does she even know if she's looking at the right one?

The bump comes out of nowhere.

There's almost no time for it to hurt. It comes so fast.

NICOLA

Nicola is fifteen years old. She's struggling with Algebra II, and she has a crush on a guy named Jeffrey in her Spanish class. She's a mediocre soccer player, a strong swimmer, a decent painter. She likes the Black Eyed Peas and her boyfriend-style ripped jeans that she used her babysitting money to buy from Abercrombie. Everything is ahead of her, and nothing is behind. She's taking her American Red Cross lifeguard course, and she's listening to the instructor, a man in his fifties, or, who knows, his seventies, because she's fifteen and those ages look the same to her.

"In a moment of panic, you will be tempted to forget everything you know," says the instructor. "Every rescue is not going to be textbook. You might be alone. You might be in the dark. Your victim might be intoxicated. Hell, *you* might be intoxicated. But I'm imprinting these words on your mind." He waves his hands over the students; it looks almost as if he's putting them under a magic spell. "Reach, throw, row, but don't go." He has them repeat this, in unison, three times, then four, then five. Reach, throw, row, but don't go. Don't go. *Don't go!*

Now, on Juliana's dock, she processes all of this in three seconds, far less time than it takes to describe it. But wow, the temptation to go is *so strong.*

The moon is one day away from being full—this is a blessing. Juliana's head is above water—this is a blessing too. Nicola pulls a pillow off the couch and throws it to Juliana. "Grab this!" she calls. "Hold on to it, you'll be safe until I can get you!" Juliana doesn't get it and it bobs away.

She turns on her phone's flashlight and yells, "Look for the light, Juliana! Face this way! I'm right here!" She knows that a nonswimmer has only about thirty seconds before panicking and starting to inhale water.

And then she remembers the kayak paddles.

For the rest of her life Nicola will look back on what happened on the dock that night, and she'll marvel at it. She'll remind herself that any situation can change in an instant (wouldn't be a cliché if it didn't hold some truth), in the blink of an eye, the slip of the foot, the miscalculation of the wheel. She'll think about this anytime she's out on a boat during her graduate work, and, when she has her own children (not so long, after all, from now, as it turns out), whom she teaches, one day, to swim out to the dock at Pokegama Lake. She'll remind herself that just as things can turn tragic in an instant, sometimes they can also turn good.

She's reaching that paddle out as far as she can, into the darkness, into the water. Juliana grabs for it, misses, goes under. That could have been it. *That could have been it!*

But that night under the full moon it seems like there's something supernatural or spiritual at work. The hand of *God,* capital, or a *god,* lowercase. Or maybe it's neither of those; maybe it's Juliana's immense inner strength, the same strength that pulled her out of her dark childhood and gifted her the grit to transform herself into who she became, who she's still becoming.

Because just after her head descends into the water it rises again, and she looks toward the light, and Nicola stretches just an inch more, maybe no more than a centimeter, and Juliana is able to wrap her shaking hand around the end of the paddle, and, with what's probably every last drop of her strength, to hold on as Nicola pulls her to the ladder of the dock, and then to pull herself up the ladder and lie, shaking and shivering, on the dock.

"What," says Nicola, as she helps Juliana sit up, wraps her in one of the towels she's pulled from the basket, "the fuck. Was that?"

Juliana shakes her head. "I don't know," she says. She's quiet for a long minute, coughing, sputtering. "I don't know anything. I don't know why I did that. I don't know who I am anymore." She inhales, closes her eyes, then opens them and lets out the biggest exhale Nicola has ever heard. It seems to Nicola as though in that exhale she's going through visible changes, as though Nicola can watch her go through all of her iterations: the girl, the teenager, the college student, the young woman, the business founder.

"You're Juliana Fucking George, and your company is about to go public and kick ass. That's who you are."

The twinkling fairy lights of the stars will soon begin to give way to striations of color. Dawn will come. Every day, a new beginning.

"Okay," says Juliana, in a tiny voice. Then she repeats it in a louder one: "Okay." Then, "I'm sorry. I'm sorry I did that."

"It's okay. I mean, yeah, I wish you hadn't. But it's okay. Are you going to go inside now?"

"I don't know. Maybe. Maybe I'll sleep out here." Juliana is still shivering, holding the towel tight around her.

"I take it back. It's not a question. You're going inside, and you're taking a hot shower, and you're going to bed."

"Okay," Juliana says one more time, obediently, like a child, and there's something childlike too about the way she lets Nicola lead her along the length of the dock, across the patio, and to her back door.

Nicola watches Juliana go inside, and she watches the lights in the house. The kitchen light goes on, then off again. This happens all the way through the house, the illumination tracing Juliana's progress, until Nicola sees a light switch on upstairs. This must be

Juliana's bedroom. Nicola has never been upstairs. She watches until that light goes out too, then she makes the short journey between their two houses that she's made so many times that summer.

It feels like the end of something, that journey, but it sort of feels like the beginning of something too.

Nicola sees now what kind of story she's been in all along. It's a story of money, yes—just look at this house Juliana has just gone into—new money, and old money, wealth and class, and the differences between the two. It's a love story too, of course, which means it's also a tragedy, as many love stories are.

Eventually she gets into her own bed and eventually, eventually, yes, she does fall asleep, but only just in time to wake up again, and to get to the Institute, and to hear, because news travels fast on a small island, that the story she's been in is also a tragedy.

NICOLA

A year passes both slowly and quickly, the way some years do. In that year, Nicola moves to Narragansett, turns thirty, joins Tinder, unjoins Tinder, joins again. Her mom buys a new car and gifts her her old Subaru. No more cycling! She lives in an apartment just one step above undergrad housing with two roommates that she found online—a boy named Travis, who is loud and drinks too much but is fairly tidy, and a girl named Maeve, who is quiet but leaves her socks in the living room and her bras in the corner of the bathroom. Also, she never unloads the dishwasher. Travis is a bartender at The Tavern, and Maeve is a graduate student in health care management at URI.

Nicola gets two jobs. The first is part-time, at the Save the Bay Exploration Center and Aquarium in Newport, where she doesn't make nearly enough to live on but is able to continue the same sort of work she did at BIMI. The second is at the storied Coast Guard House, where she works two dinner shifts a week and brunch every other Sunday. This is where the real money is, and this is where the view is too; she loves the way if you look from a certain angle out the windows that line the far edge of the dining room you can't see the rocks below and therefore you feel like you're on a ship.

Travis is never home at night and Maeve is never home in the daytime, which means that Nicola, with her irregular day-and-night schedule, is almost never alone in the house. This is mostly fine, but sometimes she longs for the relative solitude of her cottage off Corn Neck Road. What she doesn't long for is the chaos that swirled around it—that swirled around that whole island.

Sometimes she even misses the uphill, bumpy bike ride to get to Taylor and David's house.

The nine months she lives in Narragansett, she spends a lot of time near the water. On the mild days, of which there are too many (the planet is warming, which means the oceans are warming, which means every October day she doesn't need a sweatshirt her heart breaks for her aquatic buddies), she walks on the town beach, near the Coast Guard House.

You cannot, of course, see Block Island from Narragansett, the island is too far out to sea, but she imagines that she can. She thinks about how people there were careless: careless with each other's hearts, and sometimes with each other's bodies, and sometimes with their own bodies, and it ended in tragedy for Shelly, though it could easily have been any of them. It was just an accident in the dark, nobody knew what happened.

In the course of that year she goes on five dates total: three from Tinder (two terrible, one okay), and two with guys she met through friends (one okay, one terrible). She understands that this is a pretty small number of dates for a single person her age, but she's mostly fine with that.

Fall goes by; the water becomes too cold to put her feet in when she walks on the beach. In December, at the urging of her boss at Save the Bay, she applies to the Master of Arts in Marine Affairs program at her alma mater, URI.

There's a four-day period in March when she's *this close* to moving back to Minnesota. She misses her family, and she misses her home state. Rhode Island is beautiful, but it's never been home. Undergrad was so long ago she's forgotten some of the state's quirks, and now they seem quirkier than they did before. Milkshakes are called cabinets; water fountains are bubblers; milk comes in coffee flavor? Maybe marine biology isn't for her after all. March in New England can be dreary: gray-hued skies, streets of dirty melting snow, cold rain, and all of this is harder to swallow without the built-in friends and social life that come effortlessly in college.

She wonders if these last several months have been a fever dream, an overcorrection to the breakup with Zachary. Her sister Shauna is going to have a baby in May, and Nicola could be there for the birth, the first days of the baby's life. She could audition for the role of Fun Aunt.

She calls home, to take the temperature of the family. Her mom answers and tells her all about Shauna's last appointment, and how Shauna and her husband have known the sex of the baby forever but refuse to tell anyone.

"I wanted to throw them one of those gender reveal parties!" she complains. "I was really deep into my Instagram research. There was this piñata . . ." Her voice trails off. "Anyway. Never mind that. What's going on with you, sweetie?"

"I was thinking of coming home."

"Great. Yes! Book a flight. We'd love to see you. Long weekend, or could you spare a whole week?"

"No, Mom. I mean *home* home. I was thinking about *really* coming home."

"*Moving* home?"

"Well, yeah. I was sort of thinking about that."

"Hang on, Dad wants to talk to you—"

"I could use someone in the office," says her dad. "You could start with payroll and paperwork and in no time at all you'd be running the place."

Her father has tried to lure each of them into the family business at one point or another. Maybe *lure* is too strong of a word. *Invite.* That's kinder.

("*Lure* is too *gentle* of a word," her sister Kristin would say. "*Coerce* is closer.")

"I'm not a brother," she says. "You'd have to rebrand."

Nicola pictures herself in ten years, wearing, who knows, a long flowered skirt and a pastel button-down. Brow furrowed, pale from spending all of her time under fluorescent lighting, mildly depressed but too caught up in her routine to notice. She'd be single, or she'd be married to another Minnesotan, and maybe they'd have kids or maybe they wouldn't. Any weekend she didn't have to work they'd be up at the lake.

Her mom gets on the phone and says, "Nicola? I'm taking you off speaker." There's a pause, and Nicola imagines her moving from the living room, where she would have been, to the kitchen. "Don't you dare move home."

"Okay," says Nicola, taken aback. "I mean, I won't if you don't—"

"It's not that we don't want you. Of *course* we want you. We always want you. It's that you put yourself on a path for a reason. Don't get off because you got nervous. Nicola? Do you hear me?"

"I hear you," says Nicola. "I hear you."

Throughout that year, and especially during conversations like this one, Nicola thinks about what Juliana said to her when they sat on her dock that very last night.

I can tell how many different people love you. And: *People move differently in the world when they are loved by a lot of people.*

In April she's accepted to the program and given research assistant funding. After she gets her email she holds her phone, unsure who to call first. Her parents? Reina? One of her sisters? All of them would be happy to hear from her, appropriately proud and interested.

She looks at her phone, considering, and almost without thinking she's calling a number she hasn't used in nine months. She's calling one of *Forbes*'s wealthiest self-made entrepreneurs. She's not expecting an answer.

But the call connects almost immediately. *"Nicola?* I can't believe it! How are you?"

She tells her about the acceptance.

"That's amazing!" says Juliana. "I'm so happy for you! That's really fantastic, Nicola. It's the perfect thing for you." All of this feels sincere to Nicola—earned and sincere.

"So how are *you?* How's everything?"

"Good! Busy, you know. But good." Nicola kept up on news about the IPO, one of the biggest of the past few years. The numbers she read were so big they mean almost nothing to Nicola; Juliana now has unfathomable, untouchable wealth.

After that come several seconds of things they do not say. Juliana does not ask after David. Nicola does not ask about Juliana's personal life. Neither mentions Block Island or the summer before, Shelly, Great Salt, Jack Baker, any of it.

"Listen, Nicola? I have to go, okay? I have to go." A pause. "But I'm glad you called. I'm really glad. I think about you a lot. I really do. And hey—stay in touch, okay?"

"Okay," says Nicola. "Of course. You too."

"I will," promises Juliana. But she'd bet that her path and Juliana's will never cross again. Like a summer romance, like a sunset, like a snowflake, that's all in the past now.

People move differently in the world when they are loved by a lot of people. Nicola gave Juliana the gift of saving her life, sure. But Juliana gave Nicola something too: the gift of understanding this.

Travis is in the kitchen, making a peanut butter and jelly sandwich before his shift, so she tells him about her acceptance.

"Cool!" says Travis. She watches him spread a layer of potato chips on the peanut butter side, then lay the jelly side on top, gently pressing down, enough to crack some of the potato chips but not enough to break them in pieces. "I didn't even know you were into that stuff."

Nicola rolls her eyes. "Travis. I work at the Save the Bay Exploration Center and Aquarium. I go there three days a week."

He squints at her. "I thought you worked at Coast Guard House. I thought you knew my buddy Rob who also works at The Tavern with me. Want a sandwich?"

"I *also* work at Coast Guard House and know your buddy Rob who works at The Tavern with you. But the marine stuff is my passion."

"Cool," Travis says again, nodding and chewing. "Passion is good."

For some reason, it is exactly the thing she needed to hear. She says, "You know what, Travis? I *do* want a sandwich."

IN MAY SHE gives notice to her landlord. A room close to the beach won't be hard to fill for the summer, and she knows that when she comes back she wants to live alone, even if it means returning to the Coast Guard House one night a week to help cover the rent. She says goodbye to Travis, piles four of Maeve's socks outside Maeve's bedroom door, and packs up the Subaru to drive back to Minnesota.

ONE HOT DAY in August, the doggiest of the dog days of summer, Shauna is napping while Nicola and her mom pass Shauna's newborn, Jasmine, back and forth between them. They're in the screened-in porch facing the dock and the lake. Kristin and Kate were there when Jasmine was born but went back to the Cities for work. A couple of pontoons move lazily, and Nicola is alternating between watching them and marveling at Jasmine. "Look at her eyelashes," says Nicola. "I mean, come *on*."

"They're perfect," Linda confirms. After a moment she says, "You know, you look pretty natural holding that baby."

Nicola rolls her eyes. "I sweartogod, Mom."

Jasmine opens the blue saucers she has for eyes and looks at them. She's the best baby in the world, so calm and quiet, so *serene*, so wise, that Nicola worries she's ruining the reputation of babies the world over who will never live up to her example. It's actually unfair to all those other babies.

"I just don't understand," says Nicola's mother, "how this calm grandchild came from the least calm daughter." Her mother says that 76 percent of her gray hairs came from the years Shauna was fifteen, sixteen, and seventeen.

Nicola snorts, and when Jasmine looks startled at the way the snort makes Nicola's arms jump, Nicola says, "Sorry, honey," and tries to stay very still as Jasmine settles.

"Nature's correction, I guess," says Linda. Then the phone rings—their cottage is one of the last places on the planet with a landline. And they actually answer it!

"I'll get it," says Linda. In a minute she comes back and says, "You'll never believe it. That was David! He's on his way here."

"Our David?"

"Our very own David. And Felicity! Last-minute trip."

"Who takes a last-minute trip to Minnesota?" Linda shrugs. "No Taylor?" asks Nicola.

"He didn't mention Taylor. Can you do me a favor, Nic? Can you run up to Aldi and get a box of Popsicles for Felicity, and maybe a bottle of white wine? Do you think you can find something fancy enough for David?"

"You're kidding, right?"

"About buying it, or about the fancy?"

"The fancy!"

"Yes. I'm kidding about the fancy. But maybe stay away from the four-dollar bottles."

"I'd stay away from those anyway. I have some standards." She passes the baby to her mother.

Nicola has only talked to David a couple of times since the previous summer. He didn't come home for Christmas—he and Taylor and Felicity went to St. Barts with Taylor's father. Nicola knows from her lurking on the website of the *Block Island Times* and the YouTube channel that plays the planning board meetings that her little cottage has been demolished and construction on a new home is moving forward, and she also knows that the plans for the down-town hotel have been held up in a seemingly endless series of zoning meetings. It might never happen. But, knowing the Buchanans, it probably will.

At Aldi, she finds a decent bottle of Sauvignon Blanc for $22, and a box of organic Popsicles plus one of ice cream sandwiches. She's in line behind someone whose twenty-one items definitely exceed the fifteen-item limit (not that she's counting; okay, maybe she's count-ing), so she picks up one of the magazines on the endcap display and starts to read while she waits.

"You buying that?" Nicola looks up, startled, to see that her three items have moved ahead of her on the conveyor belt.

"Sorry." She closes the magazine and hands it to the clerk. She pays for her things, walks to her car, and drives home.

When she gets back, Felicity is sitting in the screened-in porch with Linda and David, quivering over Jasmine, who is sleeping like the superstar baby she is. Felicity is now four. She's a full quarter of her life older than she was a year ago. Her limbs are longer, and her curls are longer, and some of the baby fat in her cheeks has melted away, revealing a hint of what she might look like one day, as a teen and then as a young adult.

"Want to walk down to the dock, Nicola?" asks David after they all pass hugs around. "There's something I want to talk to you about."

"That sounds ominous. Is it ominous?" David doesn't answer.

"Go ahead," says Nicola's mother. "Felicity and I will bake come cookies."

"*Really?*" asks Felicity. "What *kind?*"

"Let's see what we have. Here, I'll carry the baby but you're in charge of her seat, okay?" Nicola's mom is like this, gracious and kind to small people; she'll bake with them or color with them and listen to their stories.

"You want some of this not-terrible wine?" Nicola asks David.

"You had me at *not-terrible*," he says.

They pour the wine into two plastic tumblers and walk down to the end of the dock. They dangle their feet over the edge, like they used to when they were kids and the tumblers were cans of Coke.

"So," he said. "I have something to tell you about, and I wanted to do it in person."

"Is this about Juliana again, David? Because I really don't want to get in—"

He cuts her off. "No, that's completely over. Taylor and I are making it work. We're doing great, actually."

"Yeah? For real?"

"For real. For absolute real. We got something back that we lost, you know? Trust, I guess. Kindness. We got the kindness back." He pauses. "It's something else." He looks *nervous*! David doesn't get nervous. "I want to tell you something about Jack."

She shakes her head and takes a big sip of wine. "No, thank you," she says primly. "I really don't think about Jack anymore."

His voice is urgent. "No, but Nicola. You have to listen. I have to tell you this story. I'm telling you, okay? So you just need to listen. Please? Just listen."

She squints out at the water. "Okay. I'll listen."

"Remember when Shelly Salazar died last summer?"

"Of course I remember that. Geez, David. Yeah, how could I forget? She's like the only person my age I've known who's died, basically. She washed up not that far from where I lived, you know?" Nicola, in fact, thinks about Shelly Salazar a *lot*, and how fast she went from being the object of Nicola's ire to, well, to dead. So fast.

"Okay. Sorry! That's what I want to talk to you about. Shelly— didn't drown."

"Huh? Of course she did. Her body washed up on Dinghy Beach. She was drunk and jumped off a boat. Of *course* she drowned."

"I mean, she did, of course, drown. But she didn't *just* drown."

Nicola feels prickles in her palms. Does a cloud pass in front of the sun? She says, "I'm not sure what you mean."

"Jack stayed with us for two nights right around Christmas, in Boston, before we went to St. Barts." (Taylor and David will return to Block Island in the summers, but their winter residence remains in Boston.)

"Okay?" says Nicola.

"The first night he went out, but the second night we ate at home. We drank a lot at dinner, wine, then bourbon, you know how it goes."

"I know."

"Taylor got disgusted with us and went to bed, no shocker, honestly, I don't blame her, and we just kept pouring more and more bourbon. I could tell Jack was getting pretty drunk—hell, I was getting pretty drunk too, but he was drinking faster, more, and when it was pretty late, like maybe eleven, he brought up Shelly. And he told me—"

David clears his throat, pauses, keeps talking.

"He told me that he and Taylor's friend Michael—do you know Michael? It doesn't matter. Friend from boarding school." The two *M*s, Nicola remembers. "He's sort of an asshole from my experience of him. Anyway, he told me that that night, the night Shelly died, he and Michael took the inflatable that was tied up to Johnny O'Neill's boat and tooled around in Great Salt."

"They just took an inflatable out? In the middle of a party?"

"The party on the boat was boring, I guess. I don't know. Stupid reason. Jack thinks everything is boring. Even stupider, they didn't use a light. Anyone who knows *anything* knows that you always use a light at night with an inflatable. Michael was driving. They were out in the middle of the pond, and Michael, for no reason, apparently, picked up speed. And then . . ."

Nicola has the sense of walls closing in around her, but of course there are no walls. The water is so clear at the edge of the lake, they can see all the way to the bottom. The sun is shining mightily. Far out a pontoon passes, sturdy and proud, and beyond that are the edges of Drumbeater Island. Nicola doesn't want David to keep talking. *No*, she says, but only in her head.

"And then there was a bump. Like they hit something. But they didn't have the lights, so they couldn't see. 'I thought it was a buoy, or a mooring ball,' Jack told me. They went back, tied up the inflatable, went their separate ways. But the whole time, Jack said, he didn't think it was a buoy. It didn't *feel* like a buoy. It felt like—"

"A person," says Nicola.

"Right. A person."

"My god," says Nicola. "They didn't *tell* anyone? They didn't tell the police?"

"The day Shelly's body was found, the police questioned anyone they could find who had been on the boat at the same time as Shelly. But everyone had been drinking; nobody was tracking who returned to the boat after jumping off. There was nothing to be done. And Jack's attitude, that night around Christmas when he told me this, was Shelly was already dead. 'Don't get me wrong, David,' he said. 'It's totally tragic. But what good would it be for Michael to come forward after the fact, if he doesn't even know if he hit her?'"

"He definitely hit her," says Nicola.

"That's what I thought too. But Jack's whole thing was they didn't know for sure. And even if they did, what would be the point of ruining Michael's life too? And anyway, said Jack, who's to say she wouldn't have drowned anyway? 'That girl was a total mess, she never should have been swimming. She was wasted.' That's what Jack said."

"What would be the *point*?" croaks Nicola. "The point is justice. The point is that you can't just go around killing people and going on with your life like nothing happened."

"Well, *I* know that." David shakes his head. "I'm telling you what *Jack* said. But I haven't told you the rest of it."

"There's *more*?"

David nods grimly. "In February, Michael and Mo stayed with us on their way up to ski in Vermont. Just for one night. Taylor wanted some time with Mo so she sent Michael and me to this bar around the corner. I almost couldn't look at Michael, knowing he'd done this terrible thing. I really could hardly talk to him, and he could tell. We used to hang out and get along, you know? I mean, he's an asshole, but he's a tolerable asshole, and I'm actually fine with assholes. I've known a lot of them. But like I said, he could tell, and eventually, he asked me what was up. I told him. I said, I know about the accident with the dinghy. I know what you did, and that you didn't tell anyone. And he said, What *I* did? I said, Yeah, Jack told me."

"Okaaaayy," says Nicola, drawing it out.

"And he said, 'Oh, Jesus, is *that* what Jack told you? That I was driving?'" David pauses, and his eyes flick over to Nicola. "You maybe see where I'm going here."

"I don't." Then all at once she does. All at once she understands. Her words ping over the lake. "Jack was driving the inflatable."

"Jack was driving the inflatable," says David.

Jack was driving the inflatable.

Two kayaks, far out in the distance, do their thing, and she watches them, not wanting to look at David. "I feel like I'm going to throw up. David. I wish you hadn't told me this. Why did you tell me?" She wants to put the story back in the box it came in, take it to the UPS store to return it.

David is looking at the water too. "Because I know how Jack operates. He'll pop up in your life someday—that's how he is. And I want you to know exactly who he is, so you can stay away. I used to think he was mostly harmless, you know, a playboy, of *course*, which we told you before you ever started hanging out with him."

"Taylor did say that," agrees Nicola.

"But *this* is a whole other level. This is something I didn't know he had in him."

Jack taking all of the turns in David's car too fast, shirking any responsibility. *It takes two to make an accident.* Jack beating his fist on his heart. *You got me right here.* Nicola doesn't know what to do with any of this. Her skin feels too tight on her arms. Her heart is beating uncomfortably.

Nicola's mom is at the far end of the dock now, calling out something about dinner: Will burgers do? That's all she has on hand.

They call back to her, using the false happy voices they perfected as teenagers to hide if someone was drunk, or high, or sneaking out to meet a boyfriend or girlfriend. Burgers will most definitely do. Burgers will be perfect.

"I'm sending Felicity down to you! So you need to watch her on the dock!"

"Got it!" they call back. "Send her down!"

In an instant Felicity is there, smelling like chocolate chip cookies and summer and childhood, demanding to go swimming, to go in a kayak, to get a yellow Lab puppy like her friend Sophie has. "I want to run up and down the dock," she says. "Can I do that? Can I run fast?"

Was it already a year ago that Nicola was on a different dock with Juliana, watching the green light go out on her elusive, impossible dream? Was it *only* a year ago?

"Tomorrow," she tells Felicity. "Tomorrow we will do all of that, except no promises about the puppy. Tomorrow, on flat ground, when we're not so close to the water, we will run faster."

LATER, WHEN EVERYONE else has gone to sleep, Nicola can't settle. What David told her about Jack is still roiling around in her head, her stomach, even her heart.

She goes to the bathroom, tiptoeing past the room where Shauna and Jasmine are sleeping and the one where Felicity and David are sleeping. Her mom is down the hall. She fills a glass of water in the kitchen and carries it back to her room. When she's setting it down she sees that the magazine she bought at the market has slipped onto the floor between the bed and the nightstand. She picks it up and flips through it.

And her breath catches. There's Juliana. *Juliana George, founder of LookBook, takes daughter Daisy for a walk in Malibu,* says the caption. Juliana is in sunglasses, her dark hair blowing back from her face, a baby carrier secured to the front of her body, only the back of an infant's head visible. Behind Juliana extends a vast stretch of the Pacific. Nicola has never been to Malibu or anywhere near it, but the mere name is evocative: she thinks of rum, and Barbie's pink vacation house, and Joan Didion, and movie stars in in their mansions high above the crashing sea.

Juliana's photo is on a page with six other "celebrity sightings"; no article, no other details, just the photo and the caption. No mention of a partner. No age listed for the baby, Daisy. Nicola stares for a really long time at the photo, trying to read something into it that's not there. It's impossible to read Juliana's expression. The sunglasses hide everything.

ACKNOWLEDGMENTS

This is the third book I have set on Block Island, a place I am not from but which I have come to know and love over the past several years. I've visited often and have appreciated assistance from a variety of extremely helpful locals and others in the know. As an outsider I've tried hard to listen and observe and research and get to know the essence of the place. If I erred in depicting any aspect of island life it was not from lack of effort. Beyond any unintentional mistakes and despite my efforts at verisimilitude, I hope readers recognize and accept that this is a work of fiction and that there may be houses/docks/views/water depths/pools/construction projects/ noise ordinances/town council setups created or altered in service of the story. The following people helped me with questions large and small about the island or have supported in other ways: Alyssa Giordano, formerly of Block Island Maritime Institute; Doug Gilpin; Susan Bush of Island Bound Bookstore; Dawn Holmes; Kate McConville. (Someday I'll find a glass float! I know I will!)

On the business side, Chris Giliberti, Rachel Gerring, and Mark Schwartz answered my questions about IPOs. Julia Truelove led me to them. Lindsey Ranzau suggested Pokegama Lake. Brian Moore took an initial idea from my editor and turned it brilliantly into LookBook. He also gently corrected my business mistakes. Emily

Kaiser shared with me some of her experiences as a student at Boston College's Carroll School of Management in the 2010s. Will Turner of Turner Motorsport Racing helped me with race car background (any mistakes are mine alone), and Will and Sue Turner graciously allowed me to put their perfectly named boat in the book. Kelly Doucette advised me on the details of wills and probate court. Dave Considine and Brad Mascott answered boating questions, as they have done for several books. My favorite EMT, Addie Moore (yes, she's old enough *and* strong enough to lift that stretcher!), filled in details for me.

The article "How an Ivy League School Turned Against a Student" by Rachel Aviv in the March 28, 2022, issue of *The New Yorker* was often in the back of my mind as I created and massaged Jade Gordon's backstory as an outsider in a privileged world.

F. Scott Fitzgerald's 1925 novel *The Great Gatsby* inspired this one in ways large and small.

I've been lucky to work with several talented editors over the course of my career and have been in excellent hands with each of them. This is my first start-to-finish book with Liz Stein at William Morrow, whose enthusiasm, sharp insights, eye for the big picture, and willingness to talk through any sticking points (and there were many!) made this book infinitely better draft after draft. I am also grateful to Liate Stehlik, Jennifer Hart, Julie Paulauski, and Karen Richardson, and all of the sales, marketing, and publicity people who have worked on each of my books. My agent, Elisabeth Weed of The Book Group, has been for years and years the very best cheerleader and sounding board a girl could ask for. I'm delighted to be supported by everyone else at TBG too, in particular DJ Kim.

Thank you to all of the independent booksellers, especially Jabberwocky Bookshop, Hannah Harlow at The Book Shop of Beverly Farms, and Jen Perry at Illume Books, and also to the vast universe of book bloggers and bookstagrammers who have read or posted about my books, or any books.

I'm lucky to have been involved for the past several years in the Newburyport Literary Festival, and I'm grateful to the all-volunteer group I work with there. Happy twentieth! Let's keep people reading and talking about books. Love and gratitude to the home front: my Newburyport Bad Intentions crowd (so glad you never say no to anything) and also to Katie Schickel for being my local writer friend.

Thank you to Margaret Dunn and Jennifer Truelove—for the best friendship and road trips, of course, but also for careful, thoughtful reads of this book.

One character in this book observes of another that she moves in the world like someone who's loved by a lot of people. Because of my parents, John and Sara Mitchell, my sister, Shannon Mitchell, and my vibrant, funny, smart home squad, Brian, Addie, Violet, and Josie Moore, I know what that feels like, and I love you all right back.

Meg Mitchell Moore worked for several years as a journalist for a variety of publications before turning to fiction. She lives in the coastal town of Newburyport, Massachusetts, with her husband and their three daughters. *Mansion Beach* is her ninth novel.